DARK EDGE PRESS

MURDER IN HER FIRST DEGREE

A RED BRICK MYSTERY

LIZZIE BENTHAM

Published in 2022 by Dark Edge Press.

Y Bwthyn
Caerleon Road,
Newport,
Wales.

www.darkedgepress.co.uk

A CIP catalogue record for this book is available
from the British Library.

ISBN (eBook): B0B5LZD2RS
ISBN (Paperback): 979-8-3593-9916-6

In memory of our pioneering women.

CONTENTS

Minutes of the Women's Student Union Executive Committee Meeting, The Debating Hall, Tuesday 4th September 1934, 2 p.m.

Apologies: Professor Quentin B. Smythe (University Provost), Abigail Rushton (Secretary of the Debating Society)

Present: Constance Harris (President), Iris Robinson (Vice President), Mabel Parker (Treasurer), Evelyn King (Social Secretary), Victoria Butterworth (Acting Secretary), Alexandra Cotton (Athletics Union Secretary), Mrs Gladys Adams (Advisor to Women Students)

Item 1: Minutes from the previous meeting (Tuesday 10th July 1934) accepted as accurate.

Item 2: Victoria Butterworth was welcomed to the Executive Committee as Acting Secretary by the President. A date was set for the by-election for the Secretarial position, Thursday 27th September 1934. There was discussion around holding the by-election at the same time as the elections for first-year representatives in November but there was unanimous agreement that the Secretarial position is too important to wait to appoint.

Item 3: The purchasing of a wreath and card for the family of Ethel Worksop, Outgoing Secretary of the Committee, was agreed. The Treasurer is to undertake the commission and have it delivered to Ethel Worksop's parent's house. The money for the wreath and card is to be taken from petty cash. The President hoped that all of the Executive Committee would be present at the funeral at St John's church, Friday, 14th September, at 10 a.m.

Item 4: It was agreed that the President would write to the Local Council about the dangers of fast road traffic on Oxford Road and ask them to put mitigating procedures in place. The Acting Secretary pointed out that the street lighting along that stretch of road could also be improved and that it is rather dark along there at night. This was noted by the President and will be included in the letter.

Item 5: The President updated the Executive Committee on her meeting with Detective Inspector Kydd. While the police would not necessarily divulge all their leads to a lay person regarding the progress of the investigation, it was the President's opinion that little had been achieved so far in tracing the driver of the green van that had knocked down Ethel. The van itself had been discovered abandoned in a residential area off the East Lancashire Road.

Item 6: The Vice-President put forward the motion that the Secretary of the Debating Society be asked to schedule a debate entitled: *Should hit and run drivers face the death penalty?* This was unanimously agreed by all Executive Officers.

Item 7: Any Other Business – The Social Secretary pointed out that there are only three months until the Joint Student Unions Christmas ball, and as yet no joint organising committee has been formed. The President agreed to liaise with the President of the Men's Student Union and put forward herself, the Treasurer, and the Social Secretary to sit on the Joint Ball Organising Committee.

Item 8: The Acting Secretary asked that all items for the full Committee meeting be given to her by Friday.

Item 9: The date and time of the next Executive Committee meeting were agreed for Thursday 18th September, 2 p.m. with the first full Committee meeting taking place at 7 p.m. Tuesday 11th September.

CHAPTER ONE

Comings and Goings

Saturday 8th September 1934, Evening

Click. The pre-oiled lock on the door sprang open with encouragement from an expertly wielded hairpin. Slowly and quietly the handle turned, and the door opened and closed stealthily to admit a person dressed all in black, a purposeful shadow. The shadow flitted over to the window and pulled closed the regulation halls of residence curtains but not before a fickle shaft of moonlight picked out the gleam of a wicked-looking silenced revolver and a Harlequin mask where the person's face should have been.

A torch, taped to produce a narrow beam of light was switched on and flicked around the small room, austere in its neatness. It picked out the single bed pushed up against the far wall, the snowy counterpane glinting as the torchlight caressed it.

A utilitarian desk with solid looking drawers sat next to the window and the shadow gravitated towards it with unerring determination. The hairpin came into play again and the shadow let out an audible 'Tsk!' of frustration before the desk lock finally gave way, allowing access to the room owner's correspondence. Methodically

Harlequin searched the desk, including the secret drawer, known to all students in these halls with identical desks, whose contents contained: one paper bag of Uncle Joe's mint balls, a locket with a photograph of a redoubtable looking older lady in it, a man's razor, and shaving brush, three shillings, six pence in coins and a paper clip, and drew a blank.

The wardrobe and chest of draws underwent the same thorough search and produced nothing unexpected that a young lady of an academic leaning from a well-to-do background would not own. The washbag balanced precariously on the sink and the nooks and crannies around the cold fireplace were investigated too, as potential hiding places for the something that was so dangerous to the searcher that they would risk discovery to find it. Each floorboard was tested in turn to see if it could be lifted to expose a cache beneath, but to no avail.

When Harlequin was quite satisfied that the object could not have been hidden in the room, as quietly as they had come, they left, certain of where to look next.

The lock clicked back into position behind them, sealing the fate of the room's owner.

Sunday 9th September 1934, Afternoon

Dorothea sat staring out of the window of the third-class railway carriage as the Derbyshire countryside flew by, on the way from Buxton to Manchester's London Road station. The rusty hues of autumn had begun to creep in early this year and the hedgerows, woodlands and fields were already aflame with the richness that the season of plenty brings.

It was not a long journey, barely an hour, but in ideals and philosophies a couple of hundred years separated the two places. Buxton, a Regency spa town, rediscovered by the Victorians, nestled into the verdant landscape, and hugged the railway closely. The train window like a postcard, framed the ever-changing scenery. Leaving Buxton, deep-sided verges covered in wildflowers blocked out the view of the hills and then switched places with bridges solid like the remnants of ancient fortifications. After Chapel-en-la-Frith the vista cleared and stunning views of the patchwork countryside of Derbyshire were obtained. Purple heather stood out cheerfully atop the russet moorland surrounding Castle Naze. At points just before Disley and again near Hazel Grove the track plunged into tunnels dousing the carriage in darkness momentarily, monuments to Victorian ingenuity and pig-headedness.

Dorothea was oblivious to it all. She was engaged in the cathartic exercise of introspection. It had been a rough eighteen months, a time of growing up rapidly and having to face a new reality that one does not like very much, and which one cannot change.

This time last year, Dorothea should have been on a train going in the opposite direction. She was naturally bright and had worked hard at Ashbourne Grammar School and could have chosen any academic subject to study further. Her teachers were delighted and not particularly surprised when Dorothea had won a fee only scholarship to study English at St Hilda's College in Oxford. Her headmaster had had little to do to persuade Dorothea's parents that the scholarship was large enough, with some subsidisation from them, to allow Dorothea to study so far away from home.

Dorothea's father, Graham Roberts, was a dairy farmer near the small Derbyshire village of Bradbourne. A church warden and a respected man in the community, he had married Sarah Wilkinson, 'a Woman from Chapel', and scandalised the local farming families, though why this was considered a misalliance was anyone's guess. Their first child was a stillborn son, followed in quick succession by two living girls Anna and Dorothea, with little Helen a third daughter arriving some eleven years later. Sarah Roberts never truly got over the death of her son and was prone to periods of low spirits. Having a son to pass on the farm to was what every farming family aspired to and in her grief, Sarah blamed herself for not being able to carry him.

Still, a farm is a good place for children to grow up, with good food, wide open spaces, and animals to look after, and the girls were also encouraged to acquire a decent education.

Dorothea in particular excelled both in the classroom and on the hockey pitch. After receiving excellent grades in her final school exams Dorothea was looking forward to attending Oxford in the autumn. Unfortunately, this was not to be. She picked up a serious case of pneumonia after a summer cold. The doctor did not rate her chances of survival but with careful nursing, her father supervising her care, she happily pulled through. In the circumstances it was thought advisable for Dorothea to defer her first year at Oxford until she had fully regained her health and she settled down to convalesce on the farm, with all the comforts of home.

It came as a massive blow to the family that Graham Roberts then contracted a chill from being caught in a rainstorm. Not one to look after his own health, he had thrown an overcoat on over the top and continued to wear damp clothes for the rest of the day. The chill turned into pneumonia and tragically within the week he was dead. This new grief was unbearable and brought up all the old painful memories of losing her son again, so Sarah Roberts, the girl's mother, took to her bed.

Anna, Dorothea's older sister was the heroine of the hour, calmly and with little fuss she stepped up to run the family farm. She was good at it, having had an excellent tutor in her father. After the funeral and the death duties the family would have been in pretty low water without Anna's careful stewardship of their finances. There was however not enough money in the family coffers to support Dorothea at Oxford, even with the scholarship.

In consultation with Dorothea's old headmaster, it was decided that Manchester was a more economical city in which to live, with the added advantage of being closer to home. With his help, Dorothea applied for a Board of Education grant and was successful. This allowed the recipient three years of funding for an undergraduate degree, plus a year's teacher training with the pledge that the recipient would make teaching their career for several years after graduating or else pay back the grant. With a few economies around the farm there was enough money to support Dorothea at the Victoria University of Manchester. Fortunately, the English Department and the courses they offered, was considered on a par with that taught at Oxbridge. It was therefore with a mixture of sadness, trepidation, excitement and the weight of familial expectations on her shoulders that Dorothea boarded the train at Buxton.

Gradually, moorland and fields turned into back gardens and places of work. The area around the station at Hazel Grove was surprisingly industrial and marked the beginning of the march of urbanisation. Through the carriage window at Stockport, the vista was a foretaste of what was to come. Closely packed houses interspersed with factories, and every so often a solitary church rising out of the busyness at ground level, pointing a tower or steeple heavenwards, beacons of light towards the spiritual in a grubby, soot covered landscape.

She was woken from her reverie by the carriage door sliding open and a tall, elegantly dressed, young woman hurtled into the compartment and slammed the door shut behind her. With her came a drop in temperature and a tangible atmosphere of inexplicable fear. The newcomer threw herself full-length on the floor under the seat Dorothea was sitting on. Dorothea could feel gulping, gusty breaths trying to be brought under control against the back of her ankles. She heard rapid steps in the corridor. The footsteps paused for a moment, directly outside their compartment door. Dorothea craned her neck forward to see, only to obtain the briefest glimpse of a man's navy mackintosh and fedora shading the person's face, who then hurried on past, down the passage.

Five minutes elapsed in silence. Dorothea stood up, walked to the door, and peered out into the empty corridor. She coughed delicately.

'You can come out now.'

***

The woman stirred and began to extradite herself from under the seat; this being a more involved process than Dorothea would have conceived possible as it appeared the young woman had well and truly wedged herself in place. In the end, Dorothea had to get down on hands and knees and give the slim pair of ankles a helping heave.

The woman who slowly stood up patting down her

dove-coloured travelling suit, though covered in lint and cobwebs, still presented a chic appearance. Naturally of slim build with a tendency towards being athletic and above average height, this Amazon towered above diminutive Dorothea, who at five-foot one inch had to crane her neck to look up at the stranger's face. This was partially obscured by a slightly squashed creation of charcoal felt and lace with a demi-veil covering her eyes. From what Dorothea could see, neat dark hair chopped and waved into a fashionable Garbo crop framed a squarish face. Worried grey eyes peeped through the veil at odds with the jauntily painted red lips and a very determined chin, that some would have unkindly described as insolent. At her breast a brooch glinted in rainbow colours, a non sequitur against the grey of her outfit.

The train began to slow down as it approached Manchester London Road station. The sway of the carriage becoming more pronounced and set in motion more urgent harmonics all around the two women.

'Thank you,' the woman said huskily, 'I really can't give you a reasonable explanation for this odd behaviour, I am afraid. I hope you can forgive me.'

Plot devices from her favourite crime thriller authors and Hitchcock films flitted through Dorothea's head, before she settled on the much more prosaic possibility of a scandalous divorce with recriminations on both sides, to make sense of the happenings of the last few minutes. Not having any personal experience of evidence of infidelity gathering in divorce cases, she wondered whether it would engender the level of fear so obviously apparent in the stranger's eyes.

'You are very welcome. It is none of my business, but is there anything I can do to help you?' Dorothea paused inquiringly, imagining herself as the heroine.

A range of emotions passed in rapid succession across

the woman's face. The foremost being a spark, however small, of hope.

'That is very kind of you. I wouldn't in the ordinary way ask you to do this, but it is of the utmost importance.' The woman reached down and dug a folded-up piece of paper out of one of her elegant charcoal and white Oxford shoes and handed it to Dorothea. 'Please don't read it unless it is a real emergency, it will be safer for you that way.' The woman took a step nearer to the carriage door and placed a gloved hand on the handle as the platform began to slide past the window. 'It needs to be delivered by hand or posted to Professor Aldridge of the School of Arts at the university. It is imperative that he receives this at the first opportunity.'

Dorothea took the paper from the woman's outstretched hand excitedly and thrust it deep into her old coat's pocket.

'Of course,' Dorothea replied. 'I will be joining the School of Arts myself. I am going to read English!' The pride and awe were obvious in her voice.

The stranger managed a strained smile at Dorothea's naive enthusiasm for the higher education system, pulled a pound note from her handbag and thrust it into Dorothea's hands as the train ground to a halt.

'So you are not out of pocket.'

Dorothea was about to demur when *Bang!* A muffled explosion ripped through the carriage accompanied by the sound of shattering glass, followed by *Whack!* as a bullet hit the elegant woman in the shoulder. A hole was visible in her suit jacket on the left breast, which immediately began to bleed. Dorothea was already diving for the recently vacated space under the seat when the second muffled shot rang out.

The force of the first bullet had thrown the woman against the train door and even in her shock and pain she had the forethought to continue with the movement of opening the door handle. The momentum of the impact carried her through. By the second shot her feet were on the platform and the bullet passed harmlessly overhead and hit a metal column with a *Clang* and a spark, then ricocheted off to scare the pigeons roosting on the iron trusses high up in the lofty span of glass and slate. The woman stumbled but kept walking at a brisk trot then disappeared into the crowd, clutching a handkerchief to her injured shoulder.

***

After the gun shots, the relative silence in the carriage was deafening. Dorothea cowered under the regulation railway seat, her pulse racing, with the smell of cordite tickling her nose and the wreckage of the internal window covering the floor.

Stupid, stupid mistake, she mentally chided herself straining to hear what was going on in the rest of the train. It was logical that the person following the woman would continue past their compartment to lull them into a false sense of security and then double back to catch their quarry unawares. In the distance she could hear people shouting, a whistle blowing and running feet.

Suddenly her ears picked up stealthy footsteps out in the corridor. Closer and closer they came. They paused momentarily outside the door. She held her breath and strained to hear what was happening.

Has the gunman come back? she wondered in trepidation.

Slowly, a man slid open the broken door and made his way into the compartment picking carefully through the broken glass, his tan brogue shoes stopping just level with her nose. His presence seemed to fill the whole space and Dorothea caught a waft of brilliantine, fresh sweat, and laundry soap.

The stranger started to whistle the first few bars of a jolly little tune, popular from a couple of years previously by Noel Coward entitled *Mad About the Boy* but it was eerily sinister and out of place in the wrecked compartment.

He paused, seeming to expect something to happen. Nothing happened to break the silence in the carriage. Then he whistled again.

Dorothea was starting to get cramped under the seat by this time, with dust tickling her nose. She was afraid, but at the same time a spark of anger flamed in to being.

Who is this whistler and is he a homicidal maniac? she thought.

The man spoke in a deep, refined tone, similar to the voices usually heard on the radio.

'Come on Matty, I know you are under the seat, why aren't you responding to the pre-set signal?' There was a note of worry in the stranger's voice.

With her cover blown Dorothea did not know what to do.

Do gunmen have BBC voices and whistle? Surely if this man was one and the same with the gunman, he would have beaten a fast retreat?

This thought was cut off abruptly by the man crouching down and hauling on Dorothea's ankles. His strength and the suddenness of the movement propelled Dorothea backwards at speed into the light. She was roughly dragged to her feet and spun around quickly and found herself looking up into the craggy face of a young man in his mid-twenties. Not classically handsome, still he was good looking in a dark, swarthy way and he was obviously suffering from some powerful emotions, chief amongst them being chagrin on finding Dorothea rather than the person he wanted to find.

'Who the hell are you?' he asked.

'Murderer!' The word escaped from Dorothea's lips

almost unbidden and surprised her almost as much as it did the black browed man standing before her. 'If you touch me again, I'll scream, and the guard will hear. Someone passing is bound to notice the broken glass soon.' She continued recklessly, 'Why did you shoot that woman?'

'Whoa! Just calm down a minute! There is no need to jump to conclusions.' The man's tone changed markedly, as if he was talking to a skittish horse or a frightened child. 'Shot you say? I thought I heard something. What happened? What did this woman look like?'

Dorothea eyed him suspiciously. He seemed to be genuinely at sea but maybe he was a very good actor. She looked intently at his coat and hat trying to superimpose them on the image embedded in her memory of the gunman in the corridor. All men's clothes were very similar to her untrained eye, but she thought the hat he was wearing was different.

'You know . . . really tall, dark hair, very nicely dressed. She came into this carriage to hide from someone. I saw her shot right where you are standing now!'

The man knelt down near the wreck of the external carriage door and examined some fresh splashes of crimson on the paintwork.

'Damn!' He swore fluently under his breath. 'Where is Matty now?'

'Matty?'

'Matth . . . it is short for Matilda, Matilda Abbot. I was meant to be meeting her here, but I got held up,' He looked grim. 'Where did she go?'

'Go?'

'Yes, go,' impatience rippled through the man's voice. 'There is no corpse here therefore she must have gone somewhere and probably on her own two feet.'

Stung by his tone Dorothea debated whether to

answer him. If he had been the one to pull the trigger then she certainly was not going to tell him which way Matty had gone, though she was hazy on this point anyway as all her attention had been focussed on finding cover. He was giving the impression of, if not being the woman's friend, then at least being a colleague or an acquaintance. He did genuinely seem worried by Matty's disappearance. Her hand closed tighter around the pound note that Matty had given her that she was still clutching, reminding her of the message currently residing in her pocket. Should she tell the man about it?

Stalling for time she asked, 'Did anyone pass you in the corridor?'

'No, no one.'

She had heard him come along the corridor from further down the train, away from the engine and in through the internal door. Surely then the gunman had either run along the corridor and entered the next carriage nearer to the engine or stepped into one of the other compartments in this carriage and gone out on to the platform through that compartment door and mingled with the other passengers arriving and departing on the platform. Either way, they were long gone.

'What has been happening here Sir? Miss?'

Dorothea turned with relief to the elderly guard who had just entered the compartment and who was viewing the devastation with the indignant eye of one who knows it will be his responsibility to deal with the mess.

'Oh, I am so glad you are here!' Dorothea jumped in before the dark man could speak. 'Please could you ring for the police? I have seen a woman shot at and hit. She was probably very badly wounded. This gentleman here has a gun in his coat pocket by the way. I felt something heavy in it as he was dragging me from under the seat,' she said innocently, throwing her new acquaintance well and truly under the bus.

CHAPTER TWO

A Bullet, a Funeral, and a Thief

Sunday, 9th September 1934, Evening

Detective Inspector Kydd finished writing his report after interviewing the two young people and the train guard.

It is a rum do, he decided grumpily. *A shooting, without an injured person or even a body? It shouldn't be allowed!*

There was definitely blood in the carriage, which had been sent to the laboratory for analysis and a lot of broken glass from both the inside and outside doors, so something had happened there. There did not appear to be any injury to any of the witnesses so no domestic squabble sensationalised to draw attention away from personal troubles. Though from what he had seen of the two young people they were not lying when they said they did not know each other. They did not particularly like each other either.

Obviously, there were fingerprints . . . too many fingerprints. It was a public space after all, but not outside the carriage door, which is where a gunman would have stood if he existed, which he did according to the young woman's account, though criminals today know all about fingerprints from crime novels and most have the common sense to wear gloves before going out to do something nefarious.

The guard did not have anything particularly interesting to say, as he had come upon the young people having an argument, a lover's tiff he had supposed initially until the young lady had mentioned guns.

Miss Dorothea Roberts was an interesting one. Fair and petite, with blue-grey eyes and a way of looking directly at you like she expected better of you, though she was only a slip of a young woman. She reminded him of his fifteen-year-old daughter. A bit of a teacher's pet too, top of the class no doubt, but a good kid at heart and fresh from the countryside to the big city. Apart from still being in shock by what she had witnessed and obviously irritated by that young fellow, she had given a pretty clear account of the hypothetical victim and what had happened and would make a pretty good witness if it ever came to putting her on the stand.

Pity that in all the furore the piece of paper the woman had given her seemed to have disappeared. That would have been useful evidence and maybe would have provided some fingerprints. She had not told the young fellow about the piece of paper either, probably did not trust him. He did not mention it in his account when questioned separately. She could of course be lying to make herself seem interesting but in DI Kydd's expert opinion she was not the type, too much of a swot. She had also looked utterly crestfallen when trying to pull the paper out of her pocket to show him and then having discovered that it was no longer there. Miss Roberts had even left the pound note with the inspector to give back to the woman should he find her, as she had failed in her commission. From a young lady about to start an academic career, that much money was not something you gave up easily, which pointed to an honest temperament.

The inspector chortled quietly to himself. It had not

been a gun in the young man's pocket either. Police Constable Standish had done a search of the outraged Dr Hadley-Brown's pockets when he arrived at the station waiting room. The object had turned out to be a catapult that Dr Hadley-Brown had confiscated off a second-year male student who was shooting at cans outside his office window. Miss Roberts had certainly made an impression on Dr Hadley-Brown, and it was not a good one.

He knew more than he was telling too, the inspector thought to himself.

The young man had supplied the name and address of the alleged victim, Matilda Abbot of Grangebrook Hall, a third-year student at the university studying Classics, and a fairly weak tale about why he had a meeting with her on a train coming into Manchester. Supposedly she was the daughter of a friend of his mother's, and he was meant to be picking up a birthday gift for his mother from her and this was the only mutual time and place they could meet up to hand over the present. He then clammed up and would not be drawn anymore. Yes, there was definitely something that that young fellow was not divulging.

The inspector shifted uneasily in his seat. He was not a superstitious man but there was a pricking in his thumbs that this case was linked in some way to the other university case of the student being run over and killed. It seemed that this Miss Abbot was also a member of the Women's Union Committee and two attacks in two weeks on committee members was a bit of an unswallowable coincidence.

The telephone rang on his crowded desk and after scrabbling to move three folders he located the instrument and answered it.

'Connecting you now, sir.'

The police operator worked her magic and PC Standish was on the line.

PC Standish was an enthusiastic and diligent officer, resembling a St Bernard dog to look at and had the makings of a very good detective. He would probably achieve the heady ranks of Chief Superintendent one day. At this precise moment he could not keep the excitement out of his voice.

'We have the bullet, sir!' he exclaimed. 'One of the station cleaners discovered it and passed it on to me, having heard about the incident. I have recorded where it was found and will bring you a copy of the station plan with where it was marked on it. I am just on my way to get it processed for the lab.'

DI Kydd gave a satisfied grunt in acknowledgement.

'So the young woman was telling the truth then, Standish,' he said. 'And you were ready to cast her as the villain.'

The Constable chuckled, 'Yes, sir. It seems the young lady really did see a shooting of some kind. Not sure I trust that Dr Hadley-Brown though. There is definitely something fishy about him. Do you want me to get on to the hospitals and mortuaries first thing?'

'Yes please, and doctor's surgeries. It might have been a glancing blow which could pass as a small wound or graze that might need dressing. I'll get on to the university and Grangebrook Hall before going home to see what they know about the young woman and to find out if she has headed back home.'

'Right you are, sir!' PC Standish rang off, leaving the inspector to look through a well-thumbed folder about the university and to pick up the phone again.

'Can you put me through to Dr Teresa Winterbottom, the warden of Grangebrook Hall, please?'

**

The lights from Grangebrook's Halls of Residence

twinkled out into the September evening gloom welcoming the weary, knowledge-saturated student back home into its cabbage-smelling bosom. A jazz record playing on a gramophone blared out of a partially opened sash window on the first floor and a titter of voices and laughter could be heard far away in the belly of the building.

Grangebrook Hall was not the oldest of the women's halls of residence at the university or the most architecturally pleasing to the eye, accolades usually reserved for its nearby neighbour Ashburne Hall. It was part of the Fallowfield Campus squashed between the Orthopaedic Hospital which had been set up to treat injured soldiers and sailors in the Great War and a modern housing estate, on a piece of land carved out of the Platt's estate and abutting the current Platt's Park. The students enjoyed the nearness of a tranquil green space with all the amenities of tennis courts, a boating lake and the university sports pitches nearby.

The building itself was three stories of red brick and golden-brown stone, built in a more traditional style than was currently favoured to blend in with other university buildings and was completed mainly in the late twenties. It was comparatively snug and modern compared to some of the other halls of residence and boasted a dining room, a common room and reading room.

A fine drizzle was falling, the kind which soaks right through to the skin. Droplets of water clung to Dorothea's hair and coat. Her fingers were numb from clutching the handle of her trunk and lugging it from the tram stop, past the gatehouse and up the drive with the partial quad stretching out in front of her. Her stomach was grumbling as she had not had anything to eat since lunchtime, bar the two digestive biscuits she had been given at the police station with a cup of tea. She was finally arriving at her destination after a traumatic day and was pretty sure she had missed dinner.

Dorothea entered the foyer, thumped her trunk down onto the tile floor and stretched out her arms and fingers gratefully to get some circulation back. She was not sure what to do next as the instructions for arriving at Halls, which had come in the post, had said to arrive by four o'clock, and it was now gone nine thirty. As she looked around, she spotted a young woman sitting at a table in the corner with a load of booklets on it and some keys, reading a medical textbook and scribbling in a notepad.

She looked up and smiled at Dorothea.

'Welcome to Grangebrook Hall. I am Mary Shor. Don't worry. You are not the last to arrive. What is your name and what subject are you studying please?'

'I am Dorothea Roberts, English Language and Literature.'

Mary Shor ticked Dorothea's name off a list, found a room key, checked the list again, swapped the key for another one and handed it to her along with a booklet which turned out to be a guide to the Women's Union for the current academic year.

'You are in room G11. It's a ground floor room. I had to switch you with another young woman who was meant to be in there, had a phobia of someone breaking in through the window. She's now in 115 on the first floor which you were going to have. I just have to remember to do the paperwork. I hope you don't mind me swapping you. If you go along the corridor over there and turn right, then keep going you will find it. The bathroom is past your room by about three doors. Then when you have dumped your stuff and freshened up go and knock on the door of Room G03. Maggie Forshaw is expecting you and has crumpets waiting. Sorry I can't come with you. Tabitha has just taken a young woman and her parents upstairs to find her room and I don't want to leave the desk unmanned. There are still three more first-years to arrive. If you have any problems, just come back here, and find me.'

'Thank you,' Dorothea bleated, cowed by the onslaught of information. 'Along and right, you said?'

'Yes. You can't miss it.'

Dorothea picked up her trunk again, reluctantly, and headed in the direction she had been pointed to. She counted off the room numbers under her breath as she walked along.

'G08 . . . G09 . . . G10 . . . G11 . . . G11 . . . Finally made it.' She set the trunk down again and fumbled with the key in the lock. The room was very pleasant for someone used to sharing with a sister. Lots of space, a bed made up with crisp white sheets and cream blankets and a desk by the window. Throughout the whole building, first-year students would be settling into similar rooms. For some, it was their first night away from home.

Someone had made up the fire with coal earlier in the evening and the warmth was very welcoming. Dorothea hung up her dripping coat and decided that a full change of clothes and a towel were in order before heading to room G03 as her teeth were chattering with the cold. She towelled her wet hair till it stuck up in a kind of halo, and changed into a warm tweed skirt, woollen jumper and woollen stockings and slippers. She was taking no chance of a pneumonia relapse.

Relocking the door again, she headed back the way she had come and found G03 without difficulty.

Dorothea knocked nervously and heard a voice cry out, 'I'll be with you in a minute!'

The door opened jerkily to reveal a beautiful, platinum-blonde young woman sitting in a wheelchair.

'Hello. You must be Dorothea. It is lovely to meet you. Do come in. I am Maggie and I am the Floor Rep for this bit of the building. All my other first-years arrived earlier but I haven't got as many as last year as most of the second-years have stayed on in their rooms,' she said, leading Dorothea into a room that was double the size of a normal bedroom in Halls.

It had a sitting area around the fireplace which was cheerfully ablaze and the bed over in the far corner. A door led off the main room into what was presumably a bathroom. By the bed were a couple of handrails fixed to the wall and one of the chairs near to the fire had a handrail near it, attached to the floor.

As Dorothea followed Maggie, she noticed that there were no handles on her wheelchair and that Maggie propelled herself swiftly and expertly by spinning the chair's wheels.

'I have been here for ever and know everyone. This is my fourth year, and I am doing a Master of Science in Mathematics,' Maggie said chattily. 'I have had this room since my first year. In case you were wondering, I had polio when I was tiny. I can stand up for small amounts of time but not for very long. It doesn't bother me. You don't need to stand up to do Mathematics. Anyway, enough about me, I see you are down to do English. Tell me about yourself while I put the kettle on and make a pot of tea. There are some crumpets on the table over there and a toasting fork. The butter is in a bag hanging outside the window. Jam and honey in that cupboard. Please help yourself and start toasting.'

Dorothea found herself sat in front of the fire with a crumpet speared on the toasting fork and a mug of hot sweet steaming tea next to her, telling Maggie all about her home and family life especially about her father dying the previous year and how it had turned her world upside down. Maggie was an excellent and sympathetic listener and with pertinent questions drew Dorothea out until she felt comfortable enough to tell her all about the strange happenings of her journey to Manchester and why she had been late. Some of the shock melted away under the medicinal properties of jammy crumpets, tea and kindly company.

'I don't think the inspector trusted me very much,' Dorothea said, especially since I couldn't find the piece of paper that Matty gave me.'

Maggie chuckled, 'I think that is the least or your worries. You sound like you will have made an enemy of Dr Hadley-Brown for life, with your mistaking a catapult for a gun! He is a Fellow in your Faculty by the way. Simon Culthorpe says Dr Hadley-Brown is frightfully grumpy at the best of times and rather stuck up. He did both his undergraduate and PhD at Cambridge you know.'

'Who is Simon Culthorpe?' Dorothea asked bemusedly, thinking that he must be important.

'Oh, no-one special,' Maggie replied airily. 'Just a man I know.' She changed the subject rapidly. 'Anyway, tomorrow is a big day for you so you should probably head off to bed. Breakfast is from 7 a.m., in the dining room. Medics and Agriculture students who have an early start can request a packed breakfast from the kitchen staff the night before. There is a sign-up sheet. The bus into the university leaves from outside the gate on Wilmslow Road, or alternatively the tram can take you to town. We will be having a fire drill this week, so the muster point is the tennis courts. Out the door at the end of the corridor and turn left and you can't miss them. Every Sunday afternoon I host afternoon tea here for anyone who wants to come along. We do the weekend crosswords together. I particularly like the Listener Cryptic Crossword.'

After thanking her new friend, assuring her of her attendance next Sunday and promising that if she had any problems no matter how small, at any time in the day or night she would knock on Maggie's door, she left to go to her own room.

The fire had died down to glowing coals and the room was cosy and comforting. Dorothea sighed, closed the door behind herself and locked it.

'Sanctuary,' she whispered.

The Funeral of Ethel Worksop, Friday Morning, 14th September 1934

The church of St John's was full to bursting for the funeral of Ethel Worksop who had died so young and in such tragic and mysterious circumstances. The local and academic communities were for once united in their joint grief and in some cases, crass thrill-seeking. When the slight coffin was lowered into the dank hole in the graveyard surrounded by mourners, there was a collective in-drawing of breath and Mrs Worksop clutching her husband's arm sobbed into her black edged hanky. DI Kydd who was discreetly at the back of the group was sure he saw a flash from a camera cheekily hidden by the graveyard wall.

'I might need to have a word about common decency with that journalist from the university's magazine,' he muttered under his breath.

After the funeral, the wake was held at Mr and Mrs Worksop's house and was very well attended so there was not a chair to be had in that cluttered middle-class terrace. DI Kydd was in a quandary. He held a cup and saucer of tea in one hand and a generous slab of fruit loaf in the other and therefore was totally incapacitated from eating or drinking either. The inspector had to make do with putting his cup and saucer down on a convenient sideboard and wedging his broad frame into the corner next to it while applying himself to his cake. He noticed that Mabel Parker, a pretty, plump young woman who was the Treasurer of the Women's Union was having similar difficulties to himself with a plate of beef paste sandwiches which she was devouring hungrily nearby.

DI Kydd mentally reviewed the ongoing hit-and-run case and the statements of Ethel's colleagues at the university. It was odd what had happened to Ethel Worksop. Ethel had stayed inside the Women's Union building after the Executive Officers had had their new term social, an idea of Constance Harris, the President of the Women's Union and Chair of the committee. It had included an insipid afternoon tea with limp cucumber sandwiches and dry scones and had dragged all the Executive Officers back to university two weeks earlier than was necessary for the start of term activities.

Supposedly, Ethel Worksop had wanted to use the typewriter in the committee office to type up the agenda for the first committee meeting of the year. However, it was the generally held opinion of her fellow Executive Officers that it was much more likely Ethel wanted to snoop.

The committee office was a cluttered room, filled with the detritus from past themed socials, Rag Week collecting tins and filing cabinets. It was also the hub from which all activities of the Women's Union filtered out from. All the Executive Officers had a desk in the office, though for actually doing any work the library was a much better place to be, to get away from the constant comings and goings and chatter.

Ethel Worksop had been a second-year Languages student. She had been an average, rather than an outstanding scholar, but was blessed or possibly cursed with being absolutely fascinated with everything, much to her tutors' dismay, as they had had a hard time getting her to focus. A gossip, Ethel always wanted to know what was going on and hated not knowing a secret.

On the fateful evening of the social, Tuesday the 28th of August, all the Executive Officers had hung around nibbling sandwiches and making painfully polite small talk about their summer holidays. At around 7 p.m. the other Executive Officers had gradually dispersed, leaving Ethel and the caretaker alone in the building.

The caretaker was a Great War veteran who had had his ear drums damaged by the noise of shelling so was profoundly hard of hearing. He looked after both the men's and women's union buildings which were separate but abutted each other with a door on the first floor for the Joint Common Room. He had a flat in the attic space of the women's side and didn't seem to mind the merry-go-round of dances, debates and socials happening under his feet because he could not hear the rumpus caused by the students.

Ethel had apparently worked by herself until 10 p.m. before she locked the office and let herself out the building with the spare key which she posted through the letterbox, a practice previously agreed with the caretaker for locking up. The police thought she had walked to the corner where Lyme Grove met Oxford Road and had been about to cross to the other side when having seen a van coming, she stepped back onto the pavement. The van however, mounted the pavement and ran her over and drove off. She was dead by the time PC Standish arrived on the scene; the accident having been witnessed by a couple of doctors from the Royal Infirmary on their way home from an exceptionally busy day at work. The coroner had given an open verdict on her death and the police investigation was still ongoing for the driver of the van.

At this point in DI Kydd's cogitations a wing-backed chair tucked in a dark corner of the room, became free. He was quick to jump at the chance to drink his tepid cup of tea sitting down with the saucer balanced on his knee. From the chair's solid security, he had a good view of the room and into the hallway without being easily spotted. It was the perfect place to observe people.

He considered the remaining Executive Officers dispassionately, a very disparate bunch of individuals in his opinion. These women had been in post since Easter, as elections were always held before breaking up for the Easter holidays, with new committee members taking up their posts in the summer term so that they were *au fait* with what they were doing before the new academic year began. However, even with time to bed in, this committee didn't seem to function as a cohesive unit and the inspector had picked up undercurrents of discontent when taking the young women's statements.

Apparently, Constance Harris, the President of the Women's Union, was cut from a very different cloth to previous Presidents who had tended to be hard-working and from lower-middle class backgrounds with a leaning to the left. Constance Harris was the daughter of a Baronet, the niece of a current Member of Parliament and the granddaughter of a former Chancellor of the Exchequer.

Considered dispassionately, Constance Harris was an effective leader, she knew her own mind and got results. People tended to flock to her, as they knew they wouldn't have to think of anything off their own back. If the inspector was feeling unkind, he would say Constance was a product of a class that always got their own way by talking loudly over everyone else and ignoring anyone else's ideas and feelings, especially if they were at odds with her own. She had a long face, elongated by very straight hair that wouldn't easily take a curl and had a distinctive nasal laugh that no matter where one was in a noisy room would cut across all chatter and conversation and grate on one's nerves.

DI Kydd shuddered, Constance had been ringing his office for daily updates on his enquiries into Ethel Worksop's death and wanted him to come and speak to the Committee, ostensibly to reassure them, but more likely so that Constance looked like she was taking 'decisive leadership' seriously. He really did not have the time and had been prevaricating.

Constance had backed Mrs Worksop into a corner of the room by a sad-looking, potted aspidistra and was conveying the heartfelt sympathy of the Women's Union without the insight that the dead young woman's mother was only holding herself together by force of will.

DI Kydd watched as kindly Iris Robinson intervened in what was rapidly becoming a form of torture that certainly would be outlawed by the Swiss. Iris Robinson was Vice President and had served as such under the previous President as well. Academically brilliant, but intuitive and engaged with the real world, Iris was a third-year medical student, a Marxist and involved with the University Settlement.

Under Iris's tact and skill Constance's attention was diverted from her victim, who scurried away to the kitchen as if the three-headed hound of hell was on her tail, towards the provost, Professor Quentin B. Smythe, who had just entered the room with the warden of Grangebrook Hall, Dr Teresa Winterbottom. The provost was acting as the university's most senior representative at this sad occasion and the shadow of trepidation which passed across his good-natured face was rapidly replaced with resignation, as he recognised Constance bearing down on him, knowing that any plan of escape would be futile for at least half an hour.

Dr Winterbottom prudently excused herself and went to join a group of committee members, past and present, warming themselves by the fire. Tabitha Gillespie, a retired representative who had stepped down at Easter was attempting to keep up a sparkling flow of conversation with sullen Alexandra Cotton, the Athletics Union Secretary, who was still sulking with the full Committee's decision earlier that week to hold off on charitable giving in the autumn term. It was part of Constance Harris's 'Responsible Stewardship Campaign' but quietly listening in, the inspector gathered that it was the opinion of Alexandra Cotton that, 'Constance was plain mean-spirited not to support the social projects they always did.'

Tabitha broke off from listening to Alexandra's moaning to procure Abigail Rushton, the Debating Society Secretary, a drink for a nasty sounding cough and greeted the warden's arrival with very obvious relief.

A ripple of interest was happening outside the room. A titter of laughter rapidly hushed, and voices rose in welcome. The funereal atmosphere momentarily lightened. An older woman entered the room and with her came sunlight. Mrs Gladys Adams was the Advisor to Women Students, greatly loved and respected by undergraduates and postgraduates alike. It was said that she had an eidetic memory and knew all the new undergraduate student's names within the first fortnight of term. An alumna of the Victoria University of Manchester, once a suffragette and now the widow of Hon. Mr Ferdinand Adams, a stalwart of the Foreign Office, she had had a brilliant career supporting her husband in getting differing people to talk to each other all around the globe. While the Hon. Mr Ferdinand Adams was praised for diplomatic successes that lesser men would have had trouble bringing about, people in the know knew that the chief weapon in his conciliatory arsenal was the beautiful and talented Mrs Adams who had the gift of making people feel listened to and appreciated. On her husband's sad and early demise, she moved back to Britain from the furthest reaches of the Empire much to the dismay of the Foreign Office who would have offered her a posting in her own right.

The provost was delighted and rather flattered when Mrs Adams came to him and said that as she was at a loose end and wanted to give something back to the institution that had nurtured her own academic talents, was there anything she could do to help?

Having Mrs Adams on the staff would be a large feather in the university's cap and would give him bragging rights with the provosts of other notable seats of learning. Also, Mrs Adams was a very distant cousin on his mother's side and his mother, a strident octogenarian, had strongly put it to him that, 'Cousin Gladys should be accommodated.' The provost hoped that employing Mrs Adams might go some way to make up for missing his own goddaughter's wedding, over which his mother had threatened to cut him out of her will.

Fortuitously the position of Advisor to Women Students was free, as Miss Conway had retired the previous spring, after a nervous breakdown had forced her to step down, and Mrs Adams was snapped up and installed in an office on the second floor of the Women's Union. Her duties were to sit on both the Executive Committee and Full Committee as a voice of reason, to support the Executive Officers in their decision making, to give pastoral and emotional support to any female student in need and to deal with anything of an embarrassing nature with tact and dignity, that a male tutor might find awkward to broach with a female student. This last duty encompassed a whole host of scenarios as far flung as why Mary Jameson missed lectures once a month with chronic 'headaches', what to do with Cecily Thomas's 'pash' for Dr Maddox, a Mathematics Lecturer who was a very timid and happily married man and why Jane Harden and Petunia Finnegan were absolutely inseparable.

Nodding and exchanging greetings with acquaintances as she walked through the cluttered, crowded room she meandered her way over to Mabel Parker who was just finishing off a piece of cherry cake, a waft of expensive Parisian perfume proclaiming her advance.

In his dark corner DI Kydd sat slouched a little further back into his chair and shamelessly earwigged.

'Mabel I am so glad to have caught you!' Mrs Adams exclaimed. 'You are looking lovely my dear, positively blooming. Have you and your fiancé set a date for the wedding? March? Such a lovely month to get married.

'I did so want to catch up with you regarding Evelyn King and the preparations for the Christmas ball, it's early I know but I do feel it is important to get ahead in these matters.' Mrs Adams continued, 'I know Evelyn can get a little bit carried away with her Social Secretary duties and her family are friendly with that horrible little man that the newspapers are full of. Hitler, I mean. The Germans have just made him "der Führer". I met him once in Vienna. Very overrated and pompous and that moustache! Such a silly affectation.

'Anyway, I do want to prevent a repeat of what happened at the summer fayre. The students from the Jewish Society and several international students really were quite hurt to be left out. It took a lot of smoothing over and the provost really was not pleased. We don't want to go the way of Germany and Spain. I do think we should be coming together in these times, rather than driving wedges between people. I knew if I had a little word with you that we would be on the same page and can watch out for anything of the same again and nip it in the bud.'

'Of course, Mrs Adams,' Mabel said. 'We definitely don't want any of that nastiness at the Christmas ball. I will back you up.'

'Thank you my dear. You are such a comfort.'

'There was something I wanted to ask you about too.' Mabel twisted her fingers together nervously. 'It's just that when I came to take money out of petty cash for the flowers and card for today, well, there wasn't as much in there as there should have been. I know that on Wednesday there was two pounds in the cash box as I had been to see the University Cashier to get funds for the new term. There was a new pound note in there and I didn't have a chance to go to the bank until yesterday and by yesterday afternoon it had gone. I have been worrying about it all night. Everyone knows that they should note in the ledger whenever they take any cash and write in the amount left over. I check the ledger and count the petty cash once a week to keep on top of our finances. For taking out sums like that it needs to be approved by me as Treasurer and they need a receipt.'

Mrs Adams looked thoughtful. 'When you say everyone, who precisely do you mean?'

'All the Executive Committee Officers and many of the committee members use it too, if they are given a commission by the Committee or if there is a regular outgoing like biscuits for the Debating Society. I have tried to get people to keep receipts so I can reimburse them, but some members don't have the personal finances that will allow them to be out of pocket for even a small length of time.'

'Hmmm . . . And you are sure that the money is missing?'

'Absolutely!' The sincerity true rang in Mabel's voice. 'I have triple checked the cash box and hunted around in the cupboard it is kept in, and it just isn't there.'

'Have you asked the other members of the Executive Committee?'

'I have asked around casually if anyone in the office saw anyone taking money out of the petty cash box because the ledger doesn't quite tally but no one is letting on. I didn't want to alarm the thief.' The word dropped harshly into the middle of the conversation.

'Watch and wait for now. If there really is a thief about, they won't stop with the petty cash,' Mrs Adams said, looking serious.

'What about the police?' Mabel queried. 'I saw DI Kydd here earlier. He seemed nice.'

Feeling a little bit guilty but determined not to miss a word, DI Kydd, barely six feet away, slunk even deeper into his chair.

'Not yet, we want to try and avoid a scandal if at all possible and we are still not really sure if it was taken deliberately or if the person has simply forgotten or is unable to replace it. Women's Higher Education is something we have had to fight hard for. We don't want one thief – if there is one – to give the rest of us a reputation as unhinged or troublemakers. I'll make up the money that has gone missing and you and I will be on our guard.'

'Thank you so much Mrs Adams. It feels so good to have told you. I'll sleep better tonight.'

'You are welcome my dear. It is good to talk about worries. They shrivel up under closer scrutiny!' Mrs Adams said wisely.

So there is a thief about in the Women's Union, as well as a hit and run driver and a gunman, DI Kydd thought grimly. *Something more to add to the list of crimes to solve.*

CHAPTER THREE

Crosswords and Puzzles

Fresher's Week, the Week Beginning Monday 10th September 1934, and the Start of the Autumn Term

The start of term involved a lot of standing in queues: to catch the university bus or tram, to register with your school of choice, multiple schools if you were doing some cross-disciplinary courses, then for the individual courses themselves, societies, the Women's Union, and the library. The queuing seemed interminable. Real lectures didn't begin in earnest until the following week.

Alongside academic activities, all the university societies were running tasters and events to lure new students into joining them. The temptation for first-years was to join too many and then be over-gotten with meetings and extracurricular activities and fall behind in their studies. Dorothea had thought out her strategy carefully. She joined the Athletics Union so she could try out for the hockey team, as at school she had been on the women's under twenty ones team for Derbyshire. Even having had time off training with pneumonia she was still pretty nippy and thought she could make the reserves if not the first hockey team. She also joined the Drama Society, along with many other hopefuls. She had been warned by Maggie that all the good parts in shows went to Drama Society committee members but at least being signed up meant she could audition for the smaller speaking roles and chorus.

Dorothea soon settled into life at Grangebrook's Halls of Residence. She made friends on her corridor and there were a few late nights sitting in someone or other's room in pyjamas, philosophising, putting the world to rights and drinking elderflower wine that had been a gift from home.

In that first week Dorothea spent quite a lot of her free time when she was not queueing, walking around the city centre getting to know her way around with a map provided by the joint Student Unions. It gave her a thrill to think she was walking the same streets as Elizabeth Gaskell a particular literary heroine of hers.

The Victorian architecture of Manchester, a grandiose mixture of Greek colonnades and gothic sculpture rising upwards, high into the sky, taller than Dorothea would have thought possible, left the footpath user feeling slightly claustrophobic if they glanced up.

Trams wheezed past with the electrical smell of the dodgems wafting after them, jostling for position with motor buses, motor cars, cyclists, horses and carts and pedestrians. And everywhere there were people. Businessmen with umbrellas and bowler hats, elegant ladies off to the art gallery or to play tennis, workers in their overalls let out on mass from local factories at the lunchtime and home time whistles, the homeless, mainly men, living rough on the streets, sometimes missing a limb, veterans forgotten by their peers and country. Growing up in the countryside the biggest town Dorothea had ever seen was Buxton where the extremes of rich and poor were less marked.

Lectures and tutorials began the following week. Her favourite lecturer was shaping up to be Professor

Aldridge who taught Anglo-Saxon and had the first-years for two, one-hour sessions a week. He was tall and willowy, had spikey white hair and a neat little white beard which was at least twenty years out of date. He had a dry sense of humour and his eyes sparkled at his students as he teased them for not having done the preliminary reading. Even though he felt very approachable and smiled kindly at her when she answered her name on the register, Dorothea could not bring herself to tell him about the note Matilda Abbott had given her to pass on to him. She felt a sense of guilt and failure every time she thought of the still missing Matty. There had been no news of her in over a fortnight.

Her worst lesson of the week was a two-hour tutorial with the enigmatic Dr Hadley-Brown on *Beowulf*, currently the English translation but moving to the original Anglo-Saxon later in the term when they had studied the piece some more. It had come as a shock to find out that the man from the train really was to teach her. There were only fifteen students in the group to a tutorial room rather than one hundred and twenty students in a lecture theatre so there was no way of hiding from his haughty looks of derision or icy glares when she, and to be fair, other members of the tutorial group, got something wrong, which with a subjective subject was pretty hard to do.

The Philology Lecturer had set Dorothea's year their first essay question and it was Dr Hadley-Brown's job to mark the essays when they were handed in. Dorothea was disappointed to see she had received a C – and a comment that said: *Few original ideas and mainly regurgitation of other people's work. In future, please read around the subject and then think for yourself. Good referencing.*

There was only limited consolation one could take in having good referencing.

The one event that did stand out during the first few weeks of term interspersed with hockey trials (which were successful), drama auditions (which were not), trips to the library to reserve books and lunching in the cafeteria with new course mates, was that Grangebrook Hall was broken into, and a room ransacked on the first floor.

One of the second-years came into the dining room one evening at dinner, big with news. During the day while most of the students had been in lectures and tutorials at the city centre campus, someone had gained entrance to the hall and had turned one of the first-year's rooms upside down. The porter had not seen anyone out of the ordinary come in through the main door but being a large building there was multiple side doors and fire escapes. The second-year was now a Floor Rep herself and made a beeline for Maggie Forshaw. Dorothea was sitting at Maggie's table and her ears pricked up.

'Maggie you'll never guess. Poor Freddie is having hysterics at the moment, in the warden's study. She only swapped into that room at the last minute because she was allocated a ground floor room and is terrified of someone coming through her window in the night. She is saying that she won't stay here another night.'

'Slow down. What has happened?' Maggie was calm in the face of calamity.

'Everything was thrown out of the chest of drawers and wardrobe; the mattress and pillows were slit, and the stuffing ripped out. They had pulled up some of the floorboards too. I am surprised that no one heard anything. They even ripped to pieces Freddie's new winter coat. She thinks nothing has actually been taken though.'

'That is shocking! Presumably no one heard anything because that corridor houses only first-years and they would be religiously out at lectures during the day.

Lethargy hasn't set in yet. Are the police being called in?'

'The warden told me to ring the Town Hall Police Headquarters and ask for DI Kydd. The inspector said he would be along with a police constable as soon as ever he could. The warden told me to lock the door and bring her the key. I am just on my way back to her now. She was interviewing a young gentleman when I knocked on her study door. He was a bit of a dish.'

'Which room is it?' Dorothea piped up to the second-year's retreating figure.

'115,' she called back over her shoulder. 'Whoever swapped out of it was very fortunate.'

Dorothea and Maggie exchanged startled glances. They both knew that room 115 was the room Dorothea had originally been allocated.

Tuesday 18th September 1934, Morning

DI Kydd got off the train at Euston in a surge of humanity. He had left PC Standish hunkered down using the typewriter in the inspector's own office, pulling together the latest report in the search for the missing student Matilda Abbott. All the land owned by the university had been searched along with university owned premises and large swathes of the city centre, moving progressively out towards the suburbs but all to no avail. The Chief Superintendent, at DI Kydd's request, had ordered the dredging of the city centre canals and rivers starting tomorrow. All the ports and aerodromes had been warned to stop anyone leaving the country with a passport in the name of Matilda Abbott. The story had even made the national news, possibly due to the unsolved hit and run involving the female student, and the public support both locally and nationwide was high.

The warden of Grangebrook Hall, Dr Winterbottom, was terribly upset and worried and would ring up the inspector for regular updates. This new vandalism of a student's room had really gotten under her skin. The warden's hall was definitely her castle.

It was from her that the inspector had obtained Matilda's home address and next of kin which seemed to be a maiden aunt in a very respectable suburb of London, in Sutton. He had phoned the aunt, a Miss Peterson, at home, the week before to break the bad news that her niece was missing and ask if he could come and pay his respects in person and to ask a few questions. The reception he received from down the other end of the phone was odd. It was not frosty but there was an absence of human warmth there and certainly not what he would have expected from a worried, doting aunt. The news was received as if the information had been noted, processed, and archived, and a begrudging, 'If you must,

42

but next week,' was the response he'd received when he'd asked if he could visit.

So it was that the inspector had taken a whole day away from the office to travel down to London and back, to call on Miss Peterson to see if she had any new leads on the likely whereabouts of Matilda Abbott.

He caught the northern tube line to London Bridge, a train on the Dorking line to Sutton Station and from there a taxi to Viburnum Drive which deposited him on the doorstep of a neat, fairly newly built semi-detached house with roses, asters and chrysanthemums in the front garden, in a very respectable neighbourhood.

The woman who opened the door to him was the personification of a cheerful maiden aunt. She was petite, with downy waves of white hair all over her head and contained in braids at the nape of her neck. She was wearing respectable tweeds and lamb's wool and smelt of lavender water with a hint of mothballs. She greeted him warmly but with the correct amount of worry in her voice for someone whose niece was missing.

The hairs on the back of the inspector's neck stood up on end. The voice and tone of Miss Peterson sounded very different to the woman he had spoken to on the phone just a few days before. Sensing his confusion, the woman welcomed him into an immaculate living room and offered him a cup of tea.

'I am so sorry if I was abrupt on the phone. It was such a shock you see, and I had one of my migraines so felt very under the weather.'

The inspector nodded and smiled and commiserated with her on her misfortune of suffering from such a debilitating condition and all the time marked her down as a grade one liar. It had not been this woman he had spoken to on the phone.

'Are you Matilda's only family?' the inspector asked. Miss Peterson was down as Matilda's only next of kin on her university records.

'Oh, yes, Inspector!' Miss Peterson fluttered. 'I brought her up when her parents died tragically in a train accident when she was a small girl. We are quite alone in the world the two of us.'

'Where did Matilda go to school, and did she have any particular friends that she might confide in?' the inspector asked, digging further.

'We used to live in Clapham, and she went to the local primary school and girl's grammar school. You know girls, Inspector. Matilda had a new best friend every week. So many came round for tea, one forgets all their names.'

The inspector did know girls, for as well as having two daughters himself he had three nieces. He knew the names of all their pals and while sometimes friendships came and went, most girls have one or a couple of really close friends growing up who they would do anything for.

You are lying again, the inspector thought. *I wonder why?*

'Did she have a boyfriend at all Miss Peterson?' DI Kydd continued. 'Some local lad she was walking out with?'

'Oh, no, Inspector! She was a very shy sort of girl. She would never go about with any young man especially without my knowledge. She trusted my judgement so much you see.' Miss Peterson touched a handkerchief artistically to two very dry eyes.

DI Kydd thought that Miss Peterson was overdoing it a bit now.

'Is there anyone or any place that you know of that Matilda might run to if she was in trouble?' the inspector asked, going through the motions, knowing full well that the answer he would receive wouldn't be a helpful one.

'No, Inspector. We were so close she would have come

to me, I am sure, if she was in trouble of any kind.'

The inspector noted the past tense. *She thinks Matilda is dead already*, he thought. *How does she know that?*

'Did she have any enemies?'

'Enemies? What an unusual question, Inspector,' Miss Peterson tittered. 'Of course not. She was a completely normal young woman. Normal young women do not have enemies.'

'Is there any other information that you could possibly tell me that might be pertinent to my enquiries into Matilda's disappearance? The truth could be vital to save a life,' the inspector said sternly.

'Oh, Inspector, you are scaring me now!' Miss Peterson said, promptly having a fit of the vapours.

It was a very nice performance, the inspector thought.

Why? Why is a performance necessary? She is hoping I'll take fright and run away. Well, I can play along and see what happens. He pretended to be ill at ease.

'Now, Miss Peterson, there is no need to take on so. Do you want me to call the doctor, or do you have a friend I can call? Should I put the kettle on?'

'Oh, Inspector, I think one of my migraines is coming on. I think I need to go upstairs and lie down. Do you think you can show yourself out?'

The inspector took his leave. He made a charade of closing the front door but left it ajar and walked up the path as far as the neighbour's property before bobbing down again, pretending to tie his shoelace, and counting to thirty. He then stood up, tutted, and walked back towards the house with every appearance of belonging there. He then put his ear to the gap in the open door.

All was quiet for a couple of minutes before the inspector heard a door open softly and Miss Peterson called out, 'He has gone! I saw him go down the path and out of the gate.'

He heard a man's voice in crisp, refined tones say,

'Well done, Hilary! You are a better actress than you think. He didn't suspect a thing.'

'I don't like deceiving the police, Mr George. The inspector was only doing his job and we have just made it longer and harder for him.'

'It is only for a short while. Abbott might have gone into deep cover. We need to buy time until the danger is passed. We are certainly on the right track. There is something big going on at the university,' Mr George said soothingly.

'Can we be sure Abbott is still alive? It's been nearly two weeks since we had any contact. Our information said there were shots fired at the station,' Miss Peterson sounded worried.

'Abbott is a very experienced agent. There is a very good chance that Abbott is alright. Did you hear something?'

DI Kydd had taken a step back and upset a milk bottle with a crash.

He quickly pulled the door to and simultaneously knocked smartly on it, giving the bell a ring for good measure. There was an exclamation, a door slamming; running feet and Miss Peterson's worried face peered around the door.

The inspector was everything that was apologetic. He was sorry to disturb Miss Peterson so soon, but had he left his handkerchief behind? It had been a gift from his wife, hand embroidered, and he would be sorry to lose it.

Flustered, Miss Peterson went to look for it but not before shutting the door firmly in his face.

She was back in a minute with the offending article retrieved from where he had stuffed it down the side of the sofa for just such an occasion. He made his apologies again and took his leave.

All the way back to Manchester on the train, he puzzled over the identity of Matilda Abbott, who she was

working for and what was going on in the Women's
Union.

Sunday 30ᵗʰ September 1934, Afternoon

Sunday afternoon crosswords and cake soon became a weekly diary date with Dorothea. A small group of students met in Maggie Forshaw's room bringing with them treats sent from home, or cakes and biscuits precariously baked in the communal kitchen, shared with the floor above. Maggie made tea in an odd assortment of tooth mugs and teacups, not one of them matching, and the others admired the spread and cut each offering into the same number of pieces as attendees.

A regular attendee was the Hon. Miss Tabitha Gillespie a third-year Law student who had won a place at Cambridge and had subsequently dropped out after a term due to the 'obnoxious elite'. Changing institutions, she felt more at home with the sons and daughters of shopkeepers, doctors and farmers and belonged to the Socialist Society. Flaxen and freckled and built on Valkyrie lines, she could have been the inspiration for Wagner's Brunhilde. She was a whirlwind of action by nature and had spent her first two years at the university as a year representative on the Committee fighting for the rights of her year group. Before her final year, Tabitha's tutors had had to sit her down and point out the need for a more focussed approach to her studies if she was to pass her undergraduate degree. It was with some real regret that Tabitha passed the baton of year representation to other equally capable hands and knuckled down to work. She was an alumna of Grangebrook Hall and now lived out in digs near Salford.

Then there were the two Marys. There was Mary Long, a second-year Chemist from Inverness with Celtic fiery locks, a dry sense of humour and a strict Presbyterian upbringing from which she was on the run. She liked photography and ballroom dancing but not necessarily together. Then there was Mary Short (which was long for Shor) who Dorothea had met on her first day, who was a second-year medical student from a local Jewish family. She was always immaculately turned out, with almost burgundy coloured hair that she wore crimped and waved in the latest style. Mild mannered, Mary Short was also on the hockey team with Dorothea and turned into a screaming, whirling fury on a hockey pitch. She was the team's secret weapon and had rival teams quaking in their shinpads. The two Marys were the best of friends and together they were known as 'the Long and Short of it' by their friends.

The final member of the group was Mrs Jinny Moss. She was a friend and contemporary of Maggie who had graduated the year before with a First-Class degree with honours in Music and Theology. Maggie had been one of her bridesmaids at her wedding in the summer to a local vicar, a widower with a young daughter. While no longer a member of the university, Jinny dropped in on a Sunday afternoon whenever she was able to, to 'keep my brain sharp' she said, but Dorothea thought there was a ghost of wistfulness there; Jinny really had been a brilliant scholar.

Each week the group started off with an easier crossword puzzle clipped from a daily newspaper like the Manchester Guardian or the Times, during the week it was usually pinched from the reading room, and jealously saved for such an occasion. They then worked up to the weekly Listener crossword which Maggie swore was the hardest and which made Dorothea's head hurt with the twisty nature of the clues. It was a good week if together they could do two thirds of it. It was a very good week if they very nearly completed it.

Dorothea treasured these lazy Sunday afternoons with friends. These were her home-from-home little family. They challenged her and accepted her, and she felt comfortable in their company.

'Ten across, four letters, Water Cubed,' Mary Long said, who had the neatest handwriting and who by consensus was scribe of choice.

Silence reigned as they all munched on a rich fruit cake.

'Dice?' Tabitha suggested.

'Yes of course that would fit but means eight down is Slander rather than Scandal. Twelve across, Spy – Broker, five letters, third letter is "E".'

'Agent,' they all said together and then laughed.

While this was going on, Mary Short was flicking through the latest copy of the university's student magazine, *The Worm*. She idly gave them updates on what was happening on campus.

'They still haven't found the student that went missing . . . Whatshername Thingermebob. The one who lives here, that Dorothea met on the train.'

By this time all the group knew of Dorothea's adventures at the start of term.

'Still no news? I saw the police out and about around Fallowfield Campus the other day looking for something,' Jinny said.

'Not some*thing*, some*one*!' Tabitha butted in. They were looking for a body. A load of the chaps on my course volunteered to help search. Matilda Abbott won't be alive by now if she hasn't surfaced already. Eighteen down is Blameworthy by the way,' she added callously.

'There has been nothing about the break-in in room 115 and while there is wild speculation about Ethel Worksop who got run over there is nothing new . . . Hang on. This is weird,' Mary Short said, still flicking through *The Worm*. 'I love reading the personal ads of newspapers and magazines. You know hypothesising about the author and metaphorically people watching. Well, *The Worm* doesn't usually have that sort of ad. Us emancipated female students would be ashamed to advertise for a matrimonial partner and the male students have egos the size of a planet and think that any woman they look at would want to jump into bed with them so they wouldn't need to advertise, either. Anyway, it's usually all third-years trying to sell textbooks to first-years or hard-up students trying to sell tutoring. Well, look at this!'

Crossword temporarily forgotten, they all gathered around Mary Short and peered over her shoulder at what she was pointing at.

Dorothea read out loud the following: 'Mr D seeks his Eliza for dances, companionship, and matrimony. None of her sisters need apply. 182.5.6 189.25.6, 53:28:54 2:14:46. PO Box 1315.'

'Maybe it's one of the tutors?' Mary Long said. 'Dr Hadley-Brown is very good looking and so moody, just like a certain hero from *Pride and Prejudice* . . .' she said, with a comical nod to Dorothea.

'Silly!' Dorothea was not playing along; still smarting.

'Veronica Dingle thinks she saw Dr Hadley-Brown dining at the Ritz last week and guess who with?' Tabitha added. 'You never will. It was our Mrs Adams, the Advisor to Women Students! She is quite old, poor thing. She must be pushing forty at least. Though she is terribly glamorous. He must only be twenty-six or seven.'

'I don't think it is one of the tutors,' Maggie said, bringing them back to the job in hand. 'Have any of you got any old copies of *The Worm*?'

Mary Long had some in her room and she went off to fetch them. They were from the summer term of the previous year. On her return, Mary Short turned to the personal ads and looking down the column discovered a similar missive in one of them.

'Lydia thanks Mr W for his kind offer of matrimony but has chosen to decline. She will return his ring to the following address PO Box 1030. 166.24.7 251.31.3,

53:28:6 2:12:29,' she read aloud.

'I think it is a code. Someone is using the magazine to pass on messages to someone else,' Maggie said.

'Really? Who would want to do that?' Jinny sounded surprised.

'Perhaps the same someone who would want to shoot a female student on a train.' The atmosphere in the room suddenly became very tense. 'There have been lots of odd goings-on this term, so far. We are a clever bunch; we should be able to figure this out. What can we come up with?' Maggie asked.

'Well, the characters are all from *Pride and Prejudice*,' Dorothea commented. 'Maybe the different characters are code names for people?'

'Yes, and the bit about "none of her sisters need apply" might mean that there are more of them out there reading the ad and it is specifically "Eliza" that is wanted in this case,' Mary Long suggested.

'You think it is the female character that is the focus or the male character?' Maggie asked.

'Female, obviously,' There was emphatic agreement amongst the group.

'This bit about "returning the ring" could it be an order from someone to "Lydia"? Maybe there was a drop-off last term sometime?' Jinny asked tentatively, after a while.

'Good! We are getting somewhere,' Dorothea exclaimed. 'If the "Lydia" ad is a drop-off maybe the "Eliza" one is a pick-up or meet-up? 'Declining matrimony equals drop-off and accepting offers of matrimony equals a pick-up or meeting. If only we had more of these ads.'

Mary Short and Mary Long had gone very quiet in the corner of the room where Maggie's bookshelf was. They had found a map of the local area and were working out map coordinates. After conferring for some moments, they were ready to share their findings with the group.

"53:28:54 2:14:46' and '53:28:6 2:12:29' are latitude and longitude map references,' Mary Long said. 'They are in hours, minutes and seconds.'

'For the "Eliza" advert the map reference is for St Ann's Church on St Ann's Street,' Mary Short revealed. 'And for the "Lydia" advert it is for the parcel depot on Bennett Street.'

There were exclamations of amazement from the other members of the group.

'How did you work that out?' Dorothea cried.

They looked at each other.

'We were both girl guides,' Mary Long said, with a touch of pride in her voice. 'Map coordinates just stand out.'

'What about those other numbers?' Tabitha asked. 'Are they map coordinates too?'

'No,' Mary Short replied. 'They must be some other sort of code. What other codes do spies use?' she mused.

'It isn't a simple substitution code. You know A=1, B=2, C=3,' Maggie said, busily scribbling on the back of an old envelope, 'Or a mix of a substitution code with a Caesar shift where all the letters shift by a set amount. The numbers are too high. I can't find any recognisable patterns with the numbers. If there is some form of encryption in use, then it might be impossible for us to crack it without the code word or code book.'

'I don't think it is musical,' Jinny said, leaning over Maggie's shoulder. 'I have been trying to transpose the numbers into notes on the bass cleft and treble cleft and it doesn't produce anything resembling music or language.' She sang the notes to them.

The group looked at her in awe.

'You did that in your head? You are really smart,' Mary Long said. 'Weird but smart.'

Dorothea's eyes had glazed over ever since Maggie

had mentioned code books. She left the room and returned a few minutes later with a copy of *Pride and Prejudice* which was part of the English reading list.

'I wonder if the code-setter has given us the code book in the text,' she mused. 'Can someone read out the numbers please, the way they are written. I think they might be words on a page.'

'The "Eliza" one is "182.5.6 189.25.6" and the "Lydia" one is "166.24.7 251.31.3",' Maggie said.

'So page 182, line 5, word 6 equals nothing. It finishes at line 4. Page 189, line 25, word 6, is "At". Oh. It doesn't work for the "Eliza" one,' Dorothea said with disappointment. "Nothing" and "At".'

'It was a good idea,' Tabitha said kindly. 'Maybe it has to be a specific edition. Try the "Lydia" one instead.'

'That works out to be page 166, line 24, word 7 equals "Thursday" and page 251, line 31, word 3 equals "Bag". That is more like it! Lydia, drop the bag off at the postal depot on Bennett Street on Thursday,' Dorothea exclaimed excitedly.

'At 10.30 a.m.,' Maggie added. 'I have just noticed that the "PO Boxes" are both times on the twenty-four-hour clock. We are very nearly there. It is a pity we have solved the old, coded message rather than this weeks'.'

'I have got it!' Mary Long yelled, suddenly. 'Look at the road names. "Bennett Street" goes with the code name "Lydia". Bennet is the surname of the main family in *Pride and Prejudice*. However, in the "Eliza" advertisement it is "St Ann's Church" on "St Ann's Street". Ann isn't a main character in *Pride and Prejudice*, there is a very minor character by that name, the daughter of Lady Whatshername. Ann or rather Anne is the main character in *Persuasion*. Is *Persuasion* on your reading list too?'

'Yes! I'll go and get it. That is brilliant!' Dorothea said excitedly. She ran to her room, found the book, and started flicking through the pages on the way back to

Maggie's room.

'Hurry up slow coach we are dying to know what it says,' Tabitha shrieked.

'Page 182, line 5, word 6 equals "Wednesday" and page 189, line 25 word 6 equals "Altar". So, that must mean "Eliza, go to St Ann's church, St Ann's Street at 13.15 p.m. on Wednesday and look on or under the altar!" We did it! We solved the code!' Dorothea was delirious with their success. 'It is only Sunday today we could spy on the spies on Wednesday!'

Maggie took charge as the voice of reason. 'There are two things we should try and do: One, we should ask around at *The Worm* to see who is putting these adverts in to the paper and see if we can get copies of previous adverts to look for any more patterns and get an early copy of any new ones. Mary Short, you know the Editor of *The Worm,* don't you? Do you and Dorothea want to head there first thing tomorrow?'

'Erm . . .' Mary Short looked flustered.

'Yes of course!' Dorothea agreed.

'Mary likes David Simpkins, the editor, but her parents don't approve,' Mary Long whispered in Dorothea's ear.

Maggie continued, 'Two, some of us should go to the drop-off on Wednesday and see who turns up. It needs careful planning though.'

This met with general approval from the group and together they laid their plans, the crossword forgotten altogether.

CHAPTER FOUR

A Knife in the Back

Monday 1st October 1934, Early Morning

The following morning Dorothea and Mary Short left Grangebrook Hall early and headed into the city centre on the tram, as the pale autumnal sun caused the dew covering the manicured park lawns to shimmer and steam. The only other people present were some yawning medical students that Mary Short knew, who gave sleepy greetings and a Professor of Mechanical Engineering, manically marking test scores before the first lecture of the day.

The Worm's office was situated on the top floor of the Men's Union building next to the Joint Common Room so women were allowed to visit and could get there via the Women's Union.

'He is always the first one in,' Mary Short commented. 'I do hope he is there,' she said wistfully under her breath.

They were let into the building by the caretaker. Mr David Simpkins was typing at *The Worm's* office typewriter when Dorothea and Mary Short entered the room. He was puzzling over the phrasing of a particularly gripping piece of journalism with an imminent deadline, a furrow played on his handsome brow. As the two young women came into view, his mind snapped back to the present with alacrity and his deep blue eyes focused, then he smiled engagingly at Mary Short. Mary went a becoming shade of pink and smiled at him shyly.

'Hello there, you two,' he welcomed them in a broad Lancashire accent. 'It is right nice to see you again,' he said, looking directly at Mary Short.

'Um, hello!' Mary Short really didn't know where to look, all her usual poise was gone, and she was currently looking at a depressing picture on the wall over David's shoulder of a twee cat as if it was a Royal Academy exhibit.

Dorothea looked perplexedly at her friend. Never having been in love before herself, she studied the pair in front of her like a zoologist discovering a new bug under a stone.

'Um, we were er . . . We were wondering er . . .' Mary Short stuttered.

Dorothea took pity on her friend and took the lead as Mary Short seemed to be incapable of stringing together a complete sentence.

'We were wondering if you could help us, please.' Dorothea flashed David a winning smile. 'We noticed this personal advert in the latest copy of *The Worm* and last term there was one too.' She said holding out the two advertisements for his inspection. 'We were wondering, who placed them.'

'Yes, and are these the only ones or have there been more, previously? Mary Short asked, finally pulling herself together.

David took the clippings from Dorothea and studied them. Then nodding his head, he seemed to make a decision. 'Normally journalists don't reveal their sources, but in this case, I can't reveal who submits these ads because I really don't know. I have often wondered about these. When I first started at *The Worm* two years ago, I was in charge of collating the advert pages. I think a couple of these ads came in while I looked after that section. They aren't usually in back-to-back issues. They normally come in every couple of months, though occasionally there might be a couple in a month. You can have a look at our old issues if you like? They are next door in the archive room.

'Thanks awfully, that would be great!' Dorothea exclaimed gratefully.

'So how do you receive these advertisements then?' Mary Short was puzzled.

'They always come by post, the Friday before the Tuesday that an addition of *The Worm* is due to come out. They are always typed on a typewriter and the envelopes are typed too. Here, I think I kept one.' He rooted through his desk drawers and produced a much-maligned envelope. 'This one is from when I was on the advert section. It was sent on 28th October 1932, looking at the postmark.'

'Thank you!'

The two young women put their heads together and read. 'Elinor seeks her Mr F for woodland walks, picnics and to settle down in wedded bliss at the parsonage. Marianne and Margaret are dissuaded from joining. 209.33.8 224.6.2 53:29:28 2:15:33 PO Box 1900.'

'So that means Elinor go and meet someone or pick up something from somewhere. We will have to translate it properly later,' Mary Short said. 'We didn't bring the complete works of Jane Austen and a map with us.'

'Hey, are you girls on to a story?'

'Yes!' Mary Short said.

'No!' Dorothea said simultaneously. They looked at each other.

'We might be,' Dorothea conceded. 'But it is too early to say, and we might be wrong.'

'Well, if you are, I hope you will let me have the scoop?'

'Yes, of course,' the young women agreed in unison.

'I'll show you those back issues.'

He led them to a room leading off the main office which was a glorified stock cupboard. It looked like a bomb had gone off in there.

'Oh, no! I have dissection in half an hour,' Mary Short bemoaned, taking in the magnitude of their task.

'Don't worry I don't have any lectures until the afternoon. I'll have a look through these for some more of the advertisements,' Dorothea said.

'Can I walk you to your class?' David asked Mary, 'I need to drop this article off with the publishers, urgently.'

'Um, yes please,' Mary Short said, blushing again. They left the room with David trying to persuade Mary Short to go to the pictures with him that evening.

Left by herself, Dorothea began the herculean task of sorting through stationery, reams of paper, and back issues of *The Worm* stacked haphazardly on every surface.

***

Dorothea discovered that to find anything in the cupboard she had to do a lot of tidying and sorting to impose order on the chaos that was the repository of the history of student journalism, but after a couple of hours she was winning. No one had come into *The Worm's* office but then it was not yet ten o'clock. She had managed to find a further three of the Austen themed personal advertisements even though the archive of past magazines was nowhere near complete and there were massive gaps between issues. There was only one each from the previous three academic years that she could find to add to their collection, on top of the one David had given them. The advertisements first started in the Easter term three academic years previously. She copied each one carefully into a notebook for future study.

Mr B, a young gentleman with an independent fortune is looking to meet his Jane to look after in sickness and in health and to offer his hand in matrimony. 69.10.6 134.20.6 53:31:37 2:23:53 PO Box 1300. Published 31st May 1932.

Marianne wishes to meet her Colonel B for walks to the ruined priory, duets on the pianoforte and poetry readings. Anyone else would be in the way. 128.16.6 101.14.6 53:28:47 2:14:25 PO Box 1130. Published 14th March 1933.

Emma is devastated to dash Mr E's hopes, but she is unable to accept his kind proposal. She suggests a better match would be found at PO Box 1530 332.12.4 133.22.6 53: 27:1 2:12:56. Published 21st November 1933.

Just as she was finishing off, she heard the handle turn in the outer office door. For some reason she didn't automatically call out a greeting. There was a somewhat stealthy quality about the unlocking of the door. If it was David Simpkins returning, she figured he would have called out to see if she was still there. The cupboard door was very nearly closed to give her enough space to work inside, and no one would notice the light being on as the main light inside the office was also on, so she crouched down and applied her eye to the keyhole. She could see only a limited slice of the outer office through it, including the desk that David had been working at which had a telephone on it. It was the only telephone in the office. A woman was sat at the desk with her back to Dorothea. Dorothea could only see the woman's right shoulder and hand, the furthest from the telephone. She doodled on the blotting pad as she was waiting for the call to connect. Dorothea listened for the person at the other end to answer.

In a deep voice like a man's and muffled to disguise it further the woman intoned, 'I know what you did. You will pay for your crimes.'

A squeaky voice at the other end of the telephone could be heard saying, 'Who is this? What do you want?'

The unknown woman replied, 'Wait for instructions,' before ringing off and replacing the handset.

The woman laughed. It was not a nice laugh.

There is a large dose of malice in that laugh, Dorothea thought, hoping her presence would remain hidden.

This performance was repeated four more times, sometimes the woman hung up on hearing who answered, other times when she got through to the correct person, she used the same wording as the first call. Each time, the woman would disguise her voice and ring off abruptly. Grabbing her pencil and notebook Dorothea noted down the extension numbers.

After the phone calls had ended, Dorothea heard rapid typing on the office typewriter. It sounded like a Vickers machine gun shooting off round after round of poisonous ammo that could wound just as badly as the real thing and with a lot more accuracy.

Finally, the woman picked up her bag and moved towards the door. Dorothea remained glued to the keyhole in case she could get a better view of the mystery caller but try as she might the woman's face remained out of sight.

As soon as the woman had left the room Dorothea was out of the cupboard like a shot and carefully opening the main office door to see if she could get a better look at the woman, but she had disappeared, presumably back into the Joint Common Room.

Dorothea stopped to scoop up the top sheet of the blotting paper from David's desk and what she saw made her shiver with a sudden fear. It was a basic little sketch of a hangman's noose and scaffold.

THE WORM

Edition 3: Academic Year 34/35, October 2nd, 1934

Anybody You Know?
Police Find Corpse of Mystery Man in Canal: Exclusive Scoop!

It transpired that this reporter for *The Worm* was on the spot late evening, Sunday 30th September as members of Manchester City Police dredged the canal, on Canal Street in the city centre in search of the missing third-year undergraduate student, Matilda Abbot, who hasn't been seen since the 9th of September. An extensive search has been carried out in the local area by police and student volunteers. The twenty-one-year-old is a resident of Grangebrook Hall since transferring to Manchester from Cambridge last Christmas. She studied Classics and was a third-year representative of the Women's Union Committee. She was described by her peers as a shy, hard-working young lady who kept herself to herself.

While dredging the canal police found the body of an unknown young man in his mid to late twenties. The cause of death is yet to be ascertained. If our readers have any information, please contact DI Kydd at the Town Hall Police Headquarters,

Manchester 2375.

David Simpkins (Journalist)

Tuesday 2nd October 1934, Morning

The smell of formaldehyde mingled with decay assailed DI Kydd's nostrils as he looked down at the dead face of the young man on the autopsy table, bloated and swollen from being submerged in the canal. He was pretty much unrecognisable, other than by a general description which could apply to thousands of young men in this country: about five foot ten inches with dark hair and grey coloured eyes.

Let's hope something comes of the dental record checks, he thought.

It left the whereabouts of the young woman to be accounted for and many more questions still to answer.

The pathologist entered the room with a female assistant in tow. Professor Fredericks was an expert in his field and was often used by the police in this sort of capacity. He was a gregarious, leonine sort of a fellow, with a reputation of infidelity towards his long-suffering wife.

The professor shook hands with DI Kydd.

'We are just about to get started on the dissection. Have you met Miss Robinson by the way?' he said, making the introduction.

His colleague murmured, 'Pleased to meet you,' indistinctly, before she hurried off to get ready.

Professor Fredericks leered after the retreating student doctor.

'Great girl! She is doing her current placement in pathology with me. Iris is top of her year and has a neat figure. Brains and beauty, hey! Just what I like!'

DI Kydd's right foot itched to kick the letch up the seat of his pants. Restraining the impulse he asked, 'Can you give me some idea of the cause of death?'

'I can tell you what it wasn't, old boy,' he said, whipping off the sheet that covered the cadaver from the neck down. 'It wasn't the shot wound that killed him. That can be seen from a cursory examination. That wound has been attended to with some professional skill, someone used to removing foreign objects, stitching and dressing wounds. It looks like it has started to heal over nicely too. Also, when they fished him out of the water, he was wearing a triangular bandage on his left arm over his clothes and overcoat. We shall probably find when we open him up the shot fractured his clavicle. All his clothes are there, bagged up on the side for the lab including the bandage. There were rocks in all his pockets to weigh him down. Nothing to identify him with of course.'

'So he would have been incapacitated by the gunshot wound so less likely to be able to put up a fight?' the inspector queried.

'My good man! There isn't a mark on him apart from the shot wound. He didn't struggle at all. Give us until tomorrow and I'll be able to tell you what he did die of. I'll ring you up at your office? You can of course stay if you would like to watch?'

DI Kydd hastily made his excuses and left before he had to endure a lecture and a demonstration on human anatomy.

Wednesday 3rd October 1934, Morning

Next morning the inspector didn't have to wait long before his telephone rang, and he was once again speaking to Professor Fredericks.

'It was quite an eventful autopsy, Inspector. My assistant, Miss Robinson, fainted at the sight of the body and had to be sent home and I had to find a replacement. Dashed inconvenient! It meant we were slow to get going.

'Anyway, he didn't drown. There doesn't appear to be any water in his lungs which suggests he was already dead when he hit the surface of the canal. Otherwise, he is a perfectly healthy specimen of a human male other than being dead of course.' He guffawed at his own joke. 'I had a look at his organs and the content of his stomach and sent samples to the laboratory for chemical analysis. I used my sway and got them to stay late last night to test the samples,' the professor sounded smug.

'One of the Analytic Chemists, well she is an old friend you know, told me that the last thing he ingested was coffee, jam-packed full of barbiturates. There was no alcohol in his system, and he had not eaten a meal recently.'

'Can you narrow down when the man did actually die?'

'I'd say he had been in the water for about a fortnight. That is from the level of formation of adiopocere, coupled with the water temperature. It isn't an exact science. No more than twenty days ago and no less than seven days. He went into the water fairly soon after death.'

'So it was definitely foul play and not a tragic accident or suicide?' the inspector asked, for clarity.

'In my opinion the evidence is pointing towards murder, yes. A dead body doesn't pick itself up and fling itself conveniently into the nearest body of water, weighing its pockets down with stones so it can't be found.' The smug tone was back in the professor's voice. I'll send across my full report later today. One last thing Kydd . . .'

The inspector was halted just as he was about to thank the pathologist and ring off.

'You wouldn't have seen it yesterday because the corpse was lying on his back.' The professor paused for dramatic effect. 'He had an old scar on his right hip, reaching around to his buttock, at least five years old and it looks to me like the kind of scar that one would receive when fencing.'

Wednesday 3rd October 1934, Afternoon

The six friends met in a small tea shop on Half Moon Street near to St Ann's Street, an hour before the allotted time, to finalise their plans. It had taken a bit of manoeuvring to get Maggie's chair up the two steps and in through the door, but they managed it together. It was then imperative that the group got a window table, which they did with some sharpened elbows.

While sipping tea and munching on fresh scones with cream and jam it was decided that they would make this the control room, and Maggie and Jinny would stay there to coordinate the operation. They had an excellent view up and down the eastern part of St Ann's Street, which was close to Cross Street. Dorothea left them the notebook she had copied the old personal advertisements down in on Monday, a map, and the complete works of Jane Austen to have a go at solving them.

Mary Long would sit on the bench opposite St Ann's church in the square reading a book and eating a sandwich looking like what she was: a student, studying. Fortuitously the weather was fine for early October.

Mary Short was going to linger in her favourite book shop on the corner of St Ann's Street. She often spent hours in there and was friendly with the staff so no one would worry if she spent an hour or two browsing near the window or received phone calls.

Tabitha would take up position in the telephone box on the corner where Exchange Street met Market Street, so she could keep a look out to the north of the church and square. They had all contributed to her fund of shrapnel and she had enough change to keep the telephone fed for hours. She would be able to ring the tea shop and leave a message for Maggie and Jinny and ring Mary Short in the bookshop to pass on information.

Tabitha took with her the list of phone numbers the blackmailer had rung, to try and find out who they belonged to, as something to do while she waited.

This left Dorothea to cover the inside of the church. The building was open during the day for private prayer. She had chosen to wear a dull grey skirt with a light grey mackintosh borrowed from Jinny over the top, with a rusty headscarf covering her hair so she would blend in with the ecclesiastical setting. She was going to find a good place in the nave to sit and look prayerful and keep a watchful vigil.

The plan was that Dorothea would follow whoever came to pick up the package but not look under the church altar herself in case whoever had done the drop-off was watching. On emerging from the church Mary Long would tail Dorothea allowing them to switch places if necessary or for Mary to get a message to the others.

It was agreed that unless circumstances dictated a change to their plans, they would meet back at the tea shop in two hours' time. With twenty minutes to go, Dorothea, the Marys and Tabitha left the tea shop to take up their respective positions.

Jinny and Maggie ordered more tea and some macaroons and settled down with Jinny's opera glasses to keep a look out on the street, to gossip and solve the latest advertisements.

Jinny remarked, 'If I knew vicar's wives had so much fun, I would have become one sooner!'

Maggie smiled but said nothing. She knew how hard the Reverend Moss had had to work to woo Jinny and how indecisive Jinny had been over whether to accept his proposal. She also knew that Jinny had made the right decision. The Mosses were right for each other, and Jinny adored little Arabella the vicar's precocious five-year-old daughter who had recently started day school.

'Tell me about Simon Culthorpe,' Jinny asked.

'He is an engineer, Mary Long said.'

'Oh, he is tolerable, I suppose. He has a good car, and he drives nicely. He isn't as silly as most of the mathematicians I work with. He can be amusing . . . I quite like him.'

Jinny looked at her friend in awe, 'That is the nicest thing you have ever said about any man. You must be in love.'

'Nonsense!' Maggie was emphatic.

**

At St Ann's the cool mustiness enfolded and welcomed Dorothea and she breathed deeply the smell of old hymnals, floral arrangements, and beeswax polish. The flower arrangers had been at work for harvest festival the coming Sunday and there were some beautiful arrangements in gold, yellow and white. The verger was polishing some of the brass work near the back of the church and he nodded in taciturn welcome. Not having been there before, Dorothea had asked Jinny to give her an idea of the layout of the church, Jinny having played there as an organist during her student years.

Dorothea easily found the door to the upstairs gallery and headed to a strategic position behind a column partway along the nave. She had an excellent view of the altar but from downstairs she could not be seen if she was kneeling unless someone turned around at the altar and started to walk back along the aisle, and she would have plenty of time to duck down.

While she was settling herself, she heard the church door open and a man's voice talking, presumably to the verger. Footsteps came along the aisle, and straining to see, Dorothea got a view of the familiar haughty profile of Dr Hadley-Brown as he disappeared up into the organ loft. A minute or two later the organ harrumphed into life and the strains of *We plough the fields and scatter* filled the church building with resonance. She wasn't sure if she was more shocked at his presence or his musical ability.

Dorothea then remembered as a little girl at her home church sitting on the organist's stool and pretending to play the instrument as her father had a conversation about church business with the vicar. There were mirrors angled in different directions so the organist could see the vicar's visual cues, enabling them to know what to expect to happen next during the service, while the vicar stood in different positions in the chancel.

I bet Dr Hadley-Brown has an even better view than me of the altar, Dorothea thought. *I wonder if he worked out the code like us, or is he the one pulling the strings or is it all just a massive coincidence?*

Looking at her gold wristwatch, an eighteenth birthday present, she saw the time was now ten past the hour. Dr Hadley-Brown started playing *Come, ye thankful people, come.* Dorothea took a small malicious pleasure in his slight wobble at the start of this harvest hymn.

As he was beginning the second verse the church door opened and a woman entered. She was wearing a headscarf like Dorothea and a nondescript navy skirt and twinset, and she was carrying a basket of harvest produce. Having conferred with the verger she walked up the nave into the chancel and knelt at the altar to arrange the produce at its base with some other harvest offerings from parishioners.

'Oh, well-played!' Dorothea said under her breath. No one, not even someone sitting in the choir stalls would have noticed the woman's hand feel under the altar cloth, retrieve a small package, and place it in the now empty basket.

The woman dusted off her hands on her skirt, stood up and turned around and Dorothea was looking down at a young woman who seemed vaguely familiar before she remembered she had seen her a few times in the Women's Union building. Job completed, the woman stepped confidently down the aisle to the tune of *God is working his purpose out* and Dorothea bobbed her head back down as though in fervent prayer. The young woman said a few words in farewell to the verger before leaving the church, the heavy door crashing into place behind her.

Almost immediately the organ-playing stopped, and hurrying feet could be heard descending from the organ loft. Dr Hadley-Brown flew down the aisle, black academic grown flapping. He called out to the verger something about having forgotten an important meeting and in quick succession the door of the church crashed back into place behind him too.

Dorothea, walking quickly but trying not to appear like she was hurrying, came down the stairs from the balcony. She smiled and nodded to the verger like she did not have a care in the world, dropped a coin into the collection box and then sauntered out the door. It crashed behind her for the third time in succession.

The verger, a Pentecostal on Sundays, looked after the three of them, rolling his eyes and turning them to the heavens muttered, 'See what I mean, Lord? These Anglicans are crazy!'

Once outside the church, Dorothea put on a spurt of speed as she did not want to lose her quarries. Looking up and down St Ann's Street she thought she had lost them for a moment but Mary Long signalled surreptitiously to her from over the road to turn left towards St Mary's Street. Dorothea nodded and trotted down the road in hot pursuit.

Mary Long more leisurely stood up with her book and lunch and headed after Dorothea. Unlike Dorothea she had recognised both the woman and Dr Hadley-Brown and knew where the woman had to eventually return to.

***

Looking out the bookshop window, Mary Short had been joined by David Simpkins. Their date had gone well, and David had so impressed Mary Short with his intelligence and good sense she had confided in him the strange happenings that their Crossword Club were investigating. He vowed to come with her to the bookshop to protect her from spies, aliens, and monsters and that he would not take no for an answer as he smelt the biggest story of his journalistic career to date. Together they sat by the window on bookshelf steps that they had purloined from other areas of the shop and watched the people pass them by. Sometimes they chatted about what was happening in the world and about themselves. Sometimes they just sat in amicable silence until . . .

'Did you just see who went past?'

'Yes,' Mary Short replied, 'I did, and good gracious! Is that Dr Hadley-Brown following her? Where has Dorothea got to? Oh, here she comes.'

'Is that Mary Long with the red hair just passing the lamp post now? What a farce.'

'Hang on a minute, did you see over there, there is another man keeping pace with those four. Navy mackintosh and a fedora pulled down low. What is he doing?'

The two of them pressed their noses against the glass trying to get a better look.

'I think we need to ring Maggie and Jinny!' Mary exclaimed; eyes wide with astonishment.

***

Dorothea was concentrating on keeping both the woman

and Dr Hadley-Brown in sight. The first hint she had that something was seriously wrong was turning off Southgate Street and onto Parsonage Gardens, a small park, where she was overtaken by a man dressed in a navy mackintosh wearing a vaguely familiar hat pulled down low over his face and walking very fast.

Where had she seen that hat before?

It made her feel nervous. She picked up her pace a little through the park so as not to let him get too far ahead. He was gaining on Dr Hadley-Brown coming into St Mary's Parsonage, heading towards Blackfriars Street across the river, and he made a funny flicking motion of his right wrist and suddenly there was a glint of light off a steel blade partially hidden by the sleeve of his coat.

The distance between the blade carrying man and the academic was rapidly closing and whereas the man had pulled out wide to overtake Dorothea, even stepping onto a flowerbed, he showed no sign of doing the same with the academic.

Dorothea broke into a sprint and covered the distance between herself and the sinister figure with the knife, in a time that even Eddie Tolan the reigning Olympic champion would have been impressed by. The man was unaware of her presence coming up from behind, so focused was he on Dr Hadley-Brown's shoulder blades, and he was now only a pace or two behind the academic.

Dorothea saw the man's knife-holding hand start to pull backwards as if to strike. Spurred on, she covered the remaining distance and drew alongside him and instinctively threw all her weight against the man's left shoulder in what would have been an illegal shoulder barge on the hockey pitch resulting in a sending off.

The figure totally unprepared for this unexpected attack was spun into the road and narrowly missed being hit by a taxi that swerved just in time and honked an enraged horn. The unknown assailant had just about kept his feet, but had dropped the knife in all the kafuffle, saw that the game was up and took to his heels, disappearing towards the railway station.

Dorothea's momentum carried her forward and she careered into the back of Dr Hadley-Brown knocking his feet from under him, sending them both crashing down to the pavement in a heap of arms and legs.

'Ouch! What the hell do you think you are doing you young hoodlum? Not you!' Dr Hadley-Brown swore wrathfully, sitting up and pressing a handkerchief to a grazed hand.

Dorothea sat up gingerly and made sure all her limbs were working. Apart from one scuffed knee that was bleeding gently she had come off pretty lightly as she had had a soft landing. She looked around for the man with the knife, but he was nowhere to be seen.

Mary Long jogged up behind and gave Dorothea a hand standing up.

'Are you two alright? That chap ran up Chapel Street and hopped on the back of a tram. You took him out good and proper Dorothea. Well done!' she said offering a hand to Dr Hadley-Brown who refused it ungraciously and made a show of standing up stiffly.

'He had a knife, and he was about to stick it in your back, sir,' Dorothea said calmly and with emphasis.

'Nonsense. Don't be ridiculous!' Dr Hadley-Brown snapped, peering into the distance in search of the woman's retreating figure. 'Damn lost her!'

'No, you haven't, she is over there on the bench by the tram stop getting out some sandwiches. I have been keeping an eye on her,' Mary said casually.

The look of shock followed by consternation on Dr Hadley-Brown's face was priceless.

'How did you know I was following her?'

Neither of the young women replied. Mary Long was inspecting the back of Dr Hadley-Brown's academic gown. Across the back, from waist to nearly shoulder blade was a new hole. She stuck her finger in it experimentally and waggled it only to be shooed away by Dr Hadley-Brown.

'Looks like Dorothea saved your life, sir. That would have been a nasty slash if he had landed it.'

'What? Where? Show me?' He shrugged his shoulders out of the gown, wincing a little and trying not to get blood from his grazed hand on it.

'Well, I'll be da . . .' He gave a guilty look at the two young women. 'Well, I'll be . . . er . . . well, thank you, Miss Roberts.' He looked towards the figure still eating her sandwiches waiting for a number nine tram stop. 'Well, I'd better be getting along. But how did you know I was following Evelyn King?'

'Evelyn King, isn't she the Social Secretary of the Women's Union?' Dorothea was surprised. She had heard the name mentioned and read about the committee membership in the Women's Union handbook, but she had yet to meet Evelyn.

'Let's just say we are fans of Austen, and that Worms talk too much,' Mary Long said.

Again, the shocked look returned to Dr Hadley-Brown's face, followed by a hint of wariness.

'You don't know what you are getting into. Just leave it alone. You have been clever and lucky so far, but it is too dangerous for girls like you. Go home.' He turned on his heels and walked smartly away after the retreating figure of Evelyn King who had finished her lunch and had got up to leave.

'Of all the male egotistical, chauvinistic, idiotic remarks,' Mary Long spluttered, going red in the face and sounding even more Highland than normal. 'You just saved his life, and he tells you that it is too dangerous for girls! We'll just stay at home and do some quilting shall we?' she yelled after him.

'Shouldn't we follow Evelyn King too and see where she goes?' Dorothea asked experimentally, hobbling a few steps after Dr Hadley-Brown.

'No, don't worry about her,' Mary Long sounded smug. 'I know where she'll be heading off to eventually. Let's get back to the others. We can stop off at the chemists near the cathedral and get a plaster for your poor wee knee.'

CHAPTER FIVE

A Plan, a Fire Alarm, and a Positive Identification

Wednesday 3rd October 1934, Afternoon

Tabitha and Mary Short, with David Simpkins in tow, had already arrived back at the teashop when Mary Long and Dorothea, freshly patched up with sticking plaster purchased on route, arrived. All were terribly excited and bursting to share their news, but Maggie held them all in check. Very sensibly, she suggested they pay the bill and retire somewhere more private to talk, as the waitress had been giving her and Jinny disapproving looks for staying so long.

Jinny suggested they all come back to the vicarage with her for tea, generously extending the invitation to David, who from a journalistic perspective was well and truly hooked and would not have missed it for the world, plus it had the added attraction of the opportunity of sitting next to Mary Short on the bus ride there.

There was a bus stop on Cross Street and with Jinny and Dorothea giving Maggie a supporting arm onto the bus, David wrestled Maggie's chair on board.

St Bartholomew, Lower Heaton-in-the-Marsh, was a little further out of the city than the Fallowfield Campus and was a beautiful Norman building surrounded by a green and well-maintained churchyard, an anachronism in a busy suburb, a remnant of a time when Manchester's sprawling tentacles of urbanisation had not yet reached out as far or with so much destruction. The vicarage, an airy Georgian box of a building was situated next door, hunkered down in a slightly neglected, yet still charming, formal garden. The house was cool in summer and draughty in the winter but on this mild autumnal day, with a fire burning in the parlour, it was seen at its best – both welcoming and cosy.

The Reverend, Clarence Moss, saw them coming from his study window where he was attempting to write his sermon for the following Sunday, and welcoming this new distraction bounded out of the house to greet them. He was a stocky young man in his early thirties, powerfully built and very dark of eye and hair with a shy smile and an irrepressible sense of humour. The death of his first wife in childbirth had hit him hard, causing his parishioners some sleepless nights worrying about him and the new baby. It had taken time, their friendship and support, a sensible and kindly Bishop and finally the meeting of the sympathetic and lovely Jinny to bring back his natural bounce.

A History and Classics graduate from Manchester, before undertaking theological training at Durham, the vicar often joked he was a throwback to a Sarmatian horseman auxiliary soldier passing through the Roman fort of Mamucium on his way up to Hadrian's wall for his final posting. Arabella Clarence Moss's daughter from his first marriage had inherited his colouring and he doted on her.

He welcomed them all heartily into the parlour and kissed Jinny enthusiastically in a very un-vicarly way.

Mrs O'Neil the Mosses' housekeeper bustled in and out with the tea tray and plates of freshly baked Eccles cakes and buttered bread and homemade jam.

Suddenly starving, Dorothea and Mary Long regaled those present, between mouthfuls, with a colourful account of their lunchtime adventures. Mary Long did a particularly good impression of Dr Hadley-Brown's indignant face on finding it was Dorothea who had floored him.

'Anyway, someone really doesn't like your Dr Hadley-Brown if they wanted to stick this into him.' Mary Long produced the knife wrapped in a grubby handkerchief like a conjurer producing a dove from a hat.

It was shaped like a little sword with an ornate silver handle that was set with semi-precious gems and had likely been mass-produced in the reign of Queen Victoria as a letter opener. Everyone recognised the type. They all knew an elderly relative with such a tool.

'I spotted where it fell and managed to pick it up with my hanky, so hopefully any fingerprints will be preserved,' Mary Long said proudly.

'He was wearing gloves,' Dorothea said gently, trying not to appear too dampening.

'Oh,' Mary Long deflated. 'Well maybe earlier in the day he didn't. Drat! Still, it's worth a try. I'll take it to the lab and get my friendly demonstrator to give me a hand dusting it for prints.'

Tabitha was flustered and appeared miffed to have missed all the action whilst waiting in the phone box but was big with news and could not hold it in much longer. She had spent the time fruitfully ringing up the phone numbers that Dorothea had overheard the blackmailer calling.

She took up the story. 'One was a lady's boarding house in Old Trafford where some students live. Didn't your friend live out there in her third year, Jinny? Maggie? The one who thought she could carry off a monocle but couldn't. Could you ask her to find out who is living there currently and get a list?

'The Ancoats' number was for the University Settlement at Ancoats Hall, the women's residence. There are about twenty-five female students living over there at the moment.

'Another was the office of the warden of Grangebrook Hall, Dr Winterbottom. The fourth was an extension in the Women's Union building itself which turned out to be Mrs Gladys Adams' office. The fifth you must have misheard because it was a butcher's shop in Salford and no member of the university lived there, I checked. I also had to place an order for sausages which I will need to cycle over and collect tomorrow,' Tabitha said defensively, as they looked at her in puzzlement. 'I felt it was the right thing to do.'

'While you were all running around saving lives and discovering important clues, Jinny and I have been productive too,' Maggie declared.

'Yes, we have made a timeline of all the personal ads along with their interpretations and a list of all the strange happenings this term, too. Do you want to see?' Jinny asked excitedly.

'First, add that Eliza is Evelyn King and that someone tried to knife Dr Hadley-Brown today,' Maggie ordered, a stickler for completeness, 'And those phone numbers the blackmailer used.'

Their document was as follows:

Advertisements and Strange Happenings	Advertisements Decoded	Dates
Academic Year 31/32		
Mr B, a young gentleman with an	Jane, go to the rubber works on	Received Friday 27th

independent fortune is looking to meet his Jane to look after in sickness and in health and to offer his hand in matrimony. 69.10.6 134.20.6 53:31:37 2:23:53 PO Box 1300.	Harriett Street at 13.00, on Monday.	May 1932 at *The Worm's* office, for publishing on Tuesday 31st May 1932. Pick-up Monday 6th June 1932.
Academic Year 32/33		
Elinor seeks her Mr F for woodland walks, picnics and to settle down in wedded bliss at the parsonage. Marianne and Margaret are dissuaded from joining. 209.33.8 224.6.2 53:29:28 2:15:33 PO Box 1900	Elinor, go to the pictures on Elton Street, Salford at 19.00, on Tuesday.	Received Friday 28th October 1932 at *The Worm's* office, for publishing on Tuesday 1st November 1932. Pick-up either Tuesday 1st or 8th November 1932.
Marianne wishes	Marianne, go to	Received

to meet her Colonel B walks to the ruined priory, duets on the pianoforte and poetry readings. Anyone else would be in the way. 128.16.6 101.14.6 53:28:47 2:14:25 PO Box 1130.	the Portico Library on Charlotte Street on Friday at 11.30.	Friday 10th March 1933 at *The Worm's* office, for publishing on Tuesday 14th March 1933. Pick-up probably Friday 17th March 1933.
Academic Year 33/34		
Emma is devastated to dash Mr E's hopes, but she is unable to accept his kind proposal. She suggests a better match would be found at PO Box 1530 332.12.4 133.22.6 53: 27:1 2:12:56.	Emma, post something on Saturday from Brighton Grove to catch the 15.30 post.	Received Friday 17th November 1933 at *The Worm's* office, for publishing on Tuesday 21st November 1933. Drop off

		probably Saturday 25th November 1933.
Lydia thanks Mr W for his kind offer of matrimony but has chosen to decline. She will return his ring to the following address PO Box 1030. 166.24.7 251.31.3, 53:28:6 2:12:29.	Lydia, drop the bag off at the postal depot on Bennett Street, on Thursday at 10.30.	Received Friday 21st September 1934 at *The Worm's* office, for publishing on Tuesday 25th September 1934. Drop off probably Thursday 27th September 1934.
Academic Year 34/35		
Ethel Worksop Committee Secretary died from a hit and run accident outside		*Tuesday 28th August 1934.*

the Women's Union.		
Dorothea Roberts sees Matilda Abbott 3rd Year Rep shot on the train at Manchester's London Road station.		*Sunday 9th September 1934 at around 2p.m.*
Someone broke into a first-floor room that would have been Dorothea's and searched it but didn't take anything.		*Monday 17th September 1934, in the afternoon.*
Mr D seeks his Eliza for dances, companionship, and matrimony. None of her sisters need apply. 182.5.6 189.25.6, 53:28:54 2:14:46. PO Box 1315.	Eliza, go to St Ann's church, St Ann's Street at 13.15, on Wednesday and look on or under the altar. *Eliza is Evelyn King!*	Received Friday 28th September at *The Worm's* office, for publishing on Tuesday 2nd October 1934. Pick-up

		Wednesday 3rd October 1934.
Body of an unknown young man found in canal near campus (unrelated?).		*Sunday 30th September 1934.*
Dorothea Roberts witnesses a woman sending blackmailing phone calls.	*Phone Numbers include: Ancoats Women's Residence, Old Trafford Boarding House, Grangebrook's Warden's Office, Advisor to Women's Students Office and a butcher's shop.*	*Tuesday 2nd October 1934.*
Someone tried to knife Dr Hadley-Brown while following Evelyn King.		*Wednesday 3rd October 1934.*

'Next, we need to find out what Evelyn King was picking up from under the altar cloth of St Ann's church,' Dorothea said, decisively. 'Mary, on our way here you said not to worry about where Eliza was going because you knew where she would be heading back to. Where is that?'

Mary Long chuckled, 'She is my next-door neighbour in Grangebrook Hall and has been since my first year and I know how to get into her room to look about for clues!'

She outlined a risky plan which all the friends fell in love with instantaneously but for it to work they needed to act fast and undertake it that very evening.

While they were tweaking the final details, David Simpkins was sitting quietly in the corner making copious notes.

'This is amazing! Our readers will love this. Please let me be the one to break this story! It will be the highlight of my journalism career to date.'

This simple request caused an uproar, under the cover of which the Reverend Moss slipped quietly out to pick up Arabella from school. On returning, the point was still being hotly contested by the young people with Maggie, Jinny, Mary Long and Tabitha on one side, and Mary Short and David on the other side with Dorothea being an ineffective referee hovering somewhere around the middle so the vicar thought it might be worthwhile interjecting. He cleared his throat and entered the fray.

'As a journalist, David wants this story, which is understandable, and as a group of modern women, the majority of you want to be left alone to be able to investigate this without the encumbrance of a man underfoot and think that it is too early to break the story. I, myself, am intrigued to find out what is going on at my old university while being worried about how safe this enterprise is where Jinny is concerned. A compromise is needed. How about David holds off publishing for now with the agreement of you all that he gets proprietary rights to the story, and you continue to investigate unencumbered. Along those lines, if you do need any help with any aspects of this case please do come to David and me at any time of the day or night. Now, I believe Tabitha that you are studying Law? If all agree, could you draft a simple document stating what I have just outlined? Then we can all sign it.'

His calmness and common sense brought them all down to the ground with a bump and Tabitha trotted off to the Reverend Moss's study in search of paper and a pen.

'How did you do that?' a harassed Dorothea whispered in the vicar's ear.

'Simple. Years of practice chairing Parochial Church Council meetings and refereeing disagreements between the organist and the choir,' he twinkled back at her. 'People are mostly the same you know.'

Wednesday 3rd October 1934, Evening

Mary Short, Mary Long and Dorothea were all sitting quietly in Mary Long's first-floor room in the halls of residence. They were listening intently. Both the Marys were wearing dark clothes and gloves. Mary Long's gloves were the tartan of her mother's clan, the Davidsons. At three minutes to eight o'clock in the evening they heard the door to the next-door room open and shut quietly and the rattle of keys, then footsteps retreating down the corridor. They waited a couple of minutes until they heard a gentle knock on Mary's door. The door was not locked, and Tabitha entered.

'Evelyn has taken the bait,' Tabitha whispered. 'I watched while she got safely ensconced in the music room for Maggie's tutorial about staying on for a master's degree. Maggie has got a good crowd of them. Even the warden is there.'

'Well then. Places please ladies,' Mary Long said, taking charge.

Dorothea was to stand and act as look-out at the top of the stairwell. Her scraped knee had stiffened up and precluded her from joining in with anything more active and as Mary Short said, 'You can't expect to have all the fun!'

There was a handy alcove with a cushion at the top of the stairs on which to perch. From it you could hear the door opening below and glimpse the back of the head of the person coming up the stairs to the mezzanine before they changed direction and came towards the watcher. There was just enough time to slip through the upstairs door and wave frantically to Tabitha who was standing by Evelyn King's door, ready to knock three times, the signal that Miss King was coming.

Mary Long and Mary Short were going next door via Mary Long's bedroom window. Evelyn King's room was a particularly nice one and had a bay aperture with three windows in it. Evelyn being an outdoor activity enthusiast and alpine skier of some note, she usually left the sash window nearest Mary Long's room open. The two Marys would climb out of Mary Long's bedroom window, using the ivy trellises and a narrow ledge directly under the window for hand and footholds, reach across to the ironwork drainpipe for support and then from there get a hold of the window and pull themselves through.

Once inside they would be able to search for whatever it was inside the package Evelyn had picked up from St Ann's. It couldn't be very big or heavy as it fitted inside a basket.

Dorothea and Tabitha took their places to watch and wait.

Mary Long went first. She was used to shimmying up and down the drainpipe as a form of entrance and exit to her room. She loved dancing and often came back to Halls late after the half past ten curfews. She was currently into swing and a group of her friends from the Chemistry Department frequented the Ritz on Friday nights. She was as lithe as a monkey out of the window and across the brickwork. She then pushed up the sash of Evelyn's room with one hand and it was the work of a minute to squeeze through.

Mary Short followed at a more careful pace, every movement precise and thought out. She came a bit unstuck when trying to get a leg in over the sill and after trying various combinations of legs, shoulders, and arms, eventually entered the room head-first, kicking with both legs and ended up in a tangled heap on the floor looking somewhat dishevelled.

'Shh, Shortie! Keep it down!' Mary Long was already rootling through the chest of drawers in a business-like manner. It was a neat room; everything obviously had its own place and order was imposed upon it by a ruthless hand. 'She has a rum taste in artwork, our illustrious Social Secretary.' Mary Long nodded to a flag on the wall of a hooked, clockwise cruciform on a white and red background which had had a lot of exposure recently in the tabloids.

Mary Short shivered. 'Whenever I see that flag, I feel like someone is walking over my grave.' She started to go through all the books on the bookshelf, one by one, and gave them a shake. 'My cousin Abigail is married to a German businessman, Ethan, you remember? They live in Munich, but they met here in Manchester. They are thinking of emigrating back here as there is an assiduous anti-Jewish undercurrent building up in the community and it is coming straight from the government. Ethan's sales of antiques have halved in the last three months.

'There is nothing here, though her taste in books is eclectic. Look at this section of the bookshelf: *Escapology, Cyphers, Morse Code for Beginners, Poisons, Ballistics, The Everyman's Guide to Radio Mechanics*. None of the university courses would have these as a set reading list. I'll take a look through the ashes of the fire now.' Mary Short got out a pair of tweezers and some medical sample jars from the capacious pockets of her jumper.

'I am pretty sure Evelyn King is a member of the Fascist Society. Her family certainly have links to Adolf Hitler. Look at this framed photograph,' Mary Long commented.

Mary Long gingerly handled a recently taken photo of Evelyn, and presumably, her parents and brother due to the family likeness. They were pictured in evening attire at a gala dinner and her father was shaking hands with a short, round man with a Charlie Chaplin moustache.

'Hey, the back of this is loose,' she said, giving it an experimental wiggle. 'The tape has been peeled off and resealed. I'll give it a little tug.'

'Don't break it for goodness' sake,' Mary Short warned, not looking up from her task of fettling through the cinders.

'There is a piece of paper folded up between the backing and the photograph!' Mary Long exclaimed excitedly. Hands shaking, she opened the paper and spread it out on the bed. It was an invitation but a very odd one. It read:

Dear Miss King,
Your many talents and achievements have been noted and your allegiance to the cause is unwavering. You are a particularly worthy nominee to join the Oyster Club. You are therefore cordially invited to take part in several initiation challenges. Only the bravest and the best become full members of the club. Your code name is Eliza. The Worm *will inform you of what to do next. Tell no one.*

Yours Sincerely,
The Secretary of the Oyster Society

Fishing beneath her dark cardie, Mary Long pulled out her folding Boy Scout Brownie camera which was on a leather strap around her neck and snapped a couple of photos of the invitation. She then carefully placed the paper back in the frame and resealed it as best she could with the worn packing tape, being careful to place the frame where she found it and stowed the camera away demurely in her décolletage.

An exclamation by Mary Short was cut off abruptly by three sharp knocks on the door.

'What! So soon? Quickly get the fireplace back to how it looked. There are ashes everywhere.' The strain was telling in Mary Long's voice. 'Hurry up, Shortie, we only have a minute at most.' Mary Long picked up the brush and swept some escapee cinders back under the grate.

'Go on ahead.' Mary Short was calm under pressure – an excellent trait to have as a trainee medic – as she wrestled a precious find into a sample jar.

'Tabitha knows to keep her talking. You get across and I'll be behind you. I'll just check the room is how we found it.'

Outside they could hear Tabitha's voice raised, just a little too loudly and brightly in greeting.

'Ah, Evelyn, I wanted to have a chat with you about the Christmas ball. Is now a good time? It isn't? You have a headache. You poor thing. My Aunt was a martyr to headaches . . .'

Mary Long didn't wait to hear any more. She was straight out of the window and carefully pivoting herself around the angle of the building using the drainpipe for support. Once inside, she turned back around and stuck her head and torso through to offer Mary Short a helping hand if she needed but Shortie did not appear.

The door next door opened. And the tone of Tabitha's voice while slightly more muffled went up an octave and developed a new panicked tone. No Mary Short.

Mary heard Evelyn's door bang closed. Still no Mary Short.

Outside in the corridor the signal from Dorothea had been clear and had worked but even Tabitha's excellent conversational gambits honed into the higher echelons of refined society had bought very little time with a Social Secretary who was looking a bit peaky. Evelyn managed to get the door open, with Tabitha talking all the time, but was too polite to go inside and shut the door in Tabitha's face. Just as Tabitha was starting to dry up and Evelyn was about to turn around, Tabitha noticed the door to the wardrobe in Evelyn's room closing very slowly in on itself. This momentary shock and the natural pause that went with it was just enough for Evelyn King to get through the door and bid Tabitha a good night, before shutting the door. Tabitha stood stock still. Something drastic needed to be done.

Dorothea's face appeared around the door at the end of the corridor looking wary. Mary Long stuck her head out of her door and whispered, 'Mary is still in there!'

Tabitha took the initiative, running up the corridor, away from Dorothea. There was a mechanical fire alarm point on the wall with a bell above it. She broke the glass and pulled the switch. The bell immediately rang out loudly and was answered by other bells from different wings of the building. Doors opened, and people called out to each other. Dorothea and Mary Long looked at each other and then at Tabitha in amazement.

'Come on, you two!' Tabitha ordered sharply, as doors started to open on their corridor. They shook off their stupor and headed after Tabitha towards the fire escape and down and out of the building to the tennis courts which is where the official muster point was.

Maggie rounded the building, arms and wheels whizzing at top speed.

'What did you do?' she asked, with meaning in her voice.

'I don't know what you mean?' Tabitha said, trying to look innocent, as Maggie checked them off the register.

Together they watched as the sprawling building disgorged its disgruntled occupants. They spotted Evelyn King looking sulky wrapped in a large warm-looking coat come and join the masses on the tennis courts. Almost the last person to leave the building was Mary Short. She was puffing. Between gasps for air, she explained that when the fire alarm went off Evelyn had left the room, locking the door behind her which meant that she, Mary, was locked inside.

'I had tried really hard not to lock myself in the wardrobe and there was a tricky moment when she opened the other door of the wardrobe to get her coat.

Fortunately, she wasn't really looking, and I had burrowed in between her clothes on the other side but she closed the wardrobe door, which she also didn't lock, because I was able to wiggle it open again from the inside. Then I had to climb back into Mary Long's room hoping that no one saw me and then I ran back to my room and dropped off the samples of paper from Evelyn's fireplace. I am hoping Mary Long's Chemistry friend will be able to help with testing them for any writing.

Dr Winterbottom, the warden, flitted past at that moment looking uneasy, 'It is just a false alarm, ladies. We should all be able to return to our rooms shortly when the caretaker has reset the fire alarm system.'

'Ah, Dr Winterbottom can I have a word please? I think it was me that set the fire alarm off with my bag.' Tabitha drifted away with the warden.

'She has gone to confess that it was her. She would hate it if someone else got blamed for it,' Maggie said to Dorothea quietly.

'Because she is so honest most of the time, she always gets away with it, whatever *it* is. It also helps that her family knows everyone. Did you know she had a Great Aunt on the board of trustees of the university?'

'No, I didn't,' Dorothea replied thoughtfully, realising there was such a lot to learn about her friends.

Tuesday 9th October 1934, Morning

DI Kydd had arranged for all the major fencing clubs in the country to be sent a police artist's impression of the dead man and of the dead man's scar. A few days later, he received the following letter by second-class post, written in flowing handwriting pertaining to be from a Mr Reginald Kent, Captain of the Cambridge Amateur Fencing and Swordsmanship Club:

Dear Sir,

Thank you for your inquiry. It is always a pleasure to give assistance to the police. The photograph you enclosed gave my clubmates and I some food for thought, but after some searching in the club's records and talking to some of our alumni, we may have discovered the identity of your corpse.

The incident took place round about seven years ago, between two hot-headed freshmen that were both members of our fencing club. One charged the other one with trifling with the affections of a lady that both of them were interested in and challenged the other to an old-fashioned duel with real swords (totally against club policy), in honour of the lady's virtue (non-existent).

Your corpse was the better swordsman but his opponent (whose name I won't reveal as he has a promising career working for the Foreign Office as a diplomat), was the dirtier fighter. Just as your corpse had the upper hand in the match and had bested his opponent and was walking back to his seconds, the diplomat pinked him on the behind in a fit of rage, gashing his buttock and hip and leaving his seconds in fear for his life. They called off the match and dragged off the fellow to be patched up by a local doctor. The young lady in question married the now diplomat only to divorce three years later for boorish behaviour. Having read back the above missive I have just realised that I still haven't put a name to your corpse. It is M—

PC Standish popped his head around the office door and announced, 'A Mr George of the Secret Service to see you, Inspector. He says it is urgent. Do you want me to send him in?'

'Yes please, Standish. Thank you,' DI Kydd said, upon recognising the name, and smiling grimly. Things were finally getting somewhere.

Mr George entered the room. He was a florid man, rotund as a balloon and appeared to bounce along on the balls of his feet like there was a string tethering him to the ground. There were no preliminary niceties.

'Kydd, I hear you have found the body of a young man in the canal. Have you put a name to him yet? It is important to national security that he is not identified in the press. It would undermine the vital work that he has been doing locally. This is coming right from the Minister and your Chief Superintendent agrees with me.'

'Good afternoon, Mr George, nice to meet you again. How is MI5 these days?' DI Kydd asked chattily but with an undertone of steel. He wished the Chief Superintendent had told him.

'Meet me again? I don't think I quite follow you?' Mr George was pulled up short by this unexpected greeting.

'Viburnum Drive, Miss Peterson's house. She is a civil servant I believe. She has worked as your secretary for many years.'

Mr George sagged a little bit. 'Ah. You know about that do you? Sorry and all but it was important that an agent's cover wasn't blown if they had gone into hiding.'

The phone rang. The inspector apologised and answered it. It was the Chief Superintendent. With a telephone call from the Chief only the occasional, 'Yes, sirs' were necessary.

'DI Kydd, Mr George from MI5 is on his way to you. Oh, he is there already, is he? Sorry. It seems like the cloak and dagger boys are involved in your university cases, as you thought and have been interfering with your inquiries. They have nobbled the coroner already for the young man that you pulled out of the canal so it looks like that case will be put to bed without any fuss. I do want a positive identification of the corpse though, for his sake and yours. Do you know his identity? You do? Is it who you suspected? Excellent! If the corpse was one of his men, ask Mr George to identify the body while he is there, will you? Good work Inspector!'

The Chief Superintendent rang off. DI Kydd turned to Mr George.

'So, Mr George, what can you tell me about Mr Matthew Abbott, alias Matilda Abbott of Grangebrook Hall?'

CHAPTER SIX

A Tap on the Shoulder

Wednesday 10th October 1934, Morning

Geraint Hadley-Brown was not having a great day. Mr George from headquarters had delegated the morbid and quite frankly distasteful task of officially identifying the body to him. Geraint cursed him fluently under his breath for shirking his responsibilities. There was no reason he could not have identified the body himself. He probably wanted to get off early to the golf course for a round with Sir Reginald Tewkesbury the Lord Lieutenant of one of the Home Counties. Kent, or Bedfordshire or somewhere.

Geraint had cut himself while shaving. On exiting his digs, he discovered that someone had parked a van in front of the entrance to the nearby mews where his car was garaged, which meant he had had to flag down a taxi to take him to the mortuary. He had then been held up in traffic by a brewer's dray having shed its load on Wilbraham Road so was late.

At the mortuary DI Kydd had taken him to task for hindering the police in their inquiries and to quote the inspector, 'The high-handedness of the Secret Service and the need for mutual cooperation between those that work for law and order.'

There was a lot of pressure from on high for the police to drop their investigation, but the Chief Superintendent was currently resisting. From the zealous glint in the inspector's eye, it would take a small army to stop him uncovering the truth.

DI Kydd then took Geraint through to a chilly room where a body was laid out on a gurney with a sheet covering it. At the inspector's request a technician pulled back the white sheet covering the body and Geraint was looking down at Matthew Abbott. He caught a breath and then looked away from the man's ravished features. Even after having spent a fortnight in the canal, he was recognisable. They had been to Cambridge together at the same time, though Geraint was a year younger, and had moved in similar circles. Whilst he knew Matthew as one of a particular clique and they hadn't been close, still the bit of him that should have felt something for a peer or colleague who shared mutual memories was currently numb and he resisted probing further. It would keep.

He nodded in assent to the inspector and the technician recovered his gruesome charge.

A horrible thought suddenly assailed him, causing a sharp pang in his solar plexus. *It could have been me on that slab if the knife had been on target.* His own mortality left him speechless. Thank God Miss Roberts was on hand to divert the blow. *She had behaved with considerable initiative and aplomb,* he admitted to himself grudgingly.

DI Kydd, taking pity on the young man's apparent horror at the death of his colleague took him gently by the shoulder and led him in search of a sweet cup of tea, talking to him quietly all the time. Most of it, Geraint filtered out as noise until a thought came to him through the fog and acted as a sharp slap in the face.

'I don't understand you chaps at MI5 sending in a male undercover agent to pose as a woman. Don't think the police won't find out why either! I was reading the prospectus for the university with half an idea of sending my daughter there. She is an exceptionally sharp young woman, and she runs rings around me, though there is no chance of me encouraging that now until all this business is cleared up. There are five hundred female undergraduates currently. Couldn't you have primed a current student to spy for you? That lass from the train was a smart young lady. There were no flies on her.'

Geraint sat up suddenly, snapping back into the moment.

'Inspector, you are a genius! Thank you ever so much!' He downed the rest of his tea in the chipped beige cup and grimaced at the unstirred sugar at the bottom. 'Please do let me know if I can be of any further help.'

Drat. My big mouth, the inspector thought, as he watched Dr Hadley-Brown leave the building. *What mischief is he going to get into now, and who is he going to drag into this sorry affair?*

Wednesday 10th October 1934, Late Afternoon

A young woman dressed in a non-descript tweed coat and skirt, with a knitted beret perched on her curls walked at a steady pace to a letterbox outside of the Women's Union building on her way home. Stopping in front of the red pillar box, she extracted a handful of identical white envelopes from a capacious satchel. She checked that she had not lost any: one for Constance Harris, one for Iris Robinson, one for Mabel Parker, in fact one for nearly every Executive Officer of the committee and a few members of staff too.

With a grim smile she posted them into the box and walked away quickly without a backwards glance.

Full Committee Meeting of the Women's Student Union, 11th October 1934, 7 p.m.

'Order! Order! Ladies, can I draw this meeting to order please?'

Constance Harris, the President of the Women's Union, was perspiring. Even through her innate protective layer of well-bred insensitivity, she was picking up a discernible undercurrent of panic from the committee of twenty or so fellow female students who were usually so biddable and easy to lead. Constance tapped her gavel again. No other President of the committee had ever had a gavel before. The President of the Men's Union didn't have a gavel. Even the provost of the university didn't have a gavel and looked at it longingly when he infrequently made it to their meetings.

'Order, ladies! Really, I know everyone is terribly upset that Matilda Abbott's body has been found but as I explained to you all, DI Kydd assured me the police were satisfied her death was from natural causes and they wouldn't be looking into it any further. It is of course very sad, and it will make more work for the remaining third-year reps on the committee, but we will of course run a third-year representative election alongside the first-year elections to replace Matilda. The family have asked for a private funeral and for no flowers which saves the committee some money . . .' She saw the looks of indignation on the faces of the people sitting around the table and tried to soften her previous statement with a caveat. 'Though of course we will send a card. I am sure nice DI Kydd will be able to pass it on to them. Victoria please can you organise it?'

Victoria Butterworth, taking the minutes, nodded resignedly. She had won the vote to be secretary, unchallenged, but was only now coming to realise that being so to this president was a poisoned chalice. Mrs

Adams interjected at this point, diplomatically keeping a neutral tone.

'I believe that the Classics Department want to plant a tree in Miss Abbott's memory. Maybe the Women's Union could work with them to erect a lasting memorial to Matilda in that way? I would be happy to liaise with the Head of the Classics Department.'

'Excellent idea, Mrs Adams! Thank you. You do bring such helpful suggestions to the table. Please minute that too, Victoria.'

The meeting proceeded with an air of distraction. It was not so much the confirmed death of Matilda Abbott that was spooking everyone. Apparently, according to DI Kydd, whom Constance kept quoting as if he was the Oracle at Delphi, Matilda had gone for a walk in Philips Park and along the River Medlock at Clayton Vale and had had a massive coronary attack and her body had lain unfound for several weeks in a wooded area, it was uncommon in one so young but not unheard of. Coming on top of the gruesome find of the dead young man in the canal as reported by *the Worm* and the still unsolved hit and run that had left Ethel Worksop dead, campus did not feel quite so homelike and familiar as it had done a few short weeks ago.

Iris Robinson, the committee's Vice President, looked awful. She was sitting next to Constance, out of her direct line of sight and jumped every time the gavel fell. Her eyes were red-rimmed as if she had cried herself to sleep for a week and her colour had drained away drastically to leave her an interesting grey-green, like she was about to faint or vomit imminently.

Sure enough, she got unsteadily to her feet, muttered an apology, and then dashed from the room. Unfortunately, there was a women's bathroom next door to the meeting room that the committee used, and the partition walls were not very thick and did not cut out all the noise. Everyone present could hear the muffled sounds of Iris being violently sick, followed by a thud, then silence.

Mrs Adams excused herself and hurried from the room, followed swiftly by a second-year representative who was training as a dentist, being the most medically trained person present after Iris Robinson – the patient. Muffled voices could be heard next door, followed by the return of the second-year student who primly took her seat saying, 'Mrs Adams says please continue without her and Iris. She is going to accompany Iris home to Ancoats as Iris has been a little bit unwell.'

This was the high point of the meeting. It soon descended into madness with Constance struggling to keep control with her gavel, like a ragged pirate captain at the helm of a surging galleon in a force ten gale off the Gulf of Mexico. The troublemakers were her own Executive Officers.

Mabel Parker munched her way noisily through some shortcake biscuits, rubbing her stomach and frequently excusing herself to use the bathroom.

Victoria Butterworth sighed regularly and lost her place writing down the minutes and kept having to ask people to repeat what they had just said.

Evelyn King gave a half-hearted report on the joint meetings with the Men's Union regarding the Christmas ball, but her mind was just not on it. She kept secretly smirking to herself and losing her place in her copious notes and no one was listening anyway.

Abigail Rushton, the secretary of the Debating Society, chain-smoked throughout the meeting, lighting the next cigarette from the butt of the previous one, blue smoke curling up around her head like a warped halo. Her hand shook unsteadily, and she had a rasping-sounding cough which punctuated the meeting every few minutes and grated on the nerves. By the end of the meeting everyone else was coughing and smelt like an ashtray because no one could get a window open as they had all been screwed shut.

Alexandra Cotton, Athletics Secretary, and the Representative of the Athletics Union was waspish and wanted to pick a fight with whoever was speaking, each time trying to bring the topic of conversation around to the committee's lack of charitable giving, so each item took three times as long to get through as it should.

In exasperation, Constance finally time-limited each item to get through the agenda, as it was late and no one wanted to miss the last university bus back to Halls or to lodgings, to which Alexandra took umbrage.

Tactlessly and with deliberate intent to cause offence, Abigail Rushton, whom had been relighting a cigarette looked up from her task and dropped a clanger, 'It is because of you, you argumentative, daft, socialist besom, that the president is imposing a time limit. We would have been at home in our beds half an hour ago if you could control the angst that comes out of your mouth.'

Alexandra's face crumpled up and puckered like a baby. A huge sob escaped her wobbling lips. She pressed a copious hanky to her eyes. Some misguided soul chose that moment to snicker. Alexandra took to her heels and was the final committee member that evening to run out of the room to the bathroom, but this time in floods of tears.

They could all hear gusty sobs coming through the walls. No one went after Alexandra. They were all sick of having to fight every point.

With obvious relief but looking uncomfortably guilty, Constance Harris wrapped up the meeting in record time. And with the glee of schoolchildren released for a long vacation, everyone charged out of the building, glad to be free of the baleful atmosphere.

Friday 12th October 1934, Afternoon

Dorothea had her head down in a book of Ancient Norse vocabulary in the Art's Library and was mentally over a thousand years in the past, when a tap on her shoulder caused her to turn around suddenly and to startle. The familiar and haughty face of Dr Hadley-Brown stared down at her inquiringly.

'I did call your name several times, Miss Roberts, but you appear to be away with the Norsemen.' He sounded almost apologetic. When she continued to look blank, he continued, 'Never mind. It was a joke and a poor one at that. Will you come with me please?'

'Where are we going? Am I in trouble?' Dorothea asked, getting stiffly to her feet, and stretching, thinking back, guiltily, to their breaking and entering expedition the previous week. At their weekly Sunday gathering they had turned one wall of Maggie's flat into a crime board to showcase everything they knew and talked and talked, all thought of crosswords forgotten. Mary Long hadn't heard back from her Chemistry friend so there was no new news on the knife or fragments of paper from Evelyn King's fireplace.

'Do you always ask so many questions, Miss Roberts? No in this instance you are not in trouble . . . yet. Do come along please,' interposed the academic, interrupting her train of thought.

Dr Hadley-Brown was being almost affable, and it confused her. He helped her pack away her scattered notes, raising an eyebrow at a half-started essay on *The Taming of the Shrew,* but refraining from saying anything acerbic.

He led Dorothea out of the Art's Library into the main School of Art and to a corridor on the first-floor housing some of the nicer offices belonging to senior faculty members. He knocked on the door of Professor Aldridge, waited for a muffled 'Come in,' and then, opening the door, beckoned Dorothea to go through.

'Miss Roberts, Professor,' he murmured and closed the door behind her.

'Ah, thank you, Geraint. Oh, he has gone. Oh, well, it is probably for the best. Welcome, Miss Roberts. Do come in and take a seat. Would you like a cup of tea? You would? Splendid! I'll just boil some water on my little spirit stove here. Milk and sugar? Do please help yourself to a biscuit.'

Dorothea looked around Professor Aldridge's rather large office while munching a shortbread biscuit. His office was lined in bookcases from floor to ceiling, some of them two or three volumes deep with books.

He noticed Dorothea looking at his personal library and coughed delicately.

'The great thing about a room full of books is that they act as effective sound proofing. No one will be able to listen in to our conversation. Now, Miss Roberts, Geraint has been telling me that you and your friends saved his life. For which he is naturally very grateful even if he isn't very good at showing it. It would greatly help me if you can tell me in your own words what has been happening, please? It is vitally important that you tell me everything and don't leave anything out.'

Surprised, Dorothea looked at the professor properly. That tone he had used with her was authoritative and knowing but his face towards her was gentle. She had half-thought of going back to see DI Kydd but had persuaded herself that he would be too busy to listen to her. It would be good to confide in someone with some authority.

Under the mild gaze of the professor, Dorothea told him everything, beginning with her journey to the university. She explained about meeting Matilda on the train, being passed a note to give to him and of losing the note in all the confusion of seeing Matilda shot. She told him of the break-in at Grangebrook Hall to the room which should have been hers, her friends at Crossword Club and how they had solved the riddle of the personal advertisements together. She told him about following Evelyn King and Dr Hadley-Brown from St Ann's church and pushing the knife-wielding man out of the way before he could stab Dr Hadley-Brown, and of overhearing a blackmailer at work in *The Worm's* office.

'. . . So last week the Long and Short of it . . . I mean Mary Long and Mary Shor, got into Evelyn King's room and found an invitation to join an organisation called the Oyster Club and some charred paper in the grate. Mary Long has given the charred paper plus the knife used to attack Dr Hadley-Brown to one of her Chemistry demonstrators to analyse,' she finished. 'Are we going to get in trouble, Professor Aldridge? Do you know what the Oyster Club is?'

The professor pressed his fingertips together and looked thoughtful. 'Can you keep a secret Dorothea? A really big one. Even from your friendship group, if your country needed you?'

Dorothea inclined her head hardly daring to breathe.

'It relates to Dr Hadley-Brown most acutely. Geraint Hadley-Brown has a frightfully good academic mind and recently finished his Doctorate in Philosophy at the University of Cambridge and accepted a fellowship position here in Manchester two years ago, in the summer term of 1932. However, back in 1930 while still at Cambridge, the Russians recruited him as a spy-in-waiting. He attended some lectures on communism and hung around with some friends that were devotees of Marx. He is highly educated, very well connected and is likely to have an excellent career ahead of him, whatever career he ends up pursuing, where he might benefit his communist masters with interesting information. The only thing is, Geraint isn't a traitor and came straight to me. I am by way of being his godfather you see and worked in military intelligence during the Great War. I still have connections in the Secret Service which I made use of, and it was decided that Geraint would continue on the Russian's list of agents but in fact would be working for us. A double agent if you will. Are you following me so far, Miss Roberts?'

Dorothea nodded, stunned.

'We are keeping an eye on the young gentleman who *recruited* Geraint and other members of his social group and began listening out for any other instances of similar things happening at other institutions of learning.

'Well, it came as a surprise to find out that something similar might be happening here, at this very institution. Geraint noticed the Jane Austen personal advertisements in the university's magazine and cracked their code in a very similar way to you and your friends.

'We think there is a spy-ring working out of the Women's Union and we think there are close links with the Women's Union committee membership. We don't know if they are working for the Russians or the Germans or someone else entirely, but we do know that someone very clever with links abroad is controlling the spy-ring. We have given the spy-ring the code name, the Jane's Girls, due to the obvious literary connections and the mischief they can potentially cause if left unchecked. It is however interesting to hear about the Oyster Club . . . a very apt name! An oyster turns grit into a pearl over time. Our Jane's Girls are the grit, and they will embed themselves in somewhere useful to their masters: an embassy, a large company perhaps or an advantageous marriage. In time they will yield priceless pearls of knowledge to their overlords.

'We believe the death of Ethel Worksop, the Women's Union Committee Secretary, was somehow linked to the spy-ring's activities. Either she knew too much and had gone rogue or had stumbled onto the information by accident so had to be silenced.

'So we sent an agent undercover with the job of infiltrating the Women's Union Committee. The person you know as Matilda Abbott was our spy to spy on the spies. The only thing is Matilda was actually Matthew Abbott, an experienced officer and the best female impersonator in MI5's U Branch.'

'Hang on! You sent a man pretending to be a woman to infiltrate a women's committee? Couldn't you just find a female agent? Aren't there any women that work for MI5?' Dorothea was incredulous.

The professor had the grace to look embarrassed.

'Er, yes. There are. They do vital work as secretaries and clerks and in finance.'

Dorothea looked unimpressed.

The professor tried to explain further. 'The powers that be in the Secret Service thought it was a man's job to go undercover into what proved to be a dangerous situation and a lot of the chaps back at MI5 have desk jobs at the moment so are itching to get out of the office and into the field. There are also a fair few MI5 employees who took part in amateur dramatics at Oxbridge who fancy themselves as er . . . masters of disguise, so to speak, and can't wait to get into a frock and lipstick. I am not doing a good job of explaining this, I can see,' Professor Aldridge said, mistaking Dorothea's look of bafflement at the idiosyncrasies of male leadership as incomprehension of the situation.

'Anyway, we got the sad news earlier this week that Matthew's body was found in a canal after having been missing for three weeks. It seems someone must have aided him and kept him hidden while his shoulder healed as he didn't die of his gunshot wound, the one you witnessed, rather he was poisoned with a fatal number of barbiturates on an empty stomach.

'When you met Matthew on the train, he was fearful for his life as he had in his possession a list of past and present members of the Jane's Girls posted to him by Ethel Worksop the day she died. The piece of paper he gave to you. Matthew had taken time to befriend Ethel as she, out of all the committee members liked to ferret out gossip and he thought she could be useful to him. She had previously hinted to him that she knew of a secret organisation working out of the Women's Union. Maybe she posted the list to him as some kind of insurance or maybe she had some sort of premonition that she wasn't safe. That piece of paper was dynamite. Matthew was sure that someone had searched his room the evening before you met him. Agents know these things. Tricks with talc and single hairs placed precisely to check whether drawers and bed linen have been disturbed.

'Anyway, it was imperative to pass this list on to Geraint or myself. He also thought he had a concrete lead on the unknown head of the spy-ring. Someone we have codenamed "The Matchmaking Mama" or possibly we should rename her in light of your information about the Oyster club as "The Mother of Pearl".' He gave a little laugh at his own joke.

Dorothea did not find it funny. 'Oh, no! So, I totally let Matilda, I mean Matty, Matthew down. It is my fault you don't have that list. I am so sorry. Is there anything I can do to make it up?' The devastation in Dorothea's voice was palpable.

'Well, actually, there is. I want to offer you the opportunity to serve your country. It will be dangerous. Two people have already died because of the knowledge of the Oyster Club so it is no light matter, but you have already shown great courage and intuition. As you noticed yourself, MI5 haven't been used to using female agents, but this is about to change. We want you to get yourself elected to the Women's Union Committee as one of the first-year representatives being elected in November. We need someone on the inside being our eyes and ears. If you get approached to become a member of the Oyster Club, accept the invitation, and learn what you can.'

'What about my friends? Can I tell them all of this? They are involved already,' Dorothea asked. 'I couldn't have done it without them.'

'Absolutely not. This is a matter of national security and a very dangerous situation. I can't stress this enough; you cannot trust anyone. Your friends are a remarkably talented group of young women so you can keep sleuthing with them for as long as it is on an amateur basis. You might need their help to get elected to the committee for example. However, to protect them for now, and yourself, it is best that you all appear to have no knowledge of what we are onto. The best way to appear ignorant is to be ignorant. As amateurs if you get too warm, you will seem like potential Oyster Club material rather than a major threat.'

Dorothea felt torn by this. She desperately wanted to confide in her friends and not to have secrets, but the professor's seriousness had impressed her.

'Geraint and I will be your academic sponsors for the Women's Union Committee. Here are the forms already filled in, in this envelope. I want you to keep myself and Geraint up to date with any developments. You have a tutorial class with Geraint and two lectures with me, each week. Add a note to the end of any coursework set, keeping us informed of your progress. I have added both our telephone numbers and contact addresses to the envelope. Please learn them off by heart and don't be afraid to call us if you get into difficulty.'

'What about the police?' Dorothea asked. 'DI Kydd seemed nice. Shouldn't we tell him?'

The professor looked amused. 'By this time, DI Kydd has been brought up to speed by the Head of U Branch from MI5 and I don't think he was that amused. He certainly gave Geraint an interesting time identifying Matthew Abbott's body.'

Dorothea asked the question that was burning uppermost in her mind. 'Professor Aldridge is Dr Hadley-Brown really trustworthy? He was the first person on the scene when Matty was shot. He arrived most promptly. I really did think he must have fired the shot. I know he is your godson so you will have known him since he was a baby and know him better than anyone, but people do change. Do you trust him?'

Professor Aldridge looked Dorothea straight in the eye and said firmly and with emphasis, 'I would trust Geraint with my life, Miss Roberts, and so can you.'

And that is that, and I suppose I'll have to believe the professor knows what he is talking about, Dorothea thought, *but I am watching you Geraint Hadley-Brown. I am watching you.*

THE WORM

Edition 5 Academic Year 34/35, Tuesday 16th October 1934

This magazine has learned of a delightful event occurring between two of our favourite university staff members. *The Worm's* most heartfelt congratulations go out to the happy couple on their engagement. Dr Hadley-Brown of the Department of English will wed Mrs Gladys Adams the Advisor to Women's Students.

Mrs Adams, the widow of the late Mr Ferdinand Adams of the Foreign Office, has been seen sporting a pearl and diamond engagement ring. It is thought that the couple will get married during the summer vacation at St Werburgh's, the bride's normal place of worship, with a reception at the Women's Union building. We are sure all our readers wish them well.

David Simpkins (Journalist)

CHAPTER SEVEN

Ongoing Investigations

Thursday 18th October 1934, Afternoon

Long mahogany benches stretched out either side of a central aisle, their once highly polished surfaces now patinaed with the chemical mistakes of years of undergraduates. There was a tang of vinegar mixed with burnt wooden spills in the air. Orange-flamed Bunsen burners flickered and danced, warming various strange bubbling concoctions in weird-shaped glassware, attended by efficient, white-coated demons wearing laboratory goggles. Around the outside of the room were wood and glass cupboards with sliding sashes which sucked at the air, in which the attendant white-coated demons were producing more noxious smelling gases.

This vision of hell was presided over by a Grand Demon, white coat more a beige-brown colour from years of wiping his hands, spatulas, and glassware on it, who kept pushing his safety goggles up onto his head and then wondering where he had put them. He was steadily marking his way through a gigantic pile of laboratory books presumably not for this group of students. Three Lieutenant Demons floated around their acolytes, tweaking apparatus, showing how to do complex mathematics on scrap pieces of paper and recovering substances when the demons had flushed them into the wrong bit of their funny-shaped glassware with the wrong solvent.

Dorothea felt like a fish out of water in a borrowed white coat and goggles, even though she had studied Chemistry at school. Mary Long led her through Dante's seventh circle of hell to where the smell of burning was more pronounced.

One of the Lieutenant Demons was admonishing an acolyte. 'Really, Hunt, you know that sodium gets really hot and reacts violently with water. Did you really think that putting the rest of the unused sodium into the sink and flushing it with water was the correct way to dispose of the excess? Especially when your peers insist on putting out their lit spills in the sink and then abandoning them there and then, using acetone to wash out their glassware there too. You could have set the place on fire!'

Spotting Mary and Dorothea heading towards him, the Lieutenant Demon left his quivering prey and stalked over to meet them.

'Hello, Mary,' the Lieutenant Demon said. 'I can't remember your year being quite so dopey last year. I have had a look at those bits you dropped off. Very interesting! Are you coming to the Ritz a week on Saturday by the way? It's Chubby's birthday.'

Mary introduced Dorothea. It turned out that the Lieutenant Demon's name wasn't Skullcrusher Wolfsblood III but rather Richard Dempsey and he was a doctoral student that occasionally did some analyses for the local police force. The invitation was kindly extended to Dorothea for Saturday.

Stopping by the Grand Demon, Richard Dempsey asked, 'Dr Macdonald, please can you keep an eye on my bunch of pyromaniacs. I have just got to pop to my lab for some results for these two. I'll be back in five minutes.'

The Grand Demon grunted, 'Bring me a cup of tea up from the tearoom would you please, Richard, on the way back. These lab books are soul destroying.'

'Yes, of course, Dr Macdonald.'

Out of earshot, Richard whispered, 'Poor man, his wife has made him give up smoking as they have a child on the way, and she is terrified he'll blow himself up. He is an Organic Chemist working on new fuels. Some of the compounds he is working with are a bit frisky and he is known for being absent minded,' this was an aside more for Dorothea's benefit as Mary Long was nodding sagely.

'Sweet, milky tea is what he drinks when the urge to smoke is at its greatest, poor devil.'

They had come to a small laboratory on the first floor only big enough for two or three people at most. Richard opened the door and ushered them in. There was even more odd-shaped glassware containing pale yellow concoctions bubbling away, along with a sweet smell of pear drops.

'I am interested in aldehydes and ketones,' he said, by way of an explanation.

There was a door next to the lab's only fume hood and Richard led them through to a tiny laboratory set up as a photographic darkroom. Dorothea realised why Mary and Richard got on so well, dancing and photography, a heady combination. Leading them to a messy desk he hunted around and brought out an official typed report.

'I did it properly, as knowing Mary you are probably up to something, which might end up with me stood up in court, and I don't know on which side of the dock I shall be. There were no fingerprints on the knife, sorry Mary,' he said, looking at her disappointed face. 'And no substances such as blood on the blade. It had been recently polished. Here are your photographs I have developed them for you.'

Mary squeaked in delight and flicked through some

obvious artistic shots of nature and wildlife to reach the ones she had taken in Evelyn's room of the invitation to try out for the Oyster Club.

He continued in a stilted style as one would reciting a culinary recipe, 'Visually, I have ascertained that the small pieces of burnt paper, three in total, that were supplied, were of a high density, more like good quality cardboard than paper, the kind that invitations are written on. I rehydrated the fragments then affixed them onto glass to maintain their integrity. I managed to undertake some infrared photography which is very experimental at the moment, on the fragments. See this photograph . . .? It looks like the writing on this fragment says something that looks like "Congr . . . yu . . . ave . . . pas . . . ed". The other two haven't revealed anything yet so I am currently in the process of trying the contact process with pre-irradiation using ultraviolet light. Come back in a week or so for the results of that.

'Congratulations, you have Passed! I wonder what Evelyn/Eliza passed at?' Mary Long mused.

Dorothea was just about to open her mouth to say that under the altar at St Ann's there must have been confirmation that Evelyn had passed the test or one of the tests to join the Oyster Club when she remembered the professor's words.

'Let's get the others together for an extraordinary Crossword Club meeting this evening,' she said instead. 'I'll bring biscuits.'

Thursday 18th October 1934, Evening

Crossword Club was in session and Tabitha was in full-flow character assassination of each member of the Executive Committee. She knew them all as she had had to work with most of them during her two-year stint as a year representative on the committee. Jinny was making copious notes to add to the table of events they had made in the teashop and Maggie's room was beginning to look like a full-blown police investigation with photographs, maps and text pinned to the wall.

'Firstly, let's talk about the two victims, Ethel Worksop and Matilda Abbott,' Tabitha said, warming to her role and testing out her courtroom voice. She had aspirations of being made a Member of the Bar.

'What about the dead young man in the canal and the knife attack on Dr Hadley-Brown?' Mary Long piped up.

'Quiet in court! I'll get to them later. Firstly, let us consider Ethel. She was the new secretary on the committee who had been elected back at Easter. She had previously been a year representative for the Arts, studying Languages. She was very organised and good at minute taking so was actually a very good secretary but, flipping heck she could talk! She loved to gossip and was a nosey parker. She always had to know something more than you did. Secrets, she hugged them to herself like a comfort blanket but desperately wanted to divulge them to someone.'

'Do you think she might have blackmailed someone who was vicious enough to have killed her?' Maggie said, taking a bite of a ginger snap. 'We are assuming that it was murder not an accident?'

Tabitha thought for a moment. 'No, Ethel didn't really have the temperament to be a blackmailer, but she did prattle, and she may have unwittingly come across something that her killer didn't want her to prattle on to someone else about.

'Then we come to Matilda Abbott whom Dorothea saw shot on the train. I didn't know her at all really as she had transferred here from Cambridge and, surprisingly, got voted onto the committee pretty much straight away as a third-year representative, just as I was stepping down from the committee. She supposedly died of natural causes, but it has all been hushed up very neatly. I think we can deduce that there has been foul play there too.'

Tabitha paused for breath.

'Then we come to the mysterious young man who was poisoned then thrown into a canal. Who knows how he is linked to the other two incidents but linked he must be. We don't normally get dead bodies turning up on a regular basis, a stone's throw away from the university.'

Dorothea, choosing her words carefully butted in, 'Dr Hadley-Brown must have been a target for the killer because he was Matilda's contact on the train. Maybe the killer thought Matilda had time to pass him something rather than to me. He still might be in danger.'

'Possibly.' Tabitha wasn't too happy with the interruption. 'Now let's move on to the other members of the Women's Union Committee who are all potentially suspects and may be secret members of this Oyster Club or even the Secretary of the Oyster Club herself. Someone must have been placing those advertisements in the newspaper and setting challenges for people like Evelyn King.'

'Was there any mention of the Oyster Club when you were on the committee?' Jinny asked, from an armchair in front of the cosy fireplace. 'You were on it a long time.'

Blushing slightly Tabitha thought for a moment. 'Nothing I can put my finger on. It feels a familiar phrase so I may have heard something and thought they were talking about a club for seafood connoisseurs.'

Changing the subject she continued, 'Now getting back

to our suspects, Constance Harris is the Chair of the committee this year. She is a popular leader with some but has no bright ideas herself and fobs off responsibility onto other members of the committee. She was a year rep in her first year, the Secretary to the Athletics Union in her second year and managed to cut Iris Robinson out from the position of Chair in the last election. Everyone thought Iris would win but in a surprising outcome Constance beat Iris by just five votes.'

'I was gutted when I found out,' Mary Short chipped in. 'Iris is on my course, and I know her quite well and she would have made an excellent Chair. It's strange because everyone I talked to was going to vote for Iris. If I didn't know better, I would say that the vote was rigged.'

'Who counts the votes?' Dorothea asked.

'The outgoing Chair, the Adviser to Women's Students and a senior female member of staff who for the last few years since she was appointed, has been the warden of Grangebrook Hall. I don't think any other female member of staff wants the job of vote-counting really and the warden got volunteered,' Tabitha said.

'None of those individuals sound likely to rig a vote I'll admit but I do feel there was something wrong. Iris would always stand up for the underdog and the truth. Constance might turn a blind eye to something nefarious if it was for a chum. All those public-school types stick together.' Mary Short was adamant.

'Quite.' Tabitha was a public-school type herself but did not like to admit to it. She continued, 'Iris Robinson was Deputy Chair last year under Veronica Hathaway. Veronica was a good Chair. She made sure that everyone's idea was heard. She did treat us a bit like children, but we didn't begrudge it her. Iris is very idealistic and wants to change the world. She runs herself ragged between the committee, the University Settlement, the Socialist Society, and her medical degree.

'Mabel Parker the Treasurer is an interesting one. She was a year rep last year which was her second year studying Economics. She is the daughter of a banker and really good at figures so will keep a tight hold on the committee's finances. She is engaged to be married to Ferdy Nettleton, the nephew of Lord Barnton. They are sickeningly in love. He is a bit wet behind the ears if you ask me. I've known him forever, but I have also known his Mama forever and she is a battle-axe with apron strings that would wrap around the whole world and smother Ferdy while dragging him kicking and screaming back into the familial bosom. Knowing her, she won't be too pleased that Ferdy has taken up with trade. Ferdy's family are of course as poor as church mice. They are just living off the memory of inherited money, so even Mama will have to admit that the daughter of a wealthy banker is a suitable bride for her darling firstborn, but if there is even the tiniest hint of scandal Mama will use all her influence with Ferdy (which is considerable) to break off the engagement.'

'So if there was some sort of a scandal in Mabel's past she might be willing to pay a blackmailer through the nose to keep quiet about it and not tell her future Mama-in-law,' Mary Long hypothesised. 'She would certainly be able to afford to pay up!'

'Maggie checked with our mutual friend Cecily with the monocle and found out that Mabel lives at the boarding house the blackmailer rang, so she could well be being blackmailed!' Jinny added, glancing at Maggie. 'Maybe Ethel Worksop found out something compromising about Mabel and was about to prattle it to the whole committee, so Mabel ran her over!'

'Evelyn King, the Social Secretary of the committee, we know is the "Eliza" of *The Worm*'s personal adverts and has passed at least one test to join the mysterious Oyster Club. By now she may have passed some more. We know her politics are rather right wing, and she has contacts high up in the Fascist Party, but this is no secret, everyone knows this. We don't know if she has anything that someone would want to blackmail her for or if she is the blackmailer.'

Maggie, who had been quietly studying the document that herself and Jinny had produced in the teashop, tapped the paper, and asked, 'Has anyone else noticed that there have been more than one Oyster Club members in most academic years? See "Lydia" was contacted in the summer term after the Easter changeover for the committee. That means that as well as Evelyn as "Eliza", another member of the committee could be "Lydia". In fact, all the Austen characters could have been or possibly still are committee members or ex-committee members. The Oyster Club may cream off the brightest and most talented students from the committee.'

'That is a big leap to make,' Tabitha was scornful. They could easily just be normal students at the university.'

Mary Short was flicking through the latest copy of *The Worm*. 'There hasn't been a Jane Austen personal ad since the attempted stabbing of Dr Hadley-Brown. Maybe the Oyster Club is running scared because their code has been broken by outsiders. They might find new ways to communicate which we won't know about,' she sounded wistful.

'Next, we have Abigail Rushton the Debating Society Secretary,' Tabitha said, trying to regain some control of the discussion. 'She has held this position for two years. She came to the committee through the Debating Society and didn't rise up through the ranks so to speak. Because of this she holds herself a little aloof, misses a few meetings here and there and is generally a little disdainful of committee procedures. She smokes like a chimney, and I noticed that she is looking thin when I bumped into her in the library, like she isn't eating properly.'

'Maybe she is ill?' Mary Short was concerned, her medical training coming into play.

'Drugs more like,' Mary Long butted in. 'There is a small group from the Debating Society that dabble with cocaine, heroin, hashish and the like. They want to see if they can come to some higher enlightenment by debating under the influence of drugs.'

They all looked at her, startled.

'There is some gossip going around the Chemistry Department that they asked a Chemist to manufacture them something hallucinogenic from some plant or other. The Chemist told them where to go.'

'That would explain a lot,' Tabitha mused. 'Anyway, I think we can discount Victoria Butterworth, the new Secretary who replaces Ethel Worksop. She was new to the committee at Easter as a second-year rep and by accident has been elevated to the Executive Committee.'

'Don't discount anyone. She has shown ambition and tenacity to make it onto the Executive Committee so quickly and she is very bright. Prime Oyster Club material! She could have killed Ethel Worksop to take her place as Secretary as well. She was one of my tutees in her first year,' Maggie added, by way of explanation.

'Finally, we have Alexandra Cotton of the Athletics Society. She is a very good track and field athlete and spends a lot of her time running sports clubs for children at the Settlement in Ancoats. My sources say there was a very close vote at the first full committee meeting of this term on a motion proposed by Constance Harris, the President, pertaining to freezing the committee's charitable giving to worthy causes until an audit was undertaken of the value for money of the good causes that we support. The vote went in Constance's favour by just one vote, her own. Alexandra has been furious ever since and has been disruptive at every opportunity.

Maggie was looking thoughtful. 'Our current Executive Committee is very well stocked with members and alumni of Grangebrook Hall, when we all know there are other halls of residence for women in Manchester. Maybe there is a connection that we are missing?'

'What about the members of staff that support the committee?' Mary Long asked. 'We haven't thought about them at all.'

'Well, the provost is a member of the committee by default but rarely attends. There is some resentment over that because he does occasionally attend the Men's Student Union Committee but only when he knows that they have beer. His doctor won't let him have beer, but he feels it would be rude to refuse if he is offered one by the students.'

'The Adviser to Women Students is another ex-officio member of the committee. Mrs Gladys Adams was a high-flying member of the Foreign Office before her husband died. She took up post just over three years ago. Did you see in *The Worm* that she is engaged to be married to Dr Hadley-Brown? Sorry about that Dorothea.' Tabitha threw a cheeky little barb in Dorothea's direction.

'That is about when the personal advertisements started in *The Worm*,' Jinny said, looking up from a table she was drawing out on a piece of scrap paper, 'Three years ago.'

'What's that you are making?' Mary Short asked, peering over Jinny's shoulder.

'I thought we should have something that shows our potential murder suspects and what we know about them. I thought we might all take a person and try and find out something more about them. Like if they had a reason for wanting Ethel or Matilda dead.'

'Good idea, Jinny. We can do some more investigating! We can find out where they were when Ethel and Matilda died, what their alibis are,' Mary Long said with enthusiasm.

'Maybe not Matilda's death because we don't know when that actually happened, but we do know the exact time she was shot on the train, and we know when the attack on Dr Hadley-Brown occurred.'

At this juncture Dorothea plucked up the courage to ask the question she had been waiting all evening to put to her friends.

'I think I should try and get elected to the Women's Union Committee as a first-year rep in the upcoming elections. Please will you all help me?'

There was a hush as the idea played in the young women's brains and then there was a cacophony of voices.

'Brilliant idea! You would be our eyes and ears on the inside.'

'By Jove, that's a thought!'

'You would have to be careful, but it just might work!'

'You can interview the suspects without them realising!'

'No! It's too dangerous!' Tabitha's voice was raised above all the others, and her usually cheerful face was creased with anxiety, and she was trembling. 'Two committee members have died already. It is like using yourself as bait. You would be walking into the lion's den. There must be another way!'

'But having someone on the committee might get us closer to the Oyster Club and find out who is killing off committee members. The election for first-year representatives and Matilda's third-year representative replacement is in two weeks' time. I am the only one eligible to run. In fact, I want to run. I feel that I owe it to Matilda.' Dorothea was flustered; she hadn't expected to meet with any resistance from her friends, especially not from Tabitha, a staunch supporter of the committee.

Maggie, diplomatic as ever, intervened, 'I for one will support you. As your friends, we can help mitigate some of the risk if you get elected by providing an escort to and from committee meetings and even just to and from the university.'

'Hear, hear!' the two Marys cried in unison.

'Well, I for one can't support this. You are all too reckless. You must count me out.' Tabitha grabbed her coat and bag and stormed out of Maggie's room.

Dorothea was distraught. 'I am so sorry. I didn't mean to offend Tabitha. I don't understand what just happened. She was so enjoying talking about all our suspects and then she suddenly changed.'

'Don't blame yourself, Dorothea. Tabitha obviously has something on her mind. She'll come round; you'll see. The rest of us will help you.' Jinny gave Dorothea a hug.

But Dorothea couldn't stop worrying about her friend's outburst and it was a long time before she could get to sleep that night. She had been the last to leave Maggie's rooms and something Maggie had said stuck in Dorothea's mind.

As she was about to leave, Maggie commented quite matter-of-factly, 'You do know that Tabitha was lying when she said she had never heard of the Oyster Club when on the committee, don't you? She struggles to tell lies you see so she always sidesteps a question if she can't answer it honestly. She had nowhere to hide when Jinny asked her if she'd heard of the club during her time on the committee. Her colour rose, and her cheeks and neck went red. Tabitha lied and I don't know why.'

Monday 22nd October 1934, Afternoon

The University Settlement in Manchester was a university initiative, the first outside London, and had been founded in 1897. It was based on socialist principles, where staff and students went to live in a deprived community and tried to make socioeconomic change happen by living alongside the poor and by putting on educational activities consisting of lectures, debates, concerts, and classes. There were nearly forty activities for children, young people, and adults and over one hundred voluntary helpers.

The Manchester University Settlement was based in Ancoats, Northeast of the city centre which was an overpopulated slum area where the City Council was pleased to let the university roll up its academic sleeves and get stuck in too.

At Ancoats Hall, home of the Ancoats Art Museum, an art gallery had been established to inspire and educate the locals and was a natural companion organisation to the Settlement. It let the university use its rooms for classes and debates and housed the female student's accommodation. The Round House, an old chapel, provided a large recreation room for plays and dances with the male halls of residence situated nearby on Every Street.

A van with the logo of the Manchester Corporation Gas Board pulled up outside and a gas engineer got out. When questioned later, the Ancoats Hall porter struggled to describe the nondescript gentleman. He was small to medium build, wearing baggy overalls, a cap pulled low down over his eyes, gloves and a muffler obscuring the lower half of his face. The engineer seemed to have a terrible cough which made his voice hoarse, and in a whisper, he made it known that he had been called due to the smell of gas in one of the bedrooms.

The porter, who was usually based at the Science laboratories and was only covering for a colleague who was at the dentist having an extraction, scrabbled around in the porter's cubbyhole searching for a note to explain this visitation. Shrugging and giving up on his colleague's filing system, he inquired of the engineer if he knew his way around. The muffled stranger nodded assent and mumbled something about having been sent for before.

Gratefully, the porter checked the signing in sheet, handed over the spare key for room twenty-three, pointed roughly in the right direction and retreated into the sanctuary of the cubbyhole and prayed no one else would ask him a question that he did not know the answer to.

Once inside room twenty-three, the engineer spent some time fiddling with the gas outlet on the fire. Then he added something to the biscuit jar on the mantelpiece, placed something behind the desk and dropped some rubbish into the wastepaper bin.

Then he stripped off his overalls, hat and muffler and emerged from his grubby cocoon dressed like any young female student in a slightly shabby skirt, jumper and coat with scuffed shoes and curled hair. The props of his engineering trade were consigned to his work bag which could pass as a sports bag at a push. The young woman let herself out of the room, taking care not to leave any fingerprints on the door. As she left the building, she dropped the key to room twenty-three through the hatch into the porter's cubbyhole and onto the desk, from where the sounds of a kettle whistling on a gas stove and crockery clinking could be heard.

CHAPTER EIGHT

A Sparkling Puzzle

Monday 22nd October 1934, Early Evening

'Porter, I say, Porter! We have come to visit Iris Robinson. Can we sign in please? Do you know if she is in?'

Mary Short had come with Dorothea to visit Iris at Ancoats Hall as Mary knew her from her course. They had come over on the tram one wet cold evening after dinner.

'She is expecting us.'

The porter still totally out of his depth scrabbled around for the signing in book and peered at it rheumily before passing it over to the young women. They signed themselves in and spotted immediately that Iris, their quarry, had signed in an hour ago.

'I think it is this way and up the stairs,' Mary Short said, realising that they would not get any more help from the porter. 'I came here last year to look around but then decided to stick with what I knew and stay at Grangebrook Hall.'

The first scent of trouble they got was a tiny whiff of coal gas as they entered the upstairs corridor. Dorothea picked it up first as Mary Short's nose had been desensitised to smells from her shifts in the hospital. It got stronger and stronger as they went along until outside the door of number twenty-three it was at its most potent.

Mary Short took charge. 'Dorothea, we need to see if there is anyone in there, get the window open and turn off the gas. You go for the window, break it if necessary. I'll go for the gas tap. Stay down low, coal gas is lighter than air.'

The door wasn't locked, and the handle turned easily. Taking a deep breath, the two young women rushed into the room. Dorothea's only focus was on getting to the window fast. In her haste she tripped over something that was lying prone on the floor and her fall propelled her fortuitously towards the window. Behind her she could hear Mary fumbling around by the gas fire.

Keeping low she rattled the sash window, but it was painted shut and would not budge. Silently cursing incompetent workmanship and running out of breath she grabbed the chair from by the desk and swinging it like a hammer thrower, launched it at the window with all the force that her five feet one inches could muster. There was the sound of breaking glass and the chair and a lot of the window frame disappeared into the herbaceous border below.

Dorothea stood at the window and gulped in a lungful of fresh air before turning to see Mary Short struggling to lift the bundle that Dorothea had tripped over, a huddled figure of a young woman whose lips and face had turned a sickly blue tinge. Dorothea rushed over to help. She grabbed Iris by the ankles and Mary took her shoulders. Between the two of them Iris was surprisingly easy to lift, and they manoeuvred her quickly into the corridor, closing the door behind them and coughing and spluttering as they took on board the fresher corridor air.

'Go to the porter's desk and get him to phone for an ambulance and the police. I'll start working on Iris.' Mary

Short then got to work on her patient.

Dorothea sprinted off down the corridor not waiting to see what happened. She used the banister to get downstairs quickly, sitting side saddle on it like she was a small child again at home and sliding down it to halve her time.

'Please call the police and get an ambulance.' Dorothea nearly sobbed at the startled porter. 'Someone has tried to murder Iris Robinson.'

Monday 22nd October 1934, Late Evening

Detective Sergeant Garden had finished photographing the room and PC Standish was checking the room for prints. The typed suicide note found behind the desk was bagged as evidence and the empty barbiturate wrappers were currently being extracted from the bin and bagged as well. A classic suicide attempt, cut and dried, and no doubt over a young man or poor grades and familial over-expectations and yet . . . and yet . . .

DI Kydd wasn't happy. With all the other things going on, on campus another member of the committee incapacitated was just too far-fetched to swallow. The young woman, though drugged up to her eyeballs, looked likely to make a full recovery. Luckily, she had been found in time and the dose she'd taken or been given was not enough to kill her, just knock her out while the gas did its work.

Miss Dorothea Roberts, who fortuitously had just happened to be on the scene again, had asked permission from the inspector to sit with Iris in hospital until her parents could be located. Since Iris was going to be under the careful watch of a Woman Police Constable the whole time, this idea appealed greatly to the inspector as he could keep an eye on Dorothea too.

It just didn't quite make sense. If you were taking barbiturates anyway why not take an overdose and drift into oblivion, why then turn on the gas tap? It was a risky strategy. Someone might smell the gas and rescue you. This is in fact what happened.

The young woman had been found sprawled on the floor as if she had been working at her desk and had slipped off the chair. She was wearing her everyday clothes. Normally someone who was going to take an overdose would have lain down on the bed and got dressed in to either comfortable clothes for sleep or their best clothes to make a good impression on being found, depending on how vain they were. If someone was going to gas themselves, they tended to be nearer the source of the gas than the victim had been found. He would have expected the bed to have been pushed closer to the fireplace and the victim found on the bed.

It was interesting that barbiturates had turned up again. It would be a massive job and a shot in the dark, but he made a note to find out which members of staff and students at the university had been prescribed barbiturates by their doctor.

The suicide note was suspicious too. People taking their lives on impulse didn't tend to type a note on a typewriter that was not in their possession. There was not one in the room. Essays for the medical degree were handwritten. He had already checked with Miss Mary Shor who was a course-mate of the victim. It would be more usual to handwrite a suicide note.

Then there was Miss Dorothea Roberts, who emphatically believed that what they had found was an attempted murder. The local police force normally got calls, letters and visits from members of the public on average about once a week regarding potential murders that had taken place or were about to, some were troublemakers, some were busybodies with too much spare time on their hands, some were from desperate people whose loved one had disappeared of their own free will and who didn't want to be found, and a thankfully small group of informers were genuine.

Miss Roberts was not a troublemaker, busybody or had any personal connection with the victim. Discarding the theory that Miss Roberts might be a mass murderer herself, the conclusion one came to was that she was someone to take seriously. She also had an interesting tale to tell about an attempted knife attack on MI5's finest Geraint Hadley-Brown which he hadn't reported to the police. Dorothea had seemed surprised to find out that the inspector was unaware of this.

'Can you fingerprint the gas fire, PC Standish, please? Then call a gas engineer to cap off the gas and get the whole fire sent to the lab for analysis. I am off to call the Chief Super. I think it is time to bring in retired Police Sergeant Timms.'

Tuesday Morning, 23rd October 1934, Early Hours

Sitting by Iris's hospital bed in the Manchester Royal Infirmary, late into the night, had given Dorothea time for some serious reflection. Someone was systematically and ruthlessly attacking and/or killing off members of the Women's Union Committee. Getting herself elected to that committee was looking more and more likely to be suicide, but despite that and Tabitha's grave warnings Dorothea was determined to give it a try. The WPC sat on the other side of the bed idly flicking through an old magazine.

Iris stirred, her eyelids flickered, and her eyes shot open. Weakly she tried to sit herself up on one elbow while looking wildly around the hospital ward cleared of other patients, to try and locate herself in time and space.

'What happened? Where am I?'

Then scrabbling at her regulation hospital gown unsuccessfully, 'Where has it gone?' she wailed.

'Now, Miss, you are safe enough here. You had a little accident which I will need to ask you about when you are feeling more yourself but for now just take it easy and I'll go and give Matron a shout to see if she can make you feel more comfortable.'

The WPC's tone was reassuring and seemed to calm Iris as she settled back down in the bed. However, while the WPC was at the nurse station Iris's hand shot out and imploringly grabbed at Dorothea's.

'Please, my brooch, where is it? He gave it to me. I was wearing it and now I'm not.'

'Let me take a look in your locker.'

Dorothea tried to mimic the reassuring tones of the WPC. She had a root around in the cabinet next to the bed, and to her surprise drew out a brooch that took her a few seconds to place. It was small and garish and was made up of diamonds and coloured gemstones in a wreath of multicolours. Matty Abbott had been wearing the exact same brooch when Dorothea had met her on the train. She handed it to Iris slowly, thinking hard. Iris nearly snatched it out of her hand and pinned it with trembling fingers to the inside neckline of her nightgown where it couldn't be seen. This task accomplished, she seemed to relax.

'You knew Matthew Abbott.' It was a statement from Dorothea rather than a question. 'He gave you that brooch. I saw it pinned to his chest when he was dressed as Matilda on the train when he was shot.'

'You know? Yes.'

The look of pain in Iris's eyes made Dorothea wince in sympathy and she nodded. 'Yes, I know.'

In a faltering voice which gradually got stronger, Iris explained. The WPC had slipped back quietly into her place by the bed and was taking notes.

'Matthew, in disguise as Matilda, arrived during spring term last year and was placed into the vacant room in Halls next to mine. I was in Grangebrook Hall then. I didn't know it was a disguise. He was so convincing. Though he kept himself to himself for obvious reasons, we became friends, and I helped Matilda to get elected to the committee because it was something she really wanted.

'When he got shot Matthew came to me for help. He made it across town from the station to Ancoats Hall. I am a medical student, you see. He fainted from loss of blood with the effort of getting here and collapsed on the bed. Obviously, I worked out straight away that Matilda wasn't all she seemed as soon as I stripped her. I could see that the bullet had only grazed Matthew's shoulder, so I cleaned and stitched it like we have been taught.

'When Matthew came round, he was fearful for his life. He told me that he was a member of MI5 and undercover on a mission. He said that national security would be compromised if he failed. He was very weak from the blood loss. I wanted to take him to the hospital, but he thought they would track him there, so I nursed him myself in my room. He was pretty sick for the first few days with a fever. I was pretty worried about him actually.

'In his delirium he kept talking about "The Oyster Club" and saying, "Don't let the she-devils get me" and he seemed to be frightened of being made a prisoner because he kept repeating something that sounded like "The warders are coming".

'When he was a little better, he laughed it off. He was a kind and funny man. I enjoyed talking to him. I think I fell in love with him. He seemed to know too because one day he turned serious and said, "Iris, it wouldn't work between us, old girl. If I married anyone it would be you, but I am not the marrying kind". We never spoke about it again.

'He rented a room over in New Islington for when he wasn't in disguise. One day, it was the 17th of September, when he was on the mend, and he asked me to go over there and get him some male clothes and check for any post. I was to say to his landlady that I was his sister and that Matthew had been taken ill and was recovering by the sea in Southport. Well, there wasn't much post but what there was I brought back. But something in the post made him so excited he jumped out of bed, pulled on his clothes and shoes, and left the safety of my room. As he was leaving, he gave me this brooch and said to keep it safe until he returned. He said he had designed it himself. He kissed my forehead and left and that was the last time I ever saw him alive.' Tears were welling up in her eyes.

'He must have been with me for about a week. I was dismayed to hear that a body of a young man had been found in a canal, but I still had hope. I was devastated when I walked into the autopsy room and Professor

Fredericks drew back the shroud of the dead young man and I saw Matthew lying there. I was so shocked that I fainted, and Professor Fredericks had to send me home. I knew that there must have been a cover-up by the authorities when reports that Matilda's body had been found rather than saying Matthew's body had been identified from the canal.

'Then the phone calls and letters started. Someone knew that I had had a man stay in my room. We had been so careful, but someone had found out. If they reported me, I could get sent away from the university and the disgrace would have been unbearable.'

'What did they want from you?' Dorothea asked carefully, so as not break what seemed to be a therapeutic outpouring.

'That's just it. They haven't asked for anything yet. It seems to be pure mischief-making.'

Very gently Dorothea asked, 'Did you try and take your own life because of these threats and Matthew's death?'

Two spots of colour appeared on Iris's cheeks, and she sounded quite waspish when she replied, 'No, of course not! Is that what they think?' She glanced at the WPC.

'Suicide is never the answer. I had made up my mind to take a furlough from my course and go abroad with one of the missionary societies and work in a mission hospital to gain more experience and give myself time to heal.'

'So, you didn't take barbiturates and then turn the gas on in your room?' Dorothea asked.

'Barbiturates are filthy things. I would never take them. Is that what they think I did? I know I had trouble getting the gas fire to light when I came in after my afternoon clinic, but I got it going eventually. I then made a cup of cocoa on my little camping stove and had a biscuit or two from the tin and sat down at the desk to do some work. The next thing I know is that I am talking to you.'

'Did you see anything suspicious on the night of the hit and run that killed Ethel Worksop?' Dorothea asked, changing the subject abruptly.

Surprised by the sudden change of track, Iris obligingly thought back to the night of Ethel Worksop's death. 'No, nothing I can think of. Nobody wanted to go to the Executive Committee Social because we all had to come back from vacation early for it, but we all went to please Constance Harris. Afterwards, Mabel Parker left first like a shot, followed by Abigail Rushton and I got the bus with Alexandra Cotton who lives in digs out Collyhurst way. I got off the bus first near Ancoats. Constance Harris, Ethel Worksop, and Evelyn King were all talking in the foyer when we left. Mrs Adams was with them too.'

'And had you ever heard of the Oyster Club before Matthew started talking about it in his delirium or had you ever been asked to join it?' Dorothea asked, knowing she was pushing her luck.

'No, it was unfamiliar to me.'

'Where were you at lunchtime on October 3rd by the way? It was a Wednesday.'

Iris looked confused. 'I usually help out at the baby clinic at Ancoats on a Wednesday, and I haven't missed one this term so I would have been there.'

The WPC intervened at this point. 'Miss, I have been taking down some notes. If I type them up as a statement, would you be willing to sign it?'

'Absolutely!' Iris Robinson declared emphatically. 'I did not try and commit suicide. I did not take barbiturates and I did not gas myself on purpose. I cannot explain how I ended up here.'

This was the story Iris Robinson stuck to and nothing anyone said could shake it. DI Kydd interviewed her himself and got the same statement. As a witness she impressed him. Even though there were dark smudges under her eyes, and she looked as if a puff of wind could blow her away, she had a core of inner strength and a deep-rooted resilience. Now she was clearly grieving but there was no evidence of the deep hopelessness that led to the last desperate act of finishing one's own life.

As the inspector was leaving, he asked if Matthew's brooch could be kept at the police station under lock and key as it obviously was important to the dead man. With some reluctance Iris parted with it on the promise that it would be returned to her at the end of the inquiry and was given an official police receipt.

He clenched his teeth grimly. He knew how Iris Robinson had ended up in hospital. Just before leaving for the hospital, he had had a report from the police laboratory. They had got in a specialist gas engineer to look at the gas fire from Iris's room. It had been deliberately tampered with so that the pilot light would go out during operation leaving the gas switched on.

Someone, it seemed, was systematically exterminating members of the Women's Union Committee. On the positive side this was the lead he needed to link Matthew Abbott's death to another felony committed against a member of the university. So hang the interference from MI5, Manchester's finest was back on the case.

THE WORM

Edition 6 Academic Year 34/35, 23rd October 1934

Two Women's Union Committee Members Dead and One in Hospital: Are Committee Members Being Targeted? And if so, Why?

To date, two members of the Women's Union Committee have died in suspicious circumstances, and one is under police guard at the Royal Infirmary after being given a dose of barbiturates and then being left to die from gas poisoning.

Firstly, Ethel Worksop (twenty) was the victim of a tragic hit and run accident outside of the Student Union after the first Executive Committee meeting of the year.

Then, Matilda Abbott (twenty-one) died suddenly, and her body wasn't discovered for three weeks. Last night, Iris Robinson (twenty) was discovered in her room at Ancoats Hall. She had taken a sleeping draught and the room was full of gas. Her rescuers were undergraduate members of the university who called the police. Speaking to one of Iris's rescuers, who wanted to remain nameless, there were certain anomalies present at the scene that seemed to exclude a failed suicide attempt. The police are also taking extra care to protect Miss Robinson. She is currently under round-the-clock police protection, at the hospital.

This reporter was refused entry to interview Miss Robinson by a very forceful matron who did not believe his journalistic credentials and told him with great anatomical precision where to shove them.

There was an air of expectation that another attempt on Miss Robinson's life might be made. Manchester City Police is seemingly baffled by these incidents and DI Kydd, the officer in charge of the joint investigation, would not give a comment when this reporter rang his office.

These strange and tragic happenings raise the question of how safe our university campus, and for that matter our city, is, for our female students who seem to be taking the brunt of the casualties. Members of the Men's Student Union do not seem to have been targeted.

What are the university authorities doing to keep our students safe?

David Simpkins (Journalist)

Wednesday 24th October 1934

DI Kydd had seen the article in *The Worm*. PC Standish had brought it in nervously with his mid-morning coffee and several reports to soften the blow. Disappointingly, in PC Standish's opinion, the inspector read it with his spectacles delicately balanced, showing no other emotion than a small wrinkle of his nose, in disgust. He laid it to one side and picked up a report on departmental finances.

PC Standish tried again, 'Was anything found at Matthew Abbotts' digs, sir?'

'Nothing, Standish. If there was anything to find, I think the Secret Service got there before us, by about two weeks.'

Once PC Standish had exited the room, DI Kydd picked up the article again and fumbling with the phone put a call through to retired PS Timms. He then picked up a report from the local jeweller that had made the brooch to Matthew Abbott's exact specification, the original of which was sat securely inside the safe within the Chief Superintendent's office.

DI Kydd stared down at a colour photograph of the brooch in all its garish brilliance. *Amazing what these photography wizards can do these days*, he thought. It was an expensive white gold set in the shape of a laurel wreath, studded with diamonds and seven larger precious and semiprecious gemstones. In the centre was a large pearl. It should have been elegant, and the jeweller had tried his best, but the overall appearance was somewhat discordant.

The jeweller stated that a gentleman, a Mr Matthew Abbott, had telephoned him before term had started, with exact instructions on what he wanted. He had chosen a metal and the style and had asked for the brooch to be made up with specific gemstones in a predefined order around the wreath. The gentleman had been emphatic about that. Clockwise around the central iridescent pearl there was a ruby – blood-red and sparkling, a clear diamond, a limpid deep green emerald, a creamy grass green nephrite or jade, a deep indigo blue water sapphire, and a magenta amethyst. The jeweller confirmed that there was nothing hidden within the brooch itself.

When the jeweller had politely inquired who the brooch was for, Mr Abbott had smiled somewhat wryly and had admitted that it was, 'For a lady.' The jeweller had taken that to mean it was for his mistress rather than a betrothed or family member.

So, DI Kydd thought, *Matthew Abbott is trying to tell me something from beyond the grave through the stones of this brooch and their placement. But I am damned if I know what he's trying to say.*

The Chief Superintendent popped his head round the door. 'I've got Mr George on the phone having an apoplexy that we have got Abbott's brooch. I have promised him the jeweller's report for his laboratory chaps to paw over as a sop because I don't want that brooch leaving this building, as it is part of a current case, not one that has been forcibly closed as a result of interference by the Secret Service. Solve this case, Inspector. You have my full support.' The Chief Superintendent was like a naughty schoolboy with a cream bun, having got one up on Mr George.

'Understood, sir.' The inspector grinned.

Saturday 27th October 1934, Morning

It was Saturday morning and Geraint Hadley-Brown had some errands to run in town. He picked up his car from the mews garage and set off at a sedate pace from Chorlton Park, all muffled up against the cutting wind. In town he stopped off at the university to buy a copy of *The Worm*. There hadn't been any new communication from Jane's Girls in it since the ill-fated attempt on his life. He visited his bookmakers, posted some letters at the post office, and picked up his dress suit and shirts from the dry cleaners.

When everything was done, he decided to go for a drive in the country, out towards Rochdale, to a quiet little inn he knew, which did exceptionally good pies and peas, as he had nothing on until the evening.

Wending his way through the busy city streets, stopping occasionally for a tram to pass or to nip down a shortcut, he came to Junction Street, the steepest hill in Manchester, next to the goods station. He let the Crossley Quicksilver gather speed over the cobbles, enjoying the feeling of weightlessness down the steep gradient, then pressed the brakes hard near the bottom coming up to Store Street.

There was a loud crunch, and nothing happened, the automobile continued its reckless headlong descent with no decrease of speed. Stamping on the useless brake pedal with his full weight, at the same time he tried putting the handbrake on which gave some traction as he steered around the corner on to Store Street at forty-five miles an hour. The handbrake held and slowed the Crossley's decent somewhat but sent it into a sideways slide.

What slowed the Crossley's decent more successfully was a cartload of steaming manure from the stables of the horses used to shunt trucks in the good's yard. It was parked at the side of the road in the Crossley's path. Geraint hit it side-on with an almighty crash of buckling metal and splitting wood and a shower of horse apples but did come to an effective halt.

Shaken but unhurt, Geraint extracted himself to inspect the damage to the car and cart. A crowd formed around the scene of the incident with onlookers putting in their tuppence-worth and the owner of the cart becoming more and more strident about the damage to his vehicle. Since this crash was the most interesting thing to happen all morning, a fairly big crowd developed quite quickly. A bobby on the beat stopped to ineffectually shoo the crowd away and offer unwanted advice.

Geraint appeared from under the Crossley smeared in oil and smelling of the farmyard and was not listening to the recriminations and well-meaning driving tips.

'Who is going to pay for it, that's what I want to know?'

'Use a low gear, sir, when coming down Junction Street in future, then softly on the brake, not sudden like.'

'Ten bob it will cost me to fix that cart's bent axle.'

'Make sure you check your brakes before starting on a steep downhill, too.'

'That load was promised to Father O'Connor for his roses. Now what will the Father's roses do?'

Geraint looked up and beckoned a small runny-nosed child of indiscriminate sex and offered them a shilling if they could run to the local garage and fetch a mechanic. The child, eager to please, took off at a full sprint.

While waiting, he entered complicated negotiations with the carter who gradually became less strident and more appeased as money changed hands.

'The Father's roses can wait until next week for their fertilising. Greedy shrubs roses are.'

'What's all this fuss?' The owner of the local garage

strode up, work bag in oily hand, wearing patched overalls, tatty at the hem, blissfully unaware of the smear of grease across the bridge of his nose which wrinkled at the pong.

'My brakes failed coming down Junction Street and I hit a manure cart.' Geraint was straight to the point as he was fed up with standing in as the local circus attraction. 'Please could you give me a second opinion on my car's brakes?'

The mechanic confidently switched places with Geraint and had a rummage around.

There was an intake of breath, a tuneless hum then the mechanic stood up and asked with something like awe in his voice, 'Does someone not like you very much, sir? I'll need to get it jacked up back at the garage, but it looks like someone has been tampering with the brake drum mechanism. There are file marks on the outside of the brake cylinders, and it looks like the shoes of the internal expanding mechanisms have been damaged, so that they would break on a sudden application of pressure like braking for a big hill.'

Geraint nodded. 'I thought as much. And, yes, I agree. Someone really doesn't like me at all.'

CHAPTER NINE

Dancing with Death

Saturday 27th October 1934, Evening

It was Saturday evening and Dorothea was dressed in her newest and most daring evening dress, face powdered, with a touch of lipstick, and was feeling very grown up.

There were three types of university student. Those that loved to dance and would go out of their way to attend dances multiple times a week, be they at the grand dancehalls in town or at a local church hall, either in the evening or for tea dances or dancing impromptu to a gramophone in a hall's bedroom. They lived and breathed the foxtrot, the quickstep, and the waltz. Hollywood film stars and the famous actors of the stage were their gods whose edicts they followed religiously. Then there were the students who pretended to have no time for such frivolities but secretly lapped up any opportunity to dance, though with a show of high-minded reluctance. For these a Student Union ball or a Saturday night trip to a dance hall, were a well-earned treat to be savoured and prepared for with great precision and relish. Then the third group of students were those who were so taken up with their academic subject or an ideology that there was no time, talent or

150

inclination to dance and they looked down on the first two groups, as frivolous wastrels who brought the whole of higher education into disrepute.

For someone with such a very quiet upbringing in the Highlands of Scotland, Mary Long was an exceptionally good dancer. She had natural rhythm and poise and the ability to remember a new dance routine after only a couple of practice runs. She jokingly put it down to all the Sunday School ceilidhs that she had attended growing up. Partway through her first year she had discovered a group of like-minded Chemists in the Chemistry Department, made up mainly of research students and junior staff who were just as keen on dancing as she was. They were so good that the Ritz on Whitworth Street West was their chosen haunt. It was notable for the quality of the musical talent that played there, which was matched only by the quality of the dancers who attended, who had honed their skills with many hours of practice at their local dancehalls.

Dorothea fell into the middle category of student dancers more from an uncertainty about her dancing capabilities than anything else. She was a competent technician of the art form rather than a creative genius, and while she had had dancing lessons at her grammar school and enjoyed attending dances at the local village hall growing up, she was aware of her limitations and knew she was no Adele Astaire.

It was therefore a real treat if a little bit intimidating, to be off out to the best dance hall in town. Preparation started early with a quick soak in the bathtub, so that there was some hot water left before ten other young ladies on the same floor wanted baths. Then teasing and pinning her curls into a becoming coiffure. Before spraying herself with some scent, an extravagant Christmas gift from her sister, Anna. Dressed in a long, satin, claret-coloured figure-hugging evening dress with a cape top and sleeves that she had made herself, with her old coat on for warmth as there was a frosty nip in the air, Dorothea with Mary Long, signed the out of hours Halls register and left Grangebrook Hall in high spirits.

Mary Short, who was swatting for an Anatomy test on Monday morning and wasn't going with them, had strict instructions to sign them back in before ten thirty p.m. so they did not get into trouble with the warden for overstaying the hall's curfew. Mary Short had had a tiff with David Simpkins over the article he had written for *The Worm,* that contained information she had told him in confidence, so part of not going dancing was to punish him as he enjoyed any excuse for taking Mary out.

Together with the other chattering, excited students exuberant in their dancing clothes, Mary Long and Dorothea waited at the tram stop for the tram to take them into town. It dropped them off on Oxford Street just outside the Palace Theatre where they met up with two female postgraduate students from the Chemistry Department, friends of Mary, who lodged out in Salford. The Ritz was just around the corner.

On arrival at the Ritz dance hall, they deposited their outdoor layers with the cloakroom attendant then retired to the ladies' powder room to repair the damage of travel to their apparel. Mary Long kept up a barrage of information all the while which Dorothea, wide-eyed at the glamour of the venue lapped up as she reapplied her lipstick in the gilt-edged mirror.

'Chubby Thomas is a competent dancer but look out for his right foot. He has a habit of standing on his lady's instep on spins. Did you see the new professional dancer as we came in? Standing by Dolores Markham? He was a bit of a dish! I must make his acquaintance. I wonder if he is all beauty rather than substance. Watch out for Gerry Stevenson by the way. He is doing his Master's in Physical Chemistry and is a charming fellow before he has a glass of wine, but after a drink he gets handsy. I wonder if we will see anyone famous here tonight. Last time we came we saw Alasdair Tremaine after he had done a run at the Palace Theatre in one of Noel Coward's plays. He wasn't as handsome in the flesh, as you might think. He is really quite small with loads of wrinkles around his eyes. I wonder how bad grease paint really is for the skin. I'll have to ask Richard. He'll know. The other tests he was trying on the pieces of paper we found in Evelyn's room didn't work, unfortunately. Are you ready? Good. Me too. Come on, let's find the boys. I hope they have found a good table.'

Entering the main dance hall was like stepping into a Hollywood musical. The band was already in full swing on-stage and the singer's light and jolly tones filled up the columned, cavernous room and caused one's feet to want to tap and one's hips to sway. Couples twirled around the sprung dancefloor in perfect synchronisation. The men were sartorially elegant in black and white, and the women looked beautiful, like brightly coloured butterflies on a summer's day.

The young women found the group's table with some difficulty as it was upstairs on the balcony as far from the main entrance as could be, and Dorothea was introduced to the gentlemen. Richard Dempsey, she had already met. Dr Chubby or Charles Thomas was a new lecturer, stick thin, with boundless energy and a passion for the waltz. Handsy Gerry Stevenson was a quiet inoffensive person. He had a slight hand tremor when lighting his cigarette and charming manners and very kindly offered to buy the young women a drink. As well as Mildred and Rebekah the two female postgraduate students, there was Dr Balvan Thakkar, an international scholar from India undertaking a post-doctoral fellowship with the professor of Chemical Engineering. He was light on his feet and this as well as his sultry good looks had all the ladies staring.

As the music ended, the young people paired off in readiness for the next dance. Mary Long bagged Balvan, who was the best male dancer by a long shot, and together they whirled off around the dancefloor under the admiring glances of those currently sitting out. Dorothea found herself being led to the floor by Richard Dempsey. She was naturally quite nervous of making a fool of herself in front of so many people, but her partner was an expert dancer and after a few turns of the floor she relaxed in his hold and began to enjoy herself. The music was intoxicating, and Richard was an interesting conversationalist, and she was soon enjoying herself.

She danced the next dance again with Richard Dempsey, and then Chubby Thomas gallantly claimed it was his turn to trip the boards with Dorothea so off she went around the floor again, feeling like a Hollywood starlet. She had plenty of dance partners and during a break when all four young women were back at the table for a well-needed glass of lemonade she caught up with the gossip.

Mildred was in raptures as she thought she had seen Stan Laurel coming out of the men's room. Mary Long had managed to dance with the new professional male dancer and was full of excitement.

'His name is Istvan,' she informed them. 'He dances like an angel, smells divine, has oodles of sex appeal, the charm and wit of Satan himself, and is probably a gigolo preying on lonely middle-aged ladies.'

Rebekah interjected with a catty, 'Look now, Istvan is dancing with Mrs Adams. I saw her come in with her new fiancé from the English Department. Istvan should be wary. I heard from my uncle, the one who has friends at the ministry, that there was a hint of a scandal involving Mrs Adams and a handsome young pianist. It was all hushed up, but Mr Adams died soon after of a broken heart and Mrs Adams left the Foreign Office.'

'Or maybe she poisoned him,' Mildred chipped in, 'so she could be with her musical lover.'

'Well, that didn't work, did it?' Rebekah now piqued, argued. 'Because she ended up working here at the university without her musical lover and she has taken up with Dr Hadley-Brown instead.'

'Yes, but she is free to take up with whoever she wants to be with now. I wonder if her fiancé is good in bed. He looks pretty brooding and moody. He would make a good model for a Brontë hero don't you think?'

The two older girls tittered at their supposed cleverness and were then asked to dance by a skinny youth with pimples and his red-haired, red-faced friend. As etiquette dictated that if someone asked you to dance it was poor form to refuse him without a very good excuse, they were begrudgingly whisked off to the dancefloor without further ado.

Dorothea gripped Mary Long's arm in excitement. 'Did you hear that? Maybe that is why the blackmailer rang Mrs Adam's office. She had got wind of some scandal about Mrs Adam's fidelity towards her husband.'

'Or she is a murderer,' Mary Long butted in, equally thrilled. 'We need to tell Maggie and Jinny this. They are off to try and see her first thing tomorrow morning. Maggie is taking Jinny golfing, would you believe? Have you got a tuppence that I could have for the phone? I am all out of change. Thanks. I'll quickly go and ring Jinny at the vicarage. It isn't too late, and the vicar usually stays up late on a Saturday worrying about his sermons for Sunday, so he can take a message if it is too late. There are pay phones in the lobby.' She sped off, clutching the coins on her mission.

As Dorothea was watching Mary weave her way through the tightly packed tables towards the stairs, she felt breath on her cheek that smelt strongly of alcohol.

Startled, she spun round to find Gerry Stevenson leaning towards her, nonchalantly. He laid a familiar hand on her arm as the band was striking up for the next number.

'Dorothea, I do believe this is our dance,' Gerry purred.

Unsure of what to say or do, wishing that Mary had not gone just at that moment, and that she had a really good excuse to decline his offer of a dance, like a broken ankle, Dorothea dumbly nodded and together they moved to the dancefloor.

At first, nothing untoward happened. Gerry was a good dancer, if somewhat pushy with his lead and the band was playing a moody number. It was not until they had been dancing for a few minutes that Dorothea felt Gerry's hand start moving from the small of her back downwards. With a smile fixed on her face she deliberately moved his hand and firmly repositioned it. He smiled back and again his hand started to move down. Once again, she repositioned it with an admonishing, 'No!'

This time, he pulled Dorothea tightly against him and leant in close for a kiss. Pulling away from him as much as she could and wondering if anyone would notice in this whirling throng of revellers if she gave her partner a quick kick in the shin or the unmentionables, the decision was taken firmly out of her hands when she found herself spun out of her partner's grasp and into a textbook closed hold.

A familiar voice to her ear called out, 'Learn that no means no, sir!' and away they went together leaving a bewildered Gerry alone in the middle of the dancefloor.

'Thank you for intervening.'

Dorothea thought it would be churlish to mention that at home on the farm it was her job to move Earl Primrose Alstonfield Charlie Boy III, the family's prize bull, a particularly foul-tempered beast with a vicious kick, to the field, where his harem of cows awaited him during breeding season so was quite capable of looking after herself, but was distracted by the awareness of strong muscles under the dinner jacket that her hand lay on lightly as they waltzed around the floor.

'You are welcome.' Something suspiciously like laughter danced in Dr Hadley-Brown's eyes as he looked down into hers.

'You saved my life and in return I saved you from a cad. A very heroic act. It was the least I could do.'

The tempo changed effortlessly to be more upbeat, and the singer started to sing a jazzy number by Duke Ellington, and the couple came to a halt.

'Would you like to dance the next dance with me? I realise that you might prefer to return to your party.' A hint of unsureness had entered Geraint Hadley-Brown's voice.

'But surely you want to dance with your fiancée?' The question popped out of Dorothea's mouth from sheer curiosity before she could suppress it. Geraint glanced over to where Mrs Adams was still monopolising the professional dancer.

'I think she is happily entertained for the time being.'

'Well, yes then, if you don't think she would mind.'

They swept off again, and to break the silence that had fallen, Dorothea remarked lightly, 'So you have a Doctorate in Language, you play the organ proficiently, you dance expertly, and you are a member of the Secret Service. Is there anything you don't do well?'

Dr Hadley-Brown looked amused, 'I don't make a very good cocktail, I am afraid. I can't keep the mixture in the shakers.'

'That is a shame. I won't ask you to fix me a Hangman's Blood or a Corpse Reviver then.'

Geraint looked pained.

'I am sorry, what did I say?' Dorothea was concerned.

'It's nothing. Well not nothing. Someone tampered with the brakes on my car, and I had a nasty smash this morning.'

'Are you sure that it was deliberate and not an accident?' Dorothea asked, shocked.

'Absolutely sure, my dear girl.' Dr Hadley-Brown's tone changed to the slightly acerbic one Dorothea knew best from class. 'I am rather good at mechanics too, you see. I also got the car towed to a local garage and the mechanic there agreed with my diagnosis. Someone had filed away a rather integral part of the braking system. Since Manchester is so flat, I only found out going down Junction Street. I fortuitously hit a cart containing manure. I had a soft landing you could say.'

Dorothea tried not to laugh. She really did but a chuckle burst out loud at the mental image of the strait-laced Dr Hadley-Brown covered in manure. Geraint looked scandalised then his face softened, and he started to chuckle too.

Suddenly serious again he said, 'Be careful, Miss Roberts. Whoever these people are, they mean business. Someone has tried to kill me twice. I read your report about Iris Robinson. She is very lucky that yourself and Miss Shor came along when you did. It is only a matter of time before they come after you too. That piece by Miss Shor's boyfriend in *The Worm* won't have done you any favours. By now, everyone will know that it was you who found Iris Robinson. I am sorry that I suggested you infiltrate the committee. It is not too late to pull out if you want to.'

'No, I want to find out more. We are canvassing all this week outside the Women's Union. We have badges and have baked cakes and biscuits and Jinny has made small jars of jam and marmalade to give out in return for votes.'

'Very resourceful. The way to a student's vote is through their stomach.'

The band was working up to a big finish. Up until now they had remained in hold during the dance, which was all the better for conversation. Dr Hadley-Brown now led them into a couple of spins, and they finished breathless and with a flourish.

While walking off the floor he whispered in Dorothea's ear, 'Remember, if you are ever in danger, I will do everything in my power to help.' Then he bid her goodbye and re-joined his party.

On walking back to her own party, Dorothea overheard Mrs Adams ask in an arch voice, 'Geraint, darling! Who was that? You have been neglecting me shamefully this evening.'

'One of my students and yours too my dear, Gladys. She was being harassed by a complete bounder. I thought you would want me to step in.'

'The poor dear! You did well, Geraint.' She sounded sincere. 'Come, let's dance the next one. I want to practice my tango. Istvan says my Latin dancing shows great promise.'

Mary Long came hurrying up to Dorothea as she made her way back to their group's table.

'I saw what happened. I am so sorry. It's Richard's turn to take Gerry home. He has gone to flag down a cab. Mildred and Rebekah are going with them. Chubby has his bus with him and said he will give us and Balvan a lift when we are ready. Chubby and Balvan are sweethearts.' Then she added, almost timidly, 'You were dancing with Dr Hadley-Brown. You looked very well matched you know.'

Dorothea gave her a look that spoke volumes. 'Don't be silly Longy he is as old as the hills, he is a tutor, he is engaged, and he doesn't even like me.'

'Don't be so sure of that,' Mary muttered under her breath.

Belongings were duly gathered, and the young people piled into Chubby's car, which was an old Bentley, a cavernous relic of more elegant times which he had parked badly on Whitworth Street. They were a merry party that drove back to the halls of residence with much singing and laughter and tooting of the car horn. Chubby dropped them off on Yew Tree Road to make them less conspicuous sneaking into Halls at two o'clock in the morning.

Mary Long had done this many times before and tackled getting back into Halls like a professional cat burglar. She had, with forethought, hidden two pairs of rubber-soled shoes in a bush wrapped in oilskin, before going out for the evening for them to change back into in Platt Field Park. Dorothea was glad to change out of her dainty dancing slippers into something warmer with more grip.

Leading the way, Mary Long took them on a zig-zag path through the park's shrubbery which she obviously knew by heart, keeping in the shadows and listening out for other people. At one point they heard a group of male and female students some distance away, heading back to their respective halls but making an absolute hilarious racket weaving down the main path towards the lodge. There would likely be trouble for them in the morning if the porter was awoken from his slumber.

A twig cracked loudly to the left of them making them both jump, they stood stock still and waited. An owl hooted gently on the night air, and they relaxed, thinking that they must have disturbed the bird on its nightly hunting excursion.

The young women skirted the tennis courts and came around the building from the side nearest Dorothea's ground-floor room. She, with prior instructions from

Mary, had left the window wedged open with a small piece of cardboard. There was no need to climb up the drainpipe to Mary Long's room tonight. They stopped in the shadows of an overgrown rhododendron, just a hundred yards from Dorothea's window. Just as Dorothea was about to leave cover and dart across the lawn to the window of her room, Mary laid a warning hand on her arm.

Out of nowhere, the warden, Dr Winterbottom, tall and stately, appeared, gliding silently across the grass on rubber-soled feet. Another smaller shadow, clad in a dark coat and a veiled hat emerged from around the corner of the building, presumably exiting the ground-floor side door. They stopped under Dorothea's window and seemed to have a heated discussion carried out in whispers. The conversation ended abruptly with the warden handing over a small parcel and turning on her heel and storming away in the direction of her lodge. The other person stood looking after the warden as if undecided and finally pocketed the parcel and walked away, slowly.

The two young women pressed themselves against the trunk of the beech tree, willing themselves to become invisible, as the person passed by them less than twenty yards away. They could hear her footsteps crunching away on the gravel path. Fortunately, they were hidden in deep shadow, but Dorothea still felt incredibly vulnerable to discovery. Risking a glance, Dorothea was surprised to see that the person was Tabitha Gillespie. Mary Long was shocked too, as the grip on Dorothea's arm increased until it was almost unbearable.

They waited for five minutes to make sure the coast was clear, and then at a signal from Mary, they scampered over to Dorothea's window, pushed up the sash window and clambered in over the sill.

'What was Tabitha doing receiving packages from the

warden at two o'clock in the morning?' Mary Long asked, when the window and the curtains were closed. She was getting changed into her nightgown, slippers, and dressing gown, that she had strategically left in Dorothea's room so if she was discovered on her way back to her own, she could play the 'jippy tummy, I was just going to the bathroom' card. Dorothea was impressed with Mary's duplicity.

'Dr Winterbottom looked angry. Do you think our Tabitha is the blackmailer?' Mary yawned.

'I don't think so.' Dorothea sounded unconvinced. 'I'd have recognised Tabitha's voice in *The Worm's* office that time, even if she was disguising it. I wonder if she doodles when she is on the phone. The blackmailer does.'

'I have never seen her do so. I am dead beat,' Mary yawned again. 'I'll see you and the rest of the gang for Sunday lunch,' she said. And with an airy goodnight like she had no cares in the world, Mary left, leaving Dorothea to get ready for bed.

On searching for a clean nightdress in a drawer that she didn't use much, Dorothea realised that the small bit of cotton that she had wedged in place as a marker had gone. She checked the bedroom door. It had been newly oiled and there were a few new scratches on the lock. It took her a couple of minutes to ascertain that her hunch was correct. Even though nothing was missing, someone had searched her room while she had been out and had done it very professionally too.

Dorothea fell onto her bed and dreamed confusing dreams of Professor Aldridge dancing with the warden, while Matilda and Iris played a duet on a badly tuned piano. She was engaged to Dr Hadley-Brown, but she had lost the ring he had given her, while all the while a swing tune version of *Mad about the Boy* played and would not stop.

Sunday 28th October 1934, Morning

'Four!' A young gentleman in plus fours, a garish sleeveless argyle patterned jumper, and a natty tam o' shanter set at a rakish angle on his head drove his golf ball hard and flubbed it, sending it veering off the eighth tee into the rough.

He shrugged and called good naturedly to his companions, 'I am having the worse luck today. I had better go and find it as I'll soon be all out of balls. I'll catch you up.'

With the usual banter and teasing, the rest of the group moved off up the fairway and the young fellow made a show of looking for his ball.

Jinny and Maggie were up and out early this Sunday morning.

Jinny felt slightly guilty for missing playing the organ at the eight o'clock and eleven o'clock services but as she said, 'The vicar has given me special dispensation today to do some sleuthing.'

Maggie was a keen golfer and had been encouraged by her parents to play after polio had left her body weakened and muscles wasted, as part of her rehabilitation. With the help of callipers, she was able to stand and take shots at the ball and her aim was formidable. Her wheelchair, already modified, could be modified further with extra pockets and clips for holding golf balls, tees and clubs and she was a common site on this course as she was a member of the Manchester Golf Club.

Today she had roped in Simon Culthorpe to be their caddy and though he was heavily laden he did not look too unhappy about it. As a golf club member Maggie knew that Mrs Adams regularly played a round of golf early on a Sunday morning as most of the female members knew each other quite well to speak to. Jinny and Maggie, together, had decided to tackle Mrs Adams. Their conversation starter would be that Jinny was thinking of returning to the university for a course of postgraduate study and wanted to ask Mrs Adams advice about the place of married women in academia. From there they hoped to be able to drop casually into conversation about all the happenings on campus, to try and find out where Mrs Adams had been when Matilda was shot, when Ethel was killed, and when Iris had been gassed.

It took some time and surreptitious questioning of some other club members, but they finally ran Mrs Adams to earth on the driving range where she was taking practice shots and kept impatiently checking her watch. Each tee was separated by nets to prevent an off-shot or a flying divot from braining the golfer at the next tee.

As the little group approached, a young man in a ridiculous tam o' shanter crept up behind Mrs Adams and hugged her just as she was setting up a shot. Mrs Adams jumped, and the young man was fortunate enough not to get hit by her number one wood.

Maggie and Jinny quickly chose a tee two down the line from Mrs Adams and dragged Simon Culthorpe into it. While Jinny took practice shots, Maggie tried to watch and listen to what was going on two nets away. Simon wandered off down the range to where another group were practicing and cadged a light off one of the men.

Mrs Adams did not sound too pleased by the advent of the young man whose name it became apparent was Earnest. Maggie could hear most of what was happening.

'Ah!' Mrs Adams gave a short scream quickly stifled. 'Earnest! What are you doing here? No. Don't hold onto me. We might be seen.' Mrs Adams sounded quite put out.

Earnest, having his advances rebuffed quite forcefully

was inclined to sulk, 'But Darling, I thought you liked me just a little. Didn't Blackpool mean anything to you? I haven't been able eat or sleep for longing for you.' His voice sounded absurdly young and plaintive.

She took pity on him, 'Darling of course I like you and Blackpool was special to me too but here is not the place to meet up.' A coy tone entered her voice, and she drew in close to him. 'There are too many people around who might interrupt us,' she laughed musically.

He laughed too, somewhat mollified, 'But when can I see you again? I need you Gladys, and I can't wait.'

With speed and tact Mrs Adams agreed a plan to meet up for dinner the following evening at a restaurant that was unlikely to be frequented by either of their social circles. Mrs Adams kissed Earnest somewhat chastely on the cheek and sent him on his way to join his erstwhile golfing party with promises of eternal devotion and many more weekends like Blackpool.

Maggie rolled her eyes. Earnest really was a sucker.

Mrs Adams had gone back to her driving practice once she was sure Earnest had left, with renewed viciousness.

'What's going on?' Jinny whispered impatiently, ostentatiously practicing her swing.

'Earnest has just been sent packing very expertly, I bet she phones him tomorrow to call off their date with a pathetic excuse like a headache and now she is creating a job for the groundsman by taking chunks out of his beautiful turf. Hang on a mo! Someone else is coming.'

A very dapper chap tastefully dressed in beige plus fours and a burgundy sweater stopped at Mrs Adams' tee. He was dark and shiny with Brylcreemed hair, a dancer's light and easy tread, and Slavic cheekbones. He called a greeting somewhat hesitantly in English.

Mrs Adams spun around at the sound of his voice and greeted him with both arms outstretched and kisses on both cheeks. 'Istvan!'

A conversation then ensued, fast and quietly in a language that Maggie wouldn't have been able to understand even if she could hear it.

All the while the two players took it in turns to take practice shots so that the casual onlooker would think they were just friends out for the day to play golf. When the conversation was coming to a close Mrs Adams dug into her golf bag and pulled out a misshapen package which she pressed the gentleman to take. They then embraced again and went off together towards the first hole.

'Drat!' Maggie was frustrated that she was none the wiser about what she had just witnessed.

'Where did you go to Simon?' she said, somewhat sharply, as Simon Culthorpe re-joined them quietly. 'We might have needed you.'

With a knowing smile dancing teasingly on his lips, Simon replied, 'Earnest de Grayson, a freshman at the School of Medicine, son of Sir Francis de Grayson. I asked the group over there.'

Perceivably mollified Maggie was magnanimous. 'That was very well done,' she said, patting his arm. 'We'll make a sleuth of you yet.'

Simon continued somewhat self-effacingly, 'It just so happens that I can speak a little bit of Hungarian and I am rather good at lipreading.'

He had them spellbound now.

'You can what?' Maggie and Jinny chorused.

'Mrs Adams replied at one point to the overly greasy gentleman, "You have found it?" or possibly "him". My Hungarian is pretty rusty. "How long before we are reunited?" He said something I couldn't see because he was teeing off away from me. Then she said, "Too long. I have been waiting twenty years for this". He said something else I couldn't see, and she gave him the parcel saying, "Take this with you. It will be proof of my genuineness".'

Jinny looked impressed and Maggie looked shocked, then went back to looking impassive.

'You did quite well, Simon. Only quite well mind.' And as an aside to Jinny, 'He'll do!'

Simon smiled smugly to himself.

'I wonder what it means?' Jinny asked.

'Well, she did work for the Foreign Office, so she probably does know Hungarian and have contacts all around the world. She could have lost something in another country and the greasy gentleman could be returning it to her,' Maggie mused.

'Hang on a minute!' Jinny was excited. 'Could it be a code like the Jane Austen personal ads? Being reunited? Passing over a parcel? Maybe Mrs Adams is one of the Jane Austen heroines mentioned, or the person running the show?'

'It might be, but we don't have enough information to conclude that,' Maggie said thoughtfully.

To Simon, 'How rusty is your Hungarian?'

'Pretty rusty.'

'Hmmm . . . You are demoted back to golf caddy.'

Simon just grinned.

'What should we do now?' Jinny asked wistfully.

'We could follow Mrs Adams and play a game of golf, or we could go home . . .'

'Let's play golf!' Maggie was decisive. 'You never know what you'll find on a golf course. There might be a dead body on the seventh hole!'

CHAPTER TEN

Interviews and Elections

Thursday 1st November 1934, Lunchtime

DI Kydd sat on a bench outside the town hall eating his cheese and pickle sandwich. *Mrs Kydd made a really good cheese and pickle sandwich*, he mused contentedly, and counted his blessings that such a wonderful woman, who could have had her pick of men had chosen to share her life with a humble police constable with dreams of promotion.

He was waiting for a meeting with an old friend who was currently in his employ, or rather a subcontractor of the Manchester City Police.

A heavy-set, middle-aged man in a tan trench coat with a scar that marred his left cheek from jaw to eyebrow and left one eye sightless sat down heavily on the bench next to the inspector and proceeded to get out his own packet of carefully prepared sandwiches.

'Alright, Jim?'

'Good to see you, Fred. How are Mary and the boys?'

'None too bad Jim, thanks for asking. Mary's Mother had one of her turns the other week which caused a bit of a commotion but other than that they are in fine fettle. Tim got into Salford Grammar and Henry is doing well in his apprenticeship with his uncle. Your family, are they well?'

'Oh, yes, very. The girls are doing really well at school and Mrs Kydd is on fine form.'

Opening niceties over the two men, both naturally of a taciturn turn of character, chewed their sandwiches in an amiable silence. On finishing his tongue sandwich and folding the paper wrapping carefully before placing it in his capacious pocket, retired Police Sergeant, Fred Timms, became the model of efficiency. Placing his spectacles on his nose and opening his notebook, the boss of Timms Detective Agency began his weekly report.

'Last Tuesday two of my men escorted Iris Robinson to stay with her aunt in Bournemouth. They have orders to keep a watch on her for the time being. A cabin was booked in her name with Union Castle, portside from Southampton to Mombasa, and Miss Evans my secretary boarded last Thursday under Miss Robinson's name and disembarked at the first stop, Gibraltar, to give the impression that Miss Robinson had left the country to do missionary work abroad.'

'Make sure you charge that to Mr George of MI5,' the inspector said, with the Chief Superintendent's full blessing.

'Rossi and Howard, you remember Howard? They are on Miss Dorothea Roberts's detachment. They switch every twelve hours and I relieve them when needed. After Miss Roberts' and Miss Long's late night jolly to the Ritz last week, Miss Roberts has been the model student. Howard was a bit worried that they had seen him in the shrubbery when a twig snapped underfoot but then two other women came along and they distracted Miss Long and Miss Roberts. Howard thought those two women, the warden, and a Miss Tabitha Gillespie – a retired member of the committee – were having some sort of argument and the warden, Dr Winterbottom, passed Miss Gillespie a packet of some sort.'

'An interesting time of day for a meeting,' DI Kydd interjected. 'What time was it Jim?'

'Two o'clock in the morning, Fred.'

'Hmmm . . . Nothing legitimate then. It might be time to tackle the small issue of blackmail that Iris Robinson raised. That would be a good reason for an interview with the warden and to speak to this Miss Gillespie. I'll also make it known to the committee that I am aware of the poisoned pen letter situation, and anyone affected can come and see me in confidence. Carry on Fred.'

'As it has been reading week, all Miss Roberts has done since then has been to stay in Halls, go to the library and cafeteria and to campaign for election to the Women's Union Committee as a first-year representative, with some help from her friends.'

DI Kydd pricked up his ears, 'The committee you say? I wonder what our Miss Roberts is up to? Any news of Dr Hadley-Brown?'

'Yes, Samson and Charlie Boy are tailing him. There is something that you need to be aware of, Jim, regarding Dr Hadley-Brown and you aren't going to like it.'

'What is it, Fred?'

'Someone else is also tailing him, and not very well either. We have spotted him watching Dr Hadley-Brown's lodgings for several nights this week, an average height fellow in a navy mackintosh coat and a fedora. Stands on the corner of Hardcastle Avenue in the shadow of a closed tobacconist's doorway for a couple of hours and watches the window of his lodgings.'

'That description fits with the one Miss Roberts gave of Dr Hadley-Brown's knife wielding assailant,' the inspector noted, flicking through his notebook.

'Dr Hadley-Brown almost came a cropper too last Saturday when his car brakes failed going down Junction Street. My men spoke to a nearby garage owner who worked on Dr Hadley-Brown's Crossley Quicksilver, a lovely car in my opinion. The brakes had been tampered with.'

'Can you arrange to tail the tail and find out who they are and where they come from?'

'Absolutely, Jim, if that is what you want. Same time next week?'

'Same time next week, Fred. Give my love to Mary and the boys.'

The two men shook hands and went their separate ways.

Election Day, Friday, 2nd November 1934

'Vote for Dot! Dorothea Roberts is the First-Year Rep for you! Vote for Dottie, Vote for Change!'

Mary Long could certainly project her voice if she needed to. Dorothea, with the help of her friends had set up a table outside the Student Union buildings for the whole week before the election. The table had been borrowed from David Simpkins from *The Worm's* office, so it seemed that Mary Short had patched up her quarrel with him and everything in that quarter smelt of roses.

The campaign to get Dorothea elected to the committee seemed to be going well. Lots of first-year students had stopped to talk about the issues they were having with university life, and all left with a slice of cake or home-baked biscuit and promised to vote for Dorothea. Some older female students and some male students stopped by too and all left with a homemade treat even though their vote would not count.

'You never know when a chance acquaintance will come in handy,' Maggie said wisely.

With David's article in *The Worm* highlighting all the sinister goings-on, the atmosphere on campus was a mixture of poisonous fear, with groups of female students going places together in groups for safety, and nonchalant disregard from certain students of a distractible nature. Several first-year female students voiced their concerns to Dorothea about student safety between the city centre and Fallowfield Campus. She promised that if she was elected to the committee, she would do everything in her power to make the university safer.

It was the final day of canvassing before the votes were counted that evening by members of staff and Executive Committee Officers. The results were to be announced at eight o'clock. Dorothea could feel a large pit of anxiety in her stomach that gnawed away at her. She wanted to win but winning would mean that she would be putting herself even more in danger than she already was.

Tabitha Gillespie was conspicuous by her absence in all this. She had avoided Crossword Club for the last couple of weeks and had not picked up the phone, even to Maggie. Mary Short had seen her on campus but Tabitha had darted into the Law Department before Mary had got a chance to speak to her.

The ballot box was collected for counting at five o'clock sharp and no more votes could be cast. After a final busy day of canvassing, the friends had a slap-up tea at the university's cafe while they waited for the votes to be counted.

There were five candidates who had put themselves forward to be the first-year representative for the Faculties of the Arts and Commerce, though one candidate had been disqualified for being a statue of Queen Victoria who was dead, a prank by wags from the Men's Student Union. It caused much philosophising in the Joint Common Room on the nature of candidacy and who/what counted as living.

At eight o'clock sharp the candidates for all positions who were living and breathing, with their supporters, met in the Debating Hall on the first floor of the Women's Union building to hear the results of the count.

Mrs Adams stood up and cleared her throat.

'Ladies, the results of the ballot for two first-year committee members and a third-year committee member to replace poor Matilda Abbott has now been finalised. We will start with Matilda's replacement and then come to the first-year Science representative and finally the first-year Arts and Commerce representative.'

'I don't think I can bare the suspense,' Dorothea whispered to Maggie.

Maggie grinned and gave her a quick hug.

Lilian Roth a studious looking brunette was the new third-year representative and Eunice Green from Ashburne Hall was the new first-year Science representative. Finally, Mrs Adams came to the position that Dorothea coveted.

'The results in reverse order for the new first-year Arts and Commerce representative are as follows: In fourth place with fourteen votes is Margot Paisley, in third place with twenty-seven votes is Marion Chambers, in second place with fifty-three votes is Vivian McCloud but in first place with a decisive victory of eighty-two votes is Dorothea Roberts!'

Dorothea's friends and supporters burst into raucous cheers of approval and Dorothea wilted with relief. The plan had worked. She was now a member of the Women's Union Committee and could continue investigating the weird happenings on campus from the inside.

Tuesday 6th November 1934, Morning

The warden's residence was surprisingly luxuriously furnished, for a home belonging to a humble academic, and DI Kydd secretly admired Dr Winterbottom's taste and eye for design. He had previously only been to the warden's office which was situated within the main halls of residence building and was decorated a la université, over Matilda Abbott's disappearance and subsequent demise and the break-in, so he was rather surprised by the level of comfort on offer. He was expecting something more austerely aesthete.

Dr Winterbottom noticed the inspector admiring his surroundings. 'I have some business dealings that pay very well, Inspector. I couldn't afford this on just a university salary.'

DI Kydd was disconcerted at her astuteness which made him feel uncomfortable. On trying to analyse these feelings of discomfort he had concluded that there was such a level of reserve in her manner that it precluded any natural human warmth breaking through. He was also honest enough to admit to himself that her levels of education greatly outranked his own, which only served in making him feel at a disadvantage. He had already done his homework by looking her up in *Who's Who* and making some delicate enquiries in the right corners.

An only child, her father had been a very famous Oxford scholar and her mother a sparkling society hostess, both very much in demand, so a young Dr Winterbottom had grown up in and around the greatest minds in Europe and as a child had travelled the globe in the wake of her stellar parents.

Her mother had died young of a sudden illness picked up on a trip to see Egypt's wonders and thus the young Dr Winterbottom's world changed forever. Her beloved father stopped all travel and threw himself into his research and placed her in a prestigious girl's boarding school where she excelled but only came home during the holidays to a quiet and joyless house.

She won a place at Oxford to study Political Science where she was a model student and went on to further postgraduate study and was awarded a doctoral degree for her efforts. Her father sadly did not live to see her achievements and would not have believed in awarding degrees to women even if he had.

A lectureship at Oxford went to a less qualified male colleague while this position of lecturer in Political and Behavioural Sciences at the Victoria University of Manchester was being advertised.

On meeting Dr Winterbottom, the provost knew he could solve two of his staffing vacancies in one fell swoop and installed her as Warden of Grangebrook Hall without any further interviews. The provost congratulated himself on his forethought and acumen of acquiring such an up-and-coming scholar for his institution, even though his mother would have said that he was a 'work-shy pinch penny' as Dr Winterbottom was only being paid for one role. Dr Winterbottom did not seem to mind and soon made the role her own.

Sitting down at her desk, Dr Winterbottom looked over her spectacles directly at the inspector. Deep brown eyes analysed him and judged him as inadequate.

'Well, Inspector, what news have you got to tell me regarding these shocking happenings on campus. Iris Robinson was one of my girls in her first and second year and even though she moved over to Ancoats I still consider her as part of the Grangebrook Hall family. I assume it was an unrequited love affair that drove her to it?'

She must be the only person in the whole university that doesn't read The Worm, DI Kydd thought, thinking of the piece by David Simpkins.

'The evidence so far leads us to think that she did not try to take her own life, Dr Winterbottom.'

'An accident then? We don't have many gas fires in Grangebrook Hall, but I make sure the gas company checks the ones we do have every term, as regular as clockwork.'

'No, Dr Winterbottom, we think someone deliberately sabotaged her gas fire and drugged her.'

There was a shocked intake of breath from the warden, and again the inspector wondered about her reading material.

'Attempted murder, you think Inspector? But that is horrible, truly horrible. Who would want to do that? This is a prestigious seat of learning with a worldwide reputation. Surely there isn't a psychopath on the loose.'

'Well, that is something I wanted to ask you about. It has come to my attention that several of the committee members, Iris Robinson included, received some very nasty phone calls and poison pen letters. Have you been the recipient of any of these yourself?' he asked mildly.

She gasped in surprise but quickly regained her composure. 'Unfortunately, yes, Inspector. Here, you can see them.' She opened the beautifully carved mahogany bureaux and drew out a handful of creased letters which the inspector could see were typed on a typewriter. She passed them over and the inspector, who on handling them carefully, could see that their major theme was that the warden was, 'A bluestocking, a spinster and that no man could possibly find her attractive.'

The inspector shook his head in disgust, 'These are quite vicious, Dr Winterbottom. Do you know of anyone who would have a grudge against you?'

'I thought it was probably some past student that I had disciplined who was getting her own back,' The warden looked embarrassed. 'It is not good publicity for women's higher education, so I kept it quiet. But if other people have been receiving them too . . .'

'May I keep these? There may be fingerprints.'

'Of course.'

The inspector cleared his throat, 'I have an eyewitness that saw you at 2 a.m., on the morning of the 28th of October giving a package to a . . .' He consulted his notes. 'A Miss Tabitha Gillespie. Does that have anything to do with these letters?'

The warden side-stepped the obvious trap. 'Your eyewitness must have been mistaken, Inspector, I have not met with Miss Gillespie since before the summer when she came to see me about moving into lodgings in town for this academic year. I recommended one in Salford. She is most studious, and I am sure she would not have been out of bed at that ungodly hour. I certainly was not out of bed at two o'clock in the morning.'

'Please could you give me Miss Tabitha Gillespie's address, as I should like to ask her some questions?' the inspector asked. 'She seems to be a difficult person to track down.'

'Of course, Inspector.' She jotted down an address in Salford in a surprisingly indecipherable hand. 'Now, if that is all, I have a class at eleven o'clock which I really must prepare for. Can you see yourself out?'

Minutes of the Women's Student Union Full Committee Meeting, The Debating Hall, Thursday 8th November 1934, 7 p.m.

Apologies: Professor Quentin B. Smythe (Provost), Iris Robinson (Vice President), Miss Rosana Crankshaw (Alumna), Ellen MacGruther (Year 2&3 Rep Faculty of Commerce), Sarah Morris (Year 4&5 Rep Faculty of Medicine)

Present: Constance Harris (President), Mabel Parker (Treasurer), Evelyn King (Social Secretary), Victoria Butterworth (Acting Secretary), Alexandra Cotton (Athletics Secretary), Abigail Rushton (Secretary of the Debating Society), Mrs Gladys Adams (Advisor to Women Students), Dorothea Roberts (Year 1 Rep Faculty of Arts and Commerce), Eunice Green (Year 1 Rep Faculty of Science and Medicine), Rose Abram (Year 2 Rep Faculty of Arts), Flossie Payton (Year 2 Rep Faculty of Science), Blanch Cornish (Year 2&3 Rep Faculty of Medicine), Theresa Smith (Year 2&3 Rep Faculty of Administration and Law), Lilian Roth (Year 3 Rep Faculty of Arts), May Rowlands (Year 3 Rep Faculty of Science), Ada Marsh (National Union of Students Rep), Jane Booth (Settlement Rep), Mrs Maud Liptrot (Alumna), Detective Inspector Kydd (Invited Speaker)

Item 1: Minutes from the previous meeting (Thursday 11th October 1934) accepted as accurate.

Item 2: The President welcomed Dorothea Roberts and Eunice Green to the committee as the incoming Year 1 representatives and Lilian Roth was welcomed as the Year 3 representative replacement for Matilda Abbott.

Item 3: The President announced that Iris Robinson

the Vice President would be taking a break from her studies to work at a hospital in Uganda for the foreseeable future. She strongly reminded the committee that it was their duty to support herself as President as the vacancy at Vice President would create a lot more work for her. The President showed surprise at the lack of nominations to cover the Vice President position while it was vacant.

Item 4: The President welcomed DI Kydd to come and speak to the committee. He updated the committee on where the police investigations were up to regarding the deaths of Ethel Worksop, Matilda Abbott, the break-in at Grangebrook Hall, and the attack on Iris Robinson the Vice Chair. The inspector said that it had been drawn to his attention that there had been cases of poison pen letters being received by committee members. He wanted to reiterate that the police took a very dim view of blackmail and as an offence it could carry a ten-year penal sentence. If any committee member had any knowledge or information about these letters and wanted to speak to him in confidence, he would be based in the Green Meeting room of the Women's Union building every day the following week. The President thanked DI Kydd and urged the committee to help the inspector with his enquiries.

Item 5: The new first-year representative Dorothea Roberts updated the committee on the issues that the current first-year students are facing. She proposed that a sub-committee be set up to investigate what could be done to make campus safer for female students and asked DI Kydd if he would consider being advisor to this committee. This was unanimously agreed by the committee members, but the Chair wanted it minute-taken that all ideas must come through her first and spontaneity was to be discouraged.

Item 6: Evelyn King the Social Secretary, updated the committee on the Joint Social Committee plans for the Christmas ball which will be fancy dress and take place on Saturday 1st of December so as not to clash with departmental and societies end of term parties. The merits of different venues were discussed but unanimously the committee agreed that using the two Student Unions and opening the doors between them, would be the easiest and cheapest option. Evelyn asked for each committee member to volunteer for jobs relating to the Christmas ball and said there would be a sign-up sheet outside the committee Office after this meeting.

Item 7: Any Other Business: None.

Item 8: After much debate due to end of term parties, the date and time of the next full committee meeting were agreed for Thursday 13th December at 7 p.m.

Monday 12th November 1934, Morning

DI Kydd settled himself down in the Green Meeting Room of the Women's Union with his case notes to wait.

This might be a colossal waste of time, he thought, *or it might not. Let's see which fish, if any, take the bait.*

He was only a third of the way down the second page of his somewhat complex notes when a tentative knock on the door broke the silence.

'Come in!' he called out.

Dorothea entered, balancing a cup and saucer containing steaming tea in each hand with a jar of homemade jam under her arm. Smiling, she presented one cup and saucer to the inspector while retaining one herself, then gave him the jar of jam left over from the election campaign.

'I didn't think anyone would bring you a cup of tea and I know you'll be here a while and this room has such a small fireplace.'

'Congratulations are in order, I see. You got yourself elected to the committee,' the inspector gratefully wrapped his cold hands around the cup. 'Dr Hadley-Brown put you up to it, didn't he?' he said hazarding a pretty good guess.

'You know?' Dorothea was surprised.

'No, I didn't. But I do now. You'll have to do better than that not to give the game away in future if you are going to take on undercover investigative work.'

'You do really know a lot, Inspector,' Dorothea marvelled.

'No, I don't. I didn't know you were undercover until you just told me then, by assuming I knew it to be fact. You just told me the answer to my intuitive guess. The secret to interrogation is to let your suspect talk and make them think you know more than you do.'

'I'll try and remember that. Is that what being a

detective involves, hunches and intuition?'

'No, not really. It is 70% hard slog, 25% bureaucracy, 4% useful tip-offs and 1% inspiration. Now, Miss Roberts, why have you come to visit me?'

'I wanted to know how Iris was doing. Is she well and in a safe place?'

'Yes, she is in a very safe place and has two very loyal watchdogs,' he said, remembering his conversation with retired Sergeant, Fred Timms. 'You needn't fret about her.'

'Good. I am glad.' Dorothea still looked worried.

'Is there something you wanted to tell me? You know, I know all about Matthew Abbott. Sooner or later, I'll find out why he was posted here undercover and what was on that paper he gave you.'

'I don't think I am allowed to, Inspector. I promised, and it wouldn't be right.' Dorothea looked crestfallen.

'Well then, is there a crime you want to report?' he asked kindly. 'It is right and proper for you to report a crime to the police.'

'I think someone searched my room while Mary Long and I went out dancing with friends the other week. I don't think anything was taken, but you remember the break-in at the start of term in Grangebrook? That was the room I should have had but was swapped out of because I was late and the girl who should have had my current room had a fear of someone breaking in through the window. I think that whoever shot Matty still thinks I have the paper on me. The one that Matty gave me. I am alright now, talking to you, or with my friends in a crowd, but when I am on my own, I think someone is following me and I have to lock myself into my room at night and put my trunk in front of the door and screw closed the window to get any sleep. I haven't told my friends this or Dr Hadley-Brown because it is just a . . . a hunch.'

Choosing his words carefully the inspector said, 'Miss

Roberts, you are safer than you think. Please be vigilant but believe me when I say that your safety is upmost in my mind and if you are ever in trouble, please call me.'

'Thank you, Inspector. I know I can trust you.'

Dorothea got up with her now empty cup and with a brave attempt at normality said, 'I'll leave you to the victims of your poison pen writer.' Halfway out the door she turned back and threw him a cheeky grin and added, 'I'd expect most of the Executive Committee Officers and the warden of Grangebrook Hall and Advisor to Women students to turn up to your surgery if I was you, Inspector,' before beating a hasty retreat.

Dorothea Roberts had only been gone five minutes when another knock on the door sounded, this time confidently. The door opened to reveal a glamorous woman whom he remembered seeing at the committee meeting the other evening.

'DI Kydd? Yes, I can see you are. I am Gladys Adams the University's Advisor to Women Students. I believe we met at the committee meeting the other evening.'

'Pleased to meet you again, Mrs Adams. Do come and take a seat here by the fire. There is a perishing wind blowing today.' When she was settled, he asked, 'Now Mrs Adams I can see you have something on your mind. Do you mind sharing it with me? I assume it is about these pesky poison pen letters that people connected to the Women's Union Committee have been receiving.'

'Do you think that hiding a truly terrible thing for love is justifiable, Inspector?' Mrs Adams asked with a catch in her voice.

'Respectfully, no, ma'am, I think that is the pathway to a lot more lies and a great deal of heartache.'

Mrs Adams was pensive, 'Perhaps you are right, but it would have broken my husband's heart to find out. Instead, it is my heart that has been fragmented for the last twenty years.'

The inspector waited politely, pencil poised, for the woman in front of him to tell her tale.

'I loved my late husband very much. I was eighteen when we married, and he was much older, nearly forty. We were so happy together except we were unable to have children. It was a great sadness to me. I threw myself into helping my husband's diplomatic career instead, with some success. We travelled the world together which was fascinating, but I still wanted something more, a family.

'It was just before the Great War; we were posted in Serbia when tensions were high, and my husband had been working all hours and I was lonely and bored. I met a young and talented pianist. I won't say his name, he is rather well known now you see. Something sparked between us, and we couldn't help ourselves. We had an affair which lasted a short time and ended amicably.

'Then war broke out and my husband and I moved to Romania. I saw my husband so infrequently that when I found out I was pregnant I was certain the child wasn't his and he would have known so too. He was posted to the Front indefinitely and I remained in Bucharest. He was away such a long time.

'I gave birth to my child, a beautiful little boy, and with certain deceptions no one except my personal maid and my physician knew. The physician knew of a local family who had lost a child and would gladly adopt my boy.

'It is nineteen years. Two hundred and sixty-one days and twelve hours since I gave my precious child into the arms of that doctor, and I have regretted that decision ever since.

'Embassy families got pulled out soon after. In the turmoil of war, I lost sight of my boy's adoptive family, especially during the Austria-Hungary occupation and even after war ended, I have struggled to find them again. I thought for a while that they had all perished. Those were dark days. I was reunited with my husband in London soon after and he never knew of what happened.

'Four years ago, my husband became sick, and I nursed him through his final illness. His dying wish was that I shouldn't be alone. From that moment I redoubled my efforts to find my boy.

'It was a chance conversation with a professional dancer at the Ritz which led to the best lead I've ever had regarding the whereabouts of my boy. In the Christmas vacation I am hoping to visit a small village in Romania where my intelligence suggests the child might be. I have told my fiancé, and he supports me and has offered to escort me to Arad.'

I am surprised and certainly think better of young Geraint Hadley-Brown on hearing that, the inspector thought.

'I started to receive poisoned pen letters through the post and horrid phone calls at the start of term. Someone must have found out. They threatened to go to *The Worm* with my story.' She dug in her capacious handbag and drew out some letters in their envelopes and gave them to the inspector.

'Can I keep these please? What time of day were the phone calls made?'

'Of course, Inspector, please do if it will help to catch the perpetrator. I hope to goodness that it is not one of my girls. I only received calls at night after dinner, say eight o'clock, to my home, but then I go out early most mornings to practise my golf and I get to my office in the Women's Union mid-morning.'

'Were there any demands for money?'

'No, there were no demands made. You'll keep my secret, Inspector?' Mrs Adams stood up and made ready to leave.

'I don't see why anyone should need to know, madam,' he said escorting her to the door.

A strange blackmailer that doesn't ask for anything, the inspector thought afterwards. *Maybe these letters are pure mischief making?*

A third knock at the door drew the inspector out of his reverie and a student that he recognised with some trepidation as the President of the Women's Union came purposefully into the room. He shook hands with Constance Harris and inquired what he could do for her, knowing full well how effectively she could monopolise his time and make extra work for him with very little crime prevention success.

'Inspector, I have come to see if you have an update for the committee.'

The inspector clenched his teeth to prevent an abrasive reply, 'Police work is, unfortunately, not a sprint, Miss Harris. It takes time and a lot of leg work to get results. My enquiries are ongoing.'

'Oh!' For once Constance seemed to be at a loss.

'Is there something worrying you, Miss Harris?'

'Well, yes there is rather . . . It's those beastly poison pen letters and phone calls. I didn't want to tell anyone, but I have had a couple of letters and three phone calls. I just put the phone down now if I hear that voice. Here, you can see.' She pulled out a letter. 'I burned the first couple thinking it was utter rot but then thought you should see this.'

The letter was heavily creased and typewritten like the others. It accused Constance of having fixed the election which won her the Premiership of the Women's Union.

'Is there any truth in this accusation?' the inspector asked.

Constance looked offended then wilted.

'No, Inspector. I would not cheat but I was very surprised to win. I thought Iris Robinson would win for definite. I have been so nervous and half the time I don't know what I am doing but I pretend that I do know as I don't want to let the side down. But in one of the letters I burned, I was accused of being a puppet head. Sometimes I wonder if I am playing a part that someone else has written.'

'And this came in the post? It wasn't hand delivered? When did the phone calls come?'

'Yes, they have all been posted, second-class delivery. The phone calls were either early in the morning before lectures or after dinner.'

Similar to Mrs Adams', DI Kydd thought.

'Can I keep this letter please, to compare with the other letters?'

'Absolutely, Inspector. Anything you want.'

The inspector went away feeling sorry for Constance, a feeling he never expected to feel, and was even more determined to catch the blackmailer.

The report on the poison pen letters that came back later that week, showed that the letters to Constance, Mrs Adams, and Iris Robinson were written on the same typewriter from *The Worm's* office, but the ones to the warden were written on a different typewriter altogether.

What on earth does that mean, I wonder? the inspector thought.

CHAPTER ELEVEN

The Wonders of Wireless

Tuesday 13th November 1934, Late Evening

A note slid under Dorothea's door as she was concentrating on reading *The Seafarer* in Anglo-Saxon for her tutorial the following day. She did not see the note for at least a quarter of an hour and when she finally opened the mysterious missive it merely read:

Dot,

Come to my room at 2300 hours. Bring a blanket and a tooth glass and biscuits. Mary S and Maggie are coming too. Don't knock, come straight in, but be quiet!

Mary L

Mildly interested, Dorothea did not think any more of it until five to eleven when she finally finished her tutorial prep and re-found the note under a copy of Chaucer's *The Canterbury Tales*. She collected the blanket, glass, and dug out a box of shortbread that her sister had sent from home.

Going quietly along the corridor and upstairs, she

tried Mary's door gingerly and it opened silently on freshly oiled hinges, a novelty in Halls. On entering, the room was lit only by the light of the small fire burning in the hearth and the curtains were closed.

On the floor Maggie's discarded callipers formed an obstacle course. While on the bed both Marys and Maggie had their ears pressed to glasses which were then pressed against the wall that Mary Long's room shared with Evelyn King's room.

In unison all three mimed, 'Shh!'

Mary Short made room on the bed and beckoned Dorothea over to place her glass on the wall too. Dorothea did what she was told, while mentally questioning the sanity of her friends.

However, upon listening for a few moments she was rewarded with the silence being interrupted by a pattern of faint beeps of different length. They listened for a time with Maggie and the two Marys jotting down a series of dots and dashes on scraps of paper.

After ten minutes the beeps stopped suddenly. They waited, ears pressed up to the wall, then they heard the tap of the sink running with some tooth-brushing noises, followed by the springs of the bed going *boing*.

Mary Short beckoned the others to follow her. Together they quietly left the room, Mary Long giving Maggie a piggyback, Dorothea bringing the callipers. They crept down the corridor, through a couple of doors and along another corridor and onto Primrose wing, right to the very end where Mary Short's room was.

Once inside, the friends visibly relaxed.

'Connie, my next-door neighbour, is on placement this week at the hospital, working nights, so no one will overhear us here,' Mary Short explained.

'What just happened?' Dorothea was out of her depth. 'What were all those beeps coming from Evelyn's room?'

Maggie looked at Mary Long.

'You explain Longy. You discovered it.'

'It was an accident really. I woke up the other night with my ear against the wall hearing lots of unintelligible beeps. I didn't think any more about it until I couldn't sleep last night and remembered the beeps coming from Evelyn's room, so I listened for them and heard them again. Then I remembered the rather revealing reading list on Evelyn's bookshelf which included *Morse Code for Beginners* and *The Everyman's Guide to Wireless Mechanics*. I went to the library today and picked up a book on Morse Code and invited you three over to do some sleuthing.'

Mary Short butted in, eyes shining with excitement.

'The Oyster Club has gone quiet with their personal ads in *The Worm* but maybe they are communicating via wireless sets now. This might be the clue we need to pick up their tail again.'

Mary Long was excited too, 'Evelyn or Elisa Bennet will hopefully lead us straight to her Austeny friends. Look here, Shorty, Maggie, and I tried to write down the beeps we heard as dots and dashes. We all did it independently to give us a better chance of getting it right. Come on, let's decode what we have got so far.'

With much looking at the code book, cross-referring, rubbing out and starting again, a translation of the signal was finally reached. It read:

Nothing to report oh creatures awake this silvern night which silkily wraps the dreaming earth in slumber hush for my dear one is near practice complete.

This message was repeated three times.

'Hmmm . . . Another literary code,' Maggie mused. 'Someone really likes their literature.'

'I have forgotten its name, but it is by one of the less well-known Victorian poets,' Dorothea vaguely recognised it from her reading list.

"Practice complete' I wonder if Evelyn is just learning Morse Code. I knew I hadn't made a mistake with "eremite",' Mary Long said, referring to a hotly disputed decoding error.

Dorothea was deep in thought.

'Do either of you know anything about wireless sets?'

They all shook their heads in unison.

'It seems to me that if Evelyn had a really powerful set every amateur wireless enthusiast for miles around with a receiver would be picking up her practise Morse Code attempts, which wouldn't be great for a member of the secretive Oyster Club,' Dorothea paused for dramatic effect. 'Therefore, maybe she is only transmitting a short distance and the person receiving the code is close by. We need to get ourselves a receiver too. A portable one. Next time Evelyn is transmitting, we need to listen in to see if the other person is transmitting as well and locate where they are using their wireless set. I don't know anyone who knows about wirelesses here in Manchester though.'

Mary Short was jubilant, 'Actually we do all know someone. A trip to see Jinny is in order. We need a vicar! Well one vicar in particular.'

Wednesday 14th November 1934, Afternoon

In a shed at the bottom of the vicarage garden which had possibly at one time housed the pig of a predecessor of the current incumbent, the Reverend Clarence Moss was like a child at Christmas showing off his favourite toy. He had never before had such an interested bunch of acolytes to induct in the ways of radio waves and this novelty was very nice indeed.

'Crystal wireless sets are easy to build. I did a demonstration for the boy scouts last month. If, as you say, Evelyn is transmitting Morse Code from her room it could well be that she has made the wireless set herself in which case it would only have a very limited range. Here, you can borrow this wireless receiver to play with for the time being and work out what frequency Evelyn is transmitting on. It works like a normal wireless that you pick up music on but with a few of my own modifications.'

To Mary Long he asked, 'Your room is next to Evelyn's room?' Mary Long nodded. 'It might be quite loud, and you might get feedback so you will need to use it in a different part of the building.'

'We can use my room,' Maggie offered, itching to get her fingers on the set. 'I am at the end of a corridor like Shorty's and my room is a double, so my next-door neighbour won't hear, and I am on the ground floor so we can all get outside easily to chase the other wireless user without anyone seeing us and without the need for any aerial acrobatics,' she said, giving Mary Long a dig in the ribs.'

This suggestion was universally agreeable to everyone.

'For locating the other wireless user, I should be able to cobble you together a battery powered wireless receiver that you can carry. A directional aerial might be more of a challenge but leave it with me and I'll get Jinny to ring you when it's ready. You young ladies do have some super adventures!'

The vicar sounded wistful.

'Unfortunately, I can't join you. I don't know what the bishop would do if one of his clergy was found wandering around near a female halls of residence at night with a wireless receiver. But I will help in any other way I can.'

Jinny linked her arm through the vicar's arm.

'And I will too. Always feel free to ask.'

Dorothea was very grateful to the Mosses.

***

On the bottom of an assignment set by Dr Hadley-Brown and completed later that same day Dorothea wrote her weekly update:

Evelyn King (alias Eliza) a member of the Oyster Club has been overheard using a wireless transmitter and communicating with someone, probably close by, in Morse Code. On decoding the message, it seems she was practising her Morse Code. Crossword Club members are going to monitor her communications with a wireless set from the Reverend Moss. He is going to make us a direction-locating receiver so we can discover the source of the wireless transmission. It will be ready in a few days' time.

Friday 16th November 1934, Morning

The reply she got later in the week when her assignment had been marked read as follows:

Excellent sleuthing ladies (A+) but leave this now in the hands of the professionals. I will take this forward.

'Well, he is a patronising, egocentric, annoying glory-hogging toad!'

Dorothea ground her teeth in annoyance. There was no way she was going to tamely stop with their plan now. Jinny had sent a message that the Reverend Moss had got a working prototype direction-finding receiver and tonight they were going to try it out. All week they had been monitoring Evelyn's nightly messages and the messages of the person with whom Evelyn was communicating with. At precisely midnight each night Evelyn would send out an initial string of Morse Code:

'Eliza calling, Eliza calling, Eliza calling over.'

Then an answering message would come through:

'Oyster Club Secretary receiving you, what is your report, over?'

Then Evelyn would send her report which for the last few nights had been:

'Nothing to report,' followed by a literary passage, usually a 19th century poet (they had had excerpts from Byron, Keats, and Wordsworth), followed by 'Practice complete.'

Then a final message would come from the unknown wireless user:

'Message understood, over and out.'

Friday 16th November 1934, Almost Midnight

'Please hurry! Even my woolly underwear is icing up! I have been up here for twenty minutes,' hissed Mary Long who had dressed appropriately for the adventure and had volunteered to shin up a convenient beech tree with the aerial.

In a thicket at the base of the tree, three heads were close together, craning to hear anything over the vicar's quickly manufactured, prototype, direction-finding, wireless receiver.

'I can't feel my fingers anymore,' Mary moaned ineffectually, trying to rub her hands together while holding the aerial. 'I think I might have frost bite.'

'Shh, Longy! We can't hear over your whinging,' Maggie whispered up to Mary. 'Evelyn is very late tonight with her transmission. Maybe she isn't going to transmit?'

'Hang on. Point the aerial back towards Grangebrook Hall. Yes, wait a bit, there she is. We have got her! Now slowly rotate the aerial, Longy, to see if we can pick up her contact.' Mary Short was calm under pressure.

'Nothing yet. Go around again.'

'I feel like a merry-go-round.'

'Shh! Just do it! Nothing. Wait a sec. Stop. Now go back. There! We have got them.' Mary Short was jubilant.

Dorothea jumped up and down in excitement and Maggie gave a stifled squeak of celebration.

'Where is the aerial pointing?' Mary Short asked.

'Almost exactly northeast, away from Grangebrook Hall. Hang on, I'll come down and see if we can follow the signal. Ah!' cried Mary Long losing her balance and slipping down the icy trunk and landing on Dorothea, knocking her off her feet. The aerial flopped down after her. A branch broke loudly a little further off in a patch of rhododendrons and an owl hooted eerily.

'Shh! Stop fooling around. I thought I heard something over there. Just an owl. We have heard an awful lot of owls around here tonight . . . a parliament of owls maybe. Come on, repoint the aerial in the right direction and let's go quietly.' Maggie took charge.

Maggie's chair, oiled to perfection, moved silently in the darkness. They skirted some ornamental flowerbeds, each carrying a bit of the wireless set-up linked together with wires, thankful that the moon had kindly hidden itself behind a cloud momentarily and terrified in case it would reappear before they reached the next clump of bushes. A dark square shape loomed out of the darkness.

'We are coming to the warden's residence. They must be transmitting from beyond it, outside the campus parameter. Hurry up, Evelyn will be signing off soon. We need to be in position to intercept the mysterious Oyster Club's Secretary's sign off.'

As quietly and as quickly as they could, they skirted the warden's residence and exited campus at the gate on to Wilmslow Road to take up position in the lee of an old chapel.

'Point the aerial back towards Grangebrook Hall. Dot, dot, dot, dot, dash . . . That is Evelyn. She is just signing off. Now point it that way.'

Mary Short had discovered a hidden talent of working the wireless receiver. They waited with bated breath.

'Quickly, Longy, sweep the aerial around. We are going to miss it.'

Mary Long slowly turned the aerial three hundred and sixty degrees, and just when they had given up hope they caught the last few dots and dashes when it was pointed back towards Grangebrook Hall.

'So they *are* transmitting within the grounds. We must have just missed them on the way past. Quickly, let's divide. Shortie and Maggie you dash back to Grangebrook Hall and see if you can spot anyone entering nefariously.

Longie and I will stay here and see if anyone exits this way. Leave the kit here. Meet you back in Maggie's room in fifteen minutes.' Dorothea's voice was urgent.

With a nod, Maggie, and Mary Short left silently.

Now the initial pressure was off, keeping one eye on the gate, Dorothea and Mary Long tidied up the cables and wrapped the wireless set and aerial in oilskins and stashed them in one of Mary Long's dancing hidey holes inside the roots of a tree near the gate, just inside the grounds of the halls of residence. Nobody had left through the gates.

They passed back through the shadows as silently as wraiths. As they passed the warden's residence, dark and brooding on their left, Dorothea noticed a chink of light coming through a heavily curtained window on the ground floor. She signalled to Mary who was a few feet behind and they ducked into the shelter of a convenient camellia bush.

'Look, there is a light over there in the warden's house. I don't remember seeing it on the way here.'

'Maybe she is having another late-night meeting with someone. Tabitha or someone else. We should go and see.'

'We'll get caught!'

'No, we won't! Come on, Dot!'

Daringly, Mary Long dashed across the open piece of lawn and up three steps onto the terrace that the window looked out onto. Dorothea followed, keeping a look out. Mary Long had her nose pressed up to the glass.

'I can see the corner of a piano, a drinks cabinet, and a really fancy gramophone. Looks like the fire has burnt low in the grate. I think the door is unlocked.'

'Come away, I thought I heard something, we should get back.'

At that moment the two young women were illuminated by a bright torch beam and left blinking and disoriented in its light.

'Right, you two, I have caught you breaking curfew. Miss Long you are slipping, and Miss Roberts I am surprised at you.'

The warden's voice was cool, with a large slice of sarcasm.

'Right, inside with you.'

With drooping shoulders Dorothea and Mary were marched inside and asked to take a seat on the low sofa by the fire. They sat unsure and anxious side by side. The warden stood in front of them dressed in a dark coat over a dark dress, and in a voice dripping with disappointment asked them why they thought they were above university regulations.

'The rules are there for everyone's safety and protection. What do you two think you were doing outside at this time of night?' Dr Winterbottom asked.

Mary Long thought on her feet. 'Dr Winterbottom, we are so sorry to wake you up. We saw a light and thought you might have burglars. We went to visit Jinny and the Reverend Moss at St Bartholomew's vicarage earlier this evening to help Jinny with making costumes for Arabella's nativity play. We lost track of time and the vicar said he would run us back in their Ford, but it wouldn't start. He was going to walk us back, but he got an urgent phone call on behalf of a dying parishioner and had to cycle to their deathbed instead. We managed to get a message through to Maggie, Dorothea's floor rep.'

Dorothea tried to look like she had spent the evening in sacrificial nativity costume sowing, while mentally marvelling at Mary's ability to fib.

'A very noble story, Miss Long, and I value your concern for my property. I will be checking the validity of your tale tomorrow with those people. As you know, university rules say breaking curfew is punishable by suspension from the common room for a time and for

199

repeat offences, which I am sure this is, I am particularly looking at you Miss Long, being thrown off your course. I will be talking to your tutors about your behaviour tomorrow and you can expect disciplinary action to be taken. Now leave please and go straight back to your rooms.'

'Sorry, Dr Winterbottom. We will do,' they chirruped in unison.

She held the door open to the terrace and they filed out. The door was locked firmly behind them.

'Are we really going to be sent down?' Dorothea was horrified by the thought.

'No, of course not. Dr Winterbottom, in her three years here, hasn't ever expelled anyone for breaking curfew. She has done so for other things, but not that. I think she is secretly appalled that the female students have a curfew, but the male students don't.'

'Don't we need to tell Jinny and Maggie to expect a phone call from the warden?' Dorothea was feeling very rattled.

'Again, no. That was my pre-agreed story with them in case I ever got caught coming home from dancing. Now, what I need to come up with is a new believable cover story. Did you notice what the warden was wearing?'

'No. I was distracted by getting caught.' Dorothea was acerbic.

'Oh, Dot. We are investigating. Use your eyes. She was wearing dark clothes like us, and they were day clothes not a coat hastily thrown over a nightgown. She was up and about herself. Ask yourself the question: what was she doing?'

'Maybe she had been out to a meeting or saw us from a window.'

'Or maybe she had been up to something reprehensible.'

They continued to bicker quietly all the way back to

Grangebrook Hall and climbed in through Maggie's window.

Maggie and Mary Short were waiting for them on tenterhooks and bombarded them with questions.

'What happened? Why were you so long?'

'Where did you stash the wireless gear?'

'Will the warden really kick you out?'

On their way back Maggie and Mary had not seen anyone re-entering the building, but they thought someone had sneezed a couple of times in the shrubbery.

'. . . And we got back here pretty sharpish. There were some odd noises like sneezes and some movement in the copse, but then we heard what we think was a screeching owl so thought it all must have been caused by a night creature on the hunt,' Mary Short tried to rationalise the strange noises they'd heard.

'So, to summarise what we know,' Maggie said, 'the wireless transmission was from within the grounds, the kit worked but we are not sure where along a potential trajectory the transmission came from, and two of us are now on disciplinaries for our night's work.'

They all went to bed dejectedly that night.

Over the next few days, however, there were no repercussions forthcoming, and no one queried Mary Long's fictitious tale with Maggie and Jinny. There were also no further transmissions from Evelyn King to the mysterious receiver. On submitting her report, attached to her next assignment a few days later, she got a terse reply.

Sit still, keep quiet and touch nothing.

Tuesday 20th November 1934, Lunchtime

Two academics were eating their respective lunches in the university restaurant. To all intents and purposes, it was a normal luncheon shared by two colleagues. They could have been talking about the weather or the state of politics on the continent, or who was running in the three thirty at Newbury. In fact, there was a very serious conversation occurring about the state of the nation's security from internal attack by foreign agents.

Professor Aldridge looked with distaste at his unappetising cabbage and wondered why canteen staff never seemed to be able to cook it properly. The young man opposite was in a state of repressed annoyance with the whole world in general and especially undergraduates, spy masters and MI5 budget cuts. Geraint wore a sticking plaster on the lobe of his right ear.

'It was a damnable farce, Uncle Harold, from start to finish. If it wasn't life or death, it would have been laughable. The equipment which Mr George assured me was ready for in-the-field operation was temperamental and threw a wobbler every time a drop of dew touched it. The eggheads he sent with it had the sniffles, nicotine cravings, lumbago, flat feet, and flatulence and were as quiet on manoeuvres as a geriatrics' tea dance. Why the departmental budget couldn't stretch to some technicians who were ex-military and properly trained in surveillance I don't know. Except I do know. Budget cuts. They were only marginally quieter than Miss Roberts' bumptious friends who crashed about in the undergrowth with their own wireless receiver causing our device to pick up on their radio interference. Then we got shot at. A silenced service revolver probably the same as was used to shoot Matty Abbott. We'll know for sure when they have dug the bullet out of Tobacco Addict

Egghead's thigh, who could not wait until we finished the operation to light up a cigarette. Our assailant must have been waiting in ambush. We heard an owl hoot then three shots were fired: one at Tobacco Addict Egghead, one at the wireless receiver which is now a very expensive pile of spare parts, and one at Flatulent Egghead who has a healthy sense of self preservation and threw himself to the ground so that the third bullet ricocheted off a tree sending splinters flying, one of which nicked my ear.' Dr Hadley-Brown fingered the still sore lobe gingerly.

'They must have been a pretty good shot to not kill any of you in the dark and put a valuable piece of MI5 kit out of action,' the professor remarked.

'Yes, very. They were more intelligent, better trained and more skilled than my men. I think we were being warned off.'

'"Don't mess with us, we outthink and outgun you". Yes, it does seem like that,' the professor said thoughtfully.

'I got my wounded and shaken eggheads back to the van and went back for the kit as proprietary technology. Dorothea and her partner in crime, Miss Long, were being forcibly expelled from the warden's residence as I returned through the grounds so we can be pretty sure that they were caught snooping by Dr Winterbottom. We will probably have to pull some strings with that one. Miss Robert's report on the bottom of her Bede essay (a strong B plus by the way) says that with their wireless set up they found out that the transmission was coming from within the grounds of Halls. They got as far as Wilmslow Road and the transmission was behind them. Look, I'll draw you a map. We were here, Grangebrook Hall is there, and the warden's residence is there. If I wasn't so annoyed with her for disobeying orders, I would be giving her a medal or an A minus. Significant don't you think?'

'Hmmm, very. It puts a whole new slant on things and opens up some very interesting leads.' The professor poked his crème brûlée thoughtfully.

Geraint Hadley-Brown was worried. 'I think we should call off Miss Roberts and her friends. I think they are making themselves too much of a target. I am afraid that the next body DI Kydd's men find will be Dorothea's.'

Professor Aldridge noted the use of her first name and raised a metaphorical eyebrow but continued unabashed. 'I would only call off Miss Roberts for your blood pressure, Geraint. As yet I don't think they are in any grave danger, and she is supplying us with useful information. DI Kydd has her tailed so will probably have an interesting report on his desk by now. Presumably you have a tail too? You do. Capital! DI Kydd has surpassed himself. Let Miss Roberts and her friends continue for the moment, and you and I and DI Kydd will do our upmost to look after her.'

'That's just it, sir. You and I and the inspector are all professionals. Matthew Abbott was too, for that matter. These are just young women, some barely out of the schoolroom, with no operative training and only luck and quick wits to protect them, neither of which are especially bulletproof. I don't want to have to go to one of their funerals.' Geraint shivered thinking of Matthew Abbott's lifeless face.

Professor Aldridge could see that his godson was torn. 'If that's how you feel, Geraint, then of course do what you think is best for them.' He tactically avoided saying *her*. 'Whether you can persuade the tenacious Miss Roberts to desist investigating is another matter entirely.'

'I hope I can, Uncle,' Dr Hadley-Brown prayed fervently.

As they were talking, they were surprised to see their

senior colleague, Mr George of the Secret Service, with Mrs Adams on his arm walking through the restaurant towards them. Mr George seemed to be rather struck by the handsome woman he was escorting and kept clearing his throat, and his normally somewhat pallid complexion was tinged with a hint of rose.

Professor Aldridge greeted his old friend warmly while Geraint Hadley-Brown's welcome was more reserved as befitted a meeting with his boss who was dallying with his fiancée on the back of an unsuccessful surveillance operation.

Mr George made the introductions.

'I think you both know Mrs Adams.' He glared at Geraint as he said it.

'Isn't it a coincidence?' Mrs Adams was sparkling. 'I met Mr George out on the street, and I haven't seen him since 1923, the Corfu Incident. My husband had a lot of clearing up to do after that and you were pretty busy too weren't you, Mr George? Do you remember how blue the Ionian Sea and sky are? I brought him to meet you both, but it seems he brought me to meet you! Isn't it fun that we all know each other?'

Professor Aldridge and Mr George chuckled along with Mrs Adams and Geraint smiled politely.

'Do you mind if we join you? It will be awfully jolly,' Mrs Adams asked.

'Please do, my dear, and you too George. We have a lot of catching up to do,' the professor said, as always the perfect gentleman.

Geraint looked uncomfortable. He needed to discuss state secrets with Mr George, not least the disastrous outing of Mr George's pet piece of technology. Mrs Adams, while being highly regarded in Whitehall, had had her clearance lapse since retiring from the Foreign Office and Geraint was too polite to say anything as it was his godfather who had invited the two of them to join them. He wondered what game his godfather was playing.

A very strange conversation thus ensued to avoid the lady learning how the three men were really connected in their daily lives.

'We should add Mr George to the guest list for our wedding, Geraint. You will come won't you, Mr George?' Mrs Adams asked charmingly.

'Wedding? You never told me you were engaged to this beautiful woman, Geraint.' Mr George looked thunderstruck.

'I did write to you, sir.' Geraint looked meaningfully at Mr George. *I have mentioned it in at least three weekly reports*, was what he wanted to say.

'Well, congratulations my dear,' Mr George said to Mrs Adams. 'I am sure Geraint is honoured. He is a steady young man,' he added patronisingly.

Damned by faint praise, Geraint thought. *What is the matter with the boss? He is behaving like a jealous schoolboy.*

'How do you know my lovely fiancé, Mr George?' Mrs Adams asked.

Professor Aldridge jumped in with, 'Through me my dear. George and I went to Winchester together. Both of us were choir boys.'

'My godfather put me in touch with Mr George. I am doing a research project on linguistics for his department,' Geraint stated, using his pre-set cover story. 'There is something about the project that I would like to discuss with you, Mr George, if you have a moment?'

'Sorry, my boy I promised Mrs Adams that I would discuss contacts in Romania with her.' Then turning to Mrs Adams, Mr George said, 'I don't fancy anything on this menu, my dear. I know a nice little place that cooks a wonderful lemon sole on Byrom Street. Would you care to join me?'

Apparently, university food didn't tickle Mrs Adams fancy today either, so off the pair went together as thick as thieves.

'You have been well and truly cut out there, my boy,' the professor said with a hint of smugness in his voice.

Sunday 25th November 1934, Evening

Dorothea was sitting in Maggie's room in a wing-backed chair staring moodily into the dancing fire. On the side table next to her was an open envelope with an invitation to join the Oyster Club which someone had placed into her pigeonhole that afternoon. Next to it were the names of staff and committee members written on small pieces of paper along with a telephone directory. Every so often Dorothea would sit up, stare at the names and reorganise them before moodily returning to watch the flames in the hearth.

Maggie scooted over, balancing a cup and saucer, an envelope, and tweezers on her knee.

'Here, drink this. There are three sugars in it to give you some inspiration.' Maggie carefully picked up the invitation and its envelope with the tweezers and placed them inside the larger envelope. 'Let's keep this safe for now. You never know, it might have fingerprints on it. Why has receiving it upset you so much? You should be excited that we are on the right track.'

Dorothea sighed, 'I know, it's just that part of me thinks it is a trap and the other part of me doesn't want to belong to any club that Evelyn King belongs to. I also don't like that no first challenge is given, and it says await orders.'

'What are you doing with these,' Maggie asked, pointing to the small pieces of paper with names written on them that were also on the table.

'I was seeing if anyone stood out as having the organisational genius to run the Oyster Club or have the psychological kink in them to commit murder. I have included anyone who has a connection to the case.'

'I can see that.' Maggie held up the name *David Simpkins.* 'Don't let Mary Short catch you framing her boyfriend for murder.'

'His journalism career has certainly taken off this term. Mary says he has been asked to write a piece for a national newspaper.'

'Why include Mrs Gladys Adams?' Maggie asked.

'The personal ads started after she came to the university. I checked, and she definitely has the brains and connections to run the Oyster Club.'

'And you think Constance Harris has the brains?'

'She is President of the Women's Union after all, the most powerful female student at the university. Power corrupts,' Dorothea said seriously.

'Dr Hadley-Brown? I thought you liked him?' Maggie teased.

'I don't like him and what do we really know about him? He was on the spot when Matty was shot, and we know that he has annoyed someone so much that they want him dead.'

'I don't think being annoying makes you a murderer. You have included Dr Winterbottom, the warden?'

'She is brilliant and up to something with her night-time meet ups and excursions.'

'The provost too?'

'Not really. He is basically harmless except for his dress sense. I added him for completeness.'

'Abigail Rushton. Don't tell me, she is clever and has a chip on her shoulder and would enjoy the power that the Oyster Club Secretary wields.' Scanning the other names Maggie commented. 'You have basically not ruled out anyone surrounding the committee, have you?'

'No. I think Iris Robinson is in the clear though. The doctor treating her said if she had had any more barbiturates in her system or breathed in any more coal gas, she would have been dead,' Dorothea said.

'Tabitha lied about the butcher's shop telephone number; you know? It was the telephone number of her lodgings in Salford. Why did she lie and what is she being blackmailed about?'

'What is this "X" doing on this piece of paper?' Maggie asked.

'That represents someone totally unknown to us that we have never met and that has no known connection with the university.'

'Someone that we won't ever be able to deduce and that would never be found out perhaps. It would be depressing if the murderer got away. Everyone would always be under suspicion.'

'I know. It makes me feel the weight of responsibility.' Dorothea looked worried.

'We are all in this together. It's not just on your shoulders. Is there something that is worrying you?'

'There is and I wish I could tell you, Maggie, but I promised I wouldn't.'

'Well then, tell me when you are able to and be assured that we will all help in whatever way we can,' Maggie said emphatically.

CHAPTER TWELVE

Murder at the Christmas Ball

Saturday 1st December 1934, Early Evening

Oddly enough the end-of-term Christmas ball usually ended up taking place near the beginning of December as the real end-of-term was filled with essays and tests, performances and shows, and the Christmas parties for the individual societies.

The students of the organising subcommittee for the Christmas fancy dress ball had worked tirelessly for the past three days, in shifts, to get both student unions looking suitably festive. They had scoured the local parks, university grounds and even taken excursions to the Lancashire countryside hedgerows to find fir, holly, ivy, and mistletoe with which to decorate the warren of rooms but especially the first floors of the two unions, which is where the main dances were to be held in the debating halls.

Some of the male students made an excursion to nearby Castleton to chop down an eight-foot fir tree and then tied it to the roof of one wag's car to bring it the fifty or so miles back. It looked strangely dwarfed in the Men's Student Union with its dented hand-me-down ornaments and drooping branches.

Dorothea, as a year rep, had been roped in to help make yards and yards of paper chains which she did with good grace even though it got in the way of essay writing. When it was finished the student unions did look spectacular. They were full of Christmas cheer and the promise of a smooch under the mistletoe.

The only topic of conversation on anyone's lips for weeks in advance was what costume was one going to wear to the fancy dress Christmas ball? For most people a lot of thought had gone into their costumes and Grangebrook Hall became alive with the whirr of sowing machines shared around and students popping in and out of each other's rooms borrowing a ribbon here and some taffeta there.

For those of a somewhat slapdash bent or who were time-pressured due to essays or exams the white sheets from the beds of Halls made a suitable stand-in costume. In a white bedsheet and a bit of imagination you could be Cleopatra or the Archangel Gabriel, an Egyptian Mummy, or the Oracle of Delphi or one of the Fates. Dorothea had asked her sister Anna to post from home the costume of Lady Macbeth that she had worn for her sixth form production of *Macbeth*. With a dark plaited wig, a deep green wide sleeved dress belted low on the hips, a plaid shawl, and a rugged iron crown that the local blacksmith had knocked together out of bits and pieces he had lying around the forge, she looked like she had walked straight off a Scottish heath to Dunsinane hill.

She wondered what Dr Hadley-Brown would think of her costume then chastened herself for her flight of fancy. He wouldn't be at the ball, and he was engaged to Mrs Adams who was a mature, elegant lady who oozed allure. He wouldn't have a thought left over for Dorothea Roberts.

'You do all look wonderful,' Jinny sighed.

She had volunteered the vicarage as a place where her

friends could all get ready for the ball together with lots of space and more importantly full-length mirrors, something that halls of residence were somewhat lacking in. As an alumna she wasn't entitled to attend but she wasn't too downhearted. In her own words, 'I get to see all of you dressed up looking a million pounds and I get to spend a cosy evening at home with the vicar and Arabella. I get the best of both worlds.'

The students had taken over the parlour and it was currently strewn with items of feminine apparel and an odd assortment of props and costume items.

The vicar appeared at this point somewhat bashfully with the drinks tray baring cocktails that he had mixed himself, and then he beat a hasty retreat.

'It is very kind of Reverend Moss to offer to take us in the Ford to the ball. Though we can get a taxi if it is too much bother?'

Dorothea was worried that they were putting the Mosses to a lot of trouble.

'Don't you worry at all, Dot,' Jinny said, giving Dorothea a quick hug. 'He loves being helpful. He even dug out an old chauffeur's hat earlier from his am-dram days which he is dying to wear.'

Maggie, doing her make-up in a table mirror, looked very regal as Boudicca, and proved that white bedsheets could look fabulous with some modification and accessories. Her wheelchair had been transformed into a chariot with galloping cardboard horses pulling it at the front.

'We need to remember to keep our eyes peeled for any strange happenings tonight. All the committee members will be present, and they will be under a lot of pressure, particularly the Executive Officers which could lead to imprudent outbursts. We all need to be ready to eavesdrop at any given moment,' Maggie said, the light of battle in her eyes making her look even more queenly.

Mary Long, in comparison, looked a little underdressed in a plain black dress and white laboratory coat. A name badge strategically pinned to her lapel proclaimed her to be the acclaimed Polish French Physicist, Marie Skłodowska Curie; a heroine of Mary's who had died earlier this year. If the name badge wasn't enough of a giveaway, the two cardboard Nobel Prize medals around her neck was a large clue.

'Yes, someone is more likely to slip up if they are stressed,' she agreed.

Mary Short, painting small heart patches on her cheek and by her eye, was wearing a crown and a rectangular tabard with the Queen of Hearts painted on it. David Simpkins, they had heard from Mary Short, had a matching outfit and was the Knave of Hearts. The unspoken presumption of everyone present was that things must be going very well indeed where those two were concerned. David was going to meet them at the ball, along with Simon Culthorpe.

'Are you and Simon having matching costumes too?' Jinny asked Maggie cheekily.

'In a manner of speaking.' Maggie grinned. 'He is going as a Roman soldier.'

With lots of merriment and lubricated with the vicar's excellent cocktails they eventually piled into the Mosses' ancient Ford, Model T.

'I do hope nothing untoward happens tonight and they can just enjoy themselves. Dear Lord please keep them safe,' Jinny whispered under her breath as she waved them goodbye.

Saturday 1st December 1934, Late Evening

On the first floor of the Men's Union the Debating Hall had been cleared of tables and chairs to create a large ballroom, and a swing band made up of members of the university's orchestra who got into the ball for free were tuning up along one wall.

On the first floor of the Women's Union, it was a similar story but there a jazz quartet were practising some popular dance tunes. All the fire doors between the two unions were propped open to allow the easy passage of partygoers between dancefloors, a move that had been hotly contested at the organising sub-committee meeting but had passed with a narrow margin. A buffet was going to be served in the restaurant next door and the bar in the Men's Union was already doing a roaring trade when the party from the vicarage arrived.

Dorothea had asked if they could arrive early as all the committee members had been assigned or volunteered for a job on the night, as well as all the decorating in the run up to the event. Dorothea was going to help in the cloakroom for part of the evening. This was going to be housed in *The Worm's* office, what with it being next to the Joint Common Room where fundraising stalls had been set up. Everyone therefore had to tramp past the tombola and raffle to relieve themselves of their coats and scarves and then retrieve them at the end of the night, a masterstroke of salesmanship on behalf of the organising sub-committee.

Dorothea left her friends on the ground floor as they exclaimed over the decorations and orientated themselves in the unfamiliar Men's Union building. Heading upstairs and exchanging greetings with various members of the organising committee all of whom seemed to be feeling the strain somewhat, she headed to *The Worm's* office.

Dorothea had volunteered for this role so she could spend time with some of the Executive Officers she did not know a lot about. Victoria Butterworth was already there, hanging empty coat hangers onto rails. She was dressed as Artemis the Goddess of the Hunt, utilising those very versatile bedsheets from Halls. They were soon joined by Abigail Rushton dressed as Cleopatra, and Alexandra Cotton as a snowman. Both seemed to have had the same thought and sacrificed more bedsheets.

Housekeepers and landladies in halls of residence and boarding houses all around Manchester must be tearing their hair out tonight, Dorothea thought.

'This is definitely the best job going tonight. We are away from Constance so she can't land anything on us and after the initial rush we can take it in turns to go off and dance,' Victoria said excitedly. 'It will be my first dance since having my appendix out!'

'I ended up on the clean-up crew last year. A ghastly job! The number of pot plants I had to remove vomit from really doesn't bear thinking about,' Abigail said, shuddering.

They had set up the room so that ball-goers had to come to one desk to get a ticket (they used lottery tickets) and there were two people dealing with tickets at one time. A ticket was six pence. The rails were behind the desk and two people would work at hanging up coats and pinning the other half of the ticket to the garments.

While they waited for the rush to begin, they decided on a rota for staffing the cloakroom during the evening. They would all be on duty during the initial hour which would be the busiest as most students would bring a coat of some sort to drop off. Then only one person needed to be around for the rest of the evening until the mass exodus at 11.30 p.m. to catch one of the buses back to Halls that had been laid on by the organising sub-committee. The usual curfew had been relaxed for this special event.

So Victoria Butterworth took on the first watch, which began at eight o'clock and ended at eight forty five, Abigail Rushton took eight forty five until nine thirty, Dorothea took nine thirty until ten fifteen and Alexandra Cotton took ten fifteen until eleven o'clock, and they all agreed to be back at eleven o'clock to help at the end of the evening.

The discussion was cut short by a sudden influx of students dressed as famous people, animals, and concepts from history, science, literature, art, music, theatre, and religion. It was astounding and a bit incongruous as the students dropped off their coats to be watched over and emerged from the cloakroom in character.

Nearly an hour went by before Dorothea could stop for a break. A member of the men's committee kindly dropped off a jug of lemon cordial and mince pies for them. Together they counted out the money and placed it into bags for Mabel Parker to come and lock up in the safe while munching their treats.

Alexandra Cotton had been getting progressively twitchier and more waspish throughout the evening. She repeatedly tapped an unlit cigarette on the desk and kept looking at her watch, until she suddenly excused herself and practically ran from the room.

'That is the last we will see of her tonight,' Abigail remarked, punctuating her words with a hacking cough and a drag on her own cigarette. To Dorothea she said, 'Don't book to meet a boyfriend after your stint. I bet Alexandra doesn't turn up to relieve you. She has gone to meet her dealer. We will probably hear about her exploits on the dancefloor later and find her in the morning comatose in one of the loos.' Looking at Dorothea's shocked face, Abigail added 'She takes drugs to help her athletic prowess. It's what makes her so abrasive and a real bitch sometimes. I know everyone thinks that I am the one that takes drugs. I tried them once and never again. Oh, don't worry dear, we will keep a look out for her to make sure she doesn't come to any more harm than she is doing to herself. She is a friend after all.' She coughed again and Dorothea could see she was in pain.

'That is a nasty cough, have you seen a doctor?' Dorothea asked.

'Yes, lots, and I don't like doctors very much. There is nothing they can do for me,' she replied starkly.

Mabel arriving, at this point, was a welcome diversion. She was dressed as a nun. Victoria passed over the money with a note of the total. A quarter of an hour later Mabel was back with a crease on her forehead.

'You were short with your total, you know, by fifteen shillings.'

'That can't be right. We triple checked it. I counted it, then Dorothea counted it, then Alexandra counted it. We all agreed.' Victoria was adamant.

Mabel looked perturbed, 'It has happened again then.'

'What has?' Dorothea piped up.

'All this term, small amounts of money have kept going missing. I have talked it over with Mrs Adams, but really, we must go to the police now. We can't afford to keep losing money.'

'So there is a thief around. Do you think it has anything to do with the poison pen letters and phone calls that the inspector mentioned? Have any of you been a recipient of a nasty letter?' Dorothea took the opportunity with both feet, remembering what the inspector had said about questioning suspects.

'No, I have not!' Mabel was a little bit too quick with her response and unconsciously rubbed her stomach.

'I have had a couple of letters suggesting that I orchestrated the death of Ethel Worksop to become

Secretary.' Victoria volunteered. 'It is laughable really. I was in hospital recovering from an appendicectomy at the time. Besides, I seem to have drawn the short straw being Secretary to Constance's President. I don't think she ever does anything. I won't be running for re-election next year.'

'Yes, bossy and indolent is our Constance,' Abigail added.

'Do you think the deaths of Ethel Worksop, Matilda Abbott and the incident with Iris Robinson were deliberate? I mean murder or attempted murder like *The Worm* reported?'

'No, don't be so silly. It was just the editor of *The Worm*, David Whatshisname, trying to fill space.' Mabel was derisive.

'I don't know.' Victoria Butterworth sounded more convinced. 'There has been a lot of weird things happening this term.'

'Of course, they were murdered,' Abigail Rushton stated emphatically. 'And what's more, I know who did it!'

'What? Who?' Dorothea asked eagerly.

'You are just showing off. Don't listen to her, Dot.' Mabel was sceptical.

'I am not. I just need the evidence.' Abigail sounded peeved by Mabel's lack of belief.

'If you are going to get any time at the party you all need to leave now.' Victoria's voice cut through the potential fight that was brewing and stopped the conversation short.

Resignedly, Dorothea prepared to leave but she was determined to try and get Abigail on her own when they changed watchperson in an hour or so.

Just as she was leaving to join the party Dorothea noticed a scrap piece of paper that they had been using to tally up the money on their makeshift desk. It had been scribbled on by all of them but in the corner, a doodle of a hangman's noose was now visible which was similar to the one drawn by the blackmailer. The hairs on the back of Dorothea's neck stood on end. The blackmailer had been here tonight. Checking that she wasn't being observed, she shoved the note down her décolletage and made a rapid exit.

**

Dorothea spent her hour and a half off visiting the buffet, catching up with her friends, and dancing with a couple of the young men from her course. As she was checking her wristwatch to return to *The Worm's* office to relieve Abigail Rushton, she was surprised to see Dr Hadley-Brown stalking towards her, dressed in evening attire rather than fancy dress and looking like a thundercloud.

'Miss Roberts, would you dance with me?' he almost barked.

'I have to relieve Abigail Rushton in the cloakroom at nine thirty,' Dorothea demurred not liking the look of the glint in his eye and feeling a scolding was imminent. 'I have to go back now.'

'It will be quick, I promise you.'

With an ominous sinking feeling in her stomach Dorothea let herself be led onto the dancefloor. The band struck up a sultry number.

'Can you tango, Miss Roberts?'

'Yes, of course. Everyone can.'

She was not very good at it, but she was damned if she was going to let him know that. It was a very different dance to swing-type dances. They twisted into the tango hold, strong lines in both supple bodies, and he led off with the ballroom tango: slow, slow, quick, quick, slow walking step. Dorothea felt the energy of the dance and was invigorated.

Throw it at me then Dr Hadley-Brown. I am your match, she thought, filled with confidence.

When it came, he was calmer than she expected, his temper under control.

'Miss Roberts, on the evening of the sixteenth you disobeyed a direct order from me and continued to investigate the wireless transmission from Evelyn King. While you obviously thought you knew what you were doing, your wireless equipment and the heavy-footed bumbling of your friends in the shrubbery scuppered a very expensive surveillance operation that MI5 had mounted in the grounds of the halls of residence. Our technology kept picking up you rather than anyone more nefarious. Also, you got caught by Dr Winterbottom and Professor Aldridge and I have had to pull a lot of university strings to stop yourself and Miss Long from being sent packing. Because of this you are being stood down. No more investigating. You have become a liability rather than a help.'

'A liability!?' Dorothea's response was explosive. 'We were able to discern with our equipment that the signal was coming from within the grounds of Halls and not Grangebrook Hall itself, and even its trajectory, somewhere in a line with the warden's house. You couldn't do that with your fancy equipment. Even tonight I have found out that there is a thief on the committee, and it is probably one of the Executive Officers. Abigail Rushton doesn't do drugs, but she is poorly, and Alexandra Cotton does do drugs and she is well. Abigail thinks she knows who the murderer is but didn't have the chance to say who it is because Mabel Parker cut her off. Victoria Butterworth was sick in hospital having her appendix out when Ethel Worksop was murdered, and the blackmailer is still at work as I found an identical doodle to the one the blackmailer left behind last time. Here!' With a flourish, she yanked out the piece of paper from her décolletage and tucked it into Dr Hadley-Brown's breast pocket. 'What precisely have you found out tonight, Dr Hadley-Brown?'

'Even so, Dorothea it's time to stop. You need to stop, now.' His tone was gentler.

Dorothea gritted her teeth, tears of fury pricking her eyes, but she willed herself into not replying petulantly. 'Listen, we are so near to cracking this wide open, it would be foolish to stop now. We didn't know about your surveillance operation. If you had trusted me and told me about it, then of course we wouldn't have continued. I am sorry it went wrong but you need to trust me. I am capable of doing this. Let us have some more time. One more week. Please.'

A movement in the dance allowed Dorothea to look straight into the academic's eyes for the first time and the troubled look he gave her gave her pause to reflect. 'What is it? What do you know?'

'I don't know anything for sure, I have no evidence, but I have a hunch.' He paused. 'One more week. But for your own sake, be careful. Please.'

The music grew into a crescendo before ending, and they came to a dramatic halt in one another's arms. She could feel his heart pounding in his chest pressed against hers and his breathing rather rapid against her cheek. He steadied her, his arm still around her waist as they straightened up together. Their lips almost brushing against each other's as they parted.

Startled, Dorothea took a step backwards and looked again into the man's face. He seemed equally flummoxed. Turning on her heel, her mind in turmoil, she left the dancefloor in a hurry.

***

Elsewhere in the building a Harlequin stalked through

the corridors, passing groups of students sipping cocktails and highballs, debating politics and religion in raised voices over the noise of the musicians. He skirted a mixed group fooling around under the mistletoe and sidestepped a first-year student who was retching into an umbrella stand. Taking the stairs two at a time he climbed to the first floor, a knife hidden in the ruffles at his wrist. Harlequin passed through the Joint Common Room avoiding calls to have a go at the tombola and quietly entered *The Worm's* office, pulling the door closed firmly behind.

***

Dashing back towards her cloakroom duties, Dorothea ran full pelt into Tabitha Gillespie, who was coming along the corridor outside the Joint Common Room wearing the costume of a regency lady.

'Tabitha, how are you doing? I haven't seen you for ages,' Dorothea asked breathlessly.

Tabitha was white-faced and wide-eyed as she stumbled along the corridor without stopping or acknowledging she had heard Dorothea.

'Tabitha, Tabitha!' Dorothea called after the retreating figure. She shook her head and continued through the Joint Common Room, waving to the students currently manning the raffle and tombola. On reaching *The Worm's* office she was surprised to find the door closed. Knocking in case she was disturbing a tête-à-tête or tryst she was surprised to find no one at their makeshift desk. She called out a greeting and looked between the coat rails but still there was nobody there. Thinking that Abigail Rushton must have popped out to use the bathroom, Dorothea sat down to wait.

Five minutes went by, then ten. Dorothea could not believe that Abigail would leave all the coats unwatched.

She began to get restless and remembered the archive cupboard and wondered if there was anything of interest to read in there. The door was not fully closed, and Dorothea stood in something sticky just outside it.

Opening the door, she could see that the light was off, so she felt around for the switch on the wall and encountered something wet, and again, sticky. She pulled her hand back into the light and gave a small shriek of horror as her fingertips were covered in what looked like congealing blood.

Bravely, she again reached for the light switch only to be faced with a scene of carnage. A figure in a white bedsheet costume was lying face down on the floor of the small room in a pool of her own blood. A knife stuck out of her back at a drunken angle, but Dorothea could see multiple stab wounds from what must have been a frenzied and vicious attack. She could not see the woman's face, so gingerly stepped over the body, and getting down on her knees next to her she was shocked to find that it was Victoria Butterworth and not Abigail Rushton as she had supposed. Her eyes were wide open and staring. Even so, Dorothea tried to find a pulse like she had seen Mary Short do on Iris Robinson and failed, so got out a compact mirror from her handbag and checked for breath of which there was none.

'What has happened here? Has there been an accident?'

A woman's voice close behind her made her jump. Looking up, Dorothea saw that it was a shocked Mrs Gladys Adams standing over her.

Getting to her feet slowly, Dorothea realised there was a large bloodstain on her dress and on her hands which would look incriminating, which brought colour to her cheeks and probably made her appear more guilty.

Trying to sound confident and in charge of the situation, Dorothea replied, 'Yes, there has. Please could you phone for a doctor and the police? I think Victoria Butterworth is dead. I have tested for life signs and there are none. I will stay with the body until the police arrive, so no one disturbs her. You can use the phone over there.' She pointed to the phone that the blackmailer had used on David Simpkins's desk.

Mrs Adams gave her a very odd look but moved towards the instrument, whilst obviously trying to keep Dorothea in sight.

A thought struck Dorothea then. 'Please can you ask for DI Kydd? Tell him Dorothea Roberts found the body.'

CHAPTER THIRTEEN

In a Prison Cell

Crime Scene, Sunday, 2nd December 1934, 1 a.m.

Victoria Butterworth had been a dark-haired, slim young woman of average height. She was probably considered quite handsome in life. The thin, white bedsheet makeshift robe draped around her body elegantly, and her crown of greenery was still fixed upon her brown curls making the scene somewhat surreal like a tableau gone horribly wrong.

There was nothing handsome about the young woman now, with the unsettling grinning rictus of the recently dead beginning to show, and her open eyes staring fixedly at a filing cabinet, while she lay in a pool of her own congealed blood. The police surgeon got up creakily off his knees and wrote something down in a battered notebook.

'The deceased has multiple stab wounds to her back, arms, neck, and chest. Most aren't fatal, however in one instance the knife looks like it has entered below the twelfth rib, pointing upwards through the diaphragm and looks like it may have reached her heart in one movement. Death would have been almost instantaneous. The post-mortem will reveal that for sure.

It was either a "lucky" low blow; the rib's job is to protect the body's vital organs so fairly often a rib will deflect a blow causing a nasty scratch but no real harm, or someone with some knowledge of anatomy wielded this knife with surgical accuracy.'

'Then why stab her multiple times if the murderer had anatomical knowledge?' DI Kydd asked curiously.

'How about malice, pique or hatred?' the police surgeon replied.

'Oh. Ah. When was the time of death?'

'Between three and four hours ago going by the temperature of the body and the temperature of the room, the progression of rigor mortis and the extent of congealing of her blood. I can't be more accurate at present.'

'So that would mean the murder happened around about nine thirty, give or take half an hour. Miss Roberts said she left the dancefloor at nine thirty to come and relieve Abigail Rushton from cloakroom duty and found her absent. She says she waited for ten minutes before going into the archive cupboard where Victoria's body was hidden. Mrs Adams said she left the dancefloor at around nine forty and came here straight away, so say two minutes to get here which ties in with Miss Roberts saying that Mrs Adams appeared almost immediately after she found the body,' the inspector said.

'There are no fingerprints on the handle of the knife, Inspector, even though there are traces of blood.' DS Garden had switched places with the police surgeon and was dusting away. 'I think it was wiped prior to the murder and then the murderer wore gloves.'

'Was Miss Roberts wearing gloves?' DI Kydd queried.

'No. Her hands were covered in blood too. I took a photograph of them as she wanted to wash them. Miss Roberts says that she tried to resuscitate the deceased on finding her in the cupboard.'

'Did you get to the bottom of why Miss Roberts was in the cupboard?'

'She was looking for something to read to pass the time until she was relieved, supposedly by Miss Alexandra Cotton, she says. She is studying English Language and Literature.'

This last statement was said with something akin to awe and the inspector looked bewilderedly at his sergeant who must, he thought, have the soul of a poet. He made a mental note to suggest evening classes to his sergeant at their next annual appraisal.

PC Standish knocked and entered the room, looking excited.

'Sir, I have talked to the students who were manning the stalls in the Joint Common Room. The two of them on the tombola stall are a nosey pair and it seems they took a note of who came in and out of the cloakroom as their stall was quiet at that point, which is good news for us. They saw Alexandra Cotton leave first, followed by Dorothea Roberts, Abigail Rushton and Mabel Parker leaving on mass, they saw Abigail Ruston return at about eight forty-five, and then Abigail Rushton shot out of there a couple of minutes later. They are convinced they saw someone dressed as a Harlequin entering the cloakroom after Abigail left but who didn't leave by this door into the Joint Common Room. Shortly after a Miss Tabitha Gillespie, who was on the committee last year, came into the cloakroom but left straight away back through the Joint Common Room looking shocked. Then Miss Roberts entered and didn't come out again. At around nine forty, Mrs Gladys Adams arrived and then, I quote, "All hell broke loose and half the police officers in Manchester City Police Force descended on *The Worm's* office".'

'That fire exit over there, was it locked or unlocked when you got to the scene, DS Garden?'

'Unlocked but pushed to. There is an iron fire escape that goes down to ground level.'

'So Harlequin could have disappeared down the fire escape? What did Harlequin look like, Standish?'

'The tombola pair thought Harlequin was of mid-height, lean, wearing a traditional white clown's outfit with black pompoms, a black mask, and a pointy black hat. They couldn't be sure if Harlequin was male or female.'

'That is interesting. Has either Abigail Rushton or Tabitha Gillespie turned up yet amongst the rabble in the Debating Hall who are giving their statements?'

'No, sir, but our officers downstairs know to keep a special look out for them.'

'Please could you ask around out on the street or in the properties that back onto this building whether anyone saw our Harlequin shimmying down the ladder. I think we need a word with that joker.'

'What about Miss Roberts, sir? She is still in the Green Room with Police Constable Rawlins.'

'I think that we might have some more questions for Miss Roberts that would be better asked and answered back at headquarters. Please could you request her presence there, caution her and see to her transfer? Thank you, Standish.'

Sunday 2nd December 1934, Early Morning

It was four o'clock in the morning when DI Kydd came looking for Mrs Gladys Adams. She had asked if she could wait in her office as there was a nice fire laid and she could crack on with some work. She was still dressed in evening dress but looked a little more crumpled than usual.

'Ah, Inspector, have you and your men finished taking addresses and statements from all the young people? There were at least five hundred tickets sold for the ball so you must have had your work cut out. Have they all been sent home now? Quite right too! We more mature folk cope so much better with sudden shocks than these young folk. Do come and sit here, near the fire, and warm yourself.'

Mrs Adams was as always, a gracious and charming hostess.

'Thank you, Mrs Adams that would be grand,' DI Kydd said, gratefully standing in front of the fireplace and basking in the amount of heat it generated. 'The Debating Hall is freezing when five hundred students are no longer dancing in it. How are you feeling now, as you must have had quite a shock yourself?'

'It was horrible, Inspector, but I saw worse in the war. I just feel so sorry for Victoria's parents. It is absolutely heart-breaking for them.'

'No one had a grudge against Miss Butterworth, that you noticed?'

'As I told Constable Standish, Inspector, in my statement, I know of no reason why anyone should want to kill Victoria. She was a nice girl, totally inoffensive. She had lots of friends and no enemies at all, I should think.'

'It appears that both Abigail Rushton and Tabitha Gillespie left the building before we were called in. It would be useful to have a photograph of them as they are both key witnesses. Constance Harris mentioned that you have photographs of all the committees you have worked with, up on the wall. Ah, I recognise Constance on that one up there.'

'Yes of course Inspector, here you go. This is last year's photograph. Tabitha is on the back row, second from the left. Abigail Rushford was Debating Secretary last year as well, bottom row, third from the left, so you have both on one picture.'

The inspector scrutinised the picture, carefully.

'In your opinion, Mrs Adams, would you say there was a superficial likeness between Abigail Rushton and the dead girl, Victoria Butterworth, especially from behind? Only we have heard that there were at least three young women dressed in costumes made from bedsheets, helping in the cloakroom.'

Mrs Adams paused in thought, weighing up the inspector's unspoken suggestion before she spoke. 'Yes, Inspector, Abigail and Victoria were much of the same height, slender with bobbed and curled dark hair. From the front you couldn't possibly mistake them, but from behind, in a poorly lit cupboard in a similar costume, it is possible. And Abigail is a much more plausible victim.'

'Why so?'

'She is argumentative because she enjoys it, and it goes further and is uglier than her role as Debating Secretary needs her to be. Abigail has an unkind sense of humour, deliberately taking a joke too far, and makes it her business to know everything that is going on. If I had to pick, she would be my choice as the troublesome poison pen writer and phone caller.'

'Thank you. Could I ask you why you went to the cloakroom when you did, Mrs Adams?'

'I wanted to get my coat, Inspector. My fiancé and I had been invited to a private drink reception at my fiancé's godfather's apartment which we were going to after calling in here. An old friend, a Mr George who is very high up in the Secret Service, was going to be there and I did not want to miss him. We were only going to stay here a little while to say that we had supported the student unions. These events always make one feel old don't you think, Inspector?'

'Indeed. Myself more so than you, Mrs Adams, I would think. Miss Roberts says she danced with Dr Hadley-Brown just prior to leaving the dancefloor and going to the cloakroom in *The Worm's* office. Did you see them together and see them leave the dancefloor? You can't have been too far behind Miss Roberts?'

'Yes, I do believe Geraint danced with Miss Roberts. She is one of his first-year students and he felt obliged to. I was talking to the provost just before leaving to get my coat, but I can't say that I saw when Miss Roberts left the dancefloor.'

'Did you pass anyone coming away from the cloakroom on your way there?'

'Inspector, the two unions were alive with young people having a good time. I passed lots of people on my way to the cloakroom, but no, no one specifically coming away from the cloakroom towards me. The Joint Common Room which one has to pass through, was full of young people coming and going.'

'On entering the cloakroom can you describe in your own words what you saw and heard please, Mrs Adams?'

'I entered the room and there was no one at the desk where I had previously deposited my coat. I called out and a voice answered from behind some very full coat racks saying, 'There has been an accident.' I ducked around the coat racks and behind them I found Miss Roberts dressed as Lady Macbeth, covered in blood, kneeling next to Victoria Butterworth's body. She was on her back at an odd angle, and Miss Roberts appeared to be trying resuscitation techniques to revive her. The knife was sticking out of Victoria's back, making it harder for Miss Roberts's First Aid attempts. Miss Roberts seemed agitated and asked me to ring for the police and an ambulance which I did from the phone in the same room, trying never to take my eyes off Miss Roberts. She continued to try to resuscitate Victoria Butterworth, but I could see that there was no point.'

'Was Miss Roberts wearing gloves when you saw her?'

Mrs Adam paused for a moment.

'No, Inspector I think she was gloveless. I remember seeing the blood on her hands and her costume and it reminded me of those lines from that very same Scottish play, about being unable to get the blood and it's scent off one's hands. It was most apt, I thought.'

'Ah, yes. Did Miss Roberts seem pleased to see you when you arrived, Mrs Adams?'

'She seemed nervous and jumpy, Inspector. Exactly how you would expect a murderer who had been caught in the act to behave. Have you arrested her yet? You should do. That young woman did it, Inspector. I would swear to that. I'll obviously do my best for Miss Roberts, like I would any of my students, including putting her in the way of a good lawyer but I think she must be psychopathic. She had no quarrel with Miss Butterworth that I know of, yet Victoria is dead!'

'Thank you for your help, Mrs Adams. Miss Roberts has voluntarily agreed to go with one of my constables to answer some more questions at police headquarters. It is early days yet to be making an arrest.'

Sunday 2nd December 1934, 9 a.m.

PC Standish, currently manning the duty desk, shook his head. It had been a funny old night. He yawned and rubbed his eyes. A murder in the middle of the university's Christmas fancy dress ball was one for his memoirs, especially as the prime suspect, in his humble opinion, was currently sitting resignedly in a cell helping the police with their inquiries dressed as a very bloodstained yet dignified Lady Macbeth.

He had taken contact details and statements from hundreds of students in differing states of inebriation and dressed as very different fanciful characters and the inspector was in a very good mood considering he was investigating the gory death of a young female. Normally, DI Kydd would have been like a bear with a sore head until he had a lead, but in this instance, he was humming under his breath and was positively gleeful.

'Excuse me. We want to see DI Kydd. There is about to be a miscarriage of justice. Dot wouldn't kill Victoria Butterworth. She was investigating the mysterious deaths on campus. We all were, I mean are.'

PC Standish looked at the faces of three very tired but determined young ladies that he vaguely remembered having taken statements from the previous night, and recognised trouble when he saw it.

'DI Kydd is out making inquiries at the moment but if you remind me of your names and addresses, I'll see if the inspector can see you when he returns and has a spare minute.'

'Thank you, Sergeant, that is very kind of you. We are happy to wait,' Mary Long made the mistake deliberately and was pleased to see the police constable swell with pride under the misapprehension.

'If you ladies would just wait here,' he indicated some uncomfortable-looking wooden upright chairs. 'I'll bring you all a cup of tea along in a moment.'

'Sergeant, you are an absolute angel! We missed breakfast to get here early,' Mary Long said, smiling winningly and taking a seat.

PC Standish went away with a spring in his step, determined to dig out some biscuits to go with the tea.

Maggie dug her elbow hard into Mary Long's ribs.

'You'll get us all arrested for trying to influence an officer of the law when about his duties.'

'No, I won't. PC Standish is an absolute lamb and if I am not mistaken will bring us all a slab of fruit cake or hot buttered toast.'

Sunday 2nd December 1934, Mid-morning

Dorothea, sitting miserably in the police station cell, albeit with the door unlocked, waited discontentedly, still wearing her bloodstained Lady Macbeth costume even though the smell of dried gore sickened her. The dark wig was abandoned on the floor, and she had been allowed to wash the blood off her hands but only after DS Garden had taken her photograph. She had voluntarily given her statement and fingerprints, but she was under no illusions that she was the prime suspect for Victoria Butterworth's murder. She had been placed in police custody and had been read her rights when signing her statement. No charge had been forthcoming, but she was sure that if she tried to leave, the cell door would be shut firmly and promptly.

She had phoned Professor Aldridge and had managed to get through to him. He had been reassuring, told her to sit tight and wait for Dr Hadley-Brown who was on his way, and to disclose nothing about working for Mr George of the Secret Service until Geraint arrived.

DI Kydd knocked and entered the chilly cell, carrying a large paper bag. Dorothea had not seen him since the night before, when the police had arrived at the scene. He had questioned her most thoroughly and then listened in while DS Garden had taken her statement and had arranged for her to be transferred to the police headquarters at the Town Hall. He looked tired around his eyes, but she had heard him whistle a cheery little ditty on his way along the corridor.

'Here you go, Miss Roberts,' he said, handing over a bag of clean clothes and toiletries. 'I have just had a very interesting chat with your friends. They are very intuitive young ladies. They brought you some clothes to change into. Why don't you freshen up then we will have a talk about the Oyster Club.'

He disappeared off down the corridor leaving Dorothea perplexed but very grateful for the freshly laundered tweed skirt, woollen stockings, and enclosed brogues. Returning five minutes later with PC Standish in tow, they transferred to an interview room 'to be more comfortable,' according to the inspector.

'I have reread your statement, Miss Roberts, and I think you might want to update it somewhat. Not about Victoria Butterworth's death. Your friends brought with them all your research into the mysterious Oyster Club which at least one of the current Executive Officer's belongs to. This club teaches its members covert operation skills, like using a wireless and Morse Code and has some very dubious sounding reading materials according to Miss Shor. The person who runs it is definitely someone that I, and probably the Secret Service, would want to talk with. There are several items that your friends gave to police custody that will be sent for forensic examination. Can you tell me, Miss Roberts, what you know about the Oyster Club and how it relates to the murders and murder attempts on campus? Is this what Matthew Abbott was investigating undercover?'

'Inspector, I am glad my friends brought you all our research. I have wanted you to have it for a while but as I said to you previously what I know above and beyond my friends isn't my secret to share. I have made a phone call and I hope I'll be able to tell you shortly.' She crossed her fingers and hoped that Dr Hadley-Brown would come soon.

'I won't be able to let you leave until I have a complete statement from you, Miss Roberts. Do you understand that?'

'Perfectly, Inspector. I am sorry to put you to so much trouble.'

Monday 3rd December 1934, Evening

Back at the police headquarters it was gone ten o'clock at night and DI Kydd had just returned to his office when there was an apologetic knock and PC Standish's head popped around the door.

'There is a Mr George and Dr Hadley-Brown to see you, sir. Mr George was most insistent. I said you hadn't had any sleep and were due to go home.'

The inspector rubbed his eyes and stretched. 'That's alright, Standish. Please send them in. This could be very interesting.'

Mr George blustered into the room like a small cyclone, followed more warily by Geraint Hadley-Brown.

'Ah, Inspector! Nice to see you again. Geraint has told me all about what happened at the Christmas ball. Terrible, simply terrible news. And about the young lady you are holding in your cells. He has assured me that you can be trusted so I think it is time to tell you about the biggest act of treason since wartime. I must swear you to secrecy of course.'

The inspector held up his hand to halt Mr George in his tracks. 'Thank you for your confidence, sir. Would it help if I told you that I know there is a secret society working out of the university called the Oyster Club? Members of this club solve codes and practice pick-ups and drop-offs and have books about poisons and ballistics on their bookshelves. They are literate in Morse Code and can use wireless sets to send and receive messages. Rather like the trainees of your own department perhaps, sir. It is run by someone familiar with the university and they call themselves the Secretary of the Oyster Club. It sounds like something that yourself, and the late Mr Matthew Abbott might be interested in. I can surmise from the higher-than-average mortality rate this term of prominent undergraduate students that the Oyster Club is not a benign influence on the security of the nation.'

'Ah, you know,' was all a flabbergasted Mr George could say.

'DI Kydd, I was dancing with Miss Roberts just before she went off to relieve the person in charge of the cloakroom which was when Victoria Butterworth was killed. Miss Roberts was her normal self. She definitely didn't have a knife on her person. Also, she was—'

'Working for you. Yes, I knew you were up to something when you went off suddenly after identifying Matthew Abbott's body. She was probably giving you her most recent report.'

'Has she talked? Geraint, I said it was a risky idea employing a young inexperienced woman to do a man's job.' Mr George was indignant.

'No, she hasn't talked, gentleman. She is an exemplary member of your profession. She could have been home yesterday if she had, but instead she has had to wait over thirty-six hours in a police cell for you two to come to her rescue. What has taken you so long?'

Geraint looked pained and Mr George looked guilty.

'I was at a house party over the weekend and couldn't be reached, Inspector. I left instructions with Miss Peterson, my secretary, that I wasn't to be disturbed by anything.' Mr George drew himself up to his full height of five foot four inches and tried to look dignified.

'I eventually managed to locate Mr George at Lambeth Palace after a chance phone call with the organist of Westminster Abbey, an old college friend of mine gave me a lead. I went to meet him from the station and brought him straight here.' Geraint managed to conceal his obvious suspicion of his chief's movements.

'And the Archbishop of Canterbury is a particular friend of mine. I am allowed to visit him.' Mr George sounded petulant as if he had been caught in a misdemeanour.

'Are you both willing to vouch that Miss Roberts is working for the Secret Service and is investigating these crimes rather than causing them?' DI Kydd was stern.

'By Jupiter, yes!'

'Yes, DI Kydd!'

'Well then, I think Miss Roberts would appreciate a visit from you both and if you could convince her to give me a complete statement now, that would help me a lot. I'll organise for her release while you are doing that, and it would do me a favour if you could see her home.'

Mr George and Dr Hadley-Brown meekly followed PC Standish to the cells while the inspector filled out the relevant paperwork.

What was Mr George doing at Lambeth Palace? the inspector thought, *and what an odd couple, Geraint Hadley-Brown and Mrs Adams would make. Mrs Adams is adamant that Dorothea committed the murder and Dr Hadley-Brown is equally adamant that she didn't.* He shook his head and wearily got back to his work.

***

Dorothea was lying down on her uncomfortable cot with scratchy blankets when there was a rattle of the door handle and it opened to reveal a short, rotund man who she had never met before, followed quickly by a glowering Dr Hadley-Brown. Her heart did a little wobble on seeing his familiar figure and she wanted to cry. Sitting up, she looked unsurely from man to man, looking for an explanation.

'My dear Miss Roberts, I came as soon as Geraint told me.' Not strictly accurate but reassuring in the circumstance. 'My name is George, and I am Geraint's boss and Head of U Branch at the Secret Service, so you are also under my care.' He took hold of both her hands and patted them in an avuncular manner. 'My poor child, you have been through a horrible situation and done so well not to tell anyone who you have been working for, but now I have taken DI Kydd into my confidence, and I am here to positively command you to sign a statement to say that you work for me. I have sorted everything out with DI Kydd and you are to be released into our care and we have promised too to see you safely home.'

PC Standish bustled in with his notebook and a sheaf of papers, looking a little disappointed to be losing his prime suspect.

'Miss Roberts, I have your statement here. Is there anything you would like to add after speaking to Mr George and Dr Hadley-Brown?'

'Yes, Constable!' Dorothea felt an overwhelming sense of relief. 'I do want to add something to my statement. I have been working for the Secret Service for the past few months investigating the Oyster Club, a spy-ring made up of women recruited from the university . . .'

She told the constable everything.

***

It was cold in the Crossley. Dorothea sat in the back swathed beneath blankets next to Mr George who had been most solicitous for her comfort. Mr George had asked Geraint to drop him off on Oxford Place which was suspiciously close to Mrs Adams's elegant house on Anson Road and nowhere near the Midland Hotel which was where Mr George usually stayed when he was in Manchester. Geraint wondered what the old Lothario was up to without caring much.

When Mr George had left, with a spring in his step and rivulets cascading off his sturdy umbrella, the Crossley was very quiet. Dorothea wondered what Geraint was thinking. She also realised she was starving. She hadn't been able to eat much all day.

Almost on cue, the Crossley began to slow down and stopped outside a fried fish shop. Dr Hadley-Brown hopped out and disappeared inside to reappear with a brown paper bag and two bottles of ginger ale. He placed the fragrant package next to him in the footwell and drove off. The smell of salty, vinegary goodness filled the compartment and gnawed at Dorothea's insides until she was almost sick. She thought Geraint the most selfish man ever to buy his own supper and then to taunt her with it.

The car pulled over onto Wilmslow Road, near to the entrance gate that led to Grangebrook Hall. Geraint leapt out and rummaged in the boot compartment producing a lamp, which he lit and placed on a modified hook on the Crossley's roof supports. It gave off a warm glow that made the inside of the Crossley feel intimate and safe. Geraint picked up the fish and chips and bottles of ginger ale, opened the back door and joined Dorothea in the back. He produced two tumblers, blew out a few cobwebs and dusted them with a handkerchief before filling them with ginger ale and laying the handkerchief onto the leatherwork to protect it from greasespots. He passed one glass to Dorothea and raised his in a toast.

'To freedom, Miss Roberts!'

He then dug into the brown paper bag and passed her a greasy parcel. She could have cried, and her ill will towards him evaporated instantly.

'Well, I couldn't let you go back home hungry, could I? Sorry, there is no cutlery.'

'Thank you very much,' she mumbled, with a mouth full of chipped potatoes.

They ate in companionable silence for a while.

'This takes me back. I haven't had fish and chips in a car in the rain since I was up at Cambridge. There is no finer cuisine and no finer city than this and I am sure the current company is a lot better than the rowdy college freshmen that I ran around with.'

'What was Cambridge like?' Dorothea asked curiously. 'I won a fellowship to Oxford.'

'Did you? Well, it was a privilege. It provided me with an excellent education and friends for life and instilled in me a knuckle-down work ethic, but I do have to be a bit careful not to have an insular view of the world . . . expand my horizons. But also get back to my roots, that is why I took a job up here. Why didn't you accept your place at Oxford?'

'I wanted to, but my father died last year. I got pneumonia and he nursed me, then he got pneumonia too and died from it. After that, Oxford was too expensive, and my headmaster suggested I come here instead.' Dorothea felt the stab of grief as intense as if the bereavement was fresh and blinked away sudden tears. 'Sorry, I shouldn't have mentioned my dad. I miss him terribly. I could talk to him about anything. He would have been fascinated by this Oyster Club business. I am sorry for blubbering. I must be tired after everything . . .' She looked frantically around for a handkerchief in her bag but failed to find anything that was in anyway clean or presentable.

Geraint gently drew her against his shoulder. She buried her face into him and had a really good cry, releasing great gusty, snotty sobs.

'It wasn't your fault that your father died, Dorothea.'

This caused a further wave of sobs so he held his tongue regretfully, wondering where he could get his coat cleaned at short notice. Eventually, her sobs turned into hiccups before petering out. He passed her his own handkerchief which she accepted gratefully and wiped her eyes, blew her nose defiantly, and sat up.

His eyes visibly showed his concern. 'I am sorry about your father, Miss Roberts. I didn't know. My own father died many years ago, in the war actually, and I still miss him every single day. I am lucky to have my godfather, Professor Aldridge, to speak with about anything and everything. I think I would have got into a right old mess without him.' He held out his hand and took hold of hers.

'You know you can always talk to me. I am not a monster, even if my Anglo-Saxon course was not your first choice.'

This drew a reluctant chortle from behind the handkerchief and she squeezed his fingers in return.

'Thank you for coming to my rescue again tonight, sir. I know the police constable thought I was guilty, but Victoria Butterworth was dead when I entered and fairly recently so too as she was still warm.'

'I believe you. Our murderer is very clever. The inspector said two people were seen entering the cloakroom before you, and after Abigail Rushton left. Abigail has gone missing by the way. The two people were someone dressed as a Harlequin; they are not sure whether male or female, and the other was a Tabitha Gillespie a former member of the committee. Enough about that for now though. Let's get you back to your room.'

'I can get back in by myself you know. I'll throw a stone at one of my friend's windows and they will let me in.'

'No need, I spoke to your floor rep, Maggie, earlier and she said she would wait up for you so to knock quietly on her window so she can let you in. I am going to escort you all the way there because there is a homicidal maniac at large who is a dab hand with a pistol, knife, and poison.' Geraint was firm as he helped Dorothea out of the car.

'But surely they would kill us both.' Dorothea was thinking of all the places someone with murderous intent could hide within the grounds.

So was Geraint.

'Let us think of something more cheerful instead, something like . . .' He cast around for a lively topic of conversation. 'Like current literature. What have you read recently?'

'Agatha Christie's *Murder on the Orient Express*, Margery Allingham's *Sweet Danger*, Dorothy Sayers' *Murder Must Advertise.*'

'Um, right. Remind me to make you a reading list.'

They set off through the grounds. At one point an owl hooted, causing Geraint to throw himself and Dorothea to the ground behind an old ash tree.

'It's just an owl.'

'It wasn't last time,' Dr Hadley-Brown cryptically replied.

They made it without further mishap to Maggie's window and knocked quietly. She must have been sitting on guard next to it, in her chair, because straight away she pushed up the sash to allow Dorothea to climb through.

Once this feat was negotiated Dorothea turned back to the window. 'Thank you again Dr Hadley-Brown.'

'You are welcome, Miss Roberts.'

He turned and was quickly swallowed by the shadows. Dorothea stayed at the window watching him go.

Maggie looked at Dorothea quizzically but said nothing.

Dorothea, realising she was staring, turned and gave her friend a big hug. 'Thank you so much, Maggie. I am so pleased to see you!'

'And I, you. We have all been so worried. Now no talking tonight. We will all get together in the morning and have a conference after breakfast but until such time, you need some sleep.'

Dorothea went along the corridor to her room, comforted to be in familiar surroundings.

Maggie, on the other hand, was kept awake by her

thoughts.

Wednesday 5th December 1934, Morning

DI Kydd and PC Standish entered a stark and brightly lit interview room where a young woman was sat at a table.

'Ah, Miss Gillespie, we have finally tracked you down. Good. You have been a very difficult person to get hold of. Timms Detective Agency said you were found lodging with a mill family in Ancoats. Can you tell me please when you stopped lodging at Mrs Moore's on Great Cheetham Street?'

'This is police brutality. I know my rights. Why haven't you cautioned me? I want a lawyer!'

'Miss Gillespie you are not under arrest. You disappeared so abruptly from the Christmas ball that you are one of the only people we did not get a statement from. We have information that you might be a very important witness. You are of course entitled to legal representation. Do you have a lawyer in mind? PC Standish can go and call them for you. We will terminate this interview until later.'

***

Two hours later and again DI Kydd and PC Standish entered the interview room, only this time the young woman was accompanied by a small man with a bald head and a sonorous voice.

'I am Professor Ducker of the School of Law at the University. I am a King's Counsel. Miss Gillespie is one of my third-year project students. She has asked me to act for her.'

The fellow looks more like a door-to-door salesman than a KC, the inspector thought irreverently.

'Let's get started then, Miss Gillespie. When did you move out of your lodgings on Great Cheetham Street in Salford, please?'

Professor Ducker gave a nearly indiscernible nod. Tabitha replied, 'It was on a Sunday, the 28th of October.'

'And was there a reason behind your move?'

'I decided I wanted to be closer to the university, especially the library for my final year.' Tabitha had flushed red.

'Will you endeavour to stay at your new address so that if we need to ask you any more questions after today, we can find you?'

'Of course, Inspector.'

'At two o'clock in the morning on Sunday 28th of October did you meet the warden of Grangebrook Hall, Dr Teresa Winterbottom, and have some sort of heated discussion? Did this discussion precipitate you moving to a new address?'

It was obvious to DI Kydd these questions were not expected, and some inaudible conferring occurred on the other side of the table.

'What has this got to do with the murder of Victoria Butterworth, Inspector? This seems to be an unnecessary intrusion into my client's affairs.' Professor Ducker was obviously protective of his client.

'There have been several unusual and tragic accidents happening on campus this term, Miss Gillespie, and I am interested in people who do unusual things at unusual times of the day, especially covertly. You were seen by witnesses.'

'They must have been mistaken, Inspector.'

Her colour, which had faded, flared up again strongly.

You don't realise how telling that nervous reaction is. I know you are lying, the inspector thought.

'Did you attend the Christmas ball at the student unions on Saturday the 1st of December, Miss Gillespie?'

'Yes.'

'It was a fancy dress ball. What did you go dressed as?'

Tabitha looked confused and had a whispered

conversation with the lawyer who apparently thought the question was harmless.

'A regency lady.'

'Did you go to the cloakroom at any point, Miss Gillespie?'

'Yes.'

'Could you tell us when you went to the cloakroom?'

'At about seven fifteen to drop off my coat.'

'Was there another time? You were seen going into the cloakroom at around nine twenty-five and then later in the corridor outside the Joint Common Room looking distraught at around nine thirty. If you have any evidence that could pin down the time of the murder of your colleague, then it is your duty to aid the police.'

More conferring took place.

'Professor Ducker says I should tell you I went to get my coat. I wasn't enjoying the ball very much and I wanted to leave early. No one came to the desk when I called, to serve me. I often worked in the cloakroom for events when I was on the committee, so I wondered if whoever was on duty was having a sneaky smooch with a boyfriend in *The Worm's* archive room. It has happened before. I went around the desk, still calling out and knocked on the cupboard door. My fingerprints are probably there if you look.'

DS Garden had found a clear set of prints on the door that had not been identified yet. DI Kydd made a note to ask the DS Garden to check Tabitha's against them.

'I opened the door and found Victoria Butterworth lying there in a pool of her own blood. It was awful. I thought I was going to be sick. She was still really warm like she was only asleep, but I could see her eyes were open and staring. I don't know how I got out of there. I found the nearest bathroom and was very ill. I think I might have fainted and bumped my head. When I came to and pulled myself together, I left the bathroom and the first person I met told me that a body had been found and the police were on their way. I panicked, my brain was all woolly, probably from the knock to my head and I left by the nearest exit in the furore and returned to my lodgings where I have been ever since, too scared and embarrassed to come forward.'

A nice, neat story, Miss Gillespie, the inspector thought later when he was typing up his notes, *but you were still flushed on your neck and cheeks. You were not telling me the whole truth again.*

CHAPTER FOURTEEN

A Ghost in the Cistern

THE WORM

Special Edition 1 Academic Year 34/35, December 1934

Is the Women's Union Haunted?
Students are disturbed by paranormal activity in the JCR!

Since the gruesome murder of Victoria Butterworth (20 years old) occurred at the Christmas ball and shocked the university, the Women's Union has been closed for a time to allow the police to investigate.

On reopening its door to students, this reporter has talked to several female students who are utterly convinced that the building is now cursed with paranormal activity. Three students are certain that food they have left in their lockers has gone missing.

Daisy Donaldson (20 years old) says, 'I

left a quarter of a pound of toffees and a bag of apples in my locker overnight and now there are only wrappers and apple cores left!'

Many students think that books and newspapers have been moved around in the Joint Common Room.

Patty Chandler (19 years old) says, 'Last thing on Monday night I reordered all the books on the shelves in the Joint Common Room because they were annoying me, as they were not following any library system. On Tuesday morning they were back to being a jumbled mess.'

One student who didn't want to be named thinks she saw furniture and other chattels flying around the Debating Hall (although it was after the wine club's Christmas party which if you read page seven of this magazine was a fairly wild affair in its own right).

A spokesperson for the Psychic Society has said, 'There is always a lot of excess psychic energy when someone passes in a traumatic manner. We are more than willing to aid the police by conducting a séance to contact the spirit of Victoria Butterworth to ask who murdered her. Our President's spirit guide Vlad the Impaler is very reliable. We kindly request that the Chaplaincy do not hold an exorcism service this time before we have had the chance to schedule our séance. Co-ordination of our diaries is very tricky this time of year. If they do, we will be forced to take the matter up with the provost.'

A spokesperson for the Chaplaincy responded with, 'Our thoughts and prayers are with the friends and family of Victoria Butterworth at this sad time, and we pray for the police investigating this tragedy that they will have wisdom and insight to solve this terrible crime. We do not believe that the building is haunted, and we are not in the habit of performing exorcisms. We think your source is referring to the service of dedication for the new Theology Library which just happens to be built near an old gibbet that the Psychic Society was interested in. We forgive them their obvious mistake and invite them to our upcoming carol service along with the provost. There will be mince pies and mulled wine.'

Be sure that this reporter will keep *The Worm's* readers informed of any further developments with this supernatural story.

David Simpkins (Journalist)

Agenda for the Women's Student Union Executive Committee Emergency Meeting, The Debating Hall, Monday 10th December 1934, 4 p.m.

Apologies: Victoria Butterworth (Secretary – Deceased), Abigail Rushton (Secretary of the Debating Society – Disappeared), Iris Robinson (Vice President – Sabbatical).

Attendees: Constance Harris (President), Mabel Parker (Treasurer), Alexandra Cotton (Athletics Union Secretary), Evelyn King (Social Secretary), Professor Quentin B. Smythe (University Provost), Mrs Adams (Adviser to Women Students), Detective Inspector Kydd and Police Constable Standish).

Item 1: Accept the minutes from the last Executive Committee meeting as accurate.

Item 2: An update of the police investigation by Detective Inspector Kydd.

Item 3: The withdrawal of female students in response to the murder on campus.

Item 4: Editorial decisions made by the Student's Editor, David Simpkins.

Item 5: Petty theft from around the Women's Union
Item 6: The potential 'haunting' of the Women's Union and ghostly sightings.

Item 7: The number of toilets available for students use in the Women's Union and time taken to fix toilets that are 'Out of Order'.

Item 8: Date of next Executive Committee Meeting.

Item 9: Any Other Business.

***

DI Kydd felt a mixture of foreboding and amusement as he read the hastily drawn up agenda, typed by an inexperienced hand on a blotchy typewriter. PC Standish, who was sat next to him and was being offered up on the sacrificial altar of duty as the new University Liaison Officer to attend future meetings, squirmed in his seat and felt totally out of his depth. A deflated and worried Constance Harris drew the meeting to order, supported by Mabel Parker who was acting as secretary and looked like she was not enjoying it very much. Mabel had a pile of ginger snap biscuits next to her that she demolished throughout the course of the meeting and did not share with anyone. DI Kydd wondered if she had chronic indigestion.

'We are very short of members tonight so I am very grateful to the provost for attending so that we can be quorate. Item 1, is apologies which no one has formally sent but I have taken as implied. Mabel has kindly taken up the position of acting secretary as well as treasurer until we can find someone else to replace Victoria, so it is imperative that the full committee meeting on the 13th of December goes ahead to find a volunteer replacement.

'Now Item 2, DI Kydd, please could you give us an update on your inquiry? Is Dorothea Roberts, one of our first-year representatives, still being held as a suspect?'

'Miss Roberts has been released as there is no evidence that suggests she committed the crime. We are interested in speaking to Miss Abigail Rushton who is still missing as she was the last person to see the deceased alive. Also, an unknown male or female, wearing a

255

Harlequin costume and mask who was seen entering the cloakroom around the time of the murder. If anyone has any information about the whereabouts of either of these people, please tell my officers. We are keeping an open mind and treating this death as linked to some or all the other deaths and happenings this term, possibly by the same person or group of people.'

'What? Are you actually saying that David Simpkins writing in *The Worm* is correct? That there is a link between all the tragedies happening this term? This is Item 4 on the agenda, which I wanted to raise. I thought he was just scaremongering to sell copies. I wanted some sort of check placed on *The Worm* before it is circulated. Like a sub-committee made up of the provost and members of both Student Unions.'

Alarm registered on the provost's face. He could not face any more sub-committees.

'That sounds rather like taking away free speech, don't you think?' the inspector asked. 'The Press get pretty tetchy about that.'

'Yes, but what other way can we make *The Worm* print facts?' Constance was incensed.

'But my dear, the inspector is in fact saying that Mr Simpkins has printed fact. It is probably wisest to leave *The Worm* alone and think of ways to mitigate any consequences around campus which I think touches on Item 3.' Mrs Adams was tactful yet firm.

The provost visibly relaxed.

'Well then, Item 3: it has been brought to my attention that at least twelve female students have withdrawn from their courses or have taken sabbaticals due to these happenings. As a Women's Student's Union, we need to be seen to be actively working for student's safety on and around campus. I know the police presence is particularly large on campus at the moment. Has anyone any other ideas for what we can be doing?'

'Constable Standish here can run a personal safety seminar for students if you want. He could even do a practical session on self-defence and unarmed combat,' DI Kydd said, ignoring the look of terror on his junior's face.

'Thank you, PC Standish, that would be marvellous! We can use the gymnasium. Tell Mabel when you are free, and we will make fliers to drum up attendance.'

'The Geology Society has a charabanc that they use for field trips. Some of the male students have offered to run a night bus service for female students to get them home from campus late at night,' Mrs Adams suggested. 'I promised that I would mention it here.'

'Let's take them up on that offer! Provost, would the university be able to cover the cost of fuel for the charabanc to run such a service?'

'Well, I am afraid no . . . Absolutely yes!' he said, changing his answer swiftly after Mrs Adams gave him a look that spoke volumes.

'What about a public information campaign with a slogan? Something like, "When going out at night you must take care. Always run around in pairs,"' suggested Evelyn King.

'Oh, what about, "To stay safe just listen to us, always take the night bus!?"' Alexandra Cotton contributed.

'Um, yes. Good idea on the campaign but maybe the slogan needs some work. Please could you two put a slogan sub-committee together?'

The two young women agreed half-heartedly realising that they had walked into a trap containing a bottomless pit of work.

'Any other ideas? No? Well then, let's move on to Item 5. There has been petty theft around the building. Mabel, can you tell us what you know please?' Constance asked.

Mabel began, 'It started off right at the beginning of term with a pound note disappearing from the kitty which is kept locked in the committee office. It's a sum that we as a committee can ill afford to lose. I raised it with the Executive Officers individually and no one knew anything about it. It was during Fresher's week, when students were still coming back to the university so traffic into the committee office wasn't at full capacity. I kept a careful note going forward of all committee monies and noticed a trend that is rather worrying. More often than not when money is counted, we are short. Sometimes a few pence, sometimes a few shillings but over the term we have lost five pounds five shillings and tuppence. After the terrible events of Saturday, I told the inspector, and he suggested a plan. Inspector would you like to take over please?'

'Thank you, Miss Parker. I asked Miss Parker to mention to every Executive Officer who is currently available that a donation had been made to the committee by an alumna and it had come in, in coins. This was yesterday evening. I asked Miss Parker to say that she was locking the donation in the kitty in her desk drawer as she didn't have time to count it until this morning. PC Standish then hid in the broom cupboard opposite the committee office and watched who entered and exited the office once Miss Parker had left. PC Standish found it rather informative.

'We were looking for one person in particular who had been present at the Christmas ball and helping in the cloakroom when there was an apparent mistake made when adding up the cloakroom takings. Those present included: Miss Abigail Rushton who is currently missing, Miss Dorothea Roberts who has been helping us with our inquiries, Miss Mabel Parker who spotted the mistake in the adding up, the deceased Miss Victoria Butterworth, and you Miss Alexandra Cotton. PC Standish saw you enter the office last night at eight o'clock when everyone else had gone home. You were in the office for ten minutes and then when you exited PC Standish followed you.

'You hid something in your locker and headed to the tram stop and travelled on the number eight tram to Ancoats, to St Patrick's church which was open for a confirmation class. You slipped in at the back of the church and placed something in the collection box and then left and returned home to your digs. PC Standish returned to the Women's Union and looked inside your locker and found this key. This morning PC Standish, Mabel Parker, and I used the key to open Mabel's desk. Together we counted the money inside the kitty, and it came to six shillings and six pence less than it should have. I checked with Father O'Farrell of St Patricks, and he said a donation of that size was given anonymously into their collection box yesterday.

'Miss Cotton, would you like to tell us something about this please?'

'I know what you are all thinking. She is a thief. She has taken the money and used them to buy drugs. Yes, I do take supplements to help with my athletics training. There is no law against that and yes, I have tried hashish and opioids to try and recover from athletics related injuries. I am not addicted. I can stop any time I want to. I am not so short of money that I would have to steal from the union's coffers to buy these substances.

'No. At the start of term there was a full committee vote 14:13 against, about whether to wait until later in the term to give our usual quota of money to the various charities that we support and to review what we would normally give and if we are struggling to meet it, decrease the amount. This was Constance's idea. We don't normally struggle to make ends meet and if we are then we put on a fundraising event to raise whatever it is we need, but Cautious Constance likes to have money in the bank and Cautious Constance won't take any risk. But what Cautious Constance doesn't know with her privileged upbringing and expensive education is that there are people in real need a stone's throw away from the university that benefit from the money we give as a committee; mothers who can't feed their children, older people too frail and too unwell to pay their rent and are being kicked out of their shoddy housing.

'So, I have been taking our usual tithe out of any monies raised that I can get my hands on and anonymously distributing them to the projects that we normally support that are struggling. I only took what we would have normally given by this stage of term, and I have kept a list of payments for Mabel's records. You can call me a thief if you like and arrest me, but my conscience is clear.'

'I propose a vote. This committee accepts retrospectively the responsibility for the donations to good causes that Alexandra has made on our behalf.' Mabel's voice cut across the surprised exclamations after Alexandra's unexpected announcement.

'Absolutely not! What she has done amounts to common larceny! We had a vote and decided as an Executive Committee. You can't just change the outcome of a vote if you don't like it!' Constance was irate.

'Seconded!' The provost called from across the table. 'I am genuinely shocked that charitable giving has been cut at either of the Student Unions. This university has a fine tradition of being generous.' His eyes flickered to Mrs Adams who was dabbing her eyes gently with a handkerchief and trying not to laugh. 'Also, there has been quite enough bad publicity this term and we definitely don't want to affect next year's application numbers by prolonging this scandal.'

'All in favour of including Alexandra's donation as part of this year's giving to good causes and reinstating our usual payment plan, raise your hand.' Five hands shot up.

'You aren't allowed a vote, PC Standish. His hand went down sheepishly. 'Those against.' Only Constance and Evelyn's hands went up. 'Four to two votes. That means the motion has passed. I'll minute that.' Mabel Parker sounded smug.

Flustered, Constance tried to bring some semblance of order back to the derailed meeting, embarrassment flaming on each cheek.

'Item 6, now this is laughable. There have been rumours of a ghost seen in this building. This is another example of *The Worm's* reporters making a mountain out of a molehill, I name no names. How do we want to deal with this? We can't have people saying that Victoria Butterworth's ghost is haunting the Joint Common Room just because a slightly squiffy second-year thinks they saw someone wearing white in the basement on her way to the bathroom.'

'Have there been ghostly sightings?' DI Kydd's ears pricked up.

'Yes, one or two but it is mainly furniture being moved around in the Joint Common Room and food and drink has been going missing. The Psychic Society think it might be a poltergeist and desperately want to conduct a séance, but the provost isn't too keen on the idea, are you Professor Smythe?' Constance asked.

The provost looked alarmed and started to bluster.

'Well, it's not that I don't like it, but there is no evidence of ghostly activity. The situation is a mare's egg if you ask me . . .'

The inspector cut through the academic's waffle, 'Ghostly sightings of someone who looks like the dead woman and food and drink going missing are pretty suggestive don't you think?'

Everyone around the table looked blank.

He tried again, 'I notice the next item on the agenda is about bathrooms being out of order. Can someone enlighten me on this point?'

'I wanted to raise this, Inspector,' Mabel Parker piped up. 'There never seems to be enough ladies' toilets anywhere and you always have to queue which can be trying especially if you are a bit desperate so you would think that in our own union we would be well supplied with facilities. Well, I was down in the basement just before this meeting where most of the bathrooms are and there is one bathroom in particular that has been out of order since the ball. It has got a big sign on the door. I asked the caretaker why it hasn't been fixed but he looked confused and said all the bathrooms were working perfectly. I am not sure he heard me correctly if I am honest.'

DI Kydd whispered something to PC Standish who nodded excitedly and both men stood up. The inspector was most apologetic.

'Please will you excuse us ladies and provost, for a moment? We think we may be able to clear up Items 6 and 7 for you with a little investigation.'

'Where are you going, Inspector?' Constance Harris sounded irritated that her invited guests were skipping off early.

'We are off to give a ghost an early bath,' he cryptically replied.

***

The inspector knocked loudly on the bathroom door in the basement that had an 'out of order' sign on it.

'Miss Rushton, I know you are in there. I know you are behind all the little happenings that keep plaguing the Women's Union. You are the poltergeist in the plumbing, shall we say?'

PC Standish, who was with him, added, 'The ghost in the garderobe, sir?'

'Oh, very good, Standish! The willow-the-wisp of the water closet.'

They heard the locks being drawn back behind the door and Abigail Rushton stood before them looking haggard. There were dark circles around her eyes and her hair was limp and matted, considering she had been hiding out in a bathroom for the past nine days. She wheezed noticeably and every so often her body was wracked with a coughing fit.

Glancing around the cubicle, the inspector noticed evidence that Abigail had tried to make the bathroom homely with cushions from the Joint Common Room in the bath, mugs and plates from the cafeteria in the sink and even a bottle of white wine liberated from the bar in the Men's Student Union, cooling in the cistern.

'We have been looking for you since the night of the Christmas ball. You are a very important witness, Miss Rushton. We think you are the last person to have seen Victoria Butterworth alive. Please will you come with us to the Green Room and answer some questions?'

'What if I refuse, Inspector?'

'Well then there is the little matter of pretending to be a ghost and disturbing the peace. More seriously writing poison pen letters and sending threatening telephone calls. Blackmail is an offence punishable by ten years, you know?'

She licked her dry lips nervously and visibly sagged. 'I don't have ten years, Inspector. My doctors are surprised that I am still alive.'

'Then why don't we leave these rather austere surroundings for somewhere warmer and more civilised?' She wearily agreed and together they trooped to the Green Room which seemed practically homely compared to the women's bathrooms. Seated around the fire the emaciated young woman began her story.

'I didn't kill Victoria, Inspector. She was still alive

when I left. She saw that I wasn't feeling quite myself and very kindly said she would stay on and cover my shift as well. I didn't deserve her kindness. I went straight home and took some prescribed painkillers and went to bed. I have cervical cancer with a secondary metastasis of the lungs, Inspector. No one knows except my doctors. I started to have treatment at Easter but by then it was too late. It is aggressive and now I am riddled with it. The doctors at Christies have tried everything but think I only have a month or two at best. I haven't told my parents yet. I wanted to get on with my life, what there is of it, without people feeling sorry for me.'

'I think it would be a wise move to tell your parents at the first opportunity. I would want one of my daughters to tell me. Why did you send malicious letters and make spiteful phone calls, Miss Rushton?'

'Why do anything really? It was exciting and gave me a sense of power and control over someone else while I can't control my own life. Because I enjoyed it. Because my respectable friends and esteemed tutors all have dark secrets which are fascinating. I didn't gain by it in any way other than amusement, Inspector. I never asked for money.'

'I have seen examples of your handiwork and there is menace implied and you hint that demands will come soon. One of the people you blackmailed, because that is what it was Miss Rushton, didn't take too kindly to your interference in their private life did they? You were the intended victim, not Miss Butterworth, at the Christmas ball. We couldn't find a single motive for anyone to have wanted to kill her. She was well-liked, had no known vices and wasn't a danger to anyone.'

The anguish in Abigail Rushton's voice was palpable, 'It is my fault she is dead. They were after me. All my fault.'

'There were three of you, all dressed in similar-looking costumes weren't there. Alexandra Cotton is fair, but Victoria and you have . . . Correction, *had,* dark hair.'

'The killer must have mistaken her for me. I was meant to be on duty then. Though how she . . . I mean the killer found out what rota we had drawn up . . . someone must have blabbed.'

'Miss Rushton, if you have any information about whom the killer is it is your duty to help me with my inquiries. If you shield her then you are an accessory to murder. I know several of the people you blackmailed as they came to see me, and you were overheard making several of those phone calls. One of those people is a murderer. It is only a matter of time before we catch her.'

'Inspector, I would like to help you, I really would, and if I knew for sure then I would tell you. It is just a feeling I have, and feelings aren't evidence. Also, I don't want to die before my time, what little of it that is left, and I am a lot more scared of the murderer than you.'

Nothing the inspector or PC Standish could say would make her change her mind.

'Miss Rushton, in a moment, PC Standish is going to charge you with blackmailing members of this university and perverting the course of justice. Then he will arrange for your transport to the police station. Is there anyone you would like us to call, your lawyer perhaps?'

Abigail Rushton drew herself up to her full height with an effort and smiled with genuine amusement.

'My parents please, Inspector. I'll sleep in your cell a lot better tonight than I have done for the last week or so in the bathroom here.'

She was led away with a notable spring in her step.

CHAPTER FIFTEEN

A Note, a Brooch, and a Bomb

Saturday 15ᵗʰ December 1934, Evening

It was a Saturday evening, and DI Kydd had his feet up reading the newspaper and drinking a sweet cup of tea, utterly exhausted from his week's work. His oldest daughter bounced into the room towing his niece behind her, excitement radiating from every inch of her.

'Daddy, Daddy! You'll never guess what! Rupert has proposed to Kitty, and she said yes!'

Uproar ensued in the Kydd household with all its female inhabitants having to stop whatever they were doing and admire Kitty's ring and ask about the proposal, all at once.

'Did he get down on one knee?'

'When will the wedding be? An Easter wedding? The flowers are so lovely in the spring.'

'What colour will the bridesmaids wear?'

This last one, a very important question from the inspector's youngest daughter. Happy chatter surrounded Jim Kydd and he let it wash over him while a bottle of his wife's great aunt's infamous plum wine was opened in celebration.

Kitty, vivacious and slightly tiddly on the heady mix of

stimulants; love, excitement and nearly forty percent alcohol content, was enjoying being the centre of attention.

'We went for a walk in Boggart Hole Clough yesterday on my day off. It was such a nice clear day for December, though it was right parky. We found a really lovely clearing with mistletoe growing on an old crab-apple. We sat under it to have our lunch then Rupert went down on one knee even though the grass was damp and brought out a ring box and opened it. He said, "Kitty I love you with all my heart and I want to spend my life with you. Will you be my wife?"'

A collective 'Ooh!' went around the room.

'And I said yes quickly, before he could change his mind!' She admired the ring on her finger and the way it caught the light. 'It is his grandmother's ring that he inherited. Look, the gemstones spell out "beloved". That is a beryl, that one an emerald, that one is a lynx sapphire, then an opal, then a violet sapphire, that is an emerald again and that final one is a real diamond. The Victorian's did love acrostic jewellery.'

The inspector's jaw dropped. His brow furrowed and he scratched his chin and stood up. He kissed his niece on the forehead.

'Congratulations, my dear! I hope you and Rupert will be very happy. I have always liked Rupert. Thank you for your help!' Then to his wife he excused himself and said, 'I just need to visit the office dear. I think I may have a lead,' and he was out the door and gone.

'But darling, you haven't finished your plum wine,' Mrs Kydd called out behind him. She shook her head well-used to her husband's idiosyncrasies and went back to celebrating with her niece.

***

Dorothea was sat alone in her room in Halls on a Saturday evening, trying to remodel her old winter coat. While being of very good quality, it was five years dated so not the latest model and looked a little bit scruffy. Jinny had given her some new lining fabric in a dashing dark green and she had some ribbon which would match with which to trim the collar, cuffs, and pockets.

All her friends were out tonight. Mary Long had tried to get her to come dancing with the Chemists but Dorothea was not feeling in the mood since being released from a police cell. It felt like there was a stain on her good name. Everywhere she went people's eyes were on her and she was sure she could hear whispering, 'Look over there, it's that Roberts girl. The police arrested her for the murder at the Christmas ball, you know. Look at her eyes. She is guilty, I'd swear to it,' which all got a little bit tiresome.

She started to pick out the stiches holding the old lining in place, carefully snipping each stitch with a sharp pair of work scissors.

Jinny was meant to have come over to help her, but Arabella had had chicken pox, so she was at home looking after an increasingly bored and decreasingly itchy five-year-old. Maggie and Simon had gone out to dinner and Mary Short had managed to get David Simpkins to take a long weekend off and leave *The Worm* in the capable hands of his deputy editor to go to the pictures.

Snip, snip, snip, the rhythm of the scissors was soothing, and she quite forgot everything else and just let the repetitive motion lull her into forgetting the image imprinted on her brain of Victoria Butterworth's lifeless body. She had freed up about a quarter of the lining's edge, when on giving the coat a little shake she felt a crackle inside the remaining lining. Shaking it again experimentally she managed to wiggle it into the section of the coat she was working on. Giving the coat a really rough shake, a small, folded piece of paper fell on the floor along with some fluff and a dirty handkerchief.

The room span. Hands trembling Dorothea reached towards the piece of paper which had suddenly become her whole world. Could Matty Abbott's piece of paper have fallen through the hole in her pocket and been stuck in the lining of her coat all this time? Her fingers fumbled as she tried to open it. It had stuck together from exposure to damp as she had been rained upon many times over the last few months while wearing this coat. She got some tweezers and carefully freed the delicate folds, frightened it might tear. She carefully unfolded it and looked down at the precious missive given to her by Matilda Abbott. It was addressed to Matilda Abbott in Ethel Worksop's loopy writing and was a list of named members of the Oyster Club, past and present. Dorothea recognised some of the names and they made her gasp with shock. She had to sit down, head in her hands, on her bed to try and still the ringing in her ears and the feeling of impending catastrophe.

Breathing deeply to calm herself she copied the note onto a fresh piece of paper, committing the eight names to memory at the same time.

Dorothea knew she needed to get this information to Professor Aldridge or Dr Hadley-Brown as soon as possible and the quickest way was to use the telephone. There was a payphone under the stairs in the hallway and one in the common room. She decided the one under the stairs was the more private and grabbed her purse, the copy of the list, and hid the original list temporarily underneath the mattress of her bed.

There was no one using the pay telephone under the stairs, but Dorothea soon found out why. When she picked up the handset there was no dialling tone. The phone was dead. She quickly changed plan and trotted to the common room. There were a few students in there listening to a comic piece by Norman Long on the wireless. Again no one was using the telephone, and again when she picked up the handset there was no dialling tone.

One of the female students called over, 'It's broken. I asked the porter, and he said the telephone line is down on Old Hall Lane. He said the local bobby thought someone had cut it deliberately. Probably kids.'

Another of the young women said, with a slight malicious tone to her voice, 'Dot, you are mentioned in the Christmas edition of *The Worm*. It's hot off the press. It is a bit odd really. There is a personal advertisement at the back that mentions you.'

Dorothea pricked up her ears.

'What? Where? Can you show me, please?'

A copy of *The Worm* was thrown across the room as apparently 'helping the police with their inquiries' was catching. Dot didn't have time to be offended. She flicked to the back to where the personal ads were printed. And there she read:

The presence of Miss D. Roberts of Grangebrook Hall is requested on Saturday December the 15th by General T at the Zoological Park. Miss A. Moss will be playing chaperone. Come alone. 23.5.9 63.3.4. PO Box 2030.

'Can I borrow this please?' She didn't wait for a reply. Dorothea raced back to her room to decode the message. Hands shaking, she reached for a copy of Jane Austen's *Northanger Abbey*. Turning to page 23, line 5 she read along to the 9th word which was 'Temple'. Then turning to page 63, line 3 she read the 4th word which was 'Folly'. The PO Box gave her the time of eight thirty p.m. Trembling, she tried to calm the rising feeling of nausea as she needed to think. She hadn't had time to visit the

Belle Vue Zoological Gardens yet this term, which were a major attraction in Manchester and would be especially busy in the build-up to Christmas.

She looked at the clock. It already read a quarter to eight. She had forty-five minutes to get to the Belle Vue Zoological Gardens off Hyde Road before half past eight and she still needed to ring Professor Aldridge and Dr Hadley-Brown, and now Jinny at the vicarage. She would have to take a taxi and blow the expense.

Throwing on her old coat, lining flapping, she tucked her copy of the list of names into the foot of one of her stockings for safety and put on her sturdy winter shoes. She could feel the paper pressing against her ankle, and surprisingly, it gave her reassurance. She scribbled Professor Aldridge's home address on an envelope and dug out a stamp from her purse to stick on it. She retrieved Matthew Abbott's original note from under her mattress and sealed it inside the envelope.

Dorothea was determined that whatever happened to her she would get Matty's note to the professor. Locking her room from inside, she opened the window and clambered over the frame and outside into a cold winter's night, leaving it propped open with a little bit of cardboard.

**

DI Kydd got his bicycle out and peddled like a fiend from Pendleton where he and Mrs Kydd and their family lived, to the Town Hall where he was stationed. He did it in thirteen minutes, a new record for him. He barely nodded to the sergeant in charge and dashed up the stairs, two at a time, to his office not even stopping to take off his coat though he was perspiring with the effort. From the stairwell he could hear his office phone ring imperiously, but it stopped abruptly as he entered the room.

Thinking little of it, he rummaged around on his desk and found the report from the jeweller. Impatiently, he skimmed the text looking for the names of the jewels set around the central opal in the brooch worn by Matthew Abbott and given to his friend Iris Robinson for safekeeping. He wrote the first letter or letters of the name of the gemstone and the first letter of the colour too, for good measure, down the page.

Ruby – R for Ruby or Red.
Diamond – D for Diamond or C for Clear or T for Transparent.
Emerald – E for Emerald or G for Green.
Jade/Nephrite – J for Jade or N for Nephrite or G for Green.
Water Sapphire – W for Water or S for Sapphire or I for Indigo or B for Blue.
Amethyst – A for Amethyst or M for Magenta or P for Pink or V for Violet.

Looking at the names of the colours first there wasn't enough vowels to spell a useful word, so he concentrated on the names of the gemstones. Jade gave him some trouble because its geological name nephrite was also in common use so it could be 'J' or 'N' and he was unsure whether the 'W' from water sapphire was important or not or if he needed the 'S' instead. He jotted down different connotations of the letters and looked for anagrams within.

RDEJSA
RDEJWA
RDENSA

Until it jumped out at him much sooner than he had ever expected.

He was on the phone to the Chief Superintendent within minutes.

***

Feeling genuinely frightened, Dorothea pulled her old coat around herself tightly, clasping the envelope with the precious piece of paper which had cost at least two people their lives, tightly within her hand. She checked her purse for change and walked through the grounds of Grangebrook Hall and out onto Wilmslow Road towards the city centre, crossing over the road to pop her precious letter into a post-box on the corner by Cromwell Range. Feeling relieved that her burden was committed into the hands of the Royal Mail she picked up her pace and trotted further along Wilmslow Road to a phone box outside the top end of Platt's Field Park. Reassuringly there was a dialling tone on picking up the receiver.

Remembering the numbers committed to memory such a long time ago, on connecting to the operator she asked to be put through to Professor Aldridge's home address. The phone rang on and on and no one answered. Cursing in Old Anglo-Saxon, a bonus of her studies, she hung up.

Next, she tried DI Kydd's office at the Town Hall. His number remembered from an old article in *The Worm* and once again the phone rang without being answered.

She tried St Bartholomew's Vicarage and got through to a distraught Jinny. Arabella had been put to bed as normal at half past six and Jinny had checked up on her an hour later to find her gone. The vicar was out putting a search party together of loyal parishioners.

Urgently Dorothea cut through Jinny's self-recriminations as her money was running out, and said, 'She has been taken, Jinny, by the Oyster Club. They are behind all the weird happenings on campus this term. Arabella is at the Belle Vue Zoological Park. Please ring the police and get them to look there. DI Kydd isn't picking up. I am on my way over there now. Jinny, the person behind all these things is—' Dorothea's money ran out and cut her off.

Putting her last few coins into the slot she at last tried Dr Hadley-Brown's home phone number. She had been leaving him until last and felt trepidation on hearing the dialling tone ring until someone picked up and a slightly nasal voice with a strong Mancunian accent proclaimed the speaker to be a Mrs Sheppard. On asking for Dr Hadley-Brown, Mrs Sheppard's tone turned a shade more disproving.

'He is not currently at home, Miss . . . What did you say your name was again? A Miss Roberts. Can I take a message?' Mrs Sheppard asked begrudgingly.

'Yes, please. Do you have a pen and paper? You do? Excellent. It's a list of names that he particularly wanted me to tell him. Are you ready? Frieda Hollands, Sarah Waite, Belinda Crombie, Anita Meyer, Ethel Worksop, Evelyn King, Tabitha Gillespie, and Dr Theresa Winterbottom the warden of Grangebrook Hall. That is eight names in all. Tell him I have been sent a message to meet at the Temple Folly at Belle Vue Zoological Park tonight at half past eight. I have to go.' Dorothea's voice wobbled. 'Somehow, they have kidnapped Arabella Moss, the Reverend Moss's young daughter. Please will you give him this message as soon as he comes in? It is imperative! Thank you, I have to go.'

Dorothea put the phone down, drew the collar of her coat up against the biting wind and headed into the night to find a taxi. A shadow detached itself from a gateway over the road and followed her.

274

On returning from a particularly difficult interview with Mrs Adams, where both parties had agreed that it would be expedient to break off their engagement, Geraint Hadley-Brown met with a Mrs Sheppard bristling with maternal protection and disproval.

'Dr Hadley-Brown, a young woman called for you ten minutes ago, very forward she was too in my opinion, demanding that I take down a list of lady's names and being overly dramatic about "someone having been kidnapped". I have left a note by the telephone. My Alf has choir practice this evening so there are kippers for your supper. Alf can't abide the smell of kippers. Supper is at eight o'clock sharp, mind.'

'Thank you, Mrs Sheppard' Geraint said hastily, heading for the crowded telephone stand in the hallway. 'Did you catch the caller's name?'

'A Miss Roberts. She enunciated her words properly, no mumbling. Not like that other young fellow who came round today from the gas company. He mumbled something shocking.'

Miss Roberts! You have called me at last, and with definite information, Geraint thought, as he rapidly scanned the note beautifully written in a hand that had not changed its style since cursive writing class at school. His face clouded as he read the names written with loopy flourishes on the page and in rage, he scrunched up the paper only to smooth it out again and place it carefully in his breast pocket. His hand reached for the phone, but something stopped him. Mrs Sheppard was still droning on in the background and gradually his shocked and seething brain tuned back into what she was saying.

'. . . I told him that we had only had a representative of the gas board out last week to check out our fixtures and fittings. An audit, the new chap said of the other fellow's work but Mr Mumbler, as I shall call him, spent an inordinate amount of time down in the cellar whereas the chap last week barely spent any time in there at all.'

Alarm bells that had been quietly ringing at the back of Geraint's brain slid up the octaves and became a lot louder and harsher in tone.

'In the cellar you say? I think I'll take a look. Please do not touch anything in the meanwhile, will you?'

The door to the cellar stairs was built into the space under the main staircase and was hidden behind old coats hung somewhat haphazardly on a row of pegs. Shoving aside a summer weight macintosh in a garish puce colour Geraint pushed open the cellar door and with his torch flickering and skittering around the walls, grimly descended the steps.

The dank cellar air was tinged with something else, the tang of coal gas. It took him a few minutes of searching to find what he suspected but feared to find. Hidden behind some disused packing cases and wrapped in some mouldy old blankets was a homemade explosive device attached to the house's gas line. On carefully removing its woollen wrapper the clock, previously muffled, ticked defiantly. On its face the minute hand showed that it was two minutes away from detonation on the hour.

Geraint was on his feet and sprinting across the basement and up the stairs yelling at the top of his lungs. 'Bomb! Bomb! Get outside now!'

Mrs Sheppard, who was in the kitchen, was frozen to the spot looking at him aghast and covered in flour up to the elbows having begun to make pastry.

'Whatever is happening, Dr Hadley-Brow—? Umph!'

As Geraint rugby-tackled his landlady with his shoulder, he suspected he had winded her. He hoisted her into a fireman's lift position and his momentum carried them across the kitchen, out of the scullery door and into the yard. He sprinted down the length of the scrubby lawn, hampered by his unwieldy and uncooperative burden and struggled with the lock on the garden door into the alleyway. It was padlocked in place and wouldn't budge.

Cursing and searching for some shelter he threw himself and Mrs Sheppard down behind a rather fragrant compost heap just as the clock struck eight o'clock.

A massive explosion ripped through the house, mushrooming upwards, blowing out all the windows and taking off the roof and a good portion of the neighbouring properties roofs as well.

A fire raged from within, burning fiercely and engulfing everything in flame. A fine drizzle of glass shards and cinders rained down on the prone former occupants of the building pressed in as close as they could get to the protective solidness of the compost heap.

After a few terrifying minutes two heads slowly peeped up over the top of the compost heap covered in grass clippings and vegetable peelings and stared at the raging inferno that had once been a house.

Geraint swore under his breath until Mrs Sheppard clipped him around the ears and told him to wash his mouth out with soap and water. This seemed to bring Geraint Hadley-Brown back to his senses and reignite his sense of urgency.

'I am going to phone for the police and fire brigade from the phone box on Barlow Moor Road, Mrs Sheppard and then there is something that I need to do. I might be gone some time.'

At least Alf Sheppard won't have to smell kippers when he gets home, was the idiosyncratic thought that tickled Geraint's sense of humour all the way to the phone box.

***

Belle Vue Zoological Park and Gardens on Hyde Road was a mere eleven minutes by taxi from the Fallowfield campus and only seven minutes from the main university campus by bus, but Dorothea had not yet been on a visit.

Founded in 1836 by a canny businessman, a John Jennison, as two acres of public gardens and a menagerie that fitted into one shed, Belle Vue rapidly became a pleasure playground for the upper and middle classes of Victorian society under his management, and the third largest zoological park in the country, altogether covering sixty-eight acres. There were formal gardens, exotic animals, boating lakes, firework displays, eating establishments, an athletics stadium, and grand dancehalls. The ups and downs of the turn of the twentieth century and the Great War had meant that Belle Vue had to reinvent itself many times over with the expansion of the amusement park, an exhibition hall, more diverse animals in purpose-built animal houses, scenic railways, a miniature railway, and speedway. The biggest change was the change in focus to include the working classes being targeted as customers.

Growing up on a farm and being fond of animals Dorothea had heard about Belle Vue, 'the showground of the world' all her life and was desperate to visit the zoo and see so many exotic animals in one place. Her friends at Crossword Club had talked about visiting the Christmas Circus together which was held in the Kings Hall conference venue annually, but with a serial killer on the loose she had had to abandon any thoughts of a visit – until now.

The taxi dropped Dorothea off at ten minutes past eight o'clock at the Hyde Road entrance, an imposing structure that gave little clue to the treats in-store for patrons behind its sturdy gates. The park was heaving so near to Christmas and Dorothea had to wait impatiently in a snaking queue to pay. Out of sight she could hear a fairground organ playing ever so slightly off-key and screams of excitement and terror from riders of the Bobs rollercoaster. At the kiosk Dorothea paid for general admission to the park and for a map which she pored over to find something that might fit the bill of a 'Temple' and 'Folly'. Almost immediately she spotted something that looked suitably like a fairy-tale on the map and which was impressively named the Indian Temple and Grotto. Realising she now only had five minutes left to keep her appointment she set off determinedly towards the Firework Lake trying to block out the enticing glimpses of brightly lit rides and the smell of cooking meat pies.

The Indian temple and grotto sat in what had once been the large formal gardens, but which had gradually had to give up ground to amusements of a more modern taste. The grotto was close to the amusement park and the Firework Café and had an excellent view of the Firework Lake. The temple had held various exhibits and animals on display over the years but the trend for increased animal welfare meant that all previous inmates were housed in more suitable accommodation. Nowadays it was merely an interesting folly used by courting couples for romantic trysts and in the summer, children played epic games of hide and seek in the scenic ruins. On a dark, bitterly cold December Saturday evening it was deserted, as the focus of this evening's entertainment was the Firework Lake where a battle re-enactment was taking place recreating a favourite theatrical attraction of the Victorians. Every so often a barrage of rockets would be let off to the gasps of delight and awe of an excited crowd. There were massive scenery sheets erected around the lake to give the feeling of being at Trafalgar and an armada of small boats full of actors sculling across the lake in formation.

Walking towards the Indian temple and grotto Dorothea felt very alone in this sea of festive humanity. Their laughter and frivolity at odds with the sick feeling of terror she was experiencing in the pit of her stomach. Looking up at the artificial ruins with their molten decaying appearance, she wondered if she should scout around first, find all the entrances, or just get on with it and go in the front entrance. She chose the latter. There was a polite notice from the park's authorities asking customers to refrain from clambering on the ruins in icy conditions, which she ignored. Not one member of the public noticed as she unclipped the rope barrier and slipped inside.

What Dorothea spotted first as well as the smell of damp and slipperiness underfoot, was that someone had been before her and found the electrical switch and had turned on just enough of the fake braziers and torches to make the space eerie and full of shadows without the light being obviously inviting to the crowds outside.

A spotty child was sat on a chair in the middle of the floor of the temple wrapped up in a blue coat, hat and mittens reading a comic anthology and periodically sucking a garishly coloured lollypop, noisily. She looked up when she saw Dorothea and smiled broadly.

'Hello, Dotty! I got a lolly pop! Come and look at my comic. It has funny pictures. Did you bring Daddy and Jinny? The grumpy lady said I had to sit here and be a good girl till they came, and I have been really good.'

'Hello, Arabella! Come here, sweetheart. Let me have a look at you?'

Dorothea tried to keep the fear out of her voice and keep her tone light, though inside she was shrieking. Reassured that the child was unharmed though remarkably sticky, she gave her a hug. Out of the corner of her eye she noticed that each exit was now blocked by people wearing identical fedoras on their heads and men's mackintoshes. The flickering light from the fake brazier glimmered off pistols held competently. Chilled but speaking in a calm, low voice she pulled out a shilling, the last remaining coin in her purse.

'Arabella, darling, here is some money. Go to the candyfloss stall and buy yourself some sweeties. Stay there and wait for me. If you see a policeman or a lady with children, ask them to help you ring your Daddy and Jinny at St Bartholomew's Vicarage Lower Heaton-in-the-Marsh 5788. Have you got that?'

'Mm . . . candy floss. St Bartholomew's Vicarage Lower Heaton-in-the-Marsh 5788,' Arabella's brow wrinkled, and she repeated each word with concentration.

'I will follow you shortly. I just need to speak with these ladies.'

'The grumpy lady?'

'Yes, darling, the grumpy lady.' In a loud clear voice Dorothea said, 'Off you go, darling. Go and buy some candyfloss.'

Arabella trotted happily to the main door of the temple, passed the silent figure who motioned the child on her way. The last Dorothea saw of her she was skipping happily in the direction of the amusement arcade. Feeling relieved that Arabella was safely out of the temple and severely worried why Arabella had been allowed to leave so easily, she turned back towards the altar and another figure appeared, also wearing a fedora and mackintosh.

'Hello, Dr Winterbottom. You wanted to speak with me?' Dorothea recognised the warden.

She realised belatedly that in reality Arabella hadn't been in any danger from the silent figures. Who would believe the ramblings of a five-year-old that had runaway to the fair after all?

All along it was herself that was the target and Arabella was purely the bait to get her to come to a place of the warden's choice at once. It was Dorothea who had sprung the trap and was now in grave danger. The gun held in the warden's hand was pointing straight at Dorothea's stomach, so she remained still and raised her hands above her head.

Trying to think on her feet and desperately curious in spite of the danger, Dorothea asked, 'Thank you for the invitation to join the Oyster Club. Presumably this is it and you, Dr Winterbottom are its secretary?'

'Yes, this is the current incarnation of the Oyster Club.' The wardens voice bounced around the walls of the temple impressively and she paused to enjoy the effect. 'I am its secretary, president and provost. Let me introduce you to "Elisa" who I think you already know as Evelyn King,' the shadow guarding the route out to the new reptile house nodded, 'and "Elinor" who you know very well is Tabitha Gillespie.' Tabitha remained unmoved, blocking the way that Arabella had left by. 'I had to bring her back out of retirement when the Oyster Club was threatened as "Lydia" turned out to be an abject failure. Usually, I am a very good judge of character but with Ethel Worksop who was "Lydia" I made a sad mistake. While being nosey is a useful trait for a member of the Oyster Club, not being able to take orders and being a blabbermouth are disastrous traits, especially when Matilda Abbott started to ask questions.'

Catching the eyes of Tabitha and Evelyn she said, 'Tabitha, Evelyn please can you patrol the perimeter discretely and dissuade anyone else from joining us.'

They nodded and left.

'So is Constance Harris a member of the Oyster Club?' Dorothea asked out of curiosity.

'No, of course not,' Dr Winterbottom was scornful. 'She isn't nearly intelligent enough. She is a useful puppet, much easier to work around than the last couple of presidents. Yes, Constance is worth the effort it took to get her elected.'

'You fixed the election?'

'Of course I did, Roberts! Keep up, please. You don't think that Constance would win an election against Iris Robinson on her own merit, do you?'

'Wasn't it a bit risky inviting me here tonight by personal ad? I almost didn't read the latest copy of *The Worm*.'

'I knew someone would show it to you. You were questioned and then released for the murder of Victoria Butterworth. You have notoriety and girls can be real bitches.'

'Why?' Dorothea asked, 'did you start the Oyster Club?'

'I always tell my students to be clear when asking and answering questions and that was very ambiguous. There was a niche in the market of course. I am offering a service that no one else in the country is to foreign governments. The Oyster Club is the finest spy academy for women anywhere in the world. I only choose the brightest, most keen students and tailor the programme to the individual, matching them with their . . . ahem,' she coughed delicately, '. . . sponsor. I have links to governments all over the world. Academia is so useful in that sense, along with my parents having been very internationally minded. I have links to Germany, Italy, Ireland, Japan, Russia, China, and South America, and they all are surprisingly lucrative. I am effectively a spy broker. I will match anybody who has the inclination to betray their country for a cause, or for egotism or for money with a reciprocal government. That is why it is called the Oyster Club. My clients are paying for a potential pearl that will be ready in several years' time.

'On graduating from my academy my trainee spies become dormant, in that they get on with their normal lives. They might get married or get a job and because they are very bright young women you can be assured that they will be exceptionally useful marriages and interesting jobs. No one suspects a woman, do you see? One of my girls for example is now married to an MP and another is working at the War Office.

'Think about Tabitha. She is studying the Law. Think of all the things that lawyers get to hear. Her socialist leanings make her a perfect match for sponsorship by the Russians. When my girls are in the most useful position for their sponsors then they will be reactivated and start to provide useful information. This could be in five years' time or thirty years' time.

'They obviously get paid a retainer in the meantime, to keep them on board, which becomes a useful bargaining tool if they should ever get cold feet. I obviously get paid a generous fee for brokering the partnership. That is purely why I do it and the intellectual stimulation of it. It is rather thrilling after all. I would so love to write a research paper on the psychology behind it all but alas that would give the game away.'

The warden's tone was authoritatively chatty, but the gun never wavered, and Dorothea knew that she had to keep the warden talking to give herself a chance of rescue or an opportunity to escape. She looked sadly in the direction that Tabitha had left in and felt an overwhelming sense of grief.

'Normally members of the Oyster Club would not know each other's identity and would certainly not know mine, but we are currently undergoing a bumpy transitional period. Shortly however, I have hopes that the Oyster Club will resume its cloak of anonymity.'

Dorothea didn't fancy Tabitha and Evelyn's chances. She didn't fancy her own chances either.

'Is learning how to kill a part of the curriculum of your academy?' she asked, weighing up the probability of getting out of there alive.

'Every member of the Oyster Club gets rudimentary training in firearms, knives, unarmed combat, and the use of poisons. Some choose to take advanced courses in explosives, arson, and the disposal of dead bodies. Some will never use those skills, while some show a particular talent in that area. Tabitha, rather surprisingly, is excellent with all things to do with gas plumbing but unfortunately, she has developed a conscience which is troubling for her. I, on the other hand, don't let things worry me.'

'Who killed Matthew Abbott, Dr Winterbottom? And Victoria Butterworth? And Ethel Worksop?'

Dorothea named them one by one, savouring how their names echoed around the ruins as though the dead were answering, for justice, 'And tried to kill Dr Hadley-Brown and Iris Robinson?'

'I did!' the warden announced proudly and without a hint of remorse.

CHAPTER SIXTEEN

Revelations

Saturday 15th December 1934, Evening

Geraint Hadley-Brown, having informed all the relevant authorities there was an inferno where his lodgings used to be, collected the Crossley and drove at breakneck speed through the city centre to Belle Vue Zoological Park and abandoned the car directly outside the Lake Hotel entrance to the consternation of the ticket vendor inside the kiosk. Geraint then had to move the car further up the road or face the scathing criticism from said ticket vendor who refused to sell him a ticket until, 'That monstrosity is gone!'

It was well past eight thirty p.m. when he approached the Indian temple and grotto, hot and bothered. He bought some chipped potatoes from a fish and chip stall which gave him the opportunity to casually circle the folly, munching them from a greasy newspaper cone seemingly without a care in the world but all the time reconnoitring the ground.

He soon spotted two patient figures, one on either side of the grotto, apparently loitering but still managing to exude an unconscious level of alertness and subtlety blocking the entrances to the temple. Ditching the chips into a bin he chose the smaller of the two figures and moved to a shadowed spot in the ruins where he quickly and silently climbed up the rockface, so he was above and slightly to one side of the hatted figure on an overhanging ledge. Peering down he noticed that the figure held their right arm stiffly to their side and he was pretty sure that he could see a revolver clasped tightly in the hand of one of the figures.

So that is the way of things, is it? he thought.

Positioning himself carefully on his toes on the edge of the ledge he waited until there was a barrage of fireworks to distract any onlookers then he dropped suddenly on top of the figure, felling them with an efficient chop, then disarming and pocketing the revolver in under five seconds. He dragged the prone figure further into the ruins, risking a quick flash of a torch to see who he was dealing with and showing no surprise when he recognised Tabitha Gillespie. He rapidly gagged her with his handkerchief and improvised bonds for wrists and ankles with the mackintosh belt and her shoelaces.

In the distance he could hear voices talking, so leaving Tabitha propped against a wall he crept closer to listen in.

***

The warden was in full-flow, as if she was lecturing her first-year Politics students.

'As I mentioned earlier, Ethel Worksop was a liability, especially when Matthew Abbott turned up pretending to be Matilda and asking lots of questions about the Oyster Club. Really, the Secret Service should employ some women in non-secretarial roles. Perhaps I should have a word with them.' She snorted at her own joke.

'I caught Ethel snooping around my office one day last

term when unfortunately, I had left the Oyster Club membership book out on my desk as I was in the process of inviting Evelyn King to try for the position of "Eliza" but had been called away momentarily. She denied having snooped but I could see she looked at me differently. I knew then that Ethel had to go. It was in her nature to confide in someone and that someone happened to be Matthew Abbott and when she did, she condemned him to death too. She must have had some sort of premonition of impending doom as she posted him a letter with the full list of Oyster Club members on the day of her death. I didn't know this until afterwards.

'I made an appointment with Ethel to meet after the Executive Officers' social in the Women's Union building. Disguised in our club uniform,' she indicated the coat and fedora, 'and under a fake name, I had previously hired a van. I waited round the corner for everyone else to leave. Finally, she must have given up waiting for me to come and left the building to get the tram home and I ran her down as she was crossing Oxford Road. It did make a horrible bump. I drove to a spot on the East Lancashire Road, ditched the van and hiked back to Grangebrook Hall overnight to learn the unhappy news that one of my students had met an unhappy demise. I am very clear with my Oyster Club girls that a certain level of physical fitness is needed to be a useful spy. I did the eighteen-mile hike in six hours.'

'What about Matty Abbott? Was it you who shot him on that train?'

'Absolutely. Matthew returned to Halls earlier than most students, presumably on hearing the news of Ethel Worksop's sudden death, and being suspicious, I kept him under observation and followed him to his lodgings where he must have found a letter posted by Ethel containing details of the Oyster Club because afterwards, he went to ground in his room and didn't leave it except for meals and to use the telephone, for days. I suspected that at some point Matthew would try and meet up with someone to pass on the information gleaned from Ethel Worksop. I had searched his room during dinner and there was nothing incriminating there so I knew he either had committed the information about the Oyster Club to memory or it was on his person. I thought it might be time to try out my own skills developed for a new module titled: *Phone Tapping for Beginners* and put taps on the two Grangebrook Hall's phone lines. I struck lucky as almost immediately Matthew phoned for a taxi so I knew he was leaving the building and I could follow him. He picked up a package from a jeweller in town, and then hopped on a train towards Buxton. It must have been a ruse to lose anyone tailing him because I almost missed him changing trains at Stockport. I just managed to make the swap to the Manchester train in time.

'The rest you know. How little then did I guess that you would keep sticking your nose into what shouldn't have concerned you. You and your friends. Tabitha warned me that you are a bright bunch and that I should be more careful with my Oyster Club communications in future. A pity. I enjoyed the whimsical nature of the personal advertisements.' She smirked to herself.

'Matty did hand me a piece of paper on the train, but I must have lost it in the scuffle.' Dorothea tried to get the warden back on track as like most academics she was easily diverted onto interesting tangential trains of thought.

'Yes, I had Evelyn search for that paper in what she thought was your room, but you had been swapped to a room downstairs. Evelyn showed no finesse in her search methods, she almost failed the Oyster Club entry because of that. Tabitha searched your room the second time.

'Getting back to Matthew Abbot, it was a very unlucky shot for me. I only winged him, but it was so interesting to hang around on the platform and see who turned up on the scene first. The English Department's very own Dr Geraint Hadley-Brown! I now know that the Secret Service were up to their old tricks of recruiting men from Oxbridge to their elevated ranks. Why not women from Manchester or Liverpool or Birmingham, I ask you?'

'What happened next?' Dorothea prompted, seeing another tangent looming.

'Matthew Abbott disappeared for a few weeks. I had hoped I had killed him. As the warden of Grangebrook Hall I could claim genuine worry about one of my students and was in constant touch with the police, but they were none the wiser. Matthew must have been hidden by someone somewhere. At the time I suspected Iris Robinson. Matthew was understandably a loner and Iris was the only person he had struck up a friendship with, but I had no evidence.

'Matthew didn't seem to get any post delivered to Grangebrook Hall, so I sent him a letter asking him to meet up with me to discuss my turning King's Evidence and handing the Oyster Club to the Secret Service. I was bluffing of course. I thought his post must be redirected to his lodgings address as none came to Halls. He kept the appointment with me. It was at an unfortunate time as it coincided with the discovery of the botched attempt by Evelyn to search what was meant to be your room. He came to my study so confidently. I pretended that the Oyster Club was an academic exercise in training female spies for Britain but one of my agents had gone rogue and shot at him and I needed his help to identify and capture her. He lapped it up. He stupidly let down his guard enough to drink a cup of sweet coffee with me so full of barbiturates that it would have laid out an ox. I waited until that evening and got out my car and drove his body to the canal network near the university, weighed his pockets down with stones and threw him in.'

'Was it you who tried to knife Dr Hadley-Brown? Presumably you were taking no chances and trying to eliminate anyone showing an interest in Matty?'

'Well done, Roberts. Yes, that is true. Yes, you did foil my attempt on Dr Hadley-Brown. After that I recruited Tabitha to that task. She tampered with his car brakes and earlier today set a bomb to go off at eight o'clock this evening at his lodgings. Don't expect any last-minute rescues from that quarter. I cut the phone lines to Grangebrook Hall before leaving tonight so you couldn't call for help or receive news that might stop you from coming.'

Dorothea's colour drained slowly, and she felt sick in the pit of her stomach. Dr Hadley-Brown dead? That was a thought too horrendous to contemplate and with him, the list of names of the Oyster Club gone up in smoke. She was momentarily comforted by the memory that she had posted Matty's original list of members to the professor.

'Did Tabitha try and kill Iris Robinson too?' she asked.

'Yes. Tabitha botched it up. She likes Iris and I wonder if her conscience was plaguing her. She has certainly not been herself since then.'

'It was Tabitha's job as part of our Crossword Club to phone the numbers and see who they belonged to. One was you, and she put two and two together and realised that you were the most likely candidate to be head of the Oyster Club. That is why she wanted to talk to you so urgently on the night we set off the fire alarm. Also, what she didn't tell us is that one of the telephone numbers was her own. She lied and said one number belonged to a local butcher, but I checked, and it was definitely her lodgings.' Dorothea had a moment of inspiration, 'So you were the unknown wireless operator communicating with Evelyn, teaching her Morse Code and the signal was coming from your house which is why you were up and about to catch Mary Long and myself.'

'Yes, Roberts.' The warden sighed at Dorothea's apparently slow sleuthing skills, 'My gramophone cabinet has a secret compartment to hold a serviceable wireless transmitter and receiver. All my trainees have to be competent in wireless usage. You and Miss Long were a nuisance that evening but harmless. I had just returned from dealing with interference from the Secret Service when I spotted you two peering in through my window.' Dr Winterbottom glanced impatiently down at her wristwatch.

Dorothea flung around for something to keep the conversation moving.

'You killed Victoria Butterworth. You meant to kill Abigail Rushton who has been blackmailing members of the committee and members of staff. I overheard Abigail making threatening phone calls and wrote down the numbers. Abigail is poorly and because of a warped sense of humour she derives pleasure from torturing other people.

'On the night of the Christmas ball Abigail Rushton and Victoria Butterworth were both wearing outfits made from bedsheets. They both were a similar colouring and build so it was easy to mistake one for the other, especially if Victoria Butterworth kindly came to relieve Abigail early.' Dorothea spoke precisely and slowly eking out her lifespan by each sentence.

'I really felt quite unwell when I realised that I had killed the wrong person. Poor Victoria, she was an adequate scholar.' Dr Winterbottom was almost remorseful.

'And what about Tabitha and Evelyn? Can you trust them now that they know your identity? Surely, they are a danger to you and the Oyster Club? They are both bright women. At best, you open yourself up to unlimited blackmail potential. At worst, they will realise the potential danger they are in and try to kill you before you kill them. You have equipped them to do so most thoroughly.' Dorothea was being deliberately provocative and raised her voice hoping that her words might carry to the two women on guard outside.

Dr Winterbottom laughed grimly.

'Evelyn is expendable. She is not yet halfway through her training. I shall be sorry to lose her as she showed great promise eventually. She is going skiing with her family over the Christmas holidays to Bavaria. No one would be unduly surprised if a skiing accident happened to occur to a bold young alpinist. I am due to be visiting a schoolfriend in Austria over the Christmas holidays which is not so far away. Perhaps I will visit her family while I am there to offer my condolences.

'Tabitha's performance recently has been most slip shod. I didn't like to say so earlier to her face. She will be my scapegoat. I have laid a very clever false trail to her door which proves quite conclusively that she is the psychotic, serial killer terrorising young women on campus. The gun used to shoot Matthew Abbot will be found in her belongings. She was on the spot at Victoria's murder because I sent her a message to go there. The components to make the bomb that has blown up Geraint Hadley-Brown were bought in her name. I gave them to her the night she thoroughly searched your actual room, so much better than Evelyn. Even the personal ads will all lead back to her. Her recent erratic behaviour will play into my hands. No one will believe her if she accuses me. She will be arrested and tried for murder. I will be free to restart the Oyster Club under a different name. I was thinking of Chrysalis Club.'

'Catchy,' Dorothea commented.

'And now, Roberts, I am going to have to kill you. Your repeated nosiness has left me no choice. A sad accident it will have to be. A trip and fall into the polar bear's enclosure perhaps. I'll have to give you something to make you cooperative.'

Dr Winterbottom drew out of her coat pocket a case and called out loudly for Evelyn to come and help. Evelyn marched in smartly and saluted the warden with an odd, straight-armed salute.

'Yes, thank you Evelyn, I am not the Fuhrer,' Dr Winterbottom said almost tartly.

Evelyn took over watching Dorothea with her gun trained slightly self-consciously at a point six inches above Dorothea's left elbow. The warden pocketed her own gun then opened the case and Dorothea could see a syringe inside and a vial of a clear fluid. Now was her moment to act. She knew that if she meekly stood by and let the warden administer the drug, she would be betraying all the warden's previous victims. Better a bullet in her body which would force the warden to change her plans and hopefully make a mistake that would lead DI Kydd to her door.

As the warden started to carefully draw the liquid up the syringe, Dorothea launched herself at Evelyn, aiming for her gun, and caught her completely off guard. Body slammed against body, Dorothea on top, squeezed the wrist of Evelyn's gun-holding hand and hit it repeatedly against the ground until the older girl cried out in pain. Evelyn ineffectually clawed at Dorothea's eyes and hair with her other hand trying to blind her adversary.

Dr Winterbottom was momentarily diverted; Geraint used the opportunity to quietly creep through the doorway and come up behind the warden and place the gun liberated from Tabitha to her temple while simultaneously disarming her of the syringe. It clattered away harmlessly across the flagstones. He saw her body tense and she flung herself forward suddenly, disrupting his balance then backwards knocking his chin with her head, making his teeth rattle and momentarily stunning him so he lost his grip on the woman which was just enough for her to kick him in the stomach. He went down with a groan.

Dorothea, while subconsciously aware that some sort of rescue attempt was happening at the other side of the temple, was not doing very well. Evelyn was taller and stronger than her and had managed to flip Dorothea onto her back and was trying to squash her larynx as they both still scrambled for the gun.

A dishevelled Tabitha staggered through the same doorway Geraint Hadley-Brown had entered through seconds before and paused there swaying and surveying the scene, the makeshift cords still hanging loosely from her wrists. She had heard every single word the warden had uttered, and her soul was wracked with fury and despair.

The warden had regained her poise and barked a command at Evelyn who suddenly rolled off Dorothea, causing her to gasp for air and wretch as the hands were removed from her throat.

The warden, having freed the revolver from her pocket, took aim at Dorothea, floundering and helpless on the floor, and fired.

Tabitha watching the scene unfold in front of her eyes predicted the warden's moves and leapt, shielding Dorothea. The bullet hit Tabitha in the stomach, and she hung in mid-air before falling in a heap on the floor like a broken ragdoll.

'Hold your fire! I have you all covered. Drop your weapons, please ladies,' a voice rang through the ruins. An unknown man with a Mancunian accent had entered the space. Evelyn and the warden paused in surprise by this third interruption in as many minutes and very slowly placed their weapons on the floor.

'Sir, Miss Roberts, are you alright?'

'Yes, thank you. I am very pleased to see you.' Geraint slowly stood upright massaging his painful stomach. 'You are one of the tails DI Kydd put on me, aren't you?'

'On Miss Roberts, sir. But yes, I am. My name is Timms, and I run Timms' Detective Agency. Ladies, can you put your hands in the air where I can see them. I am sorry I am a little late, sir, I stopped to phone for assistance. The park will soon be overrun with coppers.'

Dorothea was only half-aware of what was going on. She was sitting on the floor cradling Tabitha's head on her lap and trying to stem the hideous bleeding. The breath rasped in Tabitha's throat and a dribble of blood dripped pitifully from her mouth and onto Dorothea's skirt. Dorothea tenderly wiped Tabitha's mouth and held her hand which was clammy and cold.

'So sorry Dot . . .' Tabitha could not finish her sentence. Tabitha Gillespie gave a strange little sigh and then lay still.

Evelyn gave a little scream, then cried, 'she's gone!'

This momentary distraction was all Dr Winterbottom needed to run.

***

The warden ran. She ran like a hunted animal, recklessly and with no other plan but to escape imminent capture. Out of the grotto she went, clambering over precarious stones and away. In the distance but getting closer the noise of police whistles sounded shrilly and imperiously on the night air.

Geraint ran after her, himself in good shape but failing to make up any ground on the desperate woman. Dorothea was torn. Stay with Tabitha's rapidly cooling body or follow Geraint. She chose the latter.

Onto the dancing terrace which doubled up as a viewing platform for firework displays, still chock-full of excited fairgoers dazzled by the electrifying finale of the current show, the warden pushed through the crowds towards the formal gardens, ducking and dodging and trying to lose her pursuers. She jumped down off the low terrace and sprinted towards a large building, the Kings Hall, from whence the *March of the Toreadors* was gaily playing. Puffing now to keep up, Dorothea belatedly remembered the Christmas Circus which was currently being held there.

The warden aimed for what would have been the stage door in a theatre but in a setting where horses, tigers, chimpanzees, and elephants were the star performers, was a somewhat larger affair. There were two large men either side of the door whose job it was to dissuade small children from feeding the tigers and adolescents from running away to join the circus. These two gentle giants were momently broadsided when a grown woman ran past them at top speed straight into the ring, as three clowns were leaving and the stage was being set for a trampoline troupe, the most acrobatic act of the show, due to the ceiling of the Kings Hall being too low for any high-wire work. This was compounded moments later when she was followed by a man, then another woman.

Finally getting off their seats and into the ring they witnessed the crowds break into rapturous applause as the final woman bounced onto a trampoline and did a perfect vault that her gym teacher at school would have been proud of, and then continued running after the other two.

One turned to his mate and in a broad scouse accent said smugly, 'You wouldn't get that happening in Liverpool!' Thus, the merits and rivalries of the neighbouring cities were settled to his satisfaction and the gentle argument that they had been having was won.

The warden exited through the entrance, past the stall selling programmes and ice creams and changed direction suddenly, towards the amusement park, where the crowds of thrill-seekers were thickest, having been released from the historical firework battle re-enactment, desperate to spend their pennies on the rides. She discarded her fedora and mackintosh in a bid to change her appearance and kept low in the scrum of humanity to try to disappear from view.

Geraint wasn't fooled, he kept Dr Winterbottom in his sights, and Dorothea following on behind kept Geraint's head firmly in her line of vision.

The warden darted right into what turned out to be a dead end as the track of dodgem cars was blocking her exit. Exasperated, she pushed past the members of the public patiently waiting for their turn in the queue, exclaiming, 'Get out of my way!'

At the front of the queue, she grabbed a dodgem car off the surprised youth who was in charge of marshalling folk into the two-seater electric powered cars, showing him the gun clasped in her hand to prevent disobedience and sped away across the track.

There were indignant tongue clicks from further down the queue and comments about the ability of some people to wait their turn. The grumblings were intensified when Geraint appeared in hot pursuit, coat flying, and hat long gone. He proceeded to push past the same line of people and threw a shilling at the shocked youth then leapt into the next available dodgem and was away.

Dorothea who was ten seconds behind Geraint was more polite. With some 'excuse me pleases' and 'so sorrys!' she got to the front of the queue much quicker and without ruffling as many feathers. Instead of commandeering a ride she rolled her eyes on seeing Geraint's car being rammed by two high-spirited young people and jumped down onto the floor of the track. She remembered from her school science lessons that if you were not too tall and wore dry shoes you wouldn't get a shock as the electrical circuit would not be complete. She ran straight down the middle of the track, dodging dodgems and overtaking Geraint Hadley-Brown who was stuck on the side.

The youth finally waking up from his stupor shouted after her belatedly, 'Oi, you! You can't go through there!'

At the other end of the track the warden was climbing out of a dodgem car and Dorothea realised that she had made up some ground. Dr Winterbottom darted down the steps off the ride and sprinted a hundred yards to the right and into the Fun House attraction. Realising that she was at a disadvantage against an armed and dangerous person in an enclosed space Dorothea paused to weigh up the options. Did she follow on behind or run around to the end of the attraction and pounce on her at the exit?

Geraint had finally extracted himself from his dodgem car and overtook Dorothea again, plunging after the warden into the Fun House. This led Dorothea to make up her mind. Instead of following Dr Hadley-Brown she changed direction and headed for the Fun House's exit.

Looking for some sort of weapon on her way she noticed that a Punch and Judy booth was putting on the last show of the day. Only the stragglers were left watching; children who were up past their bedtimes, their attending grownups and some moderately inebriated adults who found the childish entertainment hilarious.

The crocodile had just stolen Mr Punch's truncheon and was waving it around triumphantly.

'I'll take that, thank you,' Dorothea said, snatching the truncheon off the crocodile to the bemusement of the puppeteer and the raucous applause of the audience. She raced over to the Fun House exit and hid behind the door.

***

Geraint found himself in a dark world illuminated with flashing-coloured lights. A Belle Vue employee dressed as a clown lay doubled-up by the entrance to a revolving barrel tunnel, clutching at his midriff. Concerned, as he knew the warden was still carrying a gun, Geraint checked that beneath the painted-on rictus and red nose that the clown was breathing. He was pleasantly surprised to see the clown's eyes open and watering with pain and shock, as initially he had suspected the clown had gone to the great circus ring in the sky.

'Which way did she go?' Geraint asked.

'That way,' the winded clown wheezed.

'What did she do to you?' Geraint didn't want to leave the clown on his own if he was seriously injured.

'I jumped out like I am supposed to, shouting 'Seasons Greetings!' She flipped me over like I weighed nothing, kicked me in the ribs and then she stomped on my unmentionables.'

Geraint patted the clown's shoulder sympathetically as one man to another and carefully crawled through the rotating tube feeling like a fish in a barrel and hoping the warden was not going to take a pot-shot at him.

On being dumped unceremoniously out of the other end of the rotating cylinder, Geraint saw that he was now at the bottom of a climbing frame hung with nets and ropes. At the top was a two-storey slide, the kind that you sat in an old grain sack to come down. There was no other way past the climbing frame into the next section of the funhouse. Geraint pulled at the netting to see if he could squeeze past and short-cut any acrobatics.

Bang.

A bullet hit the wall next to Geraint's shoulder, sending splinters flying. He dived for cover within the climbing frame, ultimately having the decision taken out of his hands. He heard a *whoosh* of sacking on polished wood and then footsteps running away further into the Fun House. The warden must have been waiting to see who was following her. Geraint was up the climbing frame, hand over hand like a monkey. He paused cautiously at the top to make sure Dr Winterbottom had really gone as he would be a sitting duck at the top of the slide, before grabbing a sack and racing to the bottom.

Moving into the next zone took Geraint into a room where most of the floor was a rotating cone polished and sloping to a point at the fulcrum to throw punters against the room's padded walls in random directions. On his first attempt he ran, lost his footing, slid, and got thrown against the padding close to where he had started. On his second attempt he realised his mistake and gingerly spread-eagled himself onto the rotating cone, toes scrabbling and praying that his sweaty palms would help him stick, then holding tight, Geraint rode it a hundred and eighty degrees before losing hold and sliding off in a heap on the other side of the room.

Picking himself up he moved to the exit and peered down a long corridor that contained life-size automatons that were operated by pressing switches to bring them to life. In the dim light the corridor had an eerie feeling. Gondoliers stood next to dancing regency ladies and opera singers. There were a group of particularly life-like boy scouts who Geraint passed by quickly, thoroughly unnerved. This corridor led to a distorting mirror maze. His own image first stretched and skinny, now rounded and dumpy, looked back at him claustrophobically and he could feel a cold sweat breaking out on his brow, his breath quickening.

He was in a quandary. Should he speed up and run the risk of walking straight into a loaded gun or go carefully and slowly, checking each new mirrored passage in turn but lose his prey totally?

He continued forward, grimly.

***

Dorothea, waiting patiently behind the exit door with the truncheon, was starting to get worried and a bit cold. She had nearly brained two off-duty nurses, a nun, a boy scout, and a courting couple, only aborting at the last minute and having to pretend to be a Fun House attendant, wishing them a good evening and a Merry Christmas. Fortunately, where she was standing was a fairly gloomy spot, so she had been aided by the merrymakers' lack of night vision after the garish lights inside the Fun House.

Just as she was wondering if there was another exit she had missed, she heard footsteps running towards her inside the Fun House. She paused with her truncheon raised in readiness.

This time it must be the warden, she thought. She started to bring the wooden baton down as hard as she could, only to realise that the figure emerging into the night was much taller and far manlier than she was expecting.

Dr Hadley-Brown, exiting the Fun House rapidly, had to side-step a blow that if it had landed would have cracked his skull. He caught Dorothea's swinging arm and pulled her into a headlock, sending the truncheon skidding away to rest in a pile of rubbish by an overflowing bin.

'It's me, Dr Hadley-Brown,' Dorothea squeaked through a compressed larynx.

'What the . . . You could have killed me! Never hit someone on the head. Go for the shoulder of their gun-wielding arm. You'll break their clavicle and disarm them, but you won't be done for murder.' He released Dorothea. 'Which way did she go?'

'The warden hasn't come out yet. She must still be

302

inside.' Dorothea was still breathless from being half-strangled and rubbed her throat tenderly.

'Wait here while I check for other exits and ignore everything that I have just told you. If she comes out, it's you against her.'

Dorothea waited impatiently for what seemed like an eternity but what at most was only a few minutes, while Geraint scouted around. No one else came out of the Fun House in that time. In the distance, then getting closer, she heard a familiar tune being whistled poorly and Geraint reappeared.

'No, go, I'm afraid she's managed to shake us off her tail. There are no other exits and I checked with a clown acquaintance of mine, and she definitely didn't come out the front way. Who came out of your exit?'

'A young couple, they were definitely legitimate as they had a canoodle by the Coconut Shy when they left. There were two nurses too, but I saw both of their faces in the light of the open door and the warden wasn't either of them. Then a nun with an Irish accent and a boy scout.' Dorothea was defensive.

'So a nun or a boy scout. She must have changed into clothes stashed inside the Fun House at an earlier date. I wasn't as fast as I could have been, and bar one brush with her I didn't manage to keep up with her.' Geraint was rueful. 'The warden is fairly tall. Five foot six inches in height. How tall was your nun?'

'She was petite. Smaller than me.' Light dawned. 'Dr Winterbottom was the boy scout! I thought something was wrong with him. He had the wrong sort of legs for a fourteen-year-old.' Frustrated and ashamed of her lack of foresight Dorothea cussed in Anglo-Saxon.

Dr Hadley-Brown raised an eyebrow but refrained to comment on her mispronunciation.

'Come on. We need to find DI Kydd and get the police to stop every boy scout from leaving this park.'

Taking hold of her hand he ran, setting a smartish pace over to the police telephone box near to the King's Hall dance rooms. A uniformed police constable was on duty by the police box next to the lost children collection point. By his side and tucked under his coat for warmth was a very sleepy Arabella waiting to be collected by her distraught parents. Dorothea gave a gasp of pure delight and picking up the child hugged Arabella tightly, smothering her with kisses. Arabella snuggled into Dorothea, wrapped one sticky little hand around some of Dot's curls, gave a big sigh then promptly fell asleep.

On hearing their news, the police constable blew three loud peeps on his whistle, conjuring up two more of his colleagues out of thin air. One rushed off to inform those officers on duty by the park gates of the warden's current disguise and one rang headquarters to keep them abreast of developments, while the third went to find DI Kydd at the Indian Temple, where retired Sergeant Timms was watching over a prisoner, Evelyn King, and the grisly scene of the dead body of Tabitha Gillespie rapidly stiffening in the cold night air. The inspector hurried towards them with PC Standish trotting along by his side.

'DI Kydd, Dr Winterbottom, the warden of Grangebrook Hall is behind all the killings. She is currently dressed as a boy scout. She is somewhere in this park but probably not for long.' Geraint began.

DI Kydd held up his hand to stop Geraint from continuing. 'Yes, I know. Matthew Abbott left me a clue which I was slow to work out. I want you two safely back at police headquarters, providing me with full statements of what has happened tonight, and the child back safely with her parents.' To PC Standish he said, 'DS Garden has already warned the officers at the main gates. I want Dr Winterbottom's description circulated and all ports and airfields warned.

'I have spoken to the Chief Superintendent already

and he is on his way. I want checkpoints set up on all the main roads out of Manchester and at all the railway and tram stations. I want guards on Grangebrook Hall to make sure she doesn't go back there and the Student's Union and the Department of Political Science. Also on St Bartholomew's Vicarage, we don't want Arabella Moss to go missing again.' Then he turned to Dr Hadley-Brown. 'Where are you staying tonight, sir? Professor Aldridge's? Someone needs to be on guard there too, please. Use retired Sergeant Timms' men if you are short.

'Leak the story to the press. Having the general public on the lookout for a serial killer on the run will make it harder for her to escape. That reporter for *The Worm*, David Simpkins, tell him I will talk to him exclusively. I need to inform Mr George of MI5 of developments, unless you want to?' The inspector looked hopefully at Geraint.

'I shall do it right away, Inspector.'

'Inspector, can I give you this, please?' Turning her back on the two men, Dorothea fished inside her stocking and dug out the list of names of the Oyster Club members. She glanced at Dr Hadley-Brown for reassurance, and he nodded. 'It is a copy of the letter Matty Abbott gave me on the train. I posted the original to Professor Aldridge. I thought you would want to see the membership list.'

'Thank you, Miss Roberts, I do indeed. PC Standish will take you, Dr Hadley-Brown, and the child back to headquarters. He will take your statements.' Then to Dr Hadley-Brown, he said, 'You can telephone Mr George from there. I'll join you a bit later. I need to talk to Belle View's Manager about closing early tonight so my men can work unhindered.'

He thought of the corpse of Tabitha Gillespie in the grotto and knew it was going to be a long night.

CHAPTER SEVENTEEN

Rooftop Reckonings and Fallout

Sunday 16th December 1934, Early Hours

Exhausted and suffering from shock after the day's events Dorothea was dropped off at Grangebrook Hall by a police driver at two o'clock in the morning, having given her statement at the Town Hall headquarters and returning Arabella to her parents. Crawling into bed fully dressed and shaking with reaction, sleep evaded her, and she tossed and turned until she fell into a fitful sleep. She was awakened less than an hour later by a tapping on her window. With effort she dragged herself out of bed and across the room. The knocking got louder and more urgent.

Opening the curtains, she saw Mary Long's pale face pressed up against the window. She remembered belatedly that Mary had been due to go dancing with her Chemistry friends tonight. They were going to try a new dancehall in Trafford for their Christmas shindig. Maybe she had had a fall climbing up the drainpipe to her room, it was now a very cold night so probably very icy or perhaps she had sprained her ankle doing the foxtrot so could not attempt the climb? Hurriedly Dorothea pushed up the sash and reached out to pull her friend into the room, realising too late that there was a gun nestling in the small of Mary Long's back, wielded by Dr Winterbottom who had changed again into the down-at-heel garments of a man on the tramp. The warden motioned with the gun for both women to get back into Dorothea's room and they complied in silence. The warden nimbly hopped into the room leaving the window wide open, sending an arctic blast to chill their bones.

'Sorry, Dot, she caught me shinnying over the fence by the tennis courts. There were policemen on both gate—'

Mary began to speak but the warden cut her off, imperiously.

'Silence Long. You too, Roberts. Any noise from either of you and I will shoot the other one. We will be heading for the roof, so off you go Long, lead the way. My gun is pointed at Roberts' heart so don't try anything clever.'

The strange convoy moved off out of Dorothea's room, along the corridor past Maggie's door and towards the stairwell. Up two flights of steps, passing through a room the cleaners obviously used as a storeroom-cum-staffroom and up another short flight of steps, ending in a door leading to the roof that was directly above both the dining room and common room. The warden locked the door behind her and pocketed the key, then pulled some heavy boxes across the entrance before marching the two women across the roof until they were both backed up against a low balustrade, the only thing between them and a thirty-foot drop.

'Right, let's invite some friends to this little soiree. I shall enjoy this very much. This is for spoiling my plans, Roberts.'

She pointed her gun at Dorothea and deliberately pulled the trigger. The report sounded like thunder on the night air and Dorothea gasped in pain and clutched her left upper arm dropping to her knees. It felt like a firebrand had scorched through flesh and sinew to the bone. She clamped down tightly with her right hand to stem the bleeding and Mary Long, shocked but defiant, dropped to the ground with her to help stem the flow of blood with a slightly grubby handkerchief. From down below police whistles sounded shrilly on the night air. The warden laughed in genuine amusement at the perceived chaos and fired another shot into the air to help the officers find her position.

'She wants an audience,' Mary whispered to Dorothea, who nodded in response, teeth clamped tightly shut against the pain and to prevent them from chattering.

In a loud voice, Dr Winterbottom yelled out to the small group of uniformed officers, 'I have two hostages here and have no qualms about shooting them. I will only speak to someone with the authority to grant me clemency and safe passage out of this country.'

***

Geraint Hadley-Brown, DI Kydd, the Chief Superintendent, and Mr George were all still at the police headquarters at the Town Hall when the news came in that there was a hostage situation unfolding at Grangebrook Hall.

DI Kydd was apoplectic. 'I told them that no one, not even a mouse, goes into or out of that building or grounds without my say so.'

They all scrambled into police vehicles and in under a quarter of an hour were being disgorged into a scene of chaos. Someone had pulled the fire alarm so there were nearly one hundred and twenty scantily clad, chilly, and excitable female undergraduates milling about on the lawn within firing range, giving PC Standish a headache. With the Chief Superintendent in command, a key to the dining hall belonging to Ashburne Hall across the road was procured, so PC Standish could lead his gaggle of giggling, yawning charges away from imminent danger.

Maggie and Mary Short went to find DI Kydd to ask that they be allowed to stay as it was their friends being held hostage. He took one look at their hastily thrown on dressing gowns and slippers and worried faces and kindly but firmly sent them after PC Standish, promising that they would be the first to know if anything happened. The temperature outside was one degree above freezing, and looking at the sky, the inspector thought there was a fair chance of snow. In fact, a few flakes fluttered past as he looked out over the now peaceful grounds.

Under DI Kydd's watchful eye, a cordon was drawn from calculations on the back of a cigarette packet for what the maximum range of the warden's revolver might be. The warden, seemly patient at the preparations being undertaken below, left them to it.

Mr George had procured a megaphone and after some argument with the Chief Superintendent he stepped forward to a hastily made shelter of a police van and trestle tables. 'Madam, I am the Head of the Security Service's Undercover Procedures, Infiltration, Science and Technology Branch, or U Branch for short, and the Prime Minister is a personal friend of mine. I have the necessary authority to negotiate. Firstly, we need to know that your hostages are alive and well. Only then can we come to some agreement.'

The warden reached down and grabbed the two young women by their hair and yanked them to their feet in turn. Dorothea's arm was aching horribly, and the warden jarred it deliberately. Dorothea experienced wave after wave of nausea and rather spectacularly vomited over the balustrade.

'As you can see, they are in peak condition.' After years of lecturing students in large lecture theatres, Dr

Winterbottom did not need a megaphone to project her voice. 'I want clemency and safe passage to America where I have been offered a very prestigious tenured position. In exchange, I won't kill Miss Long or Miss Roberts. If you try coming up the stairs, you will find the door locked and bolted and barricaded. I have also previously erected a high-voltage live electric wire around the building, two feet from the top. It is difficult to negotiate so please don't try anything funny with ladders. There are also poisoned caltrops in the chimneys and the windows on the floor below us are nailed shut. I have had time to prepare. I have a polar grade tent, a generator and fuel and I have stockpiled enough food and water up here for a three-month siege by which point Miss Long, and Miss Roberts will be long dead of exposure because none of the aforementioned food, water and shelter is for them. I can wait. These young women cannot. I will speak to you again in one hour. Can I suggest that you use the time wisely and ring the Prime Minister.'

At which point she very carefully took aim at where Mr George was standing and put a bullet in the police van six inches away from where his face had been. He very athletically, for someone of his girth, dived for cover. A sudden surge of activity then ensued as the makeshift barricade was moved backwards by fifty yards. The warden laughed and went inside the tent and the two young women could hear the generator start up and soon the sound of a kettle whistling on a spirit stove.

They huddled together for warmth beside the balustrade as the snow started falling in earnest for what seemed like an age. Looking around for a weapon of any sort, Dorothea spotted a short piece of lead piping lying discarded behind some of the warden's boxes of supplies by a bygone workman. Quickly and quietly, she stretched over, trying to leave no marks in the accumulating snow and not jar her left arm to hide the pipe down the coat sleeve of her uninjured right arm.

***

Mr George picked up a megaphone, his voice boomed around the hall rooftops and grounds.

'Dr Winterbottom, Teresa, please let the young ladies go then we can talk about what your requirements are. I know that you must be feeling frightened and confused and uncertain about the future. I have talked to the Prime Minister, and he wants this situation sorted out as smoothly as possible. If you come down now, I can guarantee that no court in the land would convict you of a capital crime for the deaths of the other young ladies and Matthew Abbott. I will make sure you get an excellent lawyer. A verdict of diminished responsibility, I am sure, would be reached so you need not fear the death penalty.'

Under the cover of this distraction, DI Kydd and Dr Hadley-Brown had run up the three flights of steps inside the building to investigate the locked door that led onto the roof. The inspector reached into his pocket and brought out a skeleton key. He fiddled with the lock, hoping to hear a satisfying *click*.

Out on the roof the warden was irate. She grabbed Mary Long and pressed the muzzle of the gun to her throat.

'Damn you all. I am not mad! There is no abnormality to my mental functioning. I'll pull this trigger; you see if I don't. Agree my terms or Miss Long dies,' she screamed in rage.

Dorothea saw her chance. She had one shot at this or Mary Long would die messily. Standing to her feet unsteadily, she crept quietly up behind Dr Winterbottom, the lead pipe raised in her hand and brought it down with all her weight on the warden's shoulder of her gun-wielding arm. They heard a muffled *crack* as her clavicle broke and Dr Winterbottom gasped in pain and her arm sagged. Mary Long, quick as a flash, grabbed the warden's now limp gun-holding arm causing her to scream in agony, and banged it repeatedly against the balustrade.

Bang, the gun went off, the bullet leaving the barrel harmlessly overhead as the three women struggled right on the edge of the roof. *Bang,* it went off again, less safely this time, the bullet penetrating the roofing material leaving a smoking hole in the accumulating snow. The warden managed to trip and throw Mary Long so that she landed over the balustrade rail on her midriff, winding her, her knees and toes being the only anchors on the increasingly slippery roof. Her nose was inches from the live crackling wire.

Using her uninjured arm, the warden was going to bring the gun down on Mary Long's head to stave her skull in and send her plummeting to her death. Dorothea rugby tackled Dr Winterbottom from behind and they struggled perilously close to the edge, a quickstep of death. Mary managed to scoot herself backwards and lay on the floor, spread-eagled and gasping. The warden tripped over Mary's prone figure, sending herself over the edge. Mary grasped Dorothea's waist, and with her injured arm Dorothea tried to grab at the warden's trailing ankles while holding securely to the rail with her good hand. She just managed to catch one of her heels, but the warden's weight jarred her damaged arm and dislodged her grip. The two young women heard a sickening thud from down below and saw figures from behind the barricades hurrying over.

***

The two shots rang out and caused DI Kydd to double his efforts. Praying for the safety of the two young women behind the door, under his breath, he finally heard the *click* he had been waiting for. The door opened outward so was immediately jammed by all the crates the warden had stacked in front of it. It took a few minutes to shove his way through to create enough space to squeeze out onto the roof. DI Kydd and Geraint found two freezing but very alive young ladies sitting in the warden's tent, wrapped in blankets, and sipping hot tea.

Geraint insisted that Dorothea should not walk down the stairs to the waiting ambulance and carried her down himself.

The Week Before Christmas, December 1934

Propped up in a hospital bed with her left arm bandaged, the heroine of the hour was receiving visitors after her ordeal. The first, as might be expected, was the Reverend Moss, very grateful for the safe return of his daughter Arabella, who was none the worse for her adventure. He brought with him spiritual solace and baked goodies from Jinny who was convinced hospital food was inedible.

Dorothea, while physically on the mend, still had periods of shakiness when all she wanted to do was cry, and it was when she was in a particularly wan mood that the vicar visited. Some tactful questioning by the Reverend Moss got to the heart of what was really troubling Dorothea.

'Dr Winterbottom died yesterday in this hospital, from her injuries which were horrible. Do you think there is salvation for those who do such awful things but are quite mad? The warden seemed to be so rational and everything she did was stone cold logical, but she must have been delusional, at the very least, and psychotic at most.'

Realising that there was a lot riding on his answer the Reverend Moss thought for a moment before responding. 'As human beings we all must face judgement, Scripture is explicit on that point, but Almighty God is omniscient and sees all that is in the heart of man. I am sure we can trust Him to judge justly.'

Next to visit her sick bed, was Professor Aldridge, baring a large bunch of flowers, some of Dorothea's marked essays and an assignment on *Beowulf* that needed to be written over the Christmas holidays.

'Geraint apologises but has been called away on urgent business. Well, he is moving house actually, but he sends you his best wishes for a speedy recovery and this in case you are bored.' He drew from his pocket a book on *Cynewulf's Poems*. '*Juliana* is the text for the exam in January which your course mates received on Wednesday before breaking up for Christmas. Geraint thought you would not wish to fall behind.'

Dorothea thanked the professor with a sigh. Her head was not yet in a place where she could concentrate on Anglo-Saxon.

When he took his leave, Dorothea leafed through the book looking for distraction. On the inside of the cover was a short inscription that read:

To Geraint,

On your eighteenth birthday.
I hope Cynewulf may be inspirational.

Your loving godfather,
Harold Aldridge

For some reason Dorothea felt warmed by the knowledge that Dr Hadley-Brown had lent her a book that obviously had sentimental value for him.

DI Kydd, dropping by the hospital ward, was a welcome distraction. He brought with him a bag of Everton mints and the news that the police had raided the warden's residence and it was an open and shut case. They had discovered the wireless hidden in the gramophone and the membership book of the Oyster Club in the safe. Dr Winterbottom's doctor, when questioned, confirmed that he had been prescribing her with barbiturates as she had told him she was struggling to sleep. The warden had become overconfident and had made mistakes in the belief that she was invincible and had left a partial thumbprint on the envelope of the Oyster Club invite addressed to Dorothea. The ballistics report was back, and the gun used to shoot Matilda was also the gun that killed Tabitha Gillespie.

On hearing the news that the warden was dead, Abigail Rushton had talked and had gladly shared that the poison pen letters she had sent to the warden were not the ones the warden had given to DI Kydd. It turned out that Ethel Worksop had hinted at the existence of a secret organisation that the warden was connected to, to Abigail, and that is what Abigail had put in her letters. This information was obviously too close to the mark if the police started to ask about blackmail, so the warden wrote her own blackmail letters. This explained why the warden's letters were written on a different typewriter to the other examples of poison pen letter.

'Thank you for believing I was innocent, Inspector. I am sure you had enough circumstantial evidence to think I was the murderer.'

'I knew you were honest, Miss Roberts, right from the start.' Dorothea looked confused, so the inspector continued. 'You gave me the pound note that Matty Abbot gave you because you had failed in your commission, and you felt you couldn't keep it. That act was a sacrifice on your part because you are a poor student starting out on her academic career, but you did it because it was the right thing to do.'

Dorothea's fourth visitor was Iris Robinson, looking very composed and altogether different from the last time they had met in a hospital ward, one floor upstairs, when their positions were reversed. She was proudly wearing Matthew Abbott's brooch pinned to her coat lapel. She grasped Dorothea's hand tightly and said, 'Thank you for exposing Matthew's killer, Dot. I really am truly grateful. While it will never bring him back, knowing what happened to him helps. I can get on with living. He would have wanted me to. To that end I have returned to the university to finish my course so that I can be a doctor.

'I don't know if you have heard that Constance Harris has stood down as President as she feels that it would be wrong to stay on after Dr Winterbottom's manipulation of the election last spring, so now I am the new President of the committee! I am going to need a Vice President and wondered if you might be interested?'

'No. I am happy to be a year rep for the rest of the year and serve under you, but after that I will be stepping down.' Dorothea was firm. 'I am so pleased that you are going to be President. You are exactly who we need to get the Union back on an even keel. What about Mabel Parker for Vice President?'

'Didn't you hear? No of course you wouldn't have, it is meant to be a secret. Mabel is five months pregnant. She is moving her wedding forwards to the New Year and taking an indefinite sabbatical!'

More surprise visitors came. Mr George from MI5, bringing with him the new Mrs George, previously Mrs Gladys Adams. He was so delighted at his change in circumstance and proud of his lovely lady wife that he seemed to have grown six inches taller. He accepted Dorothea's sincere, though surprised congratulations, complacently. Mrs Adams was glowing and very excited to be going on honeymoon to Romania. They seemed to be very much in love.

'Yes, well, when I clapped eyes on Gladys again after fifteen years it was as if the years rolled back. I was dashed sure I wasn't going to let it be another fifteen years before I saw her again.'

'It was very romantic. Almost a runaway wedding! Georgie, as I like to call him, had acquired an archbishop's licence and it was a very simple affair. Just us and witnesses, save that it was in Westminster Abbey and conducted by the Dean. It's so fortunate that you went to Eton with him, darling.'

'Anyway, we stopped by to say that you did an excellent job ferreting out this treasonous spy-ring and bringing Matthew Abbott's murderer to justice. Your country is very grateful indeed. If you want to come and work for me full-time when you graduate, then just say the word.'

'Thank you, that is very kind of you, sir, but I would like to serve my country in future by teaching its children English. Hopefully they will be easier to manage than mass murderers.' Dorothea was grateful but determined to keep away from anyone with homicidal tendencies for the foreseeable future.

'I shouldn't have thought so, but I admire your optimism,' Mr George said, with a twinkle in his eyes. 'I am sure I don't need to remind you that what has happened is strictly confidential and you will need to sign some paperwork shortly. Your friends have signed already.'

Mrs George had been listening intently. 'I will nominate you and your friends for a university merit award. I'll have a word in the provost's ear. The award is a shield which you'll have to share multiple ways and it will officially have to be awarded for "service to the community" or "going beyond the call of duty" but I do think we should be able to celebrate our ladies' achievements privately, even if we can't announce them publicly.'

Mr George beamed. 'An excellent idea, my love. We do need to acknowledge service and sacrifice. My department will anonymously sponsor the award a pound a person!'

Mrs George coughed delicately. 'I think five pounds each would be more appropriate, my dear.' She winked at Dorothea.

'Ah, yes, of course. That is what I meant,' Mr George replied.

Mr and Mrs George left, very pleased with their visit and with each other. Dorothea felt a little bit sorry for Mr George. He had literally met his match.

On Sunday afternoon, Mary Long, Mary Short, Maggie and Jinny all arrived for a visit. Maggie had some big news.

'Simon took me out for dinner on Saturday to that new French restaurant in Cheapside and while we were there, he asked me to marry him and more surprisingly I said "yes!". He is a bit old-fashioned so had motored over to Lytham St Anne's to ask my parents' permission last week. I don't give a fig for any of that, but I know it matters to him, and Mother and Father too, so I held my peace. We went to a jeweller on King Street and bought a ring on Monday.' She held out her hand and diamonds sparkled in profusion. 'Anyway, we will be getting married in the summer after we have both graduated and before I start a Doctorate in Philosophy. He has a job lined up, working for an engineering company a train's ride away so we should be quite well-off. Anyway, what I really want to ask is, please will you all be my bridesmaids?'

There was uproar in that bay of the ward with lots of hugging and shrieking and congratulations being given and received, so much so that the stern-looking matron had to come over and shush them.

Mary Short pulled out a newspaper and they settled down to do something together that they had not done for a long while . . . a crossword.

Monday 7th January 1935, Morning

It was a dry day with a biting wind in early January. Dorothea had just finished planting some snowdrops and crocuses that she had brought from home in pots, around the memorial tree for Matilda Abbott in the Grangebrook Hall's grounds, with a borrowed trowel from the head gardener who had sanctioned her unofficial tribute.

She sat back on her haunches and surveyed her work with a critical eye. Yes, they did look nice. They looked cheerful and full of promise. As if they had always been there.

She thought of her brief encounter with Matilda Abbott and hoped that those worried grey eyes were at peace. She still felt a massive sense of guilt and failure every time she thought of that conversation in the train carriage.

A shadow fell across her and Dorothea shivered and looked up. The familiar features of Dr Hadley-Brown looked down at her with a concerned expression on his face.

'How are you doing, Miss Roberts? Is your arm quite healed? Here, let me give you a hand up. Those flowers are quite beautiful. I am sure that Matty would have liked them.'

'Do you think so? Do you think Matthew would have minded being remembered as Matilda? You knew him so much better than anyone else here.'

Dorothea had tried to keep the wobble out of her voice, but Geraint had picked it up and he squeezed her hand which he had somehow kept hold of.

'Matthew was a very brave, clever, and funny man who served his country with distinction. He was also conflicted in many ways. He desperately wanted to fit in with the establishment but at the same time there was a part of him that wanted to take risks and rebel. It made him a very good agent when the chips were down. I think he was never happier than when he was being Matilda Abbott. She was the side of him he was most at ease with, and I would say, proud of. I think Matty would have thought your floral tribute most fitting.'

They stood in silence for a few moments looking down at the small tree, dead-looking at the present time but with the promise of new life come the spring, until Dorothea tentatively voiced a thought that had been at the forefront of her mind.

'I am sorry to hear about your engagement, did you love her very much?' and was surprised by the derisive snort she received in reply.

'Don't worry about me. I had a hunch that Mrs Adams was the leader of the Oyster Club and was totally wrong about that. It turned out that she was only trying to find her lost son. I am very pleased that the new Mrs George has made my boss happy. Besides, I never have had much luck with women.' He didn't seem too perturbed by this final remark. 'I am sorry about your friend Tabitha though.'

'She tried to kill you, multiple times!' Dorothea was indignant.

'She didn't manage it and she saved your life, and I can still be sorry for the loss of your friend.'

Controlling the treacherous wobble in her voice with some effort Dorothea asked, 'What will happen to Evelyn King?' though she wasn't sure she wanted to know.

'The university has politely asked her to leave. MI5 will keep a close watch on her and the other members of the Oyster Club, some they might try and turn to be double agents but if anyone looks likely to spy for Britain's enemies they will be put in prison.'

Looking down at the woe-begotten little face at his side and seeing her shiver and draw her new coat more tightly around her shoulders Geraint Hadley-Brown took her arm.

'Right, Miss Roberts you are freezing. Just this once I will take you for tea and cake. We will discuss *Ælfric's, The Lives of Saints* and it will give you the opportunity to try and dissuade me from giving you another C minus. Your grades have been very slip-shod last term.'

He had already marked her last piece of work and it was a strong A but now was not the time to mention this fact.

The light of battle replaced the wan look in Dorothea's eyes.

'C minus! I spent three days on that essay, and I translated the whole of *Saint Lucy* from the Old English and I read it in Latin too. In my opinion, Skeat is wrong in his translation as well.'

Off the pair of them went together, arm-in-arm, bickering companionably and so totally engrossed in the academic that they could not see the physical start of something between them.

ACKNOWLEDGEMENTS

Many thanks are due to the fabulous team at Dark Edge Press for bringing this book to life, particularly Louise, Leanne, and Jamie. Thank you to my wonderful boys Ian, Nathanael, and Samuel for all your love and support. Special thanks are due to Alan, Jean, Ian, Alex, Diana, Hilary, Tracey, Shane, Kerri, Gemma, Chantelle, Paul, Dave, Nicola, Leyton, and Ags for helpful conversations, early read-throughs, support, and encouragement throughout. And thank you to Charlotte Milne and Charlie Cochran for useful discussions about becoming an author.

BIBLIOGRAPHY

I have thoroughly enjoyed learning about 1930s Manchester, the Victoria University of Manchester, the University Settlement, MI5 and Belle Vue Zoological Gardens.

These books and sources were particularly helpful when writing about the Victoria University of Manchester in the 1930s:
- Little Wilson and Big God by Anthony Burgess, Penguin Books, 1987, ISBN 0-14-010824-6
- Portrait of a University 1851-1951 by H.B. Charlton, Manchester University Press
- Women's Student Union Handbook, 1935/6. University of Manchester Students Union Archive. University of Manchester Library. GB 133 SUA/4/2/2

These websites and sources were helpful when writing about the Manchester University Settlement:
- Manchester University Settlement, Archive of the Manchester University Settlement, 1892-2010. University of Manchester Library. GB 133 MUS
- https://minerva.manchester.ac.uk/manchester-art-museum/exhibits/show/history/p3
- Women's Student Union Handbook, 1935/6. University of Manchester Students
- Union Archive. University of Manchester Library. GB 133 SUA/4/2/2

These books and articles were really useful when writing about Belle Vue Zoological Gardens:
- Looking Back at Belle Vue Manchester by Robert Nicholls, Willow Publishing, 1989, ISBN 0-946361-29-0

- Belle Vue Manchester's Playground Second Edition by Clive Hardy, iNostagia Ltd, 2018, ISBN 978-1-84547-247-4

- Portrait, Empire, and Industry at the Belle Vue Zoo, Manchester, Ann C. Colley, Victorian Literature and Culture, Vol. 42, No. 2 (2014), pp. 167-186

This book was very helpful when writing about the Secret Service:
- In Defence of the Realm the Authorized History of MI5 by Christopher Andrew, Penguin Books, 2010, ISBN 978-0-7181-9744-5

This website was particularly helpful for figuring out the geography of Manchester in the 1930s:
- https://maps.nls.uk/os/

These websites were my go-to for fashion and jewellery:
- https://www.thecourtjeweller.com/2015/04/jewel-history-gem-alphabet-1893.html
- https://vintagedancer.com/1930s/women-1930s-fashion/

These websites were particularly useful for information about 1930s cars:
- http://www.crossley-motors.org.uk/
- https://www.supercars.net/blog/cars-by-decade/1930s-cars/

This website was particularly helpful for learning about radios:
- https://www.electronics-notes.com/

Lizzie Bentham started writing during lockdown with the aim of creating some imaginary friends to talk to, who could get out and about a bit more than she could. Originally from the northwest, she thoroughly enjoyed her time at university, so much so, she stayed on to do a doctorate in Chemistry. On graduating, so as not to leave the academic bubble, she discovered the dark side of research...

Research administration (as interesting as research but with a lot more cake). She worked in higher education helping academics to apply for research funding.

With *Murder in Her First Degree*, the first book in the *Red Brick Mystery* series, Lizzie combines her love of all things academic with another of her passions – murder mystery novels from the golden age of crime writing.

She currently lives in the west Midlands with her husband and two small children. When she is not writing, watching children's television or visiting parks, Lizzie enjoys walks in the countryside, reading, flower-arranging and crocheting.

Love crime fiction as much as we do?

Sign up to our associates' program to be first in line to receive Advance Review Copies of our books, and to win stationary and signed, dedicated editions of our titles during our monthly competitions. Further details on our website: www.darkedgepress.co.uk

Follow @darkedgepress on Facebook, Twitter, and Instagram to stay updated on our latest releases.

Printed in Great Britain
by Amazon

15743666R10194